PROJECT O.R.C.A.

SERENA J. BISHOP

Project O.R.C.A.

The Kari Chronicles
Book 1

Serena J. Bishop

Also by Serena J. Bishop

The Dreams Trilogy

Dreams

Miracles

Heroes

Other Novels

Beards

Leveled

ISBN Paperback: 979-8-9917923-1-8

ISBN Ebook: 979-8-9917923-0-1

Edited by Eanna Webb, Kilmari Publishing

Proofread by Janice C

Cover Design by May Dawney Designs

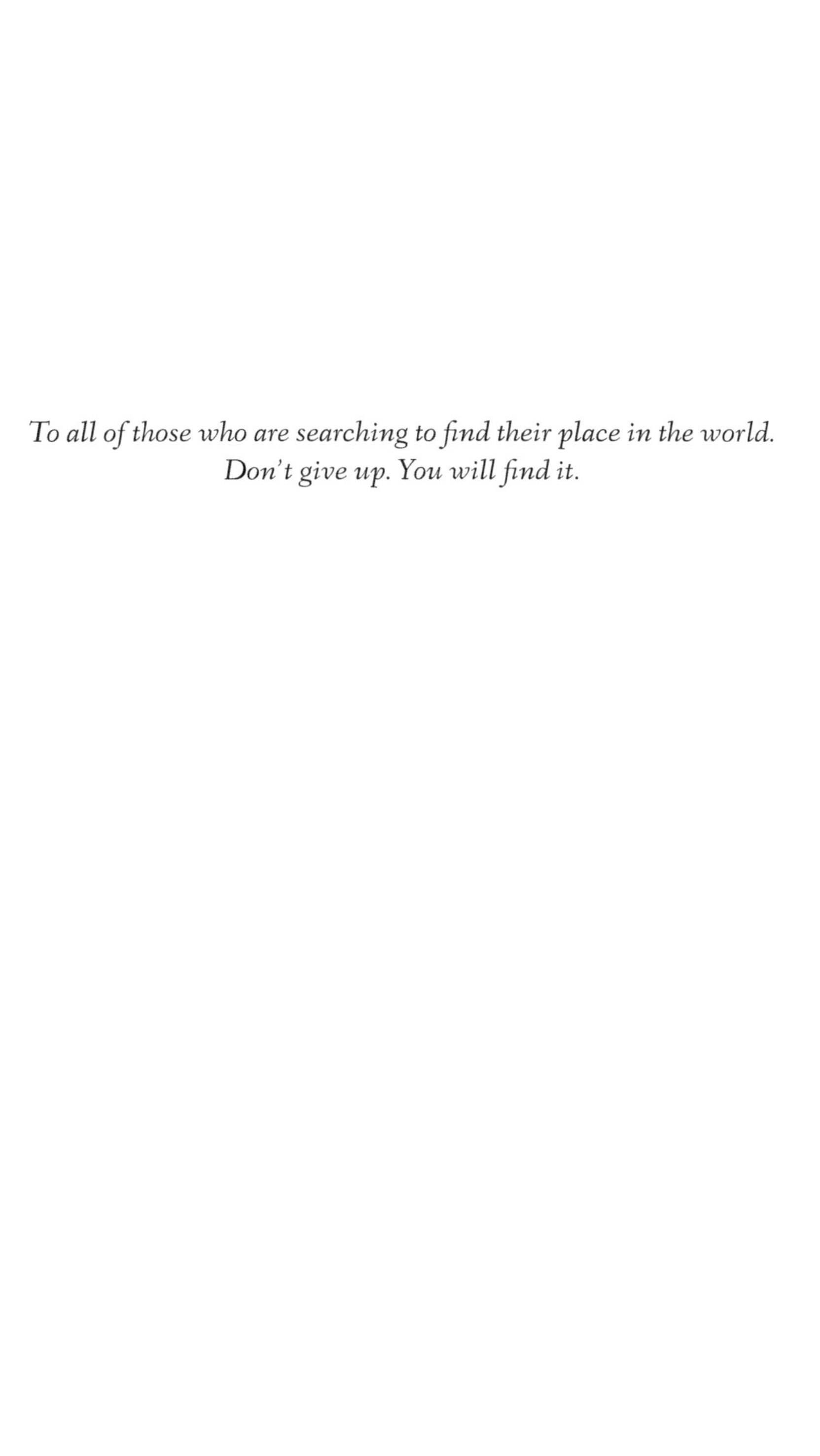

Chapter One

Kari pulled the rolling ladder with its stuck wheels across the floor with a *screech* that echoed across the mostly vacant hardware store, then climbed until she reached the height of the inaccurate clock. She removed it off the pegboard wall and made the correction. Now, it read 6:43am instead of 6:41am.

That task represented the most cerebral challenge of her graveyard shift. Now, it was back to the land of boxes because the world needed their 17 thousand different versions of light bulbs.

With every box she cut open her resentment toward the world grew. Society told her if she went to college and worked hard, she would be rewarded with a job in her chosen field. So, that's what she did. Society said that if she went to graduate school after her undergraduate degree, not only would it be easier to get a job but she'd also mature in that time and be more employable. So she did.

In the months since she defended her master's capstone,

she had applied for three dozen neuroscience jobs. That had led to a few interviews, but most came back with the feedback that she didn't have enough experience. Translation: they didn't like that she was 18.

It wasn't her fault she was a genius.

"Kari!" the daytime manager, Walt, yelled from down the aisle, clipboard in hand. "I need you to cover the contractor pick-up desk until Wes gets here. We have a line forming already."

Kari pointed to the two dozen clocks with the correct time. "But it's not supposed to open until seven!"

"Just do me this favor. The pick-up is easy," he said. "The customer will give you their name and—"

"I find out if they pre-paid, which most do. Then, I go into the back, notify the warehouse folks, and they bring the order to the front of the store with their forklift army. I've done this before, because Wes—for whatever reason—still doesn't know how to arrive on time even though you two live in the same house." She couldn't wait to hear what he thought of that, and she wouldn't have to wait much longer.

Walt took a few steps closer and his nostrils flared. *If she wasn't the mayor's daughter, I would have canned her smart-ass mouth months ago.* He traded in his annoyed look for a smile he only used when he needed to be fake nice for customers and Wes. "Glad to hear you're on board."

And that's why Kari preferred the graveyard shift. Fewer people meant fewer voices in her head. Also, it wasn't her fault one of her moms was the mayor.

In the movies, the ability to read others' thoughts was glamorized. It was a skill used to learn someone's secrets. It sounded useful, but in reality it was awful. She couldn't get away from people's thoughts—ever. When Kari had first developed telepathy when she was 11, she had to make an effort to read someone's mind. She called it her 'brain worm' because she had to focus on a person—like she was a worm crawling into their mind—until the worm found the path that allowed their brain-waves into her mind.

It was trippy.

But, when she turned 14, she no longer had to try. The thoughts—and sometimes imagery—came at once, all the time, from anyone within seven feet of her, whether she liked it or not. Living with her mothers became impossible. Friendships were a letdown because they told lies—big and small. She had only attempted one 'intimate' relationship, which actually hadn't been terrible since Nicholas had been honest to a fault. His other fault included having sex with someone who wasn't her when he went off to art school.

Such a cockwaffle.

"One last thing!" Walt yelled once he reached the end of the aisle. "Did you move that ladder by yourself? The wheels have been busted for weeks."

Did she want to gloat about her above average—some might say 'super'—strength? Yes. But doing so would complicate her life. "No. The ladder was like this when I got here."

His bushy gray brows furrowed and he gave her a slow nod. Then, he headed in the direction of the appliances section.

Kari took her time walking to the other side of the store, and while she didn't see anybody else on her trip, she did see a group of construction-like people at the contractor pick-up desk. One was cute. A little more rugged than she usually went for with the steel-toed boots and worn jeans, but they had a pretty face. However, even with a sharp jawline and pouty lips, she placed as much distance between the register and herself as possible. "What can I help you all with?"

About time. "Pick up for Hoffman and Son's Roofing and Siding." The slightly older but just as attractive blonde counterpart—probably a brother-sister duo—handed her a receipt.

"I'll go let them know in the back." She caught the eye of the brother in boots who gave her an ambiguous grin. "You can all wait out front by the loading area if you'd like."

After Kari informed the forklift team, she headed back out to the desk where they all had left, except for cute boots, who was studying the impulse buys. Now that they were closer and studying the different types of flashlights, Kari could see the faded G&C logo on the hat they wore.

You never could trust the cute ones.

G&C, or God and Country, was an extremist group who bought into believing anything someone with a loud speaker told them. They bought into the narrative that both her mothers were she-devils out to destroy jobs and 'American values'. When Kari was 11, G&C attacked both of her mothers with internet smear campaigns and someone vandalized the family home and farm property. When the police came, they took out a loaded AR-15 from the spray-paint-happy lunatic's car.

Years of therapy—for her and her mothers—and bouts of PTSD and anxiety ensued. Also, anger. The incidents, along with the telepathy, had given Kari some legit issues she constantly needed to work through.

Kari knew the customer wasn't aware she was the daughter of two of G&C's most hated women—after all, her nametag only said 'Kari', not Karishma Okpik-Bakshi—but she needed to know if God and Country had faded away in the past seven years like the letters on the hat.

She leaned her forearms against the counter. "What does your hat stand for?"

Figures someone who looks like her wouldn't know. Probably illegal anyway. "God and Country."

People often looked at her, a young woman with long, black-brown hair and mixed Indian-Indigenous ancestry and would make wild, inaccurate assumptions. Like the one this person just made. "Sounds intense and value-driven."

"It is. We share the idea that those two things should always come first in America and we'll fight anyone who says otherwise."

At the word 'fight', a graphic image appeared in Kari's mind of a team of people in combat gear terrorizing a gay pride event with assault weapons. Blood marring rainbows. Tears smearing makeup. Screams drowning out music.

Gods, she really fucking hated them. And she needed to learn if this was a planned attack or a sick fantasy. "Sticking to your guns, I see," Kari said as she struggled to maintain a conversational tone.

Lots of guns. He chortled, "You got that right."

"Any idea where I can get tickets to your next 'fight'? If it's anything like MMA, I like to watch." That part was true. As a former jiu-jitsu student, she loved grappling.

Dallas. Don't say anything. "No tickets. Just put God first, alright."

She knew what he meant and forced a smile. "You'd be happy to know I try to honor Gitchi Manitou and the many Hindu Gods on a regular basis." That part was mostly true. Kari placed herself in the spiritual not religious camp. She was more of an evidence-based person, rather than faith, but she had to be spiritual in some way since she was the product of a magical pregnancy between two women, which was how she had her paranormal abilities. Her science brain really hated that 'explanation'.

He looked more confused than Walt from earlier. "Gitchi, what?"

"Gitchi Manitou. The Creator per the Anishinaabe. Being that you're so into God and this country, you should add that Indigenous name to your list, which I'm sure already contains the thousands of worshipped Gods from human history and present day."

The fu— He took a step back, disconnecting her link. "Whatever." He turned and walked into Wes as he put on his bright red work vest. "Watch it."

"Sorry I'm late," Wes said and came behind the counter. "One of these days I'll remember to lay out what I want to wear the night before."

Kari took in his fashion ensemble of jeans, white T-shirt, and vest. She bit the inside of her cheek. "Yeah, you have a nice day. I'm out of here."

"But it's not seven yet."

"It will be by the time I'm done peeing." Kari headed to the restrooms, then to the employee locker room to turn in her vest for the day. She took out the box of nails from her locker that Mom A, the environmental activist and crafty mom, had asked her to buy so she could build a chicken coop. On her way out her eyes landed on the clock: 6:58am. She rolled her eyes. Walking out two minutes early wasn't worth the lecture from Walt. Or Mayor Mom L, if she found out about it.

So Kari took out her phone.

There were no texts from friends—she didn't have any. No texts for additional hardware supplies from Mom A. Maybe there would be an email or cute puppy video on InstaPic? She opened her mail and gasped with a smile when she saw one from Katsu Tanaka's lab with the subject line: In-Person Interview for Research Associate Position. She clicked on it.

Hello, Kari,

After reviewing your information from the screening process, we would like to invite you to our lab for an in-person interview. If you are interested, please email us back with days that work best for you in the next two weeks. Due to your age, we will book your flight and hotel accommodations to Boston (most hotels here require you to be 21).

Regards,

Chris Jenkins

Administrative Assistant, Tanaka Lab

"Yes!" she yelled to an empty room. She couldn't wait to tell the moms! And it was after seven am! Double jazzed! Kari fished her keys out of her cargo pants and then practically skipped into the parking lot's morning late May light. On the way to her hatchback she passed a massive white van with a faded God and Country bumper sticker above the license plate.

The painful images and ignorant thoughts she saw and heard from minutes earlier returned and set her heart pounding and jaw grinding. Due to working there, she knew the security cameras were awful. She tucked herself behind the bumper and opened the box of nails. Kari plucked a two-inch nail from the box and stabbed the back tire through the treads. She debated removing it, but a flat in the parking lot would bring more attention to the store, whereas a slow leak could leave him stranded on a busy highway or at the worksite after a long, hot day. It really wasn't even a contest.

The nail stayed in its new rubber home.

Satisfied with her first bit of justice, she took the scenic route to her very used car. She got in, adjusted her ponytail, and left with the kind of joy one had when they got to leave work on a high note.

On her way home, she stopped to withdraw cash from an

ATM and then drove fifteen minutes out of her way to buy a prepaid or 'burner' phone. But in a different store than last time. In that situation, it was a pedo eating lunch outside her favorite dog park. While her crime tip-line calls had never been illegal—quite the opposite—she didn't want her call traced back to her personal phone. She didn't want to answer questions in a trial of how she knew about said crimes when she was confident an answer of, 'I saw his imagery and heard his thoughts in my own brain' would aggravate the prosecuting attorney.

She called the crime tip line she knew by heart. After she consented to a recording and an actual person answered, she provided what she knew.

"Hello," Kari said, "I have reason to believe that God and Country is planning an attack at Dallas Pride. I'm not one-hundred percent if that means Dallas, Texas or some other Dallas. My source is a roofer from Hoffman and Son's Roofing and Siding in Bend, Oregon. I'm guessing this person uses he/him pronouns because of the whole hating the gays thing. Anyway, he has blond hair, blue eyes—very Aryan, which tracks—a strong jawline, and pouty lips. He spoke with a slight Pacific Northwest accent and has no visible tattoos or jewelry. Do you need any of that information repeated?"

"No, we have everything, thank you. May I ask who is—"

Kari ended the call and drove the rest of the way with the windows down and the rock music up. Even with the G&C interaction, there was a lifted weight that made her fly down the highway. So much so she winced when she caught her speed. Even being the daughter of local celebrities wouldn't get her out of a ticket going thirty over the limit.

Once she crossed the familiar railroad tracks in the rural part of the high desert, it was only a few more minutes before she turned down the gravel driveway of her home. She waved to the staff of the goat farm Mom L used to run before she turned to politics, ignored the goats—they were loud and smelled bad—and happily parked outside her tiny house.

For her sixteenth birthday, her moms turned Mom A's she-shed office where she did environmental world-saving into a tiny house for her. Living with them up until that point had barely been manageable. If they couldn't avoid each other, which was often since the moms' house was also a small single-story home, there was tension every day. The move saved their relationship to the point where Kari now considered her mothers to be her best friends. All three acknowledged this wasn't the healthiest relationship, but it was better than no relationship at all.

And better than Kari having no friends.

Like a good friend, Kari knocked whenever she wanted to visit or show up for meals. When she heard the muffled permission, she went inside. "Sorry, I'm late for breakfast. There was a thing."

"No problem, chickpea," Mom A said from the dining table with an omelet in front of her, her salt-and-pepper braid—mostly pepper—draped over her shoulder. "Yours is in the microwave. What kind of thing held you up?"

Before she made a beeline for breakfast, Kari said, "Idiots. But I don't want to talk about them, I have great news!"

"Oh!" Mom L stepped out of the bathroom in suit pants and blouse with her salt-and-pepper hair—mostly salt—still wet from her shower. "Did you see if they started construction on the new shelter?"

"No. I had to take a different way home. Although, make sure Hoffman and Son's Roofing and Siding is not involved." Kari pushed the button on the microwave to reheat her breakfast. "The good news is that I have an in-person interview in Tanaka's lab!"

Mom A made a squeak. Mom L gave her a slight smile.

"That's wonderful news!" Mom A rushed out of her seat, rounded the table, and went in for a quick hug. *So proud. This is a turning point.* She kissed Kari's cheek and then returned to the table. The scent of her evergreen soap wafted into Kari's nostrils.

Mom L continued to look at her with big, brown eyes, identical to Kari's. She stayed in the hallway with no hug intent. That was weird. And then it dawned on Kari why.

"You did it!" Kari pointed her fork at Mom L.

"I did nothing," Mom L said.

Kari didn't buy it. She put the fork on the counter and approached her. In addition to catching dangerous criminals, the other advantage to being a telepath was that her parents could never lie to her in her presence. "Mom L," she drawled.

"Okay, fine! I may have sent a follow-up email to Dr. Tanaka asking if he could bump you up in the process."

"Leela!" Mom A said in shock, back in her spot behind the table.

"I can feel that you're angry, chickpea," Mom L said. Kari got her paranormal gifts honestly. Mom L couldn't act as an empath to all, but she could with Kari. "But he's a family friend who did a bang-up job helping me with that whole coma thing I was in before you were born."

Kari's feet were frozen in place. Her mouth dropped. "I can't believe it. I got this because of you!"

"No," Mom L said with patience she had mastered over the decades and approached Kari. *Hear me out.* "I only asked that he bump you up in the process. I'm almost positive someone else still made the decision to bring you in."

The tension Kari held in her muscles started to relax.

Good. "And"—Mom L rubbed her upper arms—"Tanaka noted that he'd be gone from the lab for the next month due to a conference-vacation-conference sandwich. Trust me when I say that you still did all the work to get this interview."

"She's right, chickpea," Mom A said. "You've done the work, and nepotism has worked against people like us for centuries. I don't see the harm in using this to get your foot in the door." She narrowed her eyes at Mom L. "Although, I think that plan should have been shared with you."

I'm sorry. Mom L sighed. "I just . . . The mom in me needed to help and this was the only way I felt I could do it."

Kari wanted to be mad or at least resentful, but she loathed her current job and here was a possible way out. "I get it," Kari said over the beeping of the microwave. "You meant well, even if it was super sneaky."

Mom L put her arms around Kari, making her chin wet in the process.

It was really cute how her more petite mother needed to get on her tiptoes to kiss her cheek. It was then Kari caught the brightness of her orange-ginger soap.

I promise I won't do it again.

"I'm going to hold you to that," Kari said as Mom L retreated back down the hall. "As much as I hate the hardware store, I do want to earn my place somewhere else." She gathered her plate, poured some juice, and took it to her dining spot: a TV tray in the living room.

"When do they want you to come in for the interview?" Mom A asked over the sound of the hair dryer.

"I'm supposed to give them the best times and they're going to arrange my flight and hotel for me." Kari chewed her veggie-cheddar omelet as she thought of the logistics—and trauma—of air travel.

When her grandfather, Nana Sid, died the year before, his funeral challenged her in multiple ways. One, he was a brilliant physician-scientist whose brain had turned on him with Lewy

Body Dementia, an aggressive form of the disease. Two, his memorial service was in Florida, which meant she had to fly there. For almost fifteen hours she had been inundated with people's thoughts and images. Even the meds her therapist had prescribed for anxiety didn't help. Kari didn't believe in hell, but if there was one, it was airports and airplanes. The only positive from the whole trip was that she had caught a preteen girl's thoughts about being trafficked. Kari notified the flight attendant via napkin. When she and her moms got off the plane she saw security escorting the girl and the older woman who was with her—separately—out of the gate.

"Do you want to go back to Daryll for a refill of your medicine?" Mom A asked.

"I don't know." Kari shook her head. "It didn't do much for me. Plus, there's the whole he's probably scared of me since I blew up in his office."

When she had gone to his office seeking the medication, he had insisted on prying into the details of her life, which included not only her grandfather's death but also her dog dying and the breakup with Nicholas. Daryll kept pushing and pushing her until she snapped and revealed that the main pressure in her life was that she was a telepath. Naturally, he didn't believe her. But he eventually came around after she recited to him his own thoughts. He acted like he had seen a ghost but wrote her a prescription anyway.

She never went back.

"You could take a train to Boston," Mom L suggested and adjusted the collar on her suit jacket. "I don't know how much more expensive that would be, but you probably have enough in your account to cover the difference."

"You wouldn't cover it?" Kari asked with her mouthful.

"You get room and board for free, remember? This is all part of the wonderful world of adulting. Speaking of which . . ."

Mom L went to Mom A at the table and kissed her. "I have to go to work. Love you, sweets."

"Love you too, dreamy."

Kari was Mom L's next target and kissed her on the forehead. *Love.* "Love you, chickpea."

"Love you, too," Kari said it and meant it. She loved her mothers more than anything. They had sacrificed rooms, jobs, time, money . . . everything for her. For a child they didn't even ask for. For a child they were 'gifted' after an accidental fertility ritual.

Yeah, her science brain still couldn't come to terms with that.

Kari finished her breakfast over more travel chitchat and internet searches with Mom A. They learned that if she took a train, there would be multiple stops for transfers and the trip would be multiple days. And she'd still be surrounded by people!

It was better if she drove and camped.

"By yourself?" Mom A shrieked.

"Yes! I'm extremely capable, have loads of experience camping thanks to Michigan summers with Ata Niq and Noko Ani." Her Indigenous grandparents. "And have enough money saved so if I'm in a sketchy part or weather is terrible, I can stay in a hotel."

Mom A pursed her full lips—which Kari had inherited. She could tell she was winning her mother over.

"Not to mention the fact that I never took a break after I finished school. My trip across the country would be a great vacation. Open road. No voices. Lots of greasy spoon diners. It would be fun for me."

At the mention of diners, Mom A's lips upturned. "Okay, you've won me over, but I want to make this road trip plan with you, to include your stops for the night. I, as your very caring and protective mother, would feel better that way."

Kari supposed that was fair. "That's a deal." She took her empty plate to the dishwasher and kissed Mom A on the forehead on her way out. "See you at your dinnertime!"

Sleep. "Sweet dreams, chickpea."

The graveyard shift did have an interesting effect on her life where the moms' breakfast was her dinnertime. And like everyone's dinnertime, she had a few hours to wind down until it was time for bed. The first thing she did was say hello to Brownie.

Up until she was four she had a guardian in the form of a golden eagle looking after her. When her paranormal skills kicked in, Kari learned that she could reach out with her mind and communicate with—not control—eagles and hawks on a basic level. She stared at the trees on the Cascade Mountain in the distance and waited. After a few minutes, she saw the telltale silhouette of outstretched wings in the partly sunny sky. Then, as the bird banked to come closer, she made out its deep gold, white, and brown feathers.

It landed in front of her.

Kari approached with respect and kneeled so they were at eye level. A series of infected scratches when she was younger taught her never to ask them to land on her forearm. She didn't know if they understood her spoken words, but it made her feel like she had a friend when she did. "Hi, Brownie. I wanted to let you know that in the next few days I'll be leaving for a long trip, so don't worry that I'm not around. But maybe send the word out to your kinfolk that I might need some company, and in return I'll tell them you said hi."

She could have sworn he gave her a nod before he flew off again.

Now that she had said hello, she headed to her tiny house

for a shower and her evening entertainment, consisting of a movie and quality time with her true love: the acoustic guitar of her dreams. The low action. The clean and rich tone. The spruce top. The curvy swirls of abalone inlay in the walnut fingerboard. A companion who would never lie to her and molded perfectly to her body. After a few songs to calm her mind, she'd call it a day.

A unique and exciting day.

Chapter Two

The earthy and slightly sweet scent of woodsmoke wafted through the open window of Kari's tiny house. There was no chance her mothers had started a fire in their woodstove, especially with Mom L's hot flashes, and sunset was hours away, so the smoke wasn't from the fire pit either. That could only mean one thing: the outdoor oven.

Kari went to her window and cupped her hands around her mouth to project her voice. "Are we having pizza for dinner?"

"Yes!" Mom A yelled back. "Dinner at six, per usual."

Kari took her phone out of her cargo pants' pocket and saw the time. She only had thirty more minutes. "Okay, I think I can finish packing in that time."

Due to the possible different weather conditions Kari would encounter in her journey to the East Coast and back, her largest rolling luggage was packed to the point where she needed to sit on it to zip it closed. Her business suit and related fancies for her interview were in the garment bag on her downed Murphy bed. Satisfied her essentials were packed in an orderly fashion, Kari grabbed her bag and rolled her luggage to the door. Which happened to have Mom L on the other side of it. "I'm not late!"

Crying. "I know. I know. I just wanted to warn you." *About how emotional your Mom A is.*

"Why's she emotional?" Kari moved past her and then opened the trunk of her car. "I'm not moving for good."

"But you will be soon, and she sees this trip of yours as the beginning of the end."

"I still don't get it." Kari dropped her largest suitcase in first with a thud. "I haven't lived in the same house as you for two years."

Logical. "But that doesn't change the fact that you're our little chickpea and you're potentially leaving the nest, so"— Mom L reached for both of her hands and gave them a squeeze —"please be extra patient and sensitive."

Kari smirked. "You realize that's a challenge because I'm genetically half of you, right?"

Smart-ass. "I'm serious. You're also genetically half of your Mom A, so I know you have it in you."

"Fine," Kari drawled. Her DNA was an impossible fact to argue. She had seen the genetic test that showed she was a fifty-fifty split between her mothers. "I'll be extra gentle with Mom A."

"Thank you." Mom L released her hands and then took a step back. She shook her head. An image formed in her mind of Kari without oil smudges, clean clothes, and her hair brushed. *Not camera ready.*

"She's taking pictures?" Kari asked, surprised.

Probably a lot of them, too. "I'll see you inside in twenty minutes." Mom L peered inside her car. "Do you need help getting the camping gear in here after we eat?"

"No. Also, you *just* had back surgery." She pointed an accusing finger. "I saw you lifting lumber for the chicken coop. You have to stop trying to do so many things."

"That might be a good point." Mom L walked away. "Twenty minutes!" she yelled over her shoulder.

Kari situated the smaller luggage in her car, then went back inside for her latest camping gear employee-discounted purchase at the hardware store: magnetic solar panels for her car. Not only was their sale a surprise but so was the information that she couldn't take two weeks off work if she wanted to come back. Therefore, Kari was officially unemployed.

So long employee discount.

When she went back inside, she caught her reflection in the closet mirror. Straggly hair. Motor oil stained her cargo pants from when she fixed her car. The bottom of her tank top had been used to wipe sweat from her brow. A black smudge covered her forearm from who knows what. She was a mess. The rest of the gear would have to wait until after a quick shower.

Eighteen minutes later she emerged from her tiny house with fresh clothes and washed hair. The shower helped the mystery smudge, but the application of her fifty-fifty mix of bronze—courtesy of Mom L—and warm beige—courtesy of Mom A—foundation was what really did the trick. Clean, confident, and hungry, she made her way over to the main house.

Kari had crawled, walked, and run on the land. While she knew she wasn't saying goodbye forever to her home, the sights and smells were a far cry from where she would most likely land. There would be times she'd miss the beauty of the sun setting behind the mountains or nighttime quiet. But she wouldn't miss the goats.

And she was pretty sure she wouldn't miss the eventual chickens.

She stepped on the creaky boards of her mothers' porch and could hear both the moms talking about Mom A's upcoming interview about urban farming through the open window. Her environmental and social justice advocacy had grown to the point where she was a regular guest on multiple news channels, especially Earth News Network, or ENN as it was most commonly known. Kari knocked.

"Come in," Mom L said.

Kari did and then immediately held what she hoped wasn't an awkward smile.

"Oh, that's going to be a great picture," Mom A said, then put her phone down and rushed her at the door. Mom A's thoughts landed in her brain as kisses landed on her cheeks. *Don't cry. Don't cry. Don't cry.* "I hope you're hungry. You're in for a treat."

Kari looked across the living room to the kitchen. There was garden salad, mushroom pizza—she would have given her left arm for chicken barbeque—and a variety of berries. "Looks and smells fantastic."

"That's not everything though," Mom A said with a bounce, and then scampered to the oven. She slid on an oven mitt and took out a baking sheet that had a small stack of golden brown and crispy—yet fluffy—goodness.

"You made fry bread!" Kari usually only had versatile and culturally complicated Indigenous food when her Noko Ani made it. "I take away any disappointing thoughts I had about you not putting meat on the pizza."

Mom L chuckled. "We love you too. Now, make your plate so we can eat."

Kari didn't need to be told twice. She grabbed her plate,

made a reasonably sized salad that was heavy on the cucumbers from Mom A's garden, and added two slices of pizza. She would save the berries for her fry bread later. Kari took her plate and a glass of iced tea to her designated dining area spot.

Mom A smiled at her, but then her lips gradually flipped direction. "I'm sorry. I'm trying to keep my emotions in check." She used her cloth napkin to dab her eyes. "This isn't meant to make you feel guilty and I'm sorry if it does."

"It doesn't," Kari said matter-of-fact, only to earn a death glare from Mom L. "I mean, I know this is causing some feelings of loss for you, and I'm sensitive to that."

Mom A bit her lower lip and nodded. "Thank you, chickpea."

Mom L gave Kari a discrete thumb up. "Now that we got that out of the way. We hope you enjoy this taste of home. I know you're excited about your greasy spoon road trip adventure, but you won't get this meal anywhere else."

Kari knew that wasn't an exaggeration.

Mom L carried her loaded plate to the dining table and took her seat beside Mom A. "I hate to beat a dead horse, but are you sure you wouldn't rather take the train from Portland to Boston? You're literally driving across the entire country. And the US is a big country size-wise. We're not Belgium."

"I know, but how many other times in my life will I have the time to do this? I can see so many different places, but, most importantly, if I road trip then there's—"

"No people," both moms said in unison.

"We know," Mom A said, "too many thoughts in your head. I am curious how that'll work out for you in a lab."

It was a fair point and one Kari had already inquired about. "During my virtual interview I asked about staggered schedules because of equipment usage. The post-doc, Rabin, seemed intrigued by the idea, so I have to think that there's a chance."

Mom A stabbed a piece of broccoli with her fork. "Was he the one who asked good questions about your optogenetics capstone?"

Kari's guitar may have been her love, but optogenetics was Kari's obsession.

The technique was like having an on-off switch for different genes or proteins in the brain using the light from a fiber-optic cable. An ability like walking or a drive like hunger could be turned on or off with only a light. Based on her examination of different neurological procedures, this was the most feasible way to control her telepathy. She even wrote a procedure for it, Project Optogenetic Regulation of Cerebral Annoyance, or ORCA. However, for her master's in neuroscience capstone she left the telepathy out and instead focused on the science needed to take optogenetics beyond the optic nerve—which used light entering an eyeball—in humans.

"Both Rabin and the full-time research assistant thought my optogenetic capstone was interesting," Kari said, "but kept saying 'ambitious' like it was some kind of impossible task. It's totally possible! Genetic manipulation of cells has been done. Brain surgery has been done. Fiber-optic lights has been done. Why they keep saying it's not—"

"You know why: money and medical ethics," Mom L said. "There are proper channels for this type of research and you have to go through them. You'll learn all the details when you go to medical school in a few years."

While Kari hated agreeing with her moms, she did understand that she shouldn't go to medical school immediately after graduate school. She needed more life experiences. She needed to learn how to work with different types of people. She needed to mature—maybe work on the temper and the occasional rash decision-making, so she could tolerate the thoughts she'd hear and images she'd see.

"If I get that job in Tanaka's lab, I'll be able to put my name on some publications and earn money toward medical school." While those two factors were positives, there was a significant drawback to the Tanaka lab. "His lab seems dull though. There's nothing innovative about what he does."

"They have to play it safe," Mom A said. "Only corporations run by billionaires can afford to make those risks while the rest of the world—"

"We know, sweets." Mom L gave Mom A a soft smile and reached for her hand. "Big business is the enemy."

Mom A leaned over and kissed her cheek.

Her mothers had always been affectionate toward each other. Kari didn't believe she ever would have that kind of connection with anyone. She knew in the deepest parts of her gut that she had been created for something more profound than finding true love. Sure, she could find someone attractive along the way for some special tickles, but that was it. She wouldn't allow feelings to get in the way of her life's purpose.

She just didn't know what that purpose was yet.

Kari looked down at her empty plate and then eyed the remaining pizza on the table. "Those slices are mighty tempting."

"Go ahead," Mom A said. "Or maybe have some breakfast pizza?"

"The true breakfast of champions," Mom L said with a grin.

Mom A returned the smile but then her expression grew serious. "You're going to have a lot more temptations now. Please be smart and safe about what you choose to try, especially alcohol. You know how I feel about that."

The number of conversations she'd had with her moms about alcohol, drugs, sex, and even gambling rivaled the content of the Library of Congress. "I promise to only accept a drink from someone I know in a safe environment, drink water in between, and never drink when I'm sad. In addition, I will never try a drug made in a home lab, I know to only have safe sex and always receive and give clear consent. Lastly, I will never give money away that I need. Did I miss anything?"

Mom A smirked. "Always pee after sex to avoid UTIs."

"And on that note," Mom L said, "what time do you think you'll leave tomorrow morning?"

"I ride at dawn. I figure daylight is the element I should take advantage of the most. I'll pull off an hour or two before sundown at my campsite destination, so I have time to set up my pop-up tent and shower for the night. If I still have some energy left, maybe I'll make a fire for some peace. Like a meditative activity. Do some four-seven-eight breathing if I'm feeling overwhelmed."

The breathing technique was something she had learned to control her anxiety when voices got out of hand. Mom A used it as well when her PTSD flared. In the breathing exercise, she inhaled through her nostrils for four seconds, held the air in her lungs for seven, and then exhaled through pursed lips for eight. After a few rounds of the cycle, the stress of the situation waned.

"That's a really good idea!" Mom A said. "And speaking of your campsite, did you get a ferro rod?"

"Why would I do that when I have a lighter?"

Mom A *tsked* and left the dining table to head to their patio. She came back a few moments later and spun the firestarter from its leather cord. "I want you to take this." As Mom A came into the living room, she breached the thought threshold. *Plan B.*

Rather than argue, Kari took the firestarter and looped it around her neck. It did resemble a legit necklace. The metal was an open circle with teeth-like ridges at the bottom and a small metal rod resting on the top. "Thanks, Mom A. You've both always done a great job of keeping me warm at night." When Kari heard a loud sniffle, she glanced over at Mom L.

"That one really got to me." Mom L dabbed her teary eyes with her napkin.

Chapter Three

My baby. "I love you so much." Mom A squeezed Kari hard enough for her breakfast pizza to rise. "Please, call us as soon as you get to Twin Falls. Oh, and take pictures! The waterfall is gorgeous there."

Once the spine-crushing pressure released, Kari gave her another hug but without the chiropractic adjustment. "I promise I'll post pictures, and I'll call when I'm waiting for my steak and eggs."

Such a carnivore. Mom L laughed and went in for her goodbye hug. "I knew you'd pick your restaurant meals ahead of time."

As the sunrise cast its orange glow over them and the light breeze blew the smell of musky goats toward them, they stared at each other with uncomfortable smiles. Kari didn't understand it. She was excited to leave and her mothers were both happy for her, but it was still so hard. Kari knew she'd be back soon, but this goodbye held a weight that others didn't.

"Oh!" Mom L said with what was almost jazz hands. "Sweets, where'd you put her present?"

The soap! "I almost forgot!" Mom A reached into her hoodie pockets, pulled out two travel-sized bars of soap, and handed them to Kari.

"Thanks, but I don't think I'll need two extra bars of soap for my trip." It was then she caught the fragrance mix: evergreen and orange-ginger. "Wait, this is your soap. Why did you give me your soap?"

"In case you miss us," Mom L said.

"I've been gone longer than two weeks before."

"But in those cases," Mom A said, "you were with family. You've never been away from people who love you for so long. Even though we aren't there physically, you can close your eyes, smell a bar of soap, and imagine us there." *Might get lonely.*

Kari sighed. Dammit, that was really thoughtful. "Thank you. That's very sweet."

"It was my idea," Mom L said proudly. "But there's more, too."

Mom A smiled, reached into her hoodie pockets again and pulled out her favorite beaded earrings. It was like Mary Poppins's purse in there. "For your interview."

Kari took them with a large smile. She loved the fringe style featuring the gradual shift of the darkest aubergine to white. "Well, since I'm wearing your suit, this makes sense." It had benefited both Kari and Mom A that they wore roughly the same size clothes.

She shifted her guitar case in the passenger side to reach her backpack, where she tucked the earrings inside. "Any other gifts?"

Hugs. "Just hugs," Mom L said.

Kari wrapped her arms around her moms in one final group embrace. Over their shoulders, her eyes took in the long gravel driveway and the small buildings that made up the farm, but she also saw the images they conjured of her when she was a NICU baby and when she rode her training wheel-less bike for the first time.

Why do I think this is it? She'll come back.

Don't cry. Don't cry. Don't cry.

The fact that they sincerely saw her leaving for good began to resonate with her. If Tanaka's lab offered her the job, she'd know soon, and then she'd be packing the rest of her stuff and leaving again. "Even if I get the job," Kari said with a lump in her throat. "I will be back."

"We know," Mom A said with glassy eyes and brushed a strand of Kari's hair behind her ear. "It'll just be a little different next time."

Oh, Gods, now she's getting emotional, too. "But different can be better," Mom L said with a firm hand on Kari's shoulder. *Strong. Strong. Strong.* "Now, go forth and kick that interview's ass."

"Since I have orders, I'm giving you some." She pointed at Mom L. "You, be careful with your back. And you"—she pointed at Mom A—"don't get too attached to the chickens. There are predators out here, including Brownie."

The moms nodded their understanding of said orders.

"Good. I love you both." Kari grinned and gave each mom an individual hug, which was met with vigor and "I love you, chickpea."

She got into her car and watched them wave goodbye from her side-view mirror all the way until she made the first turn for her epic trip.

Kari put on her aviators so the sunrise didn't blind her and lowered the windows to get as much of the non-goat country air as possible. The breeze tossed her ponytail around wildly and her new music playlist, *Road Trip to the Atlantic*, blasted through the speakers. The collection of songs was from her favorite rock, blues, and pop bands. The playlist was fifty hours long, which was how long she estimated her journey would take.

As she drove her hybrid hatchback, she moved her left hand off the wheel and positioned her fingers where the different chords were while the music played. The newer songs posed more of a challenge, but by the time the second verse came around, she had the knack of it.

The first two hours she drove through the Oregon Badlands. A completely open, dry desert landscape with only a few shrubs every so often. Even with some of the cloud cover, the solar panels on the car's roof were sure to get all the juice they needed to power her laptop for her evening feature film and the electric kettle in the morning for her French pressed coffee.

Despite her outdoorsy nature, she was a coffee snob who loved movies.

After the desert was greenery and a small town. Next was Boise, followed by more desert and a touch of greenery with small towns.

Kari sensed a developing theme.

After eight hours of driving, she stretched her legs outside of Shoshone Falls and snapped some pictures of the waterfall that plunged into the river below. She received the notification that both moms loved the pictures as she submitted her order for steak and eggs to go.

The campgrounds near the falls were fine. There was no litter, the people who drank beer around their campfires weren't obnoxious about it, and she lucked out getting a spot near the bathhouses. For a nice fire to go with dinner, she bought a bundle of wood, split off corners, and used her multi-tool to make feathered wooden strips. Kari used her lighter rather than her new firestarter necklace to ignite the dryer lint, which quickly engulfed the kindling in steady, small flames. Once the first sizable log went on, she took a seat at her picnic table, sampled a steak-home fry-egg combo, and then followed through with her daughterly promise to call the moms.

Kari half listened while Mom L described their dinner plans with local politicians and once she had assured them she was safe, they ended the five-minute call. She enjoyed the rest of her dinner to the sound of her crackling fire and a group of campers laughing in the darkness. She used to laugh like that, too. But when her childhood friend, Bre, became overwhelmed with academics, they had drifted apart. There was also the issue that whenever they had sleepovers, she entered Bre's thoughts subconsciously.

After she ate, she kicked as many sticks and tripping hazards around her pop-up tent as possible. It was a basic but effective security system. Convinced she was safe, she used the campground bathhouse to take care of her nightly routine, played a few songs on her guitar, checked the news for any God and Country arrests, then called it a night with the companionship of a movie.

She missed having a dog.

The next four days followed the same travel and camp routine. The highlight was the Chicago area and its pizza. The low light was Erie. It wasn't so much the drive or the town, it was the rain and the start of her period. Heavy flow days during road trips now made her list of least favorite things along with uncontrolled telepathy, cruelty to animals, and bad jokes.

Boston couldn't come soon enough. Yes, she had saved money camping, but an actual bed and a bathroom with a shower where you didn't feel compelled to wear flip-flops awaited her. Also, there would be a TV.

It would be paradise.

Chapter Four

Boston, Massachusetts, United States

After highways and country roads, the streets of the college town were a mix of green spaces, residential, and commercial buildings. Kari recognized the brick and forest green awning of her hotel right away. She parked in the attached garage, slung on her backpack, grabbed her garment bag in one hand and her guitar in the other. There was no way she'd leave her prized possession in a parking garage overnight.

The hotel's lobby had the East Coast colonial vibe she had anticipated and dreaded. Marble, dark woods, and lots of oil portraits of probable slave owners in powdered wigs.

So tired. "Hello, miss," the young man at the receptionist desk said. Based on his pale skin, rosy cheeks, and bulbous nose, he could have been a relative of one of the men in the paintings. "Can I help you?"

"I'm here to check in. The name's Karishma Okpik-Bakshi." She slid him her driver's license.

Another football team groupie. "I'm sorry, but you're not old enough to book a room here. Minimum age is twenty-one."

"I'll keep that in mind if I ever choose to come here again. However, I'm sure you'll notice when you search my name in your system that the reservation is being held for me by someone who meets your—not at all arbitrary—age requirement."

She's got attitude, too. Great. He shot her an annoyed glare and started typing. The glare vanished and he gave her a forced smile. "So, what brings you here?" *Short answer. Short answer.*

She couldn't let his snide thoughts about her slide. "I'm a super genius with an interview at a world-renowned neuroscience lab. I'm going to take a tour of the facilities, meet the other scientists, and maybe check out the atmosphere of this charming city of yours."

"Oh." *Make this fast.* "That sounds like a full agenda."

It was satisfying watching his self-righteous face shift to one of embarrassment, and that she could draw this interaction out to cause him more discomfort. "I also want to see what all the fuss is about with your *chow-da*," she said in an adequate Boston accent. "Could you give me a list of the top ten places you'd recommend?"

Say hotel and leave. "Our hotel restaurant makes a great version of it." He cleared his throat and passed her the envelope with the keycard. "I hope you enjoy your stay."

"I'm sure it'll be great." Kari shoved her key in her pocket, picked her bag and guitar off the ground, and headed to her room.

The electronic lock clicked and she pushed the door open with her knee. Before her travel-weary eyes was a king-sized bed with a crisp, white comforter and six pillows. Across from it was a sleek desk, and above it was a wall-mounted television that put her laptop to shame.

The promised land.

Kari packed her things away but took out her toiletry bag

and carried it into the bathroom. Spa was more like it. She was pretty sure she could stretch her arms out to her sides and spin in the shower.

Kari stripped out of her clothes and threw them in a corner. Although, only after contemplating burning them. The shower spray was steamy and forceful and wonderful and—even though Mom A would disapprove because of the water usage—she planned on staying there until her fingers pruned. The hot water at the campgrounds had been fleeting, so she hadn't indulged in luxuries like conditioner or shaving.

Of all the unnecessary grooming steps many people partook in, shaving was the one she could get behind. She wasn't into fancy hair or makeup, but she loved shaving. She loved the silky-smooth feel of her legs afterward, how sweat didn't cling to her armpits, and how when she wore bikini bottoms it didn't look like a wild animal was trying to escape through the sides.

Kari stepped out of the shower refreshed but not rejuvenated. She'd need sleep for that. And as soon as her belly was full, she'd crash on those high thread-count sheets.

After sending a picture of her room to the moms, she took her room service to the bed, turned on the TV to the trashiest, dumbest movie she could find, and vowed not to do anything considered productive until her interview.

———

Kari looked skyward at the research building. The exterior of the behemoth structure was all metal and concrete with few windows, giving it both a modern and claustrophobic appearance. She pushed her way through the revolving door and saw her reflection in the glass. Today, she had let her hair fall loosely past her shoulders and wore Mom A's borrowed purple skirt suit with ballet flats. The earrings were a great touch.

"Kari?"

She turned, walked over, and extended her hand to the lead post-doctoral researcher of the lab. "It's so nice to meet you in person, Rabin. Is Dr. Singer on his way?"

I shake, but when release? He smiled and shook her hand with all the power of a dead fish. *My hand sweaty? Let go now.* "Dr. Singer had an emergency with one of his clinical trial patients. So"—he laughed with an uncomfortable smile—"you're stuck with me for the beginning."

Aw. He was nervous. That was kind of cute. "I don't mind."

He placed a hand on his chest. *Good.* "Oh good. And I hope you don't mind I ambushed you down here. Finding our labs can be a little tricky. I got lost for my interview and was late because of it." *Pit stains in my jacket.* He jerked his head in the direction of the long hallway. "I thought we'd start on the ground level and work our way up for a little tour. Then, we can have the interview with the others in our conference room," he beamed.

Others? How many people were going to be at this interview? She didn't even know that was a question she should have asked. "Sounds great."

———

"It was a hell worse than airports." Kari found that summary accurately described her time at the lab and using one of their 'wonderful' buses to commute to the clinical research area.

"But you don't believe in hell," Mom L countered.

"I do now," Kari said, as she lounged in her big, comfy hotel bed, her belly full of clam chowder and lobster roll. "The staggered schedule is a no-go. With the salary they're offering, I couldn't live remotely close to the lab, so I'd have to use public transportation with *the public*! And they basically laughed when I said optogenetics would be my first choice of research seminar topic for the grad students."

"Was there anything good about it?" Mom A asked tentatively.

"The lunch place the five-person interview firing squad suggested was excellent." To Kari's dismay, the interview wasn't only Rabin and Dr. Singer, but three others as well, including an associate researcher who didn't believe she could fluently speak the several languages she claimed to. Kari made sure her parting words to her were in Mandarin. "I'll have to send them a thank you email for the restaurant. That was at least exciting."

"I think it's crucial to remember that when you start out in a field not all jobs are great," Mom L said.

"I know, I know. I have to keep an open mind. I just . . . I don't want to be bored or uninspired." Kari pulled the comforter over her and grabbed her laptop from the other side of the bed. "I don't want a job like that to be my life."

"That's why people have hobbies," Mom A said, "but then those hobbies or passions can develop into something more. You need to give yourself time to make your mark on the world. You're only eighteen."

Kari saw her mothers' points but there had to be more. She was meant for more. She was a miracle child with supernatural gifts. She wasn't meant to spend the next four years of her life researching science that had already been scrutinized over the last several decades. "Yeah, I get it," she said, dejected, as she opened her laptop. Her eyes widened and she inhaled a sharp breath when she read the subject line of a new email: Interview invitation for inCog biostatistician and bioinformaticist.

She hadn't applied to inCog. She didn't even know what an inCog was. "I have something," Kari muttered.

"Oh!" and "What's that?" came from the moms.

"I might have a new prospect. Give me a minute." Kari opened the email and read it to herself:

Dear, Karishma,

The Chief Acquisition of Talent Officer of Wibawa Enterprises alerted us to your resume and master's capstone on NeedAJob, and we would love to speak with you about an open position of Biostatistician and Bioinformaticist at inCog. Our company divides its attention between the analysis of neurological data of other institutions and high-risk, high-reward research. We are a small team located on the *Hinewai* and are owned by Henry Wibawa.

"Shit," Kari said, flabbergasted and awestruck.

"What happened?" Mom L asked.

"Hold on." Kari continued reading the email:

If you're not familiar, the *Hinewai* is a former cruise ship turned floating business park and community. The *Hinewai* is currently docked at Manhattan Cruise Terminal; however, we depart for Newfoundland in two weeks. For your convenience, and, if you're interested in the opportunity, it would be best to schedule the in-person interview while we are in New York. Please call or email me with your availability (information in the email signature). Also, we will handle transportation and lodging costs.

Regards,

Miguel Santos, PhD, MBA, PMP

"You're not going to believe what I just read. A neurology

lab on the *freakin' Hinewai* and owned by *freakin'* Henry Wibawa wants to interview me!"

"That's amazing, chickpea!" Mom A said. "ENN recently aired a special on all the green features of the *Hinewai*. You have to go!"

"What happened to evil billionaires?" Mom L asked Mom A.

"I have a softer spot for Henry Wibawa since his mother was Māori—that's who the ship is named after—and while he does have more money than he knows what to do with, he is charitable and understands climate change more than most. The entire reason why he converted a cruise ship was because the land in Papua New Guinea, the home base for his projected new business headquarters, was flooded."

"Now," Kari said, "can you really impress me and tell me who this Santos character is?" A long silence followed. "That's what I thought. Hold on."

Kari clicked the link for the company website and went to the staff link. There were three pictures: Miguel Santos was the manager who held degrees in neuroscience and bioengineering, Milia Amos had degrees in biology and mathematics—they were probably looking for her replacement, and—"

"Shit!" Kari said, as she read the third name. "Thomas Mitchell is inCog's clinical data specialist."

"My Dr. Thomas Mitchell?" Mom L asked, shocked. "The main neurologist who helped me with my coma treatment, Thomas Mitchell?"

After uncovering the mystery of her mothers' psychic link they had shared during Mom L's coma, Mitchell had started to pursue fringe science, saw fewer patients, and further committed professional suicide by getting drunk and punching a hospital administrator. He lost his job and family in the process. He was a pariah in the neurology field. And now he worked for inCog. That was wild!

"I have to call them now!" Kari said. "We're still within business hours and if they're in New York, I have to see if I can get an interview while I'm still on the East Coast. I gotta go. Love you!"

Kari heard their echoes of 'I love you, chickpea' as she ended the call and dialed the number for inCog. After two rings, someone picked up.

"Hello, this is Santos," he said in an accent that sounded exactly like her undergraduate chemistry professor from Bogota. "You've reached inCog."

Kari sat straighter in her bed and, as a nervous habit, combed her fingers through her ponytail. "Hi, my name is Karishma Okpik-Bakshi. I'd love to set up an interview about the position you emailed me about."

Chapter Five

New York City, New York, United States

Santos had been surprised and delighted to learn that Kari was on the East Coast already. They worked it out that she could drive to New York the following day and stay in one of Wibawa's hotels until her interview the day after that. It was perfect. And, if possible, Santos sounded even more excited than she was.

The congestion of Kari's drive eventually took her to a quieter street near Bryant Park, where she parked in front of the hotel's valet and lowered her window. A blast of heat from the outside struck her like she was standing in front of the family outdoor oven.

She's younger. "Ms. Okpik-Bakshi?" the valet asked.

"Yes." Kari cocked her head to the side. "How did you know my name?"

"Madeleine provided us with a description of your vehicle. We've been expecting you." On cue, a second person in the same uniform appeared with a brass luggage cart.

Kari didn't know what was stranger: that she was treated

like royalty or that they knew her car's description when she never gave that information to anyone. "Who's Madeleine?"

They each looked at the other like Kari had said she thought the earth was flat. *Seriously?*

"She's the VIP Coordinator for the *Hinewai* and the Chief Acquisition of Talent Officer for Wibawa Enterprises," said the valet. *She's a big deal.*

"Can I help you unload your luggage?" the porter asked.

"No, thanks. I only have two bags and my guitar."

"Excellent. Then, whenever you're ready, I'll park your car in the Wibawa Tower's private garage," the valet said. "It will not be disturbed and we can retrieve it upon your request."

It's not like the customer service in Boston was poor—except for that cockwaffle at the desk—but this was leagues above. This was the celebrity treatment. Once she had her belongings, Kari took the fob off her key ring and handed it to the valet. "Oh! Would you mind putting my solar panels in the back with my tent when you get there? They're magnetic."

This is definitely not the Lambo from earlier. "Absolutely."

Kari watched as the valet drove away in the vehicle she had pieced together and fixed with Ata Niq, then headed to the lobby. Luxurious was too standard a word to describe the entrance. The space was opulent, with paintings that had their own lighting on every wall. The frames had such elaborate filigree they were art themselves. The floors were predominantly white marble tiles with a large compass star in the center made from cut black and brown marble. North, south, east, and west symbols glimmered with gold luster—probably because it was actually gold—but beyond the star stood a gorgeous person with warm umber skin, angular features, and full lips behind the reception desk.

While Kari had a list of dislikes, she also had her favorites, and beautiful people were on that list. The person's gender didn't matter. And she loved it when she could admire them from afar so her fantasies weren't ruined by their thoughts.

Muscles in that tank top. "Welcome. Our front desk staff is away at the moment, but I'd be happy to help check you in," the person said with a smoky, Italian accent. "I'm Gia, one of the hotel managers. According to Madeleine, you're staying two nights and that you're interviewing at inCog for a neuroscience position." Gia tapped a corner on the touch screen monitor built into the desk so the information faced Kari. *She must be positively brilliant.* "Very impressive for someone so young."

Kari looked at the screen, where she read her check-in information, as well as a detailed notes section that included the make and model of her car, inCog's information, and her agenda for tomorrow. Apparently, a driver was coming to pick her up at ten in the morning.

Gia tapped the screen so it flipped around again. "You have a busy day tomorrow, but that doesn't mean you can't have fun tonight. We have some wonderful theaters and clubs around here. If you tell me what you like, I can recommend a few places."

While Kari had loved The BroMancer concerts she had seen with Bre, the bawdy musical she had seen when she was 13, or playing guitar with her rock band when she was 14, she couldn't bear the thought of doing any of those things now. She wouldn't put herself through that kind of mental torture before the most promising interview she had. "I appreciate the offer, but I'll probably just walk around to find dinner and bring it back to my room while I watch a movie. I need to rest for tomorrow's big day."

"I understand." Gia touched the screen again and an empty square appeared in the center. "Please place your thumb in the square and keep it there until I tell you to lift."

"Does my thumb print count as my room key?"

"And an eight-digit code. You'll find that Wibawa properties integrate two-levels of security, including biometrics, whenever possible."

Kari did as Gia instructed and read the information about her room listed off to the side: king bed, non-smoking, park view, and more. Kari scanned her thumb, entered a code, and then headed to the elevator bank for her room on the tenth floor.

Kari placed her thumb on the scanner, typed in her code, and the small red light on the key pad turned green. The locking mechanism of the heavy door unlatched with an audible *click*. She pushed the door open to a room that was small in space but big in windows. The corner room gave her a view of—well, she didn't know what buildings she was looking at, but they were old and one had a gargoyle. There was also a sliver of green, which must have been the park view.

Kari started the business of unpacking, but before she considered all of her responsibilities done, she took out her laptop and sat on her high, firm king bed. She wanted to ensure the details for tomorrow hadn't changed.

There was an email from Madeleine, with Santos cc'd, in her inbox. The message was a brief welcome to New York, a restaurant recommendation guide for dinner, and the news Santos would meet her where her driver dropped her off and escort her on to the ship for her interview.

Kari checked the time: 2:51pm. That was just enough time for a movie before her hunt for dinner.

———

The coming-of-age drama had the dumbest ending in all of dumb endings. She should have watched the dystopian-dark comedy about artificial intelligence. At least that ending would have been realistic.

Kari went down to the lobby, noted Gia wasn't behind the desk, and meandered out onto the street. Then, she staggered.

So glad to be out of there.

Feet hurt.

I miss home.

Liars!

She should have known to prepare herself for the barrage of voices that assaulted her: Business people thinking about deals, bike messengers trying to avoid hitting pedestrians, homeless people hoping someone would acknowledge them, street musicians playing and praying for tips. It was all too much. She ran down the block until she found the haven of the park.

It was a good thing inCog was located elsewhere because city living was not for her.

On the other hand, a genuine New York City hot dog from the cart near the park entrance was right up her alley. After buying her dinner, she went into the park and found a quieter, shaded area with a bench to enjoy her meal. The New York City atmosphere was still present—there were still cars honking and people talking—but the only thoughts in her head were her own. And those thoughts were mostly about how yummy her hot dog was.

"Out of all the places in New York, this is your dinner?"

Kari recognized the voice and turned to see Gia in her casual, post-work clothes. Looped around her hand was a leash with a small, mutty-looking dog at the end of it. The maybe terrier-pug looked at her with pleading eyes and licked its chops. "I don't mind simple," she said with a broad smile, not taking her eyes off the dog.

Gia lifted her foot to avoid the leash from tangling. "And that officially makes you the complete opposite from the usual hotel clientele. Ridiculous requests are somewhat expected in the hospitality business, but sometimes the demands do get out of hand. Especially on the boat."

Did Gia mean *the* boat? "Are you talking about the *Hinewai*?"

"Indeed, I am."

"You worked there?" Kari said with a hint of awe and envy.

Gia nodded. "I was a student of World University's hospitality program, then I was a VIP assistant on the ship. The *Hinewai* was a very interesting place to work and I saw the world."

"May I ask why you left?"

Gia tugged the leash. "Come, Ollie." The little dog walked with her as she sat at the other end of the bench. "I left because . . ." *How could I possibly explain this without scaring her?*

Kari's interest piqued now, but she couldn't let that show. "Was it the no pets rule? I noticed that when I was researching the ship."

"While I do love pets, that wasn't it. I was going to say that I started to get the feeling that something odd was going on."

"What do you mean?"

Gia bit her full lower lip and looked up at the elm giving them shade. *Illegal. No proof. Paranoia. How do I say this?* "Okay, so as you walk around, take in absolutely everything. How the decks are divided, the people, their uniforms, how they behave, their access, everything. But also, don't be afraid to ask questions. Like, why do parts of the boat have armed guards?"

"That doesn't seem too weird," Kari said. "Some high schools in this country have armed guards. Plus, I'm sure the *Hinewai* would be the target of pirates if they didn't have the means to defend themselves."

But a motorized raft at midnight with no lights? "Some areas of the boat also have retina scanners."

Okay, both the midnight boat rides and that type of biometric security were a touch extreme. "Do you think something shady is happening?"

"I don't have any proof of that, but if there was, traveling the world is a great way to cover it up, don't you think?" Gia stood from the bench and Ollie started to walk away, tightening the leash. "Still, I wish you luck."

"Thank you and . . . can I give Ollie a tiny piece of hot dog?"

Gia chuckled. "Sure."

Excited, Kari tore a small piece of hot dog and leaned down until Ollie snatched it from between her fingers and then licked every molecule of it from her skin.

Gia grinned and then tugged on the leash. "Come, Ollie."

Kari watched Gia's long, muscular legs walk a leisurely pace away as Ollie's short, fuzzy ones raced to catch up. She ate the rest of her dinner while she pondered Gia's observations. Secret levels. Armed guards. Retina scanners. One of those factors by itself would raise an eyebrow, but all three had Kari intrigued.

What kind of ship was the *Hinewai?*

Chapter Six

Manhattan Cruise Terminal, New York, United States

Kari didn't want to admit that she was anxious, but the jitters, sweaty palms, and constant need to pee indicated that she was. She blew out a long breath and then headed out the main revolving doors of the hotel. Per the email, she kept her eyes peeled for a white SUV, but the vehicle approaching the hotel was more of a tank than a car. The yellow taxi in front of it looked like a toy.

The luxury SUV pulled up to the hotel curb with the driver's window down. "Karishma?" he asked. At her nod, he unlocked the rear doors. "Make yourself comfortable. It's about twenty minutes to the dock." *Traffic.*

The backseat of the limo-esque ride was as large as her entire car. The seats were dark gray leather with buttons that indicated cooling, heating, and massage. She made her butt a nice little home and turned on the massage function at the same time the driver activated the privacy screen. She didn't know what the material was made from, but it was strong enough to block his thoughts and allow her to focus on the weather station cued on the TV in front of her. A tropical storm was wreaking havoc in Miami and would most likely be upgraded to a hurricane by tomorrow. She went to the next channel and gasped at the news in the ticker box under the broadcaster: Dallas Pride terrorist attempt by God and Country thwarted by tip-line caller.

Kari smiled at the news coverage of several people in hand-cuffs and knowing so many innocent people were safe now. She laughed and pointed at the man blubbering like a child who broke his own toy. Her joy never left as they drove through Hell's Kitchen and toward the Hudson River. Soon, the terminal and marina came into view, but to her surprise there was no *Hinewai* docked alongside the other large vessels in the water.

Kari tapped on the privacy screen, then saw the intercom button. She pushed it. "Where's the *Hinewai*? I thought I'd see it by now."

"Look farther in the water."

Kari furrowed her brow and, with her nose almost touching the glass of the window, looked beyond the boats. In the distance was a white ship. "Why isn't it with the rest of the boats?"

"It docked upon arrival for unloading of waste, refueling, reloading of supplies, and pre-arranged personnel changes. They've learned that if they stay docked once all that is taken care of, the locals and other businesses get annoyed because of the amount of space it takes. I'm sure it saves money, too."

Okay, that made sense. But there was a logistical factor that did not. "So, how am I going to get on the *Hinewai*?"

"Since you're a VIP, one of the faster boats will come out. You won't wait for the tender, which is like a ferry but for boats to land."

The car slowed to a stop along the area marked for drop-offs and a pale young man—who wasn't Miguel Santos—dressed in black pants and a black button-down shirt approached the car and held a piece of paper with Kari's name typed on it. Through the glass she read his name tag: Matthew (he/him); VIP Assistant. He opened the door for her.

Kari stepped out of the car into the warm, salty breeze and shut the door, and the driver wasted no time getting out of the drop off zone. Not even a wave goodbye.

I hope she's not mad. "Welcome, Ms. Okpik-Bakshi! I'm Matthew," he said in a Queen's English British accent. "There's been a slight change of plan to your schedule. I've been asked to step in and give you a tour of the ship."

"Oh," she said, surprised. "Is everything okay?"

"Yes! I'm sorry." *Oh, I've worried her.* "A lab thing came up rather suddenly that Dr. Santos needed to tend to. Beyond that, I don't have details." *I wonder what they do down there? All the experiments.*

"Well, I appreciate you helping out and I am curious about the ship."

Oh, good. She's nice. He smiled, which caused his thin upper lip to disappear completely. "It's not a problem. Please, follow me." Matthew led the way down the dock to a boat with dual motors, seating for twelve on the outside, and a covered cabin. "Watch your step on the gangplank."

"My driver mentioned that this is the VIP boat and there is a tender. How often does the tender run?"

"Monday through Thursday we generally do three times a day. Friday through Sunday we run more often, including past midnight, so people can have a night out." *Like most VIPs.*

The captain stepped outside to untether the boat from the cleats, then took his position behind the controls and powered the motors. Over the roar of the engine she couldn't hear

Matthew, which he knew. So he smiled and looked out at the water.

She liked Matthew. He had a kind and helpful way about him, and his thoughts primarily consisted of when he was going on shore during his off hours to see a show on Broadway. He was a fan of shows on the West End in London and wanted to know how the experience compared.

As they approached the *Hinewai*, Kari craned her neck upward. "That's a *big* boat." It wasn't often the words she said sounded dumb, but this was one of those moments.

Matthew chuckled. *Cute.* "This morning's tour will be quite the experience for you."

The captain pulled alongside a garage door type opening in the *Hinewai,* then backed into the space and cut the engine. A crew member outfitted in white shorts and a burgundy polo shirt tossed the captain thick ropes who then tied them to the boat with expert knots. Through an underwater system, the boat was pulled farther into the ship and onto a loading platform. Any sea water that flowed in was drained as the garage door closed them inside the belly of the ship.

She was already a fan of the tour.

Matthew gestured to the cavernous inside. "Welcome to the *Hinewai!*" He headed into a loading area where he scanned his thumb on a pad and glanced over to Kari. "Now they know we're on board."

Kari took in the area. Nautical equipment hung on the gray walls of the spacious room and the polished cement floor was marked with directions to follow the queue. "Is that where people stand when they are waiting to get on the tender?"

"It is. Everyone who is associated with the ship must scan their thumb print whenever they come on and off the ship for tracking purposes. VIP guests, on the other hand, have to be logged in this way . . ." Matthew took his phone out of his pocket and texted. When he went to return it to his pocket, it buzzed. *This is new.* If his thought didn't give away something was amiss on his screen, his scrunched nose did.

"Something wrong?"

"No. It's just . . ." *Okay, weird, an interviewee got the VIP boat and tour, but a level A tour with lunch?* He pocketed the phone and looked back to her. "Sorry about that. After the tour, which will be rather extensive, you'll have lunch with Dr. Santos."

Lunch wasn't part of the agenda, but she wouldn't complain about a free meal. And while on the tour, she could also keep her eyes peeled for the 'red flags' Gia mentioned. "That sounds nice."

She's such a sport about it. "Alright, then. Let's start here, on deck one. Aside from the VIP boat and tender area, we also have a marine science lab and health services."

Kari followed him up the wide staircase that placed them into the interior of the ship. They walked past the landing for deck two, which, according to the sign, was classrooms and dorms for World University or WU.

As they went up the grand interior stairs Matthew said, "While this was a ship originally built for vacation cruises, the *entire* ship has been modified. There are half the number of cabins than a typical cruise ship, thereby doubling the living area. The renovation wasn't cheap, but was less expensive and built faster than a brand-new commercial build of the same square footage in Papua New Guinea, which is where the boat is registered and does its annual maintenance checks."

She marveled at the ambition and dedication to transform a cruise ship in this way. "Wasn't there a plan B location?"

"Indonesia, which is where Mr. Wibawa was raised, but the same issues existed there. I should also note that an average cruise ship travels at twenty knots while we average fifteen and use the wind kite when possible; therefore, we use much less fuel. We also take advantage of natural light, use motion sensors, and keep common areas a reasonable temperature to save energy."

No wonder Mom A loved Henry Wibawa.

They walked down the hall, between the occupied cabins, and it reminded Kari of an apartment building. Thin carpet. Shiny numbers on the doors. Some had decorations outside or welcome mats. It was homey.

He stopped at the end of the hall and gestured to a series of rooms without homey touches. *Music, board games, forget the other one.* "Each housing level has multiple clubs. We have fourteen on the ship."

Before they reached the stairwell, they passed a massive laundromat. Then, a small crowd of people on the other side of the stairwell's brass railing dressed in white pants and burgundy polos headed down. They said a chorus of hellos in different accents.

Oh, VIP tour.

Like that color purple.

Don't trip. Don't trip.

"Because we travel all around the world," Matthew said, "the diversity on our ship is only rivaled by the United Nations." He pointed to her right at the two ship stores near the next landing and headed toward the stern. *I wonder if the garbage scientists are still here.* "This is one of the business sectors, and where inCog is located. However, I'm afraid I can't show you what that looks like since I'm not coded for that office. Sorry."

"It's okay. I'll see it soon enough during my interview."

"Right you are!" he said with a grin. This guy was made of glee and sticky toffee pudding. "The interesting thing about the school and the businesses here on the *Hinewai* are that they are independent. As long as they pay their rent and abide by the rules of their contracts, they're left alone. If not, it's immediate termination of the lease and eviction of the personnel at the next port." He paused. "So, I guess that last part isn't too great, but anything that jeopardizes the safety of the ship or its people is dealt with swiftly. I heard a story about a woman who had a candle lit in Osaka and she was sent packing to Tokyo in a week's time."

Kari itched where her firestarter necklace lay against her skin.

At the next deck, the activity increased six-fold, but it wasn't only people in the ship's uniforms. It was people in pajamas, people dressed for work, one person had workout clothes and a small towel.

Getting hungry. "Welcome to the food level. We have two cafeterias, two grab and go stations, and seating for two-hundred people. It's an impressive operation mostly because of the lack of food waste. You see, everyone signs up for their meals the day before. Our TVs have the programming like a hotel, but they're working on an app for our phones."

"You have to sign up to eat?"

"Basically. Not only do you note what you'll eat, but also the time. Each meal has a three-hour range, so there is flexibility with schedule." *And less people to crowd you.*

That was so jazzed! "Do I have to choose my lunch for today?"

His brows arched. *Good question.* "Good question. Let me check." He pulled out his phone and cocked his head. *So interesting.* "I'm supposed to call Madeleine when we're done to sort that. For now, it's onward to some residential decks! There's a cabin you can see, so we're going to head to eight. Most people when they first start on the ship have to settle for an interior room and get on a wait-list for a window or balcony."

They passed a dozen cabin doors decorated with welcome mats, white boards with messages, or flags. Matthew stopped, placed his thumb on the lock, and then punched in a code. Once the green light flashed, he pushed open the door.

The bright, natural light through the balcony's sliding door flooded the room and she could see the open harbor beyond. She was pulled toward the light, slid open the door, and stepped out into the harbor air. Kari heard Matthew close the main door behind them.

"I take it you like the view."

Unlike her childhood bedroom or tiny house that gave her a view of farmland and mountains, this was open water. She could watch the sun rise and set from all over the world. She could watch seabirds fly or dolphins and whales jump out of the waves right from her own room. Even with the view of New Jersey across the river, her vantage point of the buildings and activity was unlike anything she had ever seen.

This needed to be her future.

Kari had to nail the interview with inCog. "This is so much better than goats."

"That's um . . . I've never heard that one before, but I'm glad you like it. And there's more to see than what is out the window. There is a full-sized bed with two levels of storage underneath. Wardrobe off to the side. A table that, if you add a leaf, makes it a dining area for four. The kitchen is small, but has all the basic necessities: microwave, mini-fridge, sink."

She wouldn't have to fold her bed into a wall and there was a love seat! In front of a TV! "This is *so* much bigger than my tiny house."

Tiny house? Goats? Who is this girl? Matthew formed an

image of Kari as a troll, complete with large and hairy feet. "Would you like to see the bathroom?"

"Yes, I would." Kari walked—with her reasonably sized and velvety smooth feet—in the direction of the only other door in the cabin. The bathroom was small but more than adequate. Living in such a small space for two years had prepared her well for this.

Yes, this needed to be her life.

Matthew clasped his hands together. *She's staring.* "If there's nothing else you'd like to see here, we should probably continue the tour. We're almost finished."

The next deck mirrored the seventh at the stern, but the VIP suites had two floors to call their own, and the bow had a fitness center that was better than most gyms. There was no swimming pool due to the extra maintenance and energy, so in the waterless pits there were courts for basketball and pickle-ball. The ninth deck had cabins at the stern for ship executives, including Henry Wibawa, and at the bow a theater. The tenth was dubbed the activity center and mission control deck. Lastly, towering several levels at the bow was the bridge, but at the stern . . . Kari couldn't make out what was up there.

Matthew pulled out his phone. "Time to give an update."

"But there are two more levels to see."

"Ah. Those are off-limits to the vast majority of the ship. That's where Wibawa Enterprises business operations occur, Mr. Wibawa socializes with VIPS, and his personal helicopter lands." Matthew dialed. "Hello, Madeleine. Yes, we just finished the tour . . . I don't know. Let me ask her." He looked at Kari. "How do you like your steak prepared?"

"Steak? Really?" she asked, delighted. He nodded with a grin. "Medium-rare, please."

"Got it." He winked at her, then returned the phone to his ear. "The answer is medium-rare. Where shall I take her next?"

He gaped like one of the fish in the river beneath them. *I couldn't have heard that right.* "Sorry, you want me to do what?" He rubbed his chin as he paced away from Kari. "Okay, I'll bring her up." Matthew disconnected the call and approached her once again with pursed lips. *Who is this girl?* "This must be one heck of an interview. You're going to deck eleven to have your lunch and interview with the inCog team and . . . Henry Wibawa."

Chapter Seven

Elevator with retina scan. Check.

Armed guard in a black-on-black suit with visible gun holster, taser, and soul patch facial hair waiting for them. Check.

A massive outdoor dining table with a server waiting to the side. Check.

An eccentric billionaire she recognized from his various interviews and photographs sitting at the far end and smiling at her. Check.

"Karishma!" Henry Wibawa beamed with his arms wide while he stayed seated at his charcuterie board. "Thank you for bringing her up, Matthew."

"You're welcome, Mr. Wibawa." *I don't understand anything happening here.* "Is there anything else you'd like me to do before I return to my assigned VIP duties?"

"No, that is all," Henry said. "Karishma and I have much to discuss."

Matthew bowed his head slightly and then looked to Kari.

"Good luck." He left the area and rounded the security guard to go into the ship.

What in the world was happening? This wasn't lunch with Santos and Mitchell. This was lunch with armed security, a personal server, and one of the richest people in the world.

"Please pardon me if I don't get up to shake your hand," Henry said. "I'm a bit of a germaphobe."

Henry Wibawa was thinking of shaking her hand. Her very own hand attached to her wrist. And now she probably needed to say intelligent words back to him. "Communicable diseases should be taken very seriously, especially on a relatively closed system like the *Hinewai*." There. Those were some coherent words she managed to say out loud.

He shook a finger at her and smiled. "Yes! So true. And, please, sit down."

The server pulled out her chair. *So weird. Weirder than the visit with Prince Russell.* "Ms. Okpik-Bakshi, can I offer you a beverage?"

"Um . . ." Kari sat, still stunned from the situation. The 360-degree view of the two cities and harbor from essentially the top of the ship distracted her. "Do you have iced tea?"

"We have everything, ma'am."

Of course, they did. Why wouldn't a billionaire have one of the simplest beverages in the world? "That would be nice, then."

The server left, and she stared at the man at the far end of the table with perfect teeth and crow's feet etched into his tawny skin, a glass of red wine in his hand. The sun reflected off his high forehead and cufflinks worth more than her car.

It was Henry Wibawa in the flesh.

"This is . . ." Kari couldn't find the right words within her stellar vocabulary. "I honestly don't know what to say to you."

"I understand all of this is quite overwhelming, but trust me, Karishma, when I say the pleasure is all mine."

"You can call me Kari. Also, I don't understand how that's possible."

"Oh, but it is! Do you know why I am so wealthy?" He didn't give her a chance to answer before he provided one. "I invest in the ideas I believe in. I invest in the people I believe in. Karishma, I believe in you and know that you are going to do things that will change the world!"

Clearly, he preferred to use her full first name. She let it go and leaned to the side as her server put down her iced tea with a plate of a lemon wedges and a tray of six different sweeteners, including maple syrup. She had only ever seen that at home when Mom A fixed her tea. "That's very flattering to hear, but I don't understand why. I haven't really done anything with my life yet, including getting the job at inCog."

"Isn't she humble, Josef?" he said to the soul patch guard beside him. "Yes, you are young, but my talent scout, Madeleine, found your resume and master's project for me. You see, I've been following breakthroughs in neuroscience— like optogenetics—for years because it's a science-fiction idea within our grasp! Your paper on advancing the science demonstrated how easily we could have that technology as a part of our reality if we simply put the resources toward it."

Kari's cheeks started to ache from her large smile. "You're the one who forwarded my resume to inCog?"

"Indeed. And since I own the company, they have to listen to me." He laughed and gave her that blinding smile again. "As far as I'm concerned you should have the job. You have undergraduate degrees in biochemistry and statistics, a master's in neuroscience. Your brain is absolutely brilliant! But I didn't want to step on Dr. Santos's toes too much. It's his decision, but I thought it was important that you know I support you."

A silver cloche was placed in front of her. "I can't believe you read my work and liked it."

"Loved it! I would like to talk more about it, but you should eat first."

She watched him delicately spread a soft cheese on a cracker. "Shouldn't we wait for the others? And aren't you getting a cloche, too?"

He shook his head while he chewed his cracker. "No, I have a large dinner tonight with the president."

"Oh. The president of what?"

He prepared another cracker, this time with caviar. "The United States." His meals of the day consisted of her and one of the most powerful people in the world. "Go ahead and start eating. Remember, I'm the big boss of inCog. They won't mind."

Kari couldn't argue with that. She lifted her cloche and the most perfect steak ever grilled on the planet was presented, cut at a bias in strips so she could see its perfect pinkish-red goodness. Shallow, silver pans of potatoes au gratin and roasted asparagus joined the entrée.

"My personal chef prepared that. I hope you like ribeye, but if not, he can make another."

"I'm sure that won't be necessary." Kari moaned when the rich, savory meat melted in her mouth. She had almost embraced the reality that she was sharing a meal with one of the richest and most powerful people in the world, when the why started to hound her. "I can't tell you what it means to me that you read and appreciate my ideas, but aren't there other more experienced people out there that Madeleine or inCog found?"

"Yes, you are young, but you have something that cannot be taught: imagination."

The door swung open and Miguel Santos walked onto the

deck. To contrast his light brown skin, sturdy build, and dark curly hair, behind him was Thomas Mitchell, who had a more pinkish hue, thinning blond-silver hair, and a slight beer belly. Mitchell's wire-rimmed glasses transitioned into darker lenses as he stepped into the sunlight.

Kari stood from her meal to greet him. "Hello, it's wonderful to meet you both."

Dr. Santos came closer and flashed a nervous smile. But the most dominant feature were the bags under his brown eyes. It looked like he hadn't slept in days. *I hope to God she's qualified.* "It's wonderful to meet you in person, Karishma." Santos extended his hand.

"Kari, please."

Firm handshake. "Okay, Kari. I've been told you may know my colleague, but I'd like to formally introduce you to inCog's clinical advisor and neurologist, Dr. Thomas Mitchell."

"It's true I've seen your name on a few brain scans in my house," Kari said with a smile.

An image of Mom L and Mom A looking twenty years younger appeared in his mind. Mitchell shook her hand and stared. *Spitting image both of them. The donor has to be a relative.* "It's very nice to meet you, Kari, and I'm sorry for the gawking. It's just that you share a lot of similarities to your mothers, especially Leela's eyes."

"I'm also told I have Mom L's snark." Kari returned to her seat and brought her attention back to Santos, where the server handed him a coffee.

He took a three o'clock position at the table. His tired eyes looked to her once more. "So, the schedule is that we'll have our lunch, then go down to the office for the rest of the interview."

"So, lunch is also the interview?" Kari asked.

"Think of it as a warm up," Mitchell said from the nine o'clock position.

Two more servers with cloches—complete with printed labels—came out and were placed in front of Santos and Mitchell. Everyone was out of telepathy range. Kari knew that would help her focus, but at the same time, she needed this job and was willing to manipulate the course of conversation or bend it in her favor.

"Please," Henry said, "enjoy your lunches and don't let my presence change the course of your conversation. I am happy to be an observer."

Santos had to make sure his fried oyster sandwich had the perfect distribution of tartar sauce before he spoke. "I'd actually like Kari to have the opportunity to ask questions first."

"Oh. Um, okay." Kari watched Mitchell cut the roasted half chicken with surgical precision. "I have a lot. But I guess we can start with what the day-to-day looks like? Or the research inCog is able to do on its own?"

"Great questions," Santos said. "When we aren't doing our main job at inCog—which is analyzing data and imagery from outside labs and hospitals—we investigate areas that aren't getting a lot of attention but should. We research that between contracts, but we haven't moved beyond literature reviews and brainstorming on any particular topic."

"We can't use animal models because it violates ship rules," Mitchell said. "So, we're leaning toward a pilot clinical trial to start."

"So," Kari said, "optogenetic application in humans is on the table?"

Santos paused the sandwich at his lips. "It is."

Henry didn't say a word but lifted his wine glass in a silent toast.

Kari could have danced but stayed in her seat, composed. "That's very exciting. As I'm sure you could have guessed based on my capstone topic."

"Which was impressive," Mitchell said. "We could tell you have a real passion for research."

This was when she could really pitch her abilities to Santos. "As Dr. Mitchell knows, I've grown up with science. Two of my grandparents were physicians. Plus, growing up with a mother who was a medical marvel herself, and another mother who will literally stop everything when there's an advance in green design or engineering, has not only affected my interests, but how I think. I have my other set of grandparents to thank for that as well. They really pushed me to think outside the box with problem solving."

"Can you expand on that?" Santos asked with his coffee cup in hand.

"Sure. My Ata Niq—that's my grandfather—used to say that problems are easy to solve when you have all of the right tools at your disposal, but what happens when you don't have the perfect tool? You either invent one or you have to find a new way to solve the problem. Look at it from a new angle."

The three men at the table smiled or nodded, giving her a moment to bask in her answer and enjoy another combination bite. She was about to ask about their mission statement when Santos asked, "You're close to your family, aren't you?"

Kari felt the weight of the firestarter under her blouse. "I am. They've all changed their lives to make mine better. I'd do anything for them."

Mitchell gave her a sad nod and then averted his eyes.

She knew why and didn't want to stay on a topic that brought him so much pain. "So, what kind of statistical and bioinformatic programs do you prefer to use?"

"We'll show you in the lab," Santos said. "Maybe you can even help us with a current issue. Milia had been working on it but then . . . poof."

"Did she leave unexpectedly?" she asked tentatively.

Mitchell nodded while he chewed; Santos closed his eyes and shook his head. She was at a loss as to what to say next, but she could focus on the work. Plus, if she could troubleshoot an issue during her interview, they'd have to give her the job. "I'd love to try to solve whatever problem Milia started working on."

A new security guard—no soul patch, but bald with neck tattoos—came to the table and whispered in Henry's ear. Henry nodded and stood from the table. "I'm sorry, but I must leave our lunch early. Karishma, it was a pleasure to meet you. Doctors, I look forward to hearing your decision."

"It was wonderful meeting you as well," she said, standing. She hadn't even realized that she'd stood. "Sorry. I'm a little star struck."

"I get it," Santos said. "I think I reacted the same way when I met him and won the job to manage inCog."

Kari went back to her meal and tried to think of her next easy follow-up question. "So, speaking of winning the job, may I ask how many other people you've interviewed?"

Santos swallowed and dabbed the corners of his mouth with his napkin. "That's been a bit of an issue. According to the job sites, we've had no interest, which doesn't make sense to me. Ever since Panama there's been different IT issues with either our submission or the site itself. We've contacted all the webmasters or help desks and still we have gotten nowhere." As if his wild eyes and tone didn't convey his feelings enough, he added, "I think Henry and Madeleine sensed my frustration and that's why they stepped in."

Mitchell cleared his throat. "But we're very happy you're here and open to checking out our problem."

After learning more about their data issue and how Milia basically said, 'I quit now' and ghosted them, the three of them went to the inCog lab. In the elevator, Santos's thoughts were of relief and jubilation. He hadn't expected Kari to keep up with the conversation the way she did, which made Henry's pushing of Kari's resume and capstone his way easier for him to handle. Mitchell was still fixated on the physical similarities between her and her mothers.

Hope she meets expectations. "And here we are." Santos stood beside the solid, gun-metal-gray door, pressed his thumb to the scanner, and entered the code. The interior lock shifted with a loud mechanical *clang* and he pushed the door open.

She hadn't expected translucent, frosted glass walls dividing the different regions. Through the first wall was a basic microbiology set up, the next room on the left was more biomedical, then, there was the office: a massive window made a wall, a round conference table with TV in front was in the middle of the room, and three desks lined all three main walls.

"Mitchell and I have found that this gives us each space but also allows collaboration," Santos said. "So, I have the desk by the window and Mitchell has the long wall."

Kari was too distracted by the network of large computer monitors at Mitchell's station showcasing beautiful images of brains to look at New Jersey again. "Oh!" She pointed to the black and white brain. "Is that a crow brain?"

How did she know that? "Not many people would know that without context," Mitchell said. "What gave it away?"

"I went through a phase where I was obsessed with eagles, so I learned a lot about avian biology. And since the title is about cognition, I didn't think it would be of a songbird."

Santos smiled. "I'd say that's a good use of clues. Now, onto our problem." He gestured to the conference table. "Have a seat."

For the next twenty minutes, the three discussed one specific problem that had been sent to them from universities in Switzerland and South Korea. It was a joint effort, but the two labs with the same data had somehow generated vastly different analyses. Therefore, they weren't sure what to conclude. Kari located the problem after she dug into the methodology.

"So, they both used machine learning," she said, "but they trained their systems in different ways. Geneva left out a few key demographics relevant to the study."

"What do you think?" Mitchell asked Santos.

Santos crossed his arms across his chest, his sleeves rolled up to his elbows. "This isn't the first time we've encountered this. Remember the group who trained their machines with adult data and it was a pediatric tumor study?"

Mitchell leaned back in his chair. "Oh, that's right."

"Mitchell," Santos started to stand, "join me by the auto-clave for a minute? Kari, you can enjoy the view."

But Kari couldn't enjoy the view while the two of them spoke in the next room over. Were they trying to come up with the next set of questions? Would she be given some sort of timed test? Based on Mitchell's neutral expression and casual lean against the benchtop and Santos's many hand gestures, she didn't have a clue where the rest of the interview would go.

Then, Santos took a sticky note off a yellow pad, wrote something, and walked her way. Mitchell trailed. "So, Kari, we are in a unique situation here. As you know, our previous person up and left and we are getting pummeled with work, so . . ."

Kari sat straighter and caught herself nodding as if it would encourage him to finish his thought faster.

"So . . ." He closed the distance and handed her the sticky note. *If she says no, I'm screwed. I have to sleep.* "This is our offer."

She got the job. She got the job! Kari looked at the paper:

$40,000 salary
14 days PTO
5 company holidays

Kari looked back up to Santos but was speechless.

"I know the salary seems low," Santos said, "but it's adjusted because room and board on the ship is covered."

Her mouth dropped. Did she want to work for a company who appreciated her work and shared her passion? Yes. Could she see herself living in an efficiency cabin and traveling the world while dolphins did spinny flips outside her balcony? Absolutely, yes!

"Yes! I accept the offer."

Mitchell extended his hand. "Welcome aboard."

She shook his hand and then Santos's. "I'm very excited right now. When do I start?"

"My preference is as soon as possible, but definitely before we leave New York."

"Oh." Dammit. Driving back to Oregon to get the rest of her things and driving back in that amount of time wasn't feasible. "I don't know if I can do that. I drove here and promised my moms I'd be back in a week—"

"I forgot to mention that there is a ten percent salary signing bonus."

She got $4000 just by signing? "I'm sure the moms will understand that movers will be coming to them."

"Glad to hear it!" Santos said. "But before you talk to them, we should see Madeleine to make it official. I need to send her some details and then we can go up together."

Chapter Eight

On the way to the administration office level, Santos had a more relaxed posture and fixated on sleeping well that night. And possibly with his lady friend, Charlotte, who did IT for the ship. Good for him.

"I'll sign some paperwork that relates specifically to inCog and then hand you off to Madeleine to deal with the contract of ship living." *Weird she's doing it and not the residency coordinator.*

Kari had to agree. "It's a little unexpected that she would see to those details."

"I can only think it's because she found you and wants to meet you." Santos led her through a typical business office: people in cubicles, quiet conversations with the occasional burst of volume, and the smell of coffee.

She could really go for a fancy cup to celebrate.

He stopped outside one of the doors lining the exterior. The name plate read *Madeleine Coultier*. "Here we are." He knocked lightly.

"Come in," said a muffled, cultivated Australian accent.

Santos opened the door, and a woman who looked like the ice queen she read about in Mom A's romance novels sat behind a grand desk. She was rail thin with a platinum blond bob, her fire-orange pants suit the only warm note about her. That and wisps of steam from her tea cup. Based on the squeezed lemon resting on the saucer, Kari guessed Earl Grey.

"Please, sit." Madeleine gestured to the two guest chairs in front of her. One had a small, lumbar support pink pillow that had dozens of key words about family printed in white.

"It's a pleasure to meet you." Kari was unsure if she should shake her hand, but Madeleine stayed seated, holding her tea cup. She sat in the lumbar support chair, pleased that Madeleine was out of range.

"I've been waiting to meet you for quite some time." Madeleine sipped and leaned back from her desk so she could cross her long legs. "Your inCog and ship residency contracts are ready. Dr. Santos obviously wrote in the parts specific to inCog and I wrote in your other items. If he wouldn't mind skimming it first to make sure the inCog information is correct, I'd appreciate it."

"Of course," he said and took a tablet from her. While he skimmed and Kari heard his thoughts, she took in the rest of her office. A photo of a very blond family dressed in jeans and white button-down shirts with Madeleine in the middle was featured on the wall. There was a door cracked open behind her with a towel on a shelf. "Do you have your own bathroom?"

"I do. It's a perk of the job." Madeleine brought her attention back to Santos. "Status update."

"I'm almost there." He finished and signed with the tip of his index finger.

Then, he handed Kari the tablet with her name, title of Associate Scientist, and inCog at the top. She touched her finger to the screen and recoiled when she saw the contract was

117 pages. That seemed excessive. Strange, even. Gia's words came back to her. And now that she thought about it, there were a few other things that were odd enough to prevent her from skipping to the last page and writing her digital signature.

"How did the valet at the hotel know what kind of car I drive?" Kari asked.

"I recruit for the most unique and classified projects of Wibawa Enterprises," Madeleine said. "Once I find ideal candidates from a series of exhaustive searches, an in-depth investigation is performed. Somewhere along the line the make and model of your car was discovered. How specifically was that information found? I don't know. I have staff that do that level of investigation."

Seemed reasonable enough. Kari returned her attention to the tablet and skimmed the words as she scrolled down the screen. The residency contract started today, but inCog was the next day. "I'm surprised to see the contracts have different dates."

"We've found that people enjoy that extra half-day to settle in. I believe Matthew showed you an empty cabin earlier."

"I could have *that* cabin?" Kari asked so loud Santos retracted in his chair.

Eardrums assaulted.

Madeleine nodded, with her tea cup barely covering her grin.

"That's so jazzed!" Kari went back to reading and saw that the room and board was standard and clear, but because of the nature of the ship she would need to complete a form detailing special skills in case of emergencies. There was a third section that caught her by surprise. "The Wibawa Enterprises Promise? What's that?"

"It basically extends your special skills to help other Wibawa business interests," Madeline said. "For example, there could be a VIP who wants to go scuba diving, but who wants a buddy. So, we find someone on the ship who is certified to go with them. It's paid work. Someone of your talents—I mean, you speak a dozen languages—could be very useful should we need a last-minute interpreter for Henry or something like that."

It was true that she did have crazy language skills. Kari reached the end of the contract where a black line extended above her printed name. This was it. She twirled her index finger in the air to add a bit of drama to the moment and then signed her name on the line. A strange warmth and excitement filled her. Was that . . . happiness? It had been so long she had almost forgotten what pure joy felt like.

Thank God. "And with that," Santos said, "I'll see you tomorrow at nine sharp to get you onboarded." He shook her hand with several pumps. "We're going to do such exciting work!"

He left the office and Madeleine shot her a smile. "Congratulations, and I'm sure you're excited to learn about life here on the *Hinewai*."

"I am! What Matthew showed me was very interesting. Especially that cabin." The cabin with twice the square footage of her tiny house and ocean view. "I can't believe that's mine."

"Well, it is, which brings me to security. Once you leave here, I'll ask security to apply the biometrics and code you used at the hotel to your cabin and inCog. I'll have Matthew or Finn —they're a VIP assistant too—arrange to have your belongings at the hotel, including what was in your car, brought onto the ship. I'll also get them to supply you with some linens and toiletries until you can go get your own. Are you following?"

Kari hung on to every fantastic word. "Absolutely. But, if possible, please tell them that they can donate my tent and sleeping bag."

"How kind of you," Madeleine said in a dry tone. "Now, fetching all of your items will probably take a couple of hours. In the meantime, I suggest you start the skills questionnaire on your TV. Are you following?"

"Absolutely. But I have questions." When Madeleine raised her sharp blond brow, Kari asked, "How do you recommend I get my things from Oregon onto the ship?"

"Ah, yes. I would suggest you contact home, ask what time is reasonable for a moving crew to come, tell me or a VIP assistant, and wait a day."

Next day shipping of her tiny house contents? "How much will that cost?"

Madeleine waved off the question. "Consider it part of your Wibawa Enterprise Promise signing bonus. Any other questions?" she asked with a tone that suggested she hoped there were none.

"I think I'm set."

"So glad. Well then"—Madeleine made a shooing motion with her hand—"be on your way, so I can get to the details of settling you in properly."

"Okay. Thank you." Kari stood and left her office, shutting the door behind her. When the latch clicked, Kari made a beeline to the restrooms across the cubicle farm, checked the stalls for feet, and when there were none, launched into a celebratory dance to release the abundance of positive energy that had accumulated inside her. She had a job and a new place to live! The moms would be so hap— Shit! The moms.

Kari headed for the deck with the coffee bar, because that was how she could both celebrate and tell them the news. Fortunately, today Mom L worked from home too, so she could get both of them at the same time. But she dialed Mom A's phone, since she was the one least prone to yelling.

"Chickpea!" Mom A answered. "We've been wondering

how it went, but based on the brain buzz your Mom L just reported, we think it went pretty well."

"Well, it did go very, very well. They offered me the job."

"After one interview?" Mom L shrieked.

"They're in a unique situation, but it was a *great* interview. I did a live demo of how I problem solve, and I had an endorsement from Henry freaking Wibawa."

"Wait. What?" Mom A asked in a surprised yell. "Henry Wibawa wanted them to hire you?"

"Yeah! And get this, I ate a steak lunch with him!"

After the exclamations and overlapping questions, Kari gave them a summary of her tour, the lunch, the inCog office, and then the meeting with Madeleine. Which lead to the highest frequency Kari had ever heard and may have shattered the glass screen on her cell phone.

"You're not coming home?" Mom L shrieked.

"I mean, I will eventually, but things were so exciting and I got a signing bonus and I'm so excited and we basically said a long goodbye and had a farewell dinner before I left for the road trip." Their prolonged silence caused her to bite her lower lip and wince. "Are you mad?"

"Yes, I'm mad! Why in all the goats of the underworld wouldn't I be mad?"

"Calm down, Leela," Mom A said in a poor whisper. "I'm sure chickpea had a more sound reason than she was living in the moment and money, right?"

This was Mom A taking the shovel from her so she could stop digging her hole deeper. "That's right. You see, they leave New York in less than two weeks. Driving back to Oregon and then back here again—in a car that won't fit all my stuff—is cutting the timeline really close." There were no upset screams, so she continued. "And I am sorry that I didn't discuss it with you first, but that's kind of what I have to do now, right? I'm an adult and I have to make decisions. Sometimes those decisions might not be the ones you want me to make, but I can't call or text you every time."

There was a collective sigh. "You can always reach out to us," Mom L said in a much calmer voice, "but I understand the point you're making."

"Maybe we can fly to New York before you leave?" Mom A asked. "Then, we can celebrate and send you off properly."

Leave it to Mom A to tug at the heartstrings. Kari touched her necklace. "I would really like that. Thank you."

"You're welcome, chickpea," Mom L said. "Now, how exactly are you getting your stuff to New York?"

———

After coordinating the day and time where one of the moms could direct movers, it was time for that celebratory coffee. Kari read the menu, which put most cafés to shame. There were coffees from all over the world, some she had only ever read about, and they had the price points that demonstrated that. "Can I please have a small Kona brew with cream and one sugar?"

"And a medium Italian roast," said a familiar voice from behind. "Both on me."

Kari turned and saw Mitchell. Then she watched him place his thumb on the scanner. "Thank you. So our thumb prints are tied to our bank account?"

"Basically. You need to create an account within the ship that takes a certain amount of money from your paycheck each month. It's a simple system for on-ship purchasing."

"And that's for all expenses outside of the cafeteria?"

"Correct." *If I still drank alcohol, I'd be pissed about how much they increase the price.* The barista placed their coffees on the counter, and Mitchell gestured with his ceramic mug to the edge of the deck. "Feel free to join me or go and do your own thing."

For the first time in a long time the idea of company didn't repulse her. "I'd like that."

Mitchell headed to a seating area near the railing. "I'd like to get as much fresh air as I can before I have to go back to the lab."

Kari chose a seat across from the low table between them. She took a sip of her steaming coffee and thought she died and went to utopia. This was what coffee should taste like. "Have you gone into the city much while we've been anchored?"

"Not very much. I went in to restock on some personal items and checked out a running store." He patted his gut. "I'm trying to get back into good habits. Even though they had to order the shoes for me, I ended up having sushi with one of the VIP assistants. So, that was healthy, at least."

"Oh, Matthew gave me a tour this morning."

Mitchell smiled around the rim of his coffee cup. "He's a nice kid. But it wasn't Matthew; it was Finn. And you will definitely know them when you see them. Finn has hair that is so red and wavy it looks like flames."

Kari caught the usage of 'them' and not he or she. "Matthew told me a little bit about the VIP role. Sounds like they have to work with A-list clientele."

"More like A plus. They are leaders of industry, politicians, celebrities, royalty. You name it. But the VIP assistants not only cater to the person, they also might have a family to tend to as well. That's really the only time you'll hear or see children on this ship. I'm sure you noticed that children aren't allowed."

"What happens if someone is pregnant?"

His brow raised over the rim of his glasses. "You didn't catch that in the contract you just signed?"

"I was so excited, some of the words just blurred together." Kari laughed with a nervous edge.

"Well, pregnancy beyond the second trimester is one of the medical conditions that is considered to be high-risk on the ship given the lack of specific medical care that could be needed in an emergency."

"So, they just evict you?"

Mitchell nodded. "Much like if you break safety rules." He took a sip of his coffee and made a satisfied *ahh*. "If you have other questions about the ship, please ask. But before I forget, no matter how sea-worthy you think you are, get some anti-nausea stuff from the ship store."

"Probably a good idea." Kari looked off in the distance to the towering buildings near the harbor. "Can I ask if you like it here?"

"Love it. I feel like it's given me a second chance at life." He suddenly found the tassels of his loafers interesting. "How much do you know about why I left practicing medicine?"

"I wouldn't say I *know* anything, but I know the rumors."

"The rumors are true, but I'm not embarrassed. The research I wanted to pursue was valid. However, I do regret punching my chief of staff at the hospital." He sucked in his cheek and shook his head. "I should have done it at the conference hotel when I found out he slept with my wife."

"Oh, that's . . . something."

"I think my words were a little stronger than that. On the good news front, I think my kids are starting to come around to the idea that I'm not the complete washout my ex made me out to be."

"How old are they?

"Both in their twenties. My son is an art teacher in Oregon, and my daughter is in college in California. So, they're doing well, and I'm doing well now that I'm with inCog. Santos has been good to me. I think you'll find that he's a real sweet guy."

"What did he do before he came here?"

"After graduate school in Spain he started his own outsourced data business in North Carolina, but flooding ruined his lab. Then, all I know is that Henry had been following his company and work—unbeknownst to Santos—and offered him a second chance with a new company he wanted to form, inCog. Now here we all are." Mitchell's pocket buzzed. "Excuse me for a moment." He read whatever came in and then stood. "Looks like I'll have to get the rest of the coffee to go. Santos just let me know the extra scans I needed came in."

"You two have been putting in a lot of hours, haven't you?"

"You have no idea, but thanks to you that should be a thing of the past soon enough." He headed to the counter, got his coffee to go, then turned back to her with a bright smile. "It's pretty neat we get to work together."

Kari's smile matched his. "I think so, too."

She finished her drink in solitude and then made her way back down the stairs to her cabin. Her cabin! A few people gave her a wave along the way, but most were chatting on their phone or listening to music. It really was like a city street, but with less people. When she came upon her cabin she knew there was only one way to learn if her code worked and her things had arrived. She coded herself in, opened the door, and in the middle of the room were her personal belongings.

Kari bounced where she stood. A gigantic gift basket caught her eye on the coffee table. She went over and picked up the white envelope with her name written in flowing script balanced on top. It was a standard welcome letter that laid out all the basics to life on board.

Her gift basket, on closer inspection, was a wicker trash

can. Inside was a mug, a few different teas and a small bag of instant coffee, some salty and sweet snacks, and an all-in-one body cleanser wrapped in the smallest towel she had ever seen. None of it was fancy, but it was enough to supplement her until she could go to the ship store, go into the city, or her things from home—Oregon home—arrived.

To fully embrace unpacking mode, Kari traded her suit for her least smelly tank top and cargo pants. Then, her hair went back into a ponytail. She moved her belongings against the wall. Then, she held a breath as she popped the locks on her guitar case and audibly exhaled when she saw no dings and the pick still in its appropriate location between the strings. No one had touched her baby.

Her second most prized possession peeked out of an open box: the coffee station. She placed the electric kettle and French press on the kitchen counter top at the same time there was a knock on the door. The reality of neighbors was something she had prepared herself for but hoped she had more time to get used to. She went to the door and opened it to see a Black woman with a stocky build in jeans and a plain white t-shirt holding a plate covered with foil. She kept her hair up with a colorful elastic bandana. Her smile was a tad maniacal and made her nose scrunch.

"Hi!" she said and then pushed up her pink-framed glasses. *Calm down, you screamed at her.* "I'm Jade, your neighbor."

"Kari. I'm sorry if you're coming over because you heard swearing. My shaving cream exploded in my luggage."

Jade chuckled. "That's funny—except the explosion part— I'm sorry to hear about the extra mess. But, to ease your pain, this might help." She held the plate out farther. "I hope you like apple turnovers, but if you don't, I can bring you something else tomorrow."

A neighbor who made baked goods? She could get used to

that. "Thank you. Did you just happen to have these on hand to give away?"

Yes and no. "I teach baking at WU, so when I came home and saw that I had a new neighbor, I ran back down to grab a couple from today's lesson before they made it to the student cafeteria."

"I really appreciate this. I don't know if my dining account works yet, so this might function as my dinner." She lifted the foil just enough to smell the baked cinnamon apple blend. "I thought all university people lived on the lower decks?"

"The students do. Trust me, it's best to keep students and instructors separated."

"That makes sense." Kari held her plate of turnovers and smiled. She didn't know what else to say, so she just kept smiling. Which was the same thing Jade did.

It was awkward.

This is weird. Don't know if it's her or me. "I'm going to let you get back to unpacking"—Jade started to backpedal inch by inch—"but if you have any questions or need company while you're settling in, just knock. But do it before eight in the evening, please. I don't talk to people after eight. That cuts into my me-time."

Jade went up several more points in her books: she was nice, she baked, and she respected personal space. "I promise no questions after eight."

"Great! Well, enjoy the turnovers and have a nice evening."

"You too. And thanks again." Kari shut the door, then took the foil off the plate. Perfectly golden-brown, puffy triangles laid underneath. She'd treat herself to one after she finished unpacking.

A less exciting task awaited her: dirty clothes. Hopefully, cargo pants and tank tops were acceptable work apparel for inCog because that was what she had until the rest of her clothes arrived. After her clothes were in the wash, she broke down the cardboard boxes, put the flattened pieces under her arm, and headed to the recycling shoot. Kari walked past the other cabin doors and was reminded that she needed something to decorate hers. What said, 'I'm a loner but willing to be friendly'?

"Do you need a hand getting around with those boxes?" someone asked from behind. The person was quasi-Canadian based on the pronunciation of 'around'.

Kari peeked over her shoulder and first noticed the cascading red hair. The black pants and button-down black shirt didn't showcase any physical attributes, other than they were lean. Based on the VIP assistant-style clothes and distinctive hair, though, this had to be Finn. "I got it, thanks." Of course, as soon as she declined help, the boxes slipped. She stopped to readjust her grip.

She said she didn't want help, so don't offer. Polite small talk if she makes eye contact. She's new to the boat.

Another person who respected her personal space. Kari had hope for boat society. When she reached the narrow recycling shoot, she groaned. There was no way her boxes were fitting into that as they were.

"It appears that you have a bit more folding to do. Can I cut in line so I can toss these in?" They moved the canvas bag slung over their shoulder to their feet.

"Sure." Kari stepped to the side, took her boxes, and folded them in half while the stranger put one aluminum can at a time down the shoot. "Out of curiosity, do you have to individually send them down?"

"Maintenance prefers it this way because if you do a lot at once you can jam it—like what happened near the club I just came from. Also, your question confirms my suspicion that you're new. My name's Finn." Their finger on the name tag confirmed they/them pronouns. "I'm with VIP services."

"I'm Kari—sorry, I don't have a name tag with she/her pronouns. Matthew gave me an intro of sorts to VIP services earlier."

Nice. Relaxed. "I may have given him a hand with a few phone calls to get your things. You work for inCog?"

"Technically, my first day is tomorrow, so I'm unemployed."

Finn laughed, showcasing teeth that did not have braces on them as a youth.

"Who's the VIP you're assigned to?"

An ass. "A bigtime fishery guy from Newfoundland. Has his name on everything in St. John's, but I only know that because I'm from there."

"I don't think I've ever met someone from Newfoundland." Gods, that was dumb. "Can you forget I just said that?"

Cute. Embarrassed. "Not a problem. You've probably had a long day, and I have to get back to my VIP." Finn slung the empty canvas bag over their shoulder. *It's a small place and you'll run into her again.* "Well, it was nice meeting you Kari. I'll see you around."

"It was nice meeting you, too," she said, even though Finn had started walking away.

The second pleasant interaction with a stranger in under an hour. That hadn't happened in about a decade. The ship was magical.

Once she was back in her apartment she grabbed a turnover, even though she knew she needed an actual meal. She didn't have a plate for her turnover, but she did have her collapsible camping bowl for impromptu dining.

Her butt settled into her chocolate brown loveseat and she turned on her TV. She expected to see a menu of options like the hotel, not a welcome message:

Welcome to the Hinewai, *Karishma. Please use the television remote to navigate through your options. Would you like to enter your special skills now?*

"Not really." She picked up the remote and started clicking through her priority list: money, food, and programing her favorite shows to record.

She went into her ship's spending account. The TV screen projected her current account balance of $0.00. The signing bonus would probably take a day or two or maybe a week to cycle through. After she manually entered her memorized banking information, she transferred what she felt was a reasonable amount of starter funds for her first month considering she had numerous supplies to buy: $500.

Kari went back to the main menu and found dining, which informed her that dining selections were closed for the day but she could register for her meals tomorrow. It was a simple, easy task that made her hungrier. Then, she was prompted once more if she'd enter her skills. Kari sighed and turned off the TV. It was time to visit the ship's store for her dinner and some supplies.

She hit the non-food store first. Most of the essentials were there: a dining set for one, a flatware set for one, a towel set for one, dish and hand soap, some sponges, paper towels, and binder clips because they were always useful for something.

"Yeah," the cashier said as her greeting. *She's new. I hate it when they're new.*

"Hi!" Kari said with a chipper tone, only to antagonize her, as she placed her items on the checkout counter. "This is my first purchase. So exciting!"

Are you kidding me? She began the process of ringing up her purchases. "Well, at least you figured out how to put money in your account. You'd be surprised how many people screw that up. You'll get your receipt in your ship email, with the balance of your account."

"Oh, good. Don't want to lose track."

"I think you'll be fine." *Unless she's planning on buying one of the speed boats.*

Kari cocked her head. Boats, even basic ones, were expensive. Even if her bonus had come in, that math didn't add up. "I'm sorry, but how much do I have in my account?"

The cashier squinted as she studied the screen in front of her. "You have just over $8,000."

"That's not correct."

"You're Karishma Okpik-Bakshi with inCog?"

"Yes."

"Then, it's right. Have a nice day." *Leave.*

"You too," Kari said vacantly, and meandered out of the store and across the passageway to the food store.

How could the total be right? Maybe when she entered five hundred dollars earlier, she accidentally added another zero? Then, if her signing bonus came in, that math tracked. But the large banking transfer needed tending to before she bought anything outside of the ship.

Twenty minutes later, she had more coffee, two boxes of tea, a freeze-dried mushroom pasta in a pouch that reminded her of camping, and a few more snack items. Once she was back in her cabin, she checked the balance for her ship account on the TV and saw the five hundred she added before she had left. Then, ten minutes later there were two deposits for four thousand dollars each with the notes:

inCog signing bonus
Wibawa Enterprises signing bonus

Kari's mouth dropped. She had never had so much money

to her name in her life. It couldn't be real, except it was. Her smile never left as she switched her laundry to the dryer, filled her electric kettle, and scrubbed her new dining ware. When her kettle beeped, she poured the steaming water into her meal pouch, gave it a stir, and poured the reconstituted pasta into her new bowl. The penne and mushrooms looked normal. The pink tomato-cream sauce was grainy but smelled zesty. It would do.

She took her meal over to the loveseat for a trashy movie and turned on the TV. The screen was black except for the prompt:

Would you like to enter your special skills now?

"Dammit!" she mumbled around a mouthful of mediocre pasta.

She relented and started the survey. Rather than a simple form she hoped for, she was confronted with forty questions, each with its own drop-down menu. Within the questions she confirmed she spoke many languages, had trained in Brazilian jiu-jitsu, played guitar, had training in emergency survival, could swim, and knew the basics in mechanics, electrical work, and plumbing. She did not confirm skills in other areas even if she had them. She didn't want to help everyone in a crisis.

Sometimes it was best to let natural selection sort out the situation.

When she entered No to question thirty-nine, the final question reared its ugly head:

Do you have any other skills that could be of use on the *Hinewai* or Wibawa Enterprises that you have not already listed?

Kari clicked over to No and then to the submit button.

Ecstatic that was over, but the adrenaline soars she had experienced during the course of the day had now crashed. She was exhausted. Kari set the kettle again and put on her jammies. Before she made her decaf cinnamon-vanilla tea, she went to the sliding door. She opened it with a whisper quiet motion and looked out to the city lights and the different vessels that dotted the harbor. Despite all of the activity, she felt at peace.

She could sort laundry while she watched a movie tomorrow morning. Tonight, it was tea on the balcony and a quick hello to a bald eagle who did her the courtesy of a fly by.

Chapter Nine

Maybe it was because her work experience had only consisted of online tutoring and the hardware store, but inCog's onboarding was a lengthy process. Her list of mandatory training consisted of boat safety, lab safety, anti-sexual harassment, diversity and inclusion, cybersecurity, and protected health information. She couldn't start the actual neuroscience until all of that was completed. It was annoying.

Kari waited until Santos had stopped typing before she announced her progress. "I finished the trainings."

"Already?" When she nodded, he scrunched his brow. "Let me double-check that." He spun back to his computer and went to their company portal. Kari could see her list on his monitor with green check marks beside the different modules. "I'll be damned. Well, why don't you call it a day."

It was only 3:30pm. "Are you sure? I don't mind starting an assignment."

"Which I haven't organized for you yet, because I didn't anticipate you finishing until tomorrow afternoon."

"Oh. Well, okay." She turned back to her computer, closed her windows on her double monitor setup, and logged out. "I guess I'll see you both tomorrow, then."

"But," Santos said, "since you are leaving a little early, you can catch the next tender and do a little shopping."

"I don't have any emergency items. Once my stuff gets here from Oregon I should be set."

Santos sighed. "Let's put it this way. If you could come in business casual tomorrow, that would be appreciated."

Dammit. The tanks and cargo pants weren't inCog appropriate. "Okay, I'll add that to my to-do list."

"Bye, Kari," Mitchell said. "Have fun in the city."

Kari took out her phone as she headed to her cabin to grab a canvas bag for her shopping. She stifled a laugh when she saw an email from Tanaka's lab. Too little too late when it came to that. She opened the email anyway and skimmed the first paragraph. "What?" she yelled to a small group of gym-goers on the stairway.

How could she have not gotten that job? It was the most basic job in the world. She uttered a disgusted sigh and continued on. At the next deck, her phone buzzed with a text from Mom A.

Call me ASAP. It's about the movers.

The level of urgency was rare. Kari dialed her mother. "I didn't think they'd be there until tomorrow?"

"That's what we thought, too. But they did arrive in the time window we gave them."

"So, what about the move causes an ASAP-level conversation?"

"Two questions. Do you need your bedding? And, is the

shoebox beside your nightstand that says, 'If you aren't me, do not open this even if I'm dead,' what I think it is?"

Kari stopped at the deck's landing and rubbed her face, which was much warmer than it was a moment ago. "Yeah," she drawled.

"Okay, I'll put extra packing tape around it. Also, you might want to consider getting something that has a little more structure and keeps out nasty, airborne things."

Instead of telling Mom A that her sex toys were in their own box or bag and there was a cleaner inside, she simply asked, "Is there anything else?" over the sound of packing tape being pulled from its roll.

"How was your first day?"

"A lot of trainings and my new boss, while nice, apparently doesn't find tank tops and cargo pants work appropriate."

"You'll find that's the case with most jobs."

"Speaking of jobs!" Kari's voice now filled with outrage. "It's a good thing I accepted inCog's offer, because Tanaka's lab 'decided to go another way'."

"That's a blow to the ego, I'm sure," Mom A said over a truck's engine turning over and other voices. "Okay, the movers are waving me over to sign. One second, chickpea."

After more than one second and enough time for her to reach the next deck landing, Kari heard a brief conversation that included the estimated arrival in New York. "Wait. Did he say everything should come tomorrow around noon?"

"He did. Your things will get there before we do."

"You booked your flights, already?"

"We did." The sound of a bird squawking carried over Mom A's voice. "We arrive—in theory—this Saturday afternoon and leave Monday after our ENN station tour and lunch. I just hope the hurricane coming up the coast is cooperative with our plans. Hi, baby."

Who was baby? Mom A never referred to anyone that way. It could only mean one thing. "You got the chickens, didn't you?"

"Yes! But don't worry, they'll be watched while we're gone."

"That's good to know." The caretaking of her moms' new chickens weren't in her immediate lists of concerns, but she knew how long they had wanted their own eggs. "Okay, I'm at the queue now for my trip to shore. I'll figure out how to get you two on the ship to show you my new place."

"Sounds good. Love you, chickpea."

"Love you too." Kari hung up and walked over to someone who stood by a thumb scanner and had the white and burgundy clothes of someone who worked on the ship. "Excuse me. How do we get visitors on board?"

She serious? "There are no visitors."

"You don't understand. I'm not talking about bringing strangers on board, just my moms."

She's either deaf, stupid, or entitled. "No visitors. Ever."

She was neither of those things, but considering they were the gatekeeper of the tender, she swallowed her anger and hoped he fell overboard in the near future. "Thank you for clarifying." She scanned her thumb and boarded for her trip into the city.

———

"That's a much more acceptable outfit," Santos said as she came into the office the next morning.

At least she didn't have to return her golf shirts and capri pants. "I'm glad you like it because I basically bought five versions of this outfit."

"You had a good trip out, then?" Mitchell asked.

"Yeah, I picked up a few other things, too." All except a shoe organizer. She knew she was going to need one of those for over her bathroom door. "Do I have an assignment for the day?"

"Yes," Santos said. "There's a file on your desktop that will have your work for the week. Each task has the form the client submitted so you know what they need from us. When you're finished, send it to me, so I can send it to the client. I'm the only one in the office who ever deals with clients directly."

Kari had no issues with fewer people. "I'll get started."

Her first assignment was an analysis of a clinical trial to test a drug to treat epileptic seizures in infants. The instructions were clear and the research piqued her interests. She hated her 24-7 telepathy, but at least she knew it was coming and was old enough to understand. Kari sympathized with the children who had no awareness of what was happening in their own bodies. She read more about it on her lunch break in a quiet corner of the cafeteria until she was alerted via text that her package had arrived. She shoveled the rest of her stir-fry into her mouth and headed to her cabin.

When she walked in, there was a small mountain of cardboard boxes each labeled with either the area of her tiny house or its contents: bathroom, clothes, shoes, office items, decorations and guitar stuff, and one smaller box on the peak of the mountain labeled 'Extra Special Personal Items' in Mom A's handwriting. Heat rushed to her face once again.

Why couldn't Mom L have been the point-of-contact for the movers?

With a shake of her head, Kari headed back to work. She'd finish her day at inCog, then unpack. Come the next morning, she'd wake in a place that looked and felt more like a real home.

———

The morning came too early, but the 5:30am alarm still didn't take away from the sound sleep she'd had in her new bed, complete with freshly laundered luxury sheets. She went straight to the kettle, filled it, turned it on, and then jumped into the shower. After she was clean and much more awake, she stepped out of the bathroom with a towel wrapped around herself while rivulets trickled from her hair down her neck and shoulders. She paused on her way to the wardrobe to appreciate the sunrise. It was gorgeous. The view was nothing but fire orange and blue. A big, yellow sun over the open ocean.

Wait. The ocean?

"No. No. No. No." Kari rushed closer to the sliding door. "What the . . .?"

They weren't just far away from the city. The city was nowhere to be seen.

Kari didn't know why or when the boat had moved, but Jade might. She ran across her apartment with her hand clutching the top of her towel and opened the door.

"Why good morning," Finn said with a sly grin. "Madeleine would like to see you."

Chapter Ten

Atlantic Ocean

Kari stood in her doorway, clutched her towel tighter, and set her jaw. "Where are we?"

Finn looked in both directions and up at the lights. "I'm in the passageway. You're in your cabin."

"You know what I mean." Kari pointed behind her. "We were supposed to be in Manhattan for another week."

"You didn't get a message from your cruise account last night? No pop-up on your TV?"

"I didn't check. After I finished unpacking and organizing, I looked at the skyline and played some songs on my guitar. It was very calming, unlike how I feel now!"

That does sound relaxing. "Well, to answer your question. We're on our way to St. John's, Newfoundland. We left early because the hurricane is moving faster than they anticipated."

"Weren't there people stuck in the city?"

Finn sighed and in the process their amused expression disappeared. *Why does everyone think I have answers?* "I don't know but that's a risk you take when you overnight somewhere. Now, if you could put on some clothes or not—your

90

choice—so we can leave to see Madeleine, that would be great."

"No!"

Difficult. Very angry. "She doesn't like to be kept waiting."

"And I don't like waking up in surprising places and having a conversation in only a towel!"

"If it helps, you look good wet." *Oh, poor phrasing. Now I've made her madder.*

Finn was right. The hand that held her towel was in the tightest fist imaginable. "I'm not going anywhere with you." Kari heard the squeak of a door's hinges and she whipped her head in the direction of the sound.

Jade stepped out in the hall with a toothbrush in her mouth and robe tied around her. "What in the hell is— Oh. I get it. I'll leave you two alone to figure out this morning-after business." With a quick laugh she shut the door behind her.

Dammit, now Jade thought she'd spend the night with Finn. Kari crossed her arms and then pinched the bridge of her nose. Finn couldn't answer all of her questions, which wasn't their fault, but the cryptic nature of the surprise morning visit needed some kind of explanation. "Look, I'm a bit stressed. My moms booked flights to come see me this weekend, which I was looking forward to and I'm super pissed I can't go into town to buy a shoe organizer after work today. So, I'd really appreciate some kind of explanation as to why Madeleine needs to see me this early in the morning."

"If Madeleine is involved, all I can guess is that it has something to do with an element of your contract. If I were you, I'd just get it taken care of, because you don't want to be on Madeleine's bad side." *She's vindictive.*

"Fine," Kari said, exasperated. "Give me five minutes to get ready." When they took a step forward, she put up her palm. "You stay out there."

She shut the door and stepped into the bathroom to dry her hair and put it in a ponytail. When Kari stepped out into the hall, she saw Finn leaning against the wall and studying their nails.

My cuticles are terrible.

"I'm ready for whatever it is we're doing," Kari said.

Finn pushed off the wall with the sole of their shoe that had a significant block heel. "Follow me, please."

Kari expected them to make a right to head to the elevator or stairs, but Finn went left to pass the VIP suites at the stern. Then, they headed to the cabin door labeled, VIP access – Ship Employees Only. "I've been in Madeleine's office and it's not in there."

Finn lifted their thumb and punched in a code. "We're not going to that office." The lock turned green and they opened the door for her.

Kari walked into what appeared to be a records room. Metal shelving with sturdy boxes stacked every inch. There was a desk, but through the window's light she could see its surface had accumulated substantial dust; there were cobwebs in the corners of the ceiling. "This is weird."

It gets weirder. "In here, please," Finn said at the entrance of the bathroom.

"I'm going into the bathroom with you? I don't think so."

She has a point. This is creepy. "Okay, then, take a look inside first."

Kari put a reluctant foot forward and watched Finn slide the linen closet's pocket door over to reveal not towels but an elevator. "Whoa!" Forgetting her paranoia from a moment earlier, she went into the bathroom to take in the rest. Kari saw a panel of elevator buttons inside the 'closet' but the floor was tiled like a bathroom. There was a toilet and sink, too. She turned on the faucet to learn that both the hot and the cold water flowed through the pipes. This was definitely what Gia had referred to. "What is this place?"

Secrets. "This is the way to a rather special conference room." Finn pressed the button for C, then leaned forward so their hazel eyes were aligned with a retina scanner.

"So weird," Kari mumbled as the elevator doors of the bathroom closed.

Nervous, but not scared. Interesting. "Henry and Madeleine run portions of the business with supreme secrecy. Don't worry though, you're safe."

"Do you understand that what you just said is not at all reassuring and adds more red flags? Big, wavy, crimson flags."

Finn chuckled. "I understand, and I wish I could tell you the flags get smaller, droopy, and green, but they don't." *The red flag turns into a volcano that explodes.*

Kari crossed her arms across her chest. She understood that someone like Henry Wibawa would need to have meetings that covered sensitive information, but this was ridiculous. This was along the lines of what you needed when you had illegal operations.

The elevator stopped its ascent and the door slid open to reveal a windowless conference room and long table with Madeleine at the head of it with a tea cup and saucer. One of the walls consisted of a screen that stretched from floor to ceiling. The other had a few nautical pictures and a smart board.

Madeleine wore the same cut suit as the day before, but this time it was in lavender. "Good morning, Kari. I hope you slept well."

Kari approached the table. "I slept great. The morning has been confusing though because of the lack of visible land, Finn lurking outside my door, and then being taken to a secret elevator. But at least I'm not sleepy."

"That's wonderful to hear because you need to be alert for

this conversation. Finn, is there anything I should know about your time with Kari?"

"Nothing of note, ma'am."

"Very well," Madeleine said, disappointed. "Kari is about to take on similar roles to yours, but in a part-time capacity. Do you mind if we share with her some of your backstory so she understands what we do here?"

"Um . . ." Finn locked their eyes with Kari and their slight Adam's apple bobbed. *What in the hell is going on here?* "Is that really necessary?"

"I believe it is."

Awful. Humiliation. "Alright, if you think it will help, ma'am."

"Wonderful. Please continue your duties for the day with Robert."

"Yes, ma'am." *Maybe he'll show some appreciation for once.* Finn gave Kari a short bow goodbye and stepped back into the elevator.

When the doors closed, Kari turned back to Madeleine and to the massive security guard—the neck tattoos one—who had appeared behind her. She had never seen such a square build with such a perfect, round head before. "What is all of this about and why did we leave Manhattan?"

"Please have a seat, so I can explain."

Kari took her seat at the other head of the table without taking her eyes off Madeleine. "Hopefully we can get this done within the hour. My breakfast window ends at seven."

Madeleine laughed and turned to the guard. "She's funny, isn't she, Neill?"

"Very funny, ma'am," he said with an accent that sounded South African.

Madeleine folded her hands on the table and narrowed her eyes at Kari. "You lied to us in your special skills survey."

"Seriously?" Kari rolled her eyes. "Okay, technically my certification in CPR isn't expired."

Madeleine shook her head and then locked eyes with Neill. She directed a quick motion of her index finger toward Kari. Neill moved behind her, and then Josef came out behind Madeleine like some sort of tough guy assembly line.

Kari's posture straightened. "Okay, what was all of that about?"

"Neill and Josef are going to protect me from you. Just in case."

This kept getting more ridiculous by the second. "I might have a short temper and be a bit impulsive at times, but I've never attacked someone."

"Even if that person told you that they knew you were a telepath."

She can read my thoughts? Does Josef know?

Kari focused on not reacting in any way. How could Madeleine possibly know that? The easiest way around the statement was denial, so she laughed. "You think I'm what? That's impossible. There's no such thing."

"Yes, there is. And, yes, you are."

I can't believe she's a telepath. Can she read my mind right now?

Kari ignored Neill and played it as the person she was: a scientist. "There's no evidence that anyone ever in the world has had the ability to read minds. Anyone who has ever claimed to do so has either eventually confessed to interpreting body language, used vague statements to make educated guesses, or straight-up lied."

Madeleine tapped her French manicured nails in a rolling succession against the tabletop. "Let's rewind a bit. A few years ago, I watched a documentary about the Nazis and their desire to find people with paranormal abilities." Kari's eyes widened.

"Don't worry, this has nothing to do with genocide. Anyway, that led me to think that if Wibawa Enterprises could find people with abilities like that, we could have an edge in our business dealings. I knew that Henry believed in such phenomenon, so we started a search to find these unique individuals. To do this, my assistants searched the globe's databases for certain keywords, like 'psychic', 'clairvoyant', 'pyrokinesis', 'strength'. We found Finn about two years ago."

"Finn's a part of this?"

"Indeed. They're an empath."

So sensitive to others' needs. Such a nice person.

Despite Finn's supposed and Mom L's definite empathetic abilities, Kari played dumb. "You're telling me that my elevator-ride-along-buddy can read emotions?"

"Yes." Madeleine sipped her tea. "It's a skill that has turned out to be incredibly useful, especially with our VIPs. We know in advance which conversations make people feel unsettled or uncomfortable. We can apply pressure to the right spots. Apparently, on the way up here, Finn didn't detect anything of note from you."

Kari's jaw dropped. But when Madeleine's mouth started to develop a smile, she knew she had reacted in the exact way Madeleine had wanted her to. Kari had to put her scientist hat back on. "How would you even know this is accurate about Finn?"

"Court records help."

That took Kari aback. "Those are supposed to be sealed."

"They are. Our ways of finding information are sometimes a bit unorthodox. Some would say 'illegal'. But I make the argument that illegal and immoral are different things. Putting an eighteen-year-old in jail for committing a non-violent, consensual 'crime' in order to provide for their family isn't, in my eyes, moral. But the law disagrees."

On this point, Kari agreed with Madeleine.

"But, I digress," Madeleine said. "Finn's time in jail led to certain comments in various reports. We investigated further and, with a quick visit to the corrections facility, confirmed. We told Finn that if they worked for us for five years, we'd get all charges dropped and provide financial assistance for their family during that time. Seemed like a fair trade to us, and Finn agreed."

It was a wild story, but Kari could see how it was true. But that still didn't explain how Madeleine knew she was a telepath. She never wrote it down in a manner that was uploaded to a cloud or in email. Her mothers or grandparents wouldn't have either. "I still don't understand where you would have sourced the information that led you to believe I'm a telepath. I don't have a criminal record."

"True, but you do have medical records, and your former psychiatrist's notes are a part of them. Especially that last session of yours where you brutalized a punching bag, demanded a tranquilizer for the plane ride to your Nana Sid's funeral, and, from what I gather, were in such a state of frustration that you told him you were a telepath. Sound familiar?"

A cold sweat broke out on Kari's palms and her pulse raced. She focused on 4-7-8 breathing to remain calm and not going back to that rage-filled place from almost one year ago. Kari took a moment, pieced the events together, and then cleared her throat. "So, you found the word 'telepath' in my *private* medical records and used the job at inCog to bait me here. Then, to make sure I couldn't escape once you told me, you put me in this creepy room and waited until we sailed into the middle of the ocean?"

Madeleine grimaced. "A ship without sails technically can't 'sail' but, yes, that's exactly what happened. You are quite bright."

Kari lunged out of her seat to go after Madeleine, but Neill pushed down on both shoulders to keep her seated. She used her arms to push off the chair arms but she still couldn't budge.

She's strong. Like super strong. I hope my hands don't bruise her.

"I understand that you're upset," Madeleine said.

"Upset is the understatement of the fucking year!" Kari raised her shoulders to pin Neill's hands, then twisted away giving her a millisecond to dive out of her seat. Once she scrambled to get back on her feet, Josef had a taser pointed at her. Kari stopped and raised her hands.

"Wise choice. Now, sit." The edge to Madeleine's tone was sharper than the multi-tool in Kari's pocket.

Kari did as she was told even though her chest rose and fell with heavy breaths. "What do you want from me?"

"Not much, really. I want you to read the minds of targeted individuals and report back what you 'heard'. You can have your job at inCog and live quite nicely on this ship. You're welcome for your start-up bonus, by the way."

This was insane. Madeleine was insane. "You want me to read the most private thoughts of people *intentionally*. I don't claim to be the most ethical person in the world, but I'm not doing that."

"I think you will."

"No, I won't! And as soon as we dock in Newfoundland, I'm gone, and I'm telling everyone about how you're illegally accessing private files."

"I doubt you'll do that." Madeleine leaned back in her chair and crossed her legs. "Because you . . . like . . . justice."

"What do you mean by that?"

"It means that I've seen your internet search history. You searched 'God and Country' paired with 'Dallas' obsessively for the last week, and lo and behold what did I see in the news the other day but an anonymous tip in Oregon that prevented a massacre. Or perhaps the times you scoured the sex offender database looking for specific people who were caught with anonymous tips. I mean, how many other times have you done something like this?"

Oh wow. Neill gave her a light pat on the shoulder.

Kari wasn't sure if he did that because of a job well done or because she hadn't answered Madeleine's question. She wanted to lie, but she was also proud that she had stopped tragic events from taking place and stopped sexual predators. Who knew how many other examples Madeleine had? "I . . . I stopped counting."

"That's what I thought. You see, in this situation on the *Hinewai,* you can read the minds of powerful people who may be committing serious crimes on a global scale or who are engaged in morally repugnant behavior, like mistreatment of animals—which is not illegal everywhere, and you can help stop it. How's that sound?"

Madeleine just had to mention animals. To Kari's ears, the arrangement didn't sound awful, but there was always a catch. "What do you get out of it?"

"I get to watch the Wibawa empire grow and reap the benefits of success once these people are out of the way."

Always want more.

Kari found herself nodding at the deal even though she wanted as normal a life as she could get. That was why her job —wait. Were Santos and Mitchell in on this? Surely their thoughts would have given something away, but they hadn't. "Santos and Mitchell don't know about this, do they?"

"The people on this ship who know about your abilities are confined to this room, plus Henry. Finn doesn't even know yet."

There was no coincidence of her being offered a job at inCog that no one had responded to. That vacancy had been orchestrated by Madeleine and Henry. "You sent Milia packing without Santos knowing about it and then blocked Santos's posting of the job. That's why no one applied!"

"I will not confirm nor deny that, but that does sound brilliant. However, we're getting off track. Once you get your first assignment—"

"But I haven't even said yes yet!"

Madeleine sighed and looked to Josef. "I hate it when they don't understand that there are consequences to not cooperating."

Major consequences. Cooperate.

Kari's back stiffened. "Consequences?"

"Indeed." Madeleine's focus shifted back to Kari. "But I'd rather not get into a discussion of what happens when there is either a lack of obedience or discretion, since it's rather . . . messy. I'd rather focus on the fact that you can do good with little inconvenience to your life."

If you can hear me, you should just accept it already. There are worse ways to be manipulated.

Neill had a point. "Okay," Kari said. "That's fair. When will I know I have an assignment? Is there like a signal or something?"

"Yes. We shine a light in the shape of a brain into the sky." Madeleine cackled at her joke. "Sorry, I couldn't help myself. When we need you, I'll send for you, and I'll do my best not to interfere with your business hours at inCog. Do you have any other questions?"

"How long do I have to do this? You said Finn has five years of this."

"Your specific residency contract, thus your Wibawa Enterprises Promise, is good for one calendar year. After that, we'll reassess. Honestly, for a genius, you should read more carefully. I mean, Neill understands his contract."

"I do," Neill said, "but I also understand how people have different types of intelligence."

Even though Neill prevented her from getting in Madeleine's face, she liked him. "I'll go back and reread the contract. I don't think I have any other questions."

"Excellent!" Madeleine beamed. "Neill, please escort her out. Enjoy your breakfast."

When she still hadn't moved, Neill tapped her shoulder. Taking the hint, she made her way into the same elevator as before.

She's a mind reader. That's crazy. "So, you know what I'm thinking?" he said to her once the doors closed.

"Yes."

Wild. "Are you trying to do it?" *Peanut butter-banana sandwich.* "What did I just think?"

"No, I don't try, and peanut butter-banana sandwich."

Wild! "People's thoughts come at you all the time and you can't control it?" *So annoying.*

"Yes, it is annoying. So, can I ask what you're here for?"

Wanted South African military. "Kak. You know now don't you."

"Yeah, but don't worry. I won't tell or ask why." The elevator door opened to the office storage. "Can I leave here like a normal room or do I have to do something special like talk into the faucet for a voice identification?"

"Nothing special, but if someone sees you and asks a question, just say that it's VIP-business only."

"Understood." Kari walked to the cafeteria in a daze. She was a player in Henry Wibawa's plot to gain more power by learning the dirty secrets of the most successful and influential people in the world.

She grabbed a tray, got her yogurt parfait, and made her way to the beverage station for a ginger ale. She needed any assistance she could get to calm her upset stomach. Fortunately, there were plenty of seats to choose from at the early hour. Good. She could place herself in the farthest corner booth and no one would accuse her of being anti-social.

"Good morning!" Mitchell said with a chipper lilt and grin, but his optimism diminished. *Looks ill.* "Are you okay?"

There was no point denying her emotions since she was going to have to work with him all day. "I got some news this morning that was . . . surprising. I'm still processing it."

He nodded. "Was it that we're in the middle of the ocean? Because I was surprised when I saw that update last night." *Can't get my new running shoes that came in.*

"That was certainly part of it. I'm just very . . . stressed right now."

I know what this is. Mitchell did the thing she least wanted him to do which was put his tray down and took a seat across from her. "I understand. This is a big change. The ship, the job, leaving home for the first time. Do you have a friend you can call?"

"My moms are my only friends and I can't talk to them about this." Oh Gods, would they be the 'consequences' Madeleine alluded to? Because she was definitely the type of person who would murder the chickens to 'send a message'.

Understand no friends. "You can consider me a friendly ear, and if I can't help, I might be able to find someone on the ship who can."

She stifled a laugh. "No one who'd I'd talk to would believe me if I told them."

"You'd be surprised what I'll believe. You of all people ought to know that."

Mitchell had a point. A great point, actually. Her telepathy wasn't a giant leap from the psychic link he helped discover between her mothers during Mom L's coma. He might be able to help her. She might even be able to leverage this new situation to her advantage in some way.

Kari stirred her parfait and crunched on the granola as a plan formed. If she came clean about her abilities, maybe Santos and Mitchell would be willing to make ORCA happen if she could get the money. Henry and Madeleine were by far the easiest source of funds if she could convince them.

But first, she needed Santos and Mitchell on board.

Looks less sick.

Kari sipped her soda and then brought her attention back to Mitchell, who still regarded her like she was a patient. "So," she drawled, "here's a fun fact about me. I'm a telepath."

He laughed. *Better mood, at least.* "Are you also able to bend that spoon you're using with your mind?" He laughed again, but then stopped when she didn't join in. His brow rose. "You're serious?"

She liked that his first response wasn't denial. "Yes."

Mitchell sat back in his chair with a *huh*. "I did not see that coming."

"Well, I wasn't expecting to tell anybody, but here we are." Mitchell stared at her with thoughts of how that could be anatomically and physiologically possible while she continued to eat her breakfast. Her parfait tasted better now. The blueberries were fresh. "I'd be happy to continue the conversation in the lab. For now, we can talk about regular things, like do you have a plan B of how to get your running shoes?"

His brow furrowed. "How did you know?"

"Take a wild guess."

Shit. It's real. Behind his wire-rimmed glasses his eyes widened. "Not to sound like a jerk, but would you mind if I left. This will take some getting used to for me."

That was the best news she had heard so far that morning. "Please do. I'll see you in the office."

Chapter Eleven

Not only was Kari grateful for the chance to finish her breakfast in peace, but she was even able to settle into her meal enough to notice the nuances in the ship's honey granola versus Mom A's superior maple-based recipe. Kari would have to tell her that to soften the blow that she was in the middle of the ocean, not New York.

After Kari finished her breakfast, she paced the decks of the ship. Before she spilled her guts to Santos and Mitchell, she needed a clear plan. And a clear head. She stood along the railing breathing in the clean sea breeze, focused on the horizon, and let her mind work unpressured.

Santos and Mitchell didn't need to know everything about her, only the parts that were relevant to her telepathy. They didn't need to know she was a magic birth or that she had enhanced strength or that she could communicate with birds of prey. They also didn't need to know about Madeleine and Henry's scheme.

After she formed her plan, it was time to issue some bad

news. She wanted to text, but that would only result in a call. "Hey, Mom L."

"This is unexpected. Is everything okay?"

"So . . . there's a minor problem with your agenda when you arrive in New York. I won't be there."

After a few seconds of shouting and talks of air miles and apologizing to Mom A for waking her due to the shouts, Kari was able to explain the early departure due to the hurricane.

Once the moms got over their disappointment, even though they were pleased ship safety was taken so seriously, Mom L asked, "Is there anything else pressing we should know?"

"Mom A makes better granola than the ship."

"Aw, thanks, chickpea."

After the call, Kari went to work pleased she had taken one massive item off her to-do list. Now, it was time for a second. She walked into the office where Santos and Mitchell spoke about the ship's abrupt departure and the hurricane's category upgrade. "Good morning," she said.

"Good morning," Santos said. "I hope you didn't have plans to go into Manhattan."

"Not anymore." She didn't want to distract from the morning's key issue, so she didn't mention her mothers' visit or need for a shoe organizer. Kari went to her desk chair and settled in. "I started to tell Mitchell something at breakfast and you should know too."

Santos's cheery disposition vanished. "Is something wrong?"

"I think I'll let you be the judge of that." She glanced over to Mitchell who sat on the literal edge of his seat. At least he was excited. "Okay, here's the deal. The reason I'm interested in neuroscience is because I have telepathic abilities."

Santos stared ahead with a crease in his brow, then burst

into laughter. He pointed at Mitchell. "Did he put you up to this?" He continued to chortle.

"I can prove it if you want me to."

"Oh, please do," Santos said, amused.

Kari rolled her chair closer. Both of her colleagues were within thought distance, but she focused on Santos. "Think of and picture an animal."

"Alright." *Most absurd animal? Mutant anteater outside of Pacoa.*

"Mutant anteater!" Kari said. "And you," she turned to Mitchell, "thought it was the hairy frog."

"That's right," Mitchell confirmed. "I learned about it when my son did a report."

Santos's wide smile disappeared and his face shifted into one of wonder. "How did you do that?"

"I wish I knew. If I knew, then I could control it. As of now, the only way I know how to stop it is distance."

Santos rubbed the dark stubble at his chin. "I'm sorry, I need a moment to let this sink in." His 'moment' was more like ten seconds of staring at her. *Can't be possible. But it is possible. Does she know that I'm thinking right now about how not possible this is?*

"Yes, I know how you're thinking about how it's not possible." She rolled back in her chair so she only had her own thoughts to contend with. "There. Now you have more privacy."

Santos shook his head, slack jawed. "When did you discover this?"

Kari gave them the history of her telepathy and the adjustments she had made to her life because of it. To their credit, they didn't interrupt her even though she could see on their faces that they had dozens—if not hundreds—of questions.

"That sounds both fascinating and awful at the same time," Santos said.

"Correct. I haven't had a normal relationship with another human in over seven years."

Mitchell crossed her arms. "At least your mothers know. Their support has probably been a life saver."

"Yeah, they've been great about it. But all of this is why I've been obsessed with finding a way to control it. I'm convinced that optogenetics is the best path forward."

"Not deep brain stimulation?" Mitchell asked.

"Deep brain stimulation is too broad. Optogenetics works with a specific molecular target."

Santos cocked his head. "But how could you possibly know what the target in your brain is?"

"You're right, I don't know. But I know how I can figure it out. I need an EEG and functional MRI when I'm actively telepathic and when I'm not, so I can locate the region of activity. Then, I'll need neurosurgery to remove a sample of the cells from that identified region." Kari paused to choose her words carefully. So far, they seemed on board and she didn't want to say anything that would deter them. "I know the cells there are different than the others, so we find a difference and target that. Then, we can design the vector for said target with the light-activated molecule. We go back inside my brain, put everything back in there, and turn on a little light with a remote control and that tells my telepathic neurons to shut up. Easy peasy."

Mitchell leaned back and folded his arms. "That actually makes sense."

"The theory does, but the other details . . ." Santos shook his head. "Did you give any thought to the approval side of this? Because you can't just get these tests and surgeries."

"I mean, technically, you can," Mitchell said. "You just have to go about it in a non-traditional way, in theory."

"I don't want theory," Kari said. "I want to do this. With you two."

"Whoa," Santos said with his hands waving. "We can't do this!"

"Why not?" she asked. "Isn't this the high-risk, high-reward research inCog is all about?"

"Well, yes, but . . ." Santos looked over to Mitchell. "It's illegal, right?"

"Taking images, biopsies, and performing surgery on a willing participant of sound mind in a pilot clinical trial by a licensed physician is not illegal; however, to go through with the logistics of all of that would probably require some rather questionable ethics."

"What do you mean?" Kari asked.

"Finding locations where there are not only available rooms or equipment, but who won't ask questions. You can't just call someone and ask to borrow their equipment for a few hours."

Kari cocked her head. "But, isn't that what you did with Mom L when you couldn't get her out of her coma?"

Santos sat straighter, his eyes focused on Mitchell. "Is that true? You just called a friend?"

Mitchell sighed. "He's not my friend now, but yes, I did. And I was desperate. I don't really have those kinds of connections now."

"I might," Santos said. "I'm not saying I'm totally on board with this, but I've made several contacts over the years. All over the world."

"Do you trust these contacts?" Kari asked.

"Most. They have everything you would need and won't ask any questions as long as the approval paperwork is there."

Kari was never much of a hacker—it just didn't interest her —but in this case, she'd make an exception. "Hypothetically speaking, I could probably find a way into any human research protections office and get a digital rubber stamp. If anyone asked." Both their eyes widened. At least she knew they were moral folk, unlike the lady upstairs.

Santos laughed again. "I can't believe we are talking about this *and* that I am actually entertaining this idea. Would you do this, Mitchell?"

He pursed his lips. "I'm split, to be honest. On one hand, the three of us would single-handedly revolutionize what is known about the brain and, if everything worked as hoped, Kari could live the life she so desperately wants. You've had to lead an isolated life and I know what that's like, but at least it came to me as an adult and at the cost of my own choices. On the other hand, something could go wrong." He gestured to Kari. "You might not die, but this could make your situation so much worse."

"That would only be if we got to the surgery part," Kari said.

"True," Santos said while nodding his head. "There would be no harm to some basic testing and imaging studies. It would be fascinating, really. Plus, I know how clinical trials work. Or don't work." When Kari cocked her head, he explained, "When Charlotte was younger, she couldn't get into a migraine study, even though she had met all the criteria and someone had dropped out. She's had to live with extra pain most of her adult life because of bureaucracy. Luckily, the ship has been very flexible with her needs, even if people are frustrated the *Hinewai* app isn't developed yet."

"I'm sorry to hear that," Kari said. Now she felt bad for thinking that the IT team on the ship was lazy.

"Mitchell," Santos said, "you're the clinician here, but I'm willing to try this."

Mitchell still held a pensive expression. "I think you're right and I'm on board with at least doing the imaging work."

Kari tapped her feet in a happy dance, then clapped her hands together. "Thank you! When are we going to do this? What's the schedule?"

"Let's calm down just a bit," Santos said. "We just learned about this. There is a lot to consider and we have to keep in mind our scheduled stops. But, off the top of my head, I don't see why Mitchell couldn't get general baseline vitals here on the ship."

"And we can schedule blood work in Newfoundland," Mitchell said. "After that we could do the EEG and MRI in Europe. A functional MRI will be harder to get, but seeing the structures of your brain won't be good enough. We need to see how your brain is actively changing when you're doing tasks."

"I'm pretty sure I have an fMRI source," Santos said, "but there is another logistical element we need to work out: money."

"I might have an idea there," Kari said. "I'll let you know soon how feasible it is."

"Good," Santos said. "We also need you to write up the details of this research proposal and then pass it to us for review. This is serious, so I want us to have our own internal guide to show that we've thought through every step."

"Sure. I can send it once I'm back in my cabin."

Mitchell's brow raised. "You have it written already?"

"Well, yeah. I can only play guitar for so many hours. Is there anything else I can do?"

"Yes," Santos said with a smile, "your originally planned assignment for the day: data from a Parkinson's mini-pig model."

———

Kari stood from her seat, placed her hands on her lower back, and stretched. Mitchell appeared to be working on a separate project, as colorful PET scan images of a spinal cord were on his largest monitor. Santos clicked away at his keyboard. "I just emailed you my report. Is it okay if I call it a day?"

"Fine by me," Santos said. "We'll see you tomorrow and remember to send us that proposal."

"Will do."

Kari shut her computer down and headed out. First, she'd go to her cabin to send them her proposal and then go to Madeleine's office near the main admin center. Surely, if she tried to open the secret VIP door the security team would be alerted. Josef would tase her for sure.

She turned the corner and nearly walked right into Finn. This time she wasn't aggravated by the surprise. "I need you to take me to Madeleine."

She's not annoyed to see me at all. "I was coming to get you."

"Oh, good. This works out, then."

Finn walked to the stairs. *Attitude is a major shift.*

"What can I say? Attitudes change with motivation."

How . . .? Mind reader? Finn stopped and turned to her. Their eyes showed a mix of surprise, confusion, and horror.

"The answer is yes." Kari gestured to the hall. "Can we continue, please? I really want to talk with her and, apparently, she wants to see me again even though I have no idea what it's about."

"Your skills are needed with one of our VIP guests." *Telling Henry how our guest feels isn't good enough anymore, apparently.*

"I hope me being here isn't a blow to your ego."

Intrusive! Finn stopped on the stairs. "I'd appreciate it if you didn't read my mind."

"I'm not trying, but I'll keep my distance so I can't." Kari dropped a few paces behind them. For a trim build, Finn did have a muscular ass.

Wish I could do that.

"You can never shut it off?" she asked. Finn shook their head. "Doesn't that give you a headache?"

"Only if there are a lot of conflicting feelings. I like harmony."

Kari was true to her word and kept her distance until they were forced to be in the secret elevator together. The only thing that could have made the situation more awkward was if a woodwind version of *Love in an Elevator* played. However, the time did allow her to appreciate Finn's angular jaw and pouty lips. "So, you're from Newfoundland?"

Hate small talk. "I am."

Kari rocked on her heels. "Do you know a place where I can get a shoe organizer?"

They looked at her with a furrowed brow as the elevator doors opened to the conference room where Neill waited.

"Hi, again," he said with a wave. "Finn, you can go. Kari, please come with me."

"I'll see you soon." Finn left through a door adjacent to the elevator.

"This way." Neill's massive frame lumbered to the rear of the conference room where there was another door. He pressed a button on an intercom.

"Let her in," came Madeleine's voice through the small speaker.

He opened the door and gestured for her to go inside. She stepped into . . . a stairwell? "What is this?"

"Down the steps," Neill said. "You can't miss it. I'm heading to the lounge area now."

Kari walked down the half dozen curved steps and into

Madeleine's other office? Her smaller and sparse office. There were no windows. The only item on the walls was a digital map of the world with different colorful dots. Newfoundland was yellow, as were regions in Sweden, Libya, India, and Japan. Green and red were sprinkled across the globe. On her desk, there was a single closed laptop, not a scrap of paper, and a single coaster. And there were no visitor chairs.

Kari stood before her. The desk between them kept Madeleine's thoughts out of range. "I have a proposition for you."

Madeleine's head tilted back and she cackled. "You are one-of-a-kind, aren't you? I am thoroughly intrigued, go ahead."

"Okay. This morning we didn't discuss the details of these assignments."

"No, we didn't, because the details are minimal. You're confined to the ship and placed near someone. Simple."

"Okay, but what if you could do more with me? Like, what if you could send me places in exchange for some research assistance?"

Madeleine leaned back in her chair and folded her hands in her lap. "Keep talking."

Here it went. "So, Santos and Mitchell are no strangers to odd phenomenon, so I may have told them that I'm a telepath."

"Were you day drinking or high?" Madeleine said in an octave higher than usual.

"Does that make me telling them better?"

Madeleine looked as though she gave the question consideration. "No."

"Well, I wasn't. Anyway, I told them and they were surprised to say the least, but it got all of us talking. Long story short: we'd like to—"

"You want money for Project ORCA?"

"How do you know about that?" Kari asked, shocked.

"Oh, please. Haven't you figured it out by now that I know everything about you! Even your taste in erotic stories, which is . . . diverse." Madeleine silently rotated back-and-forth in her swivel chair while Kari processed that humiliating information. "So, in this new deal you get money for ORCA and I can move you all over the world to learn secrets. Is that it?"

"Yes!"

"No."

Kari's optimism deflated. "Well, what else would you want in exchange for the money?"

"Oh, I love that question. What do I want?" Madeleine tapped her tented fingers against each other in a slow rhythm and swiveled in her chair some more as she pondered her answer. She took a few more seconds and then stopped her swivels to level her icy gaze at Kari. "For the project funds—because I do understand that happy workers are better workers —I want to send you on any assignment, telepathic or not, anywhere in the world for . . . four years."

"You said one year earlier today!"

"That was before you wanted money for your brain experiment which may fail and leave you completely useless to me once you get to the surgery bit. So, that's the deal. Four years, regardless of your inCog employment. After each successful assignment, I'll drop money for your little project. Take it or leave it."

Four years. Gods, that was a long time to take orders from someone. But millions of people her age around the world did the same thing when it came to the military or other types of service. "To be clear, you're not going to ask me to do any criminal acts?"

"No. I have other, more qualified people for that."

Kari took a moment to mull it over. But really, she would do anything to see ORCA come to fruition. "Then, we have a deal. Do we rewrite my contract now?"

Madeleine winced. "Writing things down is . . . messy. I prefer verbal agreements, and I trust that when I send inCog the money for your 'seizure' funding along with a renovation bonus *and* the fact that you still understand that there are consequences to a lack of obedience and discretion as a signed 'contract.'"

"That's fair."

"I'm so glad you approve. I can sleep at night now. Do you have any other questions before we get started with your first assignment?"

Kari pointed to the map. "Why is Newfoundland yellow?"

"The reason why you are here." Madeleine approached the map and touched the Canadian island until it zoomed in on a corporate building. She tapped the building and its company information displayed, including an organizational chart. "One of our VIP guests, Robert MacDonald, is the CEO of this $400 million fishing enterprise. We think there are a few details he's left out in his conversations with Henry, who happens to be a shareholder. Your job is to learn those details when Henry plants the seed during conversation. They're meeting right now on deck ten."

"Won't that be very suspicious? I'm eighteen and have never once been to one of their business chats."

"Henry often has attractive, young adults in the hot tub or lying about sunbathing when there are guests."

"Do these young adults have sex with the guests?"

"Only the sex workers do, which you are not, so stop worrying about that detail."

Kari nodded. "Who else is there right now? Because the fewer minds I have to sift through the better."

"I hadn't thought of that." Madeleine tapped her chin with

her index finger. "Finn is doing the preliminary work and knows to leave when they see you. I can ask Neill to escort the others out."

"That'll work. How long will I need to be there?"

"Well, due to the new and improved contract you stay until you get the information. No information, no money." Madeleine pointed to the closet door on the other side of the room. "You can use my other office's bathroom to change into the suit hanging for you. The closet is a gateway, an eyehook opens a sliding door."

"The bathroom is a secret passage?" Madeleine opened her mouth to answer but Kari held up her hand. "Never mind. Of course, it is." They stared at each other in silence for a long moment until Kari realized why. "You want me to do this now?"

"That is preferable, yes."

"But I just found out!"

"You can ruminate all you want while you change clothes or do you need chickens in Oregon to get dropped into a fryer to get your feet moving?"

Sure, Kari didn't have a bond with the chickens, but they didn't deserve that. Kari opened the door and proceeded to the closet where there were office supplies on side shelves. She saw the eyehook in the back wall and slid the pocket door, which put her in a bathroom closet where there were cleaning products, a box of tampons, and extra toilet paper. After Kari slid that door open, she saw a sporty, orange bikini hung on a towel rack. Kari was surprised by two things about the suit: there was a top and it wasn't made of strings.

Kari changed and folded her clothes in a neat pile on top of a corner shelf dedicated to lotion and perfume. On the top, she placed her multi-tool and her firestarter necklace.

Before Kari left, she checked her reflection in the mirror

above the sink. Then, she flexed. The cut definition in her arms and upper abdomen was there, but she hadn't had a good sweat in a while. She'd start a workout routine tomorrow. Or at least check out the gym. That counted.

Kari went back to the secret office in her bikini and bare feet and saw a more casual version of Madeleine. Her suit jacket was off. Her sleeves were rolled up showing off a rose gold and diamond watch, and she had her top button undone. A pair of large, stylish sunglasses perched on her head.

"Oh, that fits you very well!" Madeleine said. "You can keep it, by the way."

"Really?" That was an unexpected treat. "It's super comfortable. Do I always get to keep the clothes?"

"Yes, but that doesn't include shoes. I like shoes and we're the same size. I checked."

Kari wouldn't have any place to put those new shoes anyway. "Now, what do we do?"

"You're going to go out to the deck where you had lunch yesterday and learn what you can from the man who isn't Henry. How you do that is up to you. And, if you're feeling shy, remember that he is *not* a good person. There is plenty of evidence to dig up to bring him to some sort of justice."

"Understood." Kari stood with her hands on her hips and scanned the office. With the exception of the elevator and bathroom door, she couldn't see a clear exit for where she needed to go. "How do I get there from here?"

Madeleine went to the digital map and pressed a series of buttons at the bottom. The map pushed out enough for a person to fit. "Make a right and open doors along the way. You can't miss it."

"This is an elaborate exit." Kari approached Madeleine and the passageway.

Walking out in a bikini would get another lecture from HR.

"There is a more direct path from my other office, but then you'd pass the real ship staff. Do you have any *other* questions?"

Kari heard the exasperation in Madeleine's voice, but it was interesting knowing that HR had needed to lecture her in the past. "No questions."

"Good. I'll be a minute behind you."

Kari slipped through the narrow passage illuminated by red lights along the floor and padded along in her bare feet up the steps again. How was this her life now? On one hand, it was terrifying. On the other hand, she was free. She had the chance to do her dream science. She could travel the entire world. She didn't have to hide her biggest secret from her new colleagues. She could help expose the illegal secrets of the rich and powerful.

All things considered, her new life was kind of neat.

Once she reached the end, she used the glowing eyehook to slide the door and revealed yet another bathroom closet and stepped inside. Were all bathrooms on the ship part of secret passageways? As a test, she turned on the faucet to test its functionality. Convinced the plumbing worked, she headed to the toilet to relieve herself.

There was no telling how long she'd be on the deck.

With her bladder empty and hands washed, Kari exited the bathroom to step on the outer perimeter of the ship. Kari uttered a quiet squeak when the air of the open ocean struck her. It may have been June, but the more northern latitude didn't get the memo. Despite the goosebumps, she took a moment to look over the railing to the deep blue of the ocean below. It was a long way down.

Kari headed to the ship's bow where the server who gave her the iced tea tended the bar. Henry wore similar clothes as the day before—suit with no tie—while his guest, Robert, was in more cruise-ship appropriate attire: khaki shorts and a white linen shirt. He donned a pair of dark sunglasses with reflective lenses and a neck cord. The two men sat in a lounge area for four while an electric heater glowed in a pulse over them. A hot tub was behind them.

The occupied hot tub.

She made eye contact with Finn, who had their long hair up in a bun and gave her a slight nod. Then, their ivory skin and long, lean muscles emerged from the steaming water. Kari didn't hate the view of the deep V of their Adonis belt plunging into either side of the cherry red, square-cut swim shorts. But the show was short-lived when Finn picked a puffy white towel up off the step and walked in the opposite direction toward Madeleine, drying themself off with each step.

As Finn and Madeleine debriefed on the far side of the deck, Kari took a longer route so she caught Robert's attention as Henry spoke about stocks.

Eye candy nipping out. "This beautiful young lady looks like she could use some time near the heater," Robert slurred with a grin.

Since she wanted secrets, it was best to pretend that she didn't speak English. "I'm only here for the hot tub," Kari replied in Hindi.

Oh, a foreign girl.

Kari tested the water by dipping her toes and verified Creeper McStare was in telepathy range. Then, she lowered herself into the exquisite sensation of hot jets pulsating against her back. Yeah, her new life was pretty neat. She focused on the shallow conversation about business meetings and drinking, and kept her peripheral vision on the business duo.

"I think your focus has deteriorated with that drink," Henry said to Robert. "I invited you here so we could talk business and problem solve."

Such a gullible idiot. Thinks I'm drunk. "I know why I was invited. I just don't see the harm in some people-watching, too." *Wonder if the red head will come back.*

Kari rolled her eyes, then turned her head when she saw movement off to her other side.

Madeleine sauntered toward the bar where the server had a martini with three skewed olives ready for her. She took it without thanks and then sat beside Henry. "Something tells me we're not talking about last year's stocks."

The bitch is back.

Kari laughed but then coughed to cover up her faux pas.

Damn. Only see the top of her head. "Our conversation may have taken a turn," Robert said.

"Indeed, it did," Henry said. "Actually, your company's profit has improved every year for the past four years, but last year it went through the roof. I know I'll hear the summary at the board meeting, but I was hoping to get a preview."

What's his angle? "My company maintains great relationships with local fishermen around the world and pays them a fair price."

"Oh, come on," Henry said. "There has to be more to it than that. Your competitors aren't doing nearly as well as you."

Use legal nets. "Maybe they aren't trying as hard."

Kari quickly dipped her mouth under the water to stifle her chuckle. Both because Robert was an ass, but also because she pictured Mom A's face if she had heard that.

"I suppose sometimes it is a matter of effort." Henry grinned with his head cocked. "You've certainly been able to enjoy the spoils. In the past few years, you've been able to buy an apartment in New York, matching Aston Martins for you and your wife—who doesn't have to know about your fun last night, by the way—and a cattle ranch!"

She was fun. "What can I say except I'm expanding into

surf and turf." Robert laughed again and then clinked the ice around in his glass.

Kari accepted that some people were driven by greed, but there was no excuse for making bad jokes. None.

Time to figure out his angle. "I'm flattered you've noticed my purchase power," Robert said. "But why are you so interested in my assets when you own ten percent of the world?"

"I track who I'm in business with so I'm not surprised. I hate surprises."

He'd hate to learn about the dock worker bribes. Robert traded his empty glass for a full one. He didn't thank the server either. "I understand that."

"I'm glad we see eye to eye," Henry said. "So, what's the secret to your personal success?" he asked in a tone that lost its conversational playfulness.

This is getting annoying. "I thought I just answered that."

"Not the details," Madeleine said.

Not her now too. "You know what"—Robert put his drink on the table—"my muscles are starting to feel a bit tense." He stood and took off his shirt and shorts, leaving him only in his gray boxer briefs. "I think I'll get into the hot tub for a bit."

For the first time, Kari watched Henry's eyes lose their twinkle and become black pinpoints. His slight grin morphed into tight-lipped distain. But as quickly as his face transformed into fury, it returned to the pleasant billionaire she had been introduced to. "Do what you'd like, Robert. You're our guest here." He stood and buttoned his suit jacket. "I'll see you at dinner." Henry left the lounge.

Did that mean she stayed with Robert alone? Madeleine seemed to understand her conundrum because she mouthed, *Stay,* and pointed to Neill who was on guard.

To Robert's credit, when he finally got into the hot tub, he sat across from her, not beside her. "By any chance, do you speak French?" he asked in French.

Even though she was fluent, she viewed this as an opportunity to flatter him. "Yes, I do, but probably not as good as you," she said with inaccurate pronunciation.

After boosting his ego, Kari created the cover that she was another VIP guest—the daughter of a hotel entrepreneur—and turned the conversation to travel. He said he loved exploring and eating his way around the world, but she also learned he had several offshore bank accounts and secret children in multiple countries. While she found that morally repugnant, it wasn't illegal. That information came in the fact that he used an Icelandic climatology team who rented one of his fishing boats to smuggle drugs inside ice core samples.

Convinced she had siphoned enough incriminating information to cause him mountains of legal trouble, it was time to excuse herself from the hot tub. "This was nice, but I'm afraid my dinner will be ready soon." When she braced her hands against the sides to stand, he put his hand over her forearm.

"But we're having such a good time."

"We were, and now I have to leave." She lowered her gaze to his hand, hoping he'd get the hint. He did not. "Please, move your hand."

Robert sent her a smarmy grin. "You look strong, I think you should make me."

Kari watched Neill inch closer to the hot tub. "Okay." She rotated her forearm toward his thumb and easily twisted out of his grasp. "Bye."

Smart-ass bitch. He grabbed her forearm again. This time tighter.

Neill rushed to her, but she was faster. With her free hand, Kari delivered a hard palm strike to Robert's face. She heard the crunch.

He released her as blood erupted from his crooked nose and into the hot tub. "You fucking bitch!" Robert wailed while he covered his face and she got out of the hot tub. "You broke my nose!" He looked at Neill. "She broke my nose!"

"She did." *That might need some ice.* Neill pointed to her arm where her skin was discolored from his grip. "Are you okay?"

"I'm fine," she whispered in English. "I just want to get out of here." She picked up a towel and wrapped it around herself. "Should I take the same way in?" she asked over Robert's cries that he was going to sue her rich, hotel family.

"Yeah. I'll take Robert down to the medical bay."

———

Getting out of wet tops in a dignified way was impossible. Kari changed clothes in Madeleine's bathroom as she gave her the rundown of the bank accounts, the children, and the ice core samples. And him pretending to be drunk.

"You did good work today," Madeleine said, "but, in the future, if anyone gets handsy, please don't hit them in the face. It raises . . . questions. Neill could have intervened."

"But that would have been less satisfying."

Madeleine laughed. Not the one Kari had heard before, but one that suggested genuine amusement. "Oh, I understand that. Trust me."

With the bikini top finally off and twisted in an orange mound at her feet, Kari dried with a hand towel. Her stomach grumbled. She didn't want to come off whiny but this was an issue that needed addressing.

"Out with it," Madeleine said. "You've been quiet far too long."

"Well," Kari said as she shimmied on her underwear, "it's

just that while I'm grateful I got an amazing bikini out of this assignment, it threw off my plans for after work."

"Is there a question in there? Or are you simply complaining in a roundabout way?"

Kari zipped her pants and then pulled on her shirt and necklace. "Would it be possible to have a twenty-four-hour heads-up so I can plan? Say this happens when we're docked and I'm on land. That'd be really inconvenient for you."

"You make an interesting point, and I like how you made it about me." Madeleine paused a few seconds more. "I will do my best to give you proper notice before assignments."

"Thank you." She slipped on her shoes, tucked her multi-tool in her pocket, then went into the office, damp bikini in hand. "So, are you done with me?"

"Almost." Madeleine motioned with her finger to follow her up the stairs and across the conference room. "For the sake of my own convenience and Finn's schedule, I'm going to give you elevator access, so you need a retina scan."

"That's so jazzed!"

I hate slang. "I don't like or always understand slang, but I'll interpret that as agreement of some kind." Madeleine pressed the button for the elevator and stepped inside, but she held a hand up for Kari to halt. After a few seconds of button pushing, she waved Kari inside. "Stand in front of the panel and look into the scanner." Madeleine moved to the side to give her breadth.

Kari did as instructed. A red dot appeared but she knew it was really an infrared beam mapping the back of her eyes.

"Congratulations, you now have access to the VIP office and elevator during the time slots I designate."

"So, I can't come up here whenever I want?"

Why would she do that? "Why would you do that?"

Kari shrugged. "I don't know. Maybe Neill needs me because you passed out from low blood sugar or something."

Madeleine's manicured eyebrows raised. Then, as she stepped out of the elevator, she pushed the button for the doors to close. "Goodbye, Kari."

Kari descended in solitude and reflected on the past two hours. There had been surprise after surprise coming at her from all directions. But a pleasant surprise was that, for the first time in a long while, Kari had found someone who said what they thought. Madeleine was a narcissist and a possible psychopath, but at least she was honest.

Chapter Twelve

Even if the day ended in catastrophe, at least Kari could say she attempted to start healthy habits by hitting the gym before work. She strode into the inCog office, her muscles tired from exertion and her finger sore from getting it pinched between free weights. Kari found both Mitchell and Santos at the conference table, their attention focused on the large TV screen with the research proposal she had sent them the night before. Some areas were highlighted.

"Why the highlights?" Kari noted the uncomfortable looks they shared with each other. "What?"

"I'll start," Santos said to Mitchell, then turned his attention to Kari. "You did a decent job, but for a proposal we 'submit' for approval, we need to restructure it. This needs to blend in. We really don't want to stand out in any way in case someone were to start digging. So, you'll need to take out any reference to 'cerebral annoyance' or 'ORCA'."

Kari loved that acronym but she did see his point. "Okay. Wh—"

"And because of your age, Parkinson's is unheard of, so I've sent you two proposals for deep brain stimulation on an individual with treatment-resistant depression and another who had seizures. I think DBS is the way to go to explain the stereotactic surgery element. Not all brain surgeries require computer-guidance drilling and biopsy. Mitchell and I will do the deep dive of the procedures once the regular inCog work is done."

Kari nodded. "What's on deck for today, anyway?"

"Cocaine-addicted rats," Santos said with more optimism than most people would.

Kari went over to her work station and brought her computer to life. "Oh!" She hadn't told them the most exciting news. "I was able to talk to Madeleine about financing our study."

"I know," Santos said. "I received a call from ship management this morning. You must have made a compelling argument."

"I did, but I also had to barter some of my non-inCog time to serve my Wibawa Enterprises Promise on a regular basis. Like yesterday after work, I helped translate Hindi and French. How much money did they give us for that?"

"I didn't check since I didn't think there would be anything yet. Hold on a second." Santos went to his computer and typed a few codes. "Jesus Christ! We have an extra $50,000 in our account." His head whipped around to Kari. "What in the world did you translate for?"

She hated playing dumb, but it was best. "Business deal of sorts. I guess when Henry makes several million dollars due to my skills, we get a percentage of that."

Santos went back to the figure on the computer screen and rubbed the back of his neck. "How does an eighteen-year-old who has never worked before waltz into Madeleine Coultier's office and get us this amount of money with a seizure clinical trial pitch just by translating?"

"I also promised them four years of my services. It was deemed a fair trade."

Mitchell whistled a long note. "That's quite a commitment."

Kari shrugged. "It's what I'm willing to do to see my dreams realized."

———

The image of a substance abuse rehabilitation facility for rodents entered her mind as she headed to her cabin. When she arrived outside her door, a pink sticky note faced her at eye level.

Come over for happy hour if you see this before 5pm. (This is Jade, btw)

A small thrill coursed through her. She had never, ever been invited to a happy hour before. Mostly because of being under the legal age to drink in the US. Kari peeled the note off her door and then walked the few feet to Jade's cabin. She knocked and a second passed before she heard a muffled, "I'm coming," from behind the door.

No one ever responded to an invite. "You came over!"

"It seemed a fun thing to do. I've never put in time 'working for the man' and then had a real happy hour before."

Has she never had a job? Jade stepped to the side. "Well, come on in! I think you'll find my place is a lot like yours. Just a bit more lived in."

Kari stepped inside and observed the identical yet cozier

space. Where Kari's entire apartment was painted a generic off-white, Jade had an accent wall of brick red. Kari's white place setting for one versus Jade's over the sink four-piece place settings in four vibrant colors. Where Kari had a love seat, Jade had a large recliner and end table. She couldn't even see Jade's bed because a folded room divider—complete with shelves full of knick knacks and photographs—acted as a barrier.

"This is amazing!" Kari said. "There's so much personality. My place says, 'a human might live here.'"

Jade chuckled as she meandered into her kitchen. "It takes time. And bribing our hallway representative with baked goods helps. You would have thought I wanted to tear down a wall with the way he reacted to the recliner. So, what can I get you? I don't have much of a selection, but I do have wine and a great bottle of rum I picked up when we were in Miami. With the strawberries I just bought I could make daiquiris."

"I don't really have much experience in the way of alcohol. Wasn't really a thing in my house growing up and I never was invited to parties." She saw a look of sympathy cross Jade's features. "Don't feel bad, I wouldn't have wanted to go anyway."

"Not even in college?"

"I lived at home for undergrad and on-line grad school. Plus, there's the whole only being eighteen thing."

"You're eighteen?" Jade shouted, as if Kari had committed some atrocity.

"Plus a few months. If you're worried about if I'm legal to drink, we're in the clear due to international waters and PNG law. Cheers!"

"Hold on. We need to rewind a bit." Jade moved her hands in a rapid circle. "But you're a neuroscientist with inCog."

"Technically, my title is 'associate scientist.'" When Jade

continued to stare, Kari added, "I finished school quickly." Now Jade added an eyebrow quirk. "Okay, I'm a genius."

"You must be! I can't believe you're young enough to be my daughter."

"Wait." Given Jade's energy and youthful features, that didn't track. "How old are you?"

"Forty-four."

"No way!"

"What can I say? I drink lots of water, get plenty of sleep, and take care of my skin." Jade went to her mini fridge and pulled out a container of pre-cut strawberries. "These berries are the absolute best. I go to every single farmers' or street market I can find when we're on land. The colors, the smells, the bartering. I just love it."

"I think I had to go to the farmers' market every weekend of my life before I moved away, so I get it. Mom L was the president of it for a while."

Jade stopped dropping berries into the blender. "What's a mom-el?"

"Oh, I have two moms: an Aurora and a Leela. So, Mom A and Mom L."

"Got it." Jade added some ice and rum then mixed it. "If you want it sweeter," Jade said over the whirring motor, "I have some honey." She took off the lid, dipped in a spoon, and handed it to Kari. *This is so weird. It's like drinking with Diana.*

Kari sampled the pink drink. The strength of the rum overpowered the berries, not enough to contort her face, but enough for a slight burn to travel down her throat. "Maybe a little honey. And, if you don't mind, some more ice."

Jade tossed in a few more ice cubes, drizzled a thick, gold ribbon from a glass jar in the mix, and then blended it again. She poured two glasses, and handed one to Kari. Jade held her glass up. *I hate coming up with toasts.*

"To feeling your age," Kari said.

"Yes!" Jade clinked her glass and then went over to her recliner.

Kari sipped her drink. The extra ice and honey transformed the beverage into a brilliant burst of dessert in a glass. "This is amazing."

Jade stifled a laugh. "It's just a basic daiquiri, but you're welcome."

Kari went to a dining chair that had a homemade cushion on it. Or at least she assumed it was homemade given that it looked like an old college sweatshirt.

"You can bring your chair over here," Jade said.

"That's okay. I actually like having a lot of personal space. Did you make these cushions?"

"I sure did. I realized one day that I was never going to wear those sweatshirts again, but at the same time, I couldn't part with them. So, I repurposed them in a way that gave the place more personality."

Kari observed Jade's cabin again. Personality covered the apartment, from the sketches and recipes framed on the walls, pictures of Jade and a young woman in a cap and gown, to the little area rug in the kitchen. "How much of this did you bring on the ship with you when you first started?"

"I had a suitcase of clothes, a couple of boxes, and my chef knives. I've accumulated the rest over the past two years." Jade pointed at her. "You might want to slow down."

Kari looked into her glass which was already half empty. "Oh, wow. Compliments to the chef."

"I appreciate that, but it doesn't sound like you know what your tolerance level is, and that can be a very uncomfortable lesson to learn."

That was good advice and made her think of all the mini-lectures Mom A had given her about temptation before she left for her road trip. At the time, she had been annoyed, but now a sense of longing struck. It wasn't so much that she missed her moms. She missed her best friends. She brought her hand to her necklace and thought of them.

"Are you okay?" Jade asked. "You look like you just got really sad."

"I'm okay. It's just that I got this job kind of suddenly and I was going to see the moms in New York for a more proper goodbye, but that didn't happen. The longest I've been away from home has been for a month. It'll be weird."

"You'll probably get a little home sick, but you have plenty of nice folks here to keep you company if you get lonely. There are all kinds of clubs you could join."

"I don't really do that."

Jade's drink paused at her lips. "You don't have hobbies?"

"I do. I play the guitar and love movies. It's just people. Like I told you, I need my space."

"But you're okay with me."

"Because you've been generous and you're over there. Most of the people I've met . . . they don't understand or respect my need for space."

"When you put it that way I do seem like fabulous company." Jade waited a few moments in silence. "So, before I suggest something and sound pushy, do you want to meet more people?"

"Eh. It's just that if I meet people, then they might want to be friends, and my brain gets overwhelmed easily with lots of people around, too." That was enough information to be considered truthful and allow Jade to draw her own conclusions. But Jade continued to look at her for more details. "If my brain gets stressed, I have seizures."

"Oh, I've read about that! That's a shame." Jade had a

thoughtful look about her. "How do you feel about physical activity?"

"Like sports?" Jade nodded. "Again, the people and personal space issue, but I like competition."

"Great!" Jade pushed down her recliner and stood. "Let's go!"

"What's happening?"

Jade poured more from the blender into her cup and then gestured for Kari to hand hers over. "We're polishing off what's in the blender and heading to club six."

Kari stood and felt the slightest wobbles in her legs. She handed her glass to Jade and got a little closer than usual to see if her telepathy was affected by the alcohol. "What's in club six?"

Table tennis. Jade handed her back a full glass. "It's a surprise."

———

Even though it wasn't a surprise, Kari played along and sipped her drink on the way while she kept a firm grip on the railing. "I can understand why I shouldn't drive or operate heavy machinery."

Or text exes. "It's important to learn your limit in a safe environment, and two drinks is clearly your limit."

Kari focused on putting one foot in front of the other and followed Jade down the hall until they stopped outside of Club 6: Tabletop Sports. Kari cleared her throat and tried to sound as uncertain as possible. "Is this like table tennis or something?"

She guessed right! "You betcha!"

Jade opened the door to a room with vintage arcade game posters covering the walls, a shuffleboard table pushed against the back wall, an air hockey table in front of that, and a foosball table where two men focused on their game and moved their grips with rapid, aggressive spins. Beside that was a vacant table tennis table.

"Want to play?" Jade asked.

The others were far enough away for their thoughts not to be a problem. "Sure. I've never really played much before and my coordination is a little questionable at the moment, but I'll try."

Jade handed her a paddle then pulled down a loose net hung high on one side and extended to the other to divide the spaces. It was a simple and cheap solution to having their ball go to the other side of the room.

Kari bounced on her heels as she took in the fun atmosphere. And Jade was far enough away where she didn't have to hear her thoughts. "This place is jazzed!"

Jade laughed. "I haven't heard that word since my daughter was in middle school."

Two things caught Kari. One, was her slang out of date? And she hadn't asked about Jade's daughter. Actually, she didn't know much about Jade. "I just realized you know much more about me than I know about you."

"What would you like to know? This'll be our warm up." Jade served the ball to Kari.

She returned the ball with a soft lob. "How did you end up on the *Hinewai*?"

"Ah. When Diana left for college, it felt like a time for a fresh start. We like to say we started a new adventure together, but separate. And because I know you're doing the math in your head to figure out when I had her, I got married and pregnant right after I finished culinary school. When she was twelve, the ex and I got divorced."

Kari stretched to the far corner but missed the ball. "I'm sorry to hear that." She tossed the ball back over to Jade.

"It's fine. I missed out on a lot starting a family so young, so I'm seeing all the sights now." She served again.

"Do you get to talk to Diana much?" Kari asked with a soft underhand.

"Not as much as I'd like because of time zone issues and her class schedule, but we text or email pretty often. Eventually, I'd like to settle near her once she figures out where she wants to land. Family is important." The ball hit the net and slowly dribbled to a stop. Jade leaned across the table to get it.

"So, the *Hinewai* isn't a forever thing for you?"

Hell, no. Jade returned to her spot to serve. "I think the *Hinewai* offers a lot, especially for younger people, but there's just something about this place . . . I get a weird vibe sometimes." Jade shook her head. "But enough of that talk. I'd say our warm-up is done. It's on now!"

They continued their laughs as they increased the level of intensity to their play. Kari knew she was terrible, but Jade didn't care. She wasn't very good either. They spent the majority of their first game chasing the white ball under the table and around the perimeter of the netted room. The last time she'd had this many laughs was when she had watched her cousin Wade fall out of a canoe and he couldn't get back in.

Gods, she really hated him.

"Ready for another game?" Jade asked.

"Yeah, let's do one more before—Oh, hold on. My phone." Kari pulled her vibrating phone out from her back pocket. "It's Mom L."

"Are you sure you want to answer that right now?"

"Wouldn't you want to talk to your daughter if she called?"

"Yeah, but you're drunk, and that's a parent. Different dynamic."

"It's fine." Kari put the phone on speaker. "Hi! I put you on speaker, so don't go spilling any super-secret mayoral secrets. Oops, I shouldn't have said secret twice. Don't go spilling any small-town government secrets."

"I wasn't planning on it." After a small pause, Mom L asked, "Are you okay?"

"I'm great! I'm playing table tennis with my neighbor, Jade. Say hi, Jade."

"Hi!"

"You can tell her I said hi back and I don't want to keep you, because you sound like you're having fun—"

"I'm having so much fun!"

"Right," Mom L drawled. "So, I'm calling because your Mom A and my anniversary is coming up, and I wanted to get your opinion on an idea I had today."

"I'd love to help!" Kari caught Jade pointing to herself. "Sorry, *we'd* love to help. Shoot!"

"Are you sure you're okay? You almost sound . . . drunk."

"There's a *really* good reason for that, but don't worry because we've concluded that two drinks is plenty."

"If you're anything like me—and you *are*—chug some water or sports drink before bed."

"Then I'll have to pee."

"A small price to pay to avoid the sensation of your head in a vice. How about you give me a call back when it's convenient for you?"

"That would be great. We want to get in another round of table tennis before dinner."

"It's a plan, then. And . . . I'm glad you're having fun, chickpea. I love you."

"Love you back, Mom L." Kari hung up, tucked her phone back into her pocket and put her game face back on, but Jade appeared amused, not competitive. "What?"

"That was so cute!" Jade lobbed a serve her way. "How long have your moms been together?"

Kari returned it with a gentle swat of the paddle. "Married for almost nineteen. Together for twenty-two, and they're *still* into each other."

Jade hit the ball back. "That's hot."

"Please, don't call my moms hot."

"Hot! Hot! Hot!" Jade chanted even when Kari laughed until her sides ached.

———

Once their paddles were put away and they had their empty glasses in their hands, they meandered back up the stairs to the cafeteria for dinner. Kari loved the time she spent with Jade, but she was exhausted.

I'm so beat. "If you don't mind," Jade said, "I'm going to head up to my room with our glasses, get my plate, then get my dinner before it's lights out for me."

"I was just thinking the same, but what do you mean you're getting a plate? You don't use the cafeteria's stuff?"

"The ship only uses generic white, so what I do is take my own place settings to the cafeteria on a tray—also one I bought—and then take it home. I just have to wash it myself, but that's not a major hassle."

This could be a major game changer. "So, we don't *have* to eat there?"

"No. But they hate it when you take their dining ware, which is why mine are colorful. Even my utensils are this iridescent, rainbow-like color. They're real pretty."

"You are a genius, too!"

Jade chuckled. "I don't know about that, but I do know how to live on the ship and can teach you what I know."

"I'd really appreciate that."

"Then, how about I let you borrow a dining set, and show you how it's done?"

"Yes! Show me how to live!"

Chapter Thirteen

St. John's, Newfoundland, Canada

The urge to pee appeared in her dream and then brought Kari into reality. She tossed her covers off and dragged her feet to the bathroom in the near blackness of her room. But on the return to her bed, a sparkle outside the sliding door caught her eye. In the violet sky she saw a light, but not from the stars. A lighthouse. She had no idea how far away they were, but they'd drop anchor soon.

Kari turned to her cabin door when she heard a rustle against the carpet. A white envelope lay on the inside. She picked it up, pulled out the handwritten note out of the sealed envelope, and read.

Use the elevator to come to my office, Saturday at 1:00 pm. Wear the suit and shoes from your interview.

Who would she be tasked with spying on this time? And where? At least the requested wardrobe didn't raise any alarms.

She picked up her charging phone on the nightstand: 5:01am. Kari exhaled a noise of disgust and glanced at her unmade bed. She knew even if she were able to fall asleep, it would be poor. She turned off the alarm, then turned on her electric kettle for coffee. She might as well start her day.

———

"Morning, Kari," Santos said as soon as she walked into inCog. "How are you feeling this morning?"

"Fine." If she didn't know better, she'd say he was smirking at her. That was new. "Why do you ask?"

"Because I saw you get your dinner last night. You were very happy about the colorful reflection of yourself in your spoon and table tennis."

Kari cleared her throat. "Well, learning that I don't have to have all my meals surrounded by people and that there's a sport available on the ship that allows a healthy distance between others was very exciting." She turned on her computer and saw a new file on her desktop. "Is this study about ferrets on amphetamines or something?"

"Actually, it's the ORCA study and your examination schedule for today. Mitchell's down in the medical bay waiting for you now. If he needs a follow-up, we can use the resources here rather than when we get to Iceland for the EEG."

"Okay, so I do that, and then what?"

Now, Santos really did smirk. "I believe you said something about getting into a system to gain the necessary approvals."

"Gotcha. I'll start that when I return."

Kari strolled down to deck one, past the marine science lab, and to the medical bay. Its red sign with a white cross in the center jutted out from above the door and inside the room a woman spoke to Mitchell.

Mitchell greeted her with a raise of his coffee cup. "Good morning, Kari. This is Dr. Zakharov. Zak's one of the three full-time physicians on the ship."

"Hello, Kari, call me Zak. Or Dr. Zak." Her smile was warm in the chilly room. *She matches the description of the person who broke that VIP's nose. I'll have to notify ship security.* "Dr. Mitchell explained that you need a routine physical as a requirement of your work. Would you rather I perform it? Or perhaps like me to stay and chaperone?"

At least she had ethics even if she was a poor judge of character. "No, that's not necessary."

"Alright, then. I'll be in my office if either of you need anything."

She looks exhausted. Mitchell grinned but then it disappeared. "Are you feeling well?"

"I woke up earlier than I wanted to, but I'm good to go."

Good. He motioned for her to follow him to the far side of the room, behind the curtain divider. "I thought maybe you'd be hungover, but now that I think about it, I could shake those off pretty easily when I was eighteen, too."

Kari groaned. "Does everyone know I had too much to drink last night?"

"Only those at the seven o'clock dinner service. Your enthusiasm over honey mustard was pretty comical, but don't worry, I think everyone on board has an embarrassing story like that. Mine was falling off a treadmill. Have a seat." He gestured to the table.

Kari got on and peered out the porthole. Several boats dotted the water and the larger of St. John's waterfront buildings stood in the near distance.

Tell her about the blood test. "You have an appointment on shore tomorrow morning for a blood panel, so you'll need to get on the first tender and fast for twelve hours." He brought over a laptop and turned it to her. "Can you punch in your height and weight."

Kari saw the fields she needed to enter and did the quick unit conversions into the metric system in her head. She was a smidge over five and a half feet, so that was 170 centimeters, and she was 150 pounds, so 68 kilograms. "I should probably tell you before we start that my heart rate is crazy low. Don't be alarmed."

"Okay, I'll try not to freak out." Mitchell took the cuff off the wall and put the plugs of the stethoscope in his ears. He proceeded to take her blood pressure and oxygen saturation levels. *Those are good.* "I appreciate the note about your heart rate. Have you ever investigated that?"

"Nope. It's been like that since before I was born."

I bet she has even more abilities we don't know about.

"But where would the fun be if I disclosed all of my secrets?"

Mitchell looked over the frames of his glasses. "I keep forgetting you can do that, even though it's why we're doing all of this."

"If it helps, I'm still getting used to the fact that I can talk about it openly. At least to some people." He shined a pen light in her eyes, then she blinked away the colorful spots. "It's so much easier, and I don't feel like I'm lying because I'm withholding the truth. Therapy was awful because of that."

"You were in therapy?"

"Yeah. After G&C trespassed on the farm and threatened the moms, we did family and individual therapy. Mom L insisted I go. Said she had benefited from it—even though it took her awhile to admit that—and thought I would too."

He typed in a note and took the stethoscope off his neck. "I think you should include that in the rewrite of the proposal. It shows that you have a family history—I doubt someone would dig far enough to learn which mother of yours is biological—and that you've been to a therapist, so it provides extra credibility to a surgical procedure. Were you ever on any medication?"

"No. Although my therapist did talk to Mom L about it. She told me it was my choice, but I didn't want the side effects. It was easier removing myself from people."

Sad. He plugged his ears with the ends of the stethoscope again. "Breathe normally, please."

Kari sat straight and breathed, then took deeper breaths when prompted. "What's"—she inhaled—"after this?" She exhaled.

"Vision, hearing, and reflexes. Then, we're tapped out with what we can do here today."

Given the basic equipment in the room that made sense. "Out of curiosity, is there anything that you would find in this or my blood work which would prevent you from being the clinician in this study?"

Good question. He took a moment to think. "Not that I wouldn't do it, but we'd have to have a serious conversation if you were pregnant."

Despite her magical birth origins, Kari released a quick laugh. "Not happening here. The self-serve kiosk has been my go-to for service for well over nine months."

Preaching to the choir there. Then he looked at her with wide eyes. "I . . . um . . . I'm sorry, you probably heard that."

Kari simply nodded. Then, they stared at each other for an awkward moment before he blurted, "Let's check your ears."

———

After a superficial exam, which proved that her major systems were normal or superior, Kari continued her day. Between revising different sections of her research proposal, she would sneak glances of St. John's harbor out the office window and daydream. Some of it was practical, like what her new plates or shoe organizer would look like. Some were more fantasy, like what her new life would be like if ORCA worked. She could have fun with people beyond table tennis. Possibly enjoy sex with someone other than herself. But mostly, Kari wondered what sort of assignment awaited her tomorrow.

"Hey, honey mustard!" a guy yelled with a wave from across the stairs leading away from inCog.

She waved back and continued to her cabin. Dammit, was this going to be her nickname on the ship? Even chickpea would be leagues better than that. Her childhood nickname reminded her that she owed Mom L a return call. She took her phone out and dialed.

"How are we feeling today?" Mom L asked.

Kari couldn't see her mother but knew she was amused. "I took your advice about the water and was fine for my physical." She stopped walking as soon as the words left her mouth and knew what Mom L's next question would be.

"You needed a physical? Shouldn't they have done that sort of thing before they made you live on a boat?"

Kari did want to tell her moms at least part of the plan. She was living out her dream, they would be happy for her. "Before we get into all that, what's this anniversary idea of yours?"

Kari listened as she walked up to her deck and took another sticky note off her cabin door. This time, Jade told her to keep the dishes until she got her own set. Nice.

"So, what do you think, chickpea?"

Yes, that nickname was light-years better than honey mustard. "I think it's nice that you want to take her to Alaska. Even if your timeline is almost a year from now. Are you going to visit Ata Niq's stomping grounds?"

"Time permitting, and that's sort of up to him if he wants to visit."

Kari kicked off her shoes and sat on her loveseat. "I'm by far not an expert in romance, but usually a couple's getaway doesn't involve inviting someone's parents along."

"Or their child."

"Huh?" Leave it to Mom L to add some twists and turns to the conversation. "I'm coming, too?"

"I hope so. I figured your Mom A and I can have couple's time for a few days before the rest of the family gets there. It coincides with when the *Hinewai* is supposed to be in Anchorage. You know, assuming no weather emergencies or the Ring of Fire doesn't decide to erupt at once."

Alaska was almost 360 degrees from where she was now. It was difficult to imagine she'd be cruising around that much of the world. "Then, you get my seal of approval."

"Great! I'll book it after you tell me why you had to have a physical because I did *not* forget you said that."

Dammit. She thought she had escaped. "It goes like this . . . Remember when I started therapy with Daryll, and you wanted me to tell him about my telepathy because you thought it would help me?"

"You mean as opposed to when you told him in a completely unplanned way because you had let your emotions bottle up and you exploded? Yes, I remember."

Mom L would have to phrase it that way. "Well, Mitchell and Santos know now, too."

"Whoa! How did that happen?"

This was where she had to tread with caution. They deserved to know about the plan, but for their own safety they couldn't know all of the details. "We were talking about the two of you and the dreams; Mitchell asked if I exhibited any abilities. So, figuring he was the safest person on Earth to know, I told him." After several seconds of silence, Kari held her phone away from her ear to see if the call dropped. It hadn't. "Mom L?"

"Yeah, I'm here. I'm just . . . I'm shocked. How did he react?"

"Fantastic, actually. It led to a rather interesting conversation with Santos, which has led to some big news." Kari blew out a breath. "We're going to try it."

"What do you mean 'it'? Like the ORCA 'it'? The surgery 'it'?"

"Yes," Kari said with much less confidence than she should have.

"What? When?" she asked, panicked.

"Calm down. There are no firm dates, because there is a lot of analysis that needs to be done. But my physical this morning was a part of it, and I'm having a blood draw tomorrow in St. John's—I'm in Newfoundland, by the way. Then, it's brain imaging in Europe." Kari stopped to allow her mother to process the news. After there was silence on the other end of the phone for several seconds, Kari prepared herself for the mother's opinion. "Are you mad?"

"I feel many things right now, but anger isn't one of them. I know how badly you want this, I just . . . I honestly thought this was a decade or two in the future. I'm a little scared." After a brief pause, she added. "Okay, I'm a lot scared, but I don't think I'm scared enough to tell you not to do it, especially if the surgery part isn't definite."

Kari collapsed back on her loveseat. "I'm so glad. I wasn't going to tell you—"

"How could you not tell us?" Mom L yelled.

"Because this could lead to drilling a hole through your daughter's head and I thought that might be upsetting to you."

"Well, they aren't drilling holes yet. What *would* be upsetting is if you hadn't told me or your Mom A."

"Speaking of her, can you tell her?"

"No! This is something that needs to come from you while I hold her hand. Plus, she's going to want to talk about your hair if and when you do the surgery part, and I don't feel comfortable doing that."

Kari rubbed her forehead. Mom L was right. Hair held a great significance for her ancestors, and surgery meant she would have to shave at least a portion of her head.

"Sweets!" Mom L yelled. "Chickpea needs to talk to you!"

"I didn't think I'd have to talk to her now!" Kari said, outraged.

"I'm full of surprises, just like you. Love you. Bye."

"Hi, chickpea!" Mom A's voice practically sang. "How's life on the ship?"

"Well"—Kari propped her feet up on her coffee table—"it goes like this."

Kari spent the next few minutes repeating everything she had told Mom L, and like her, Mom A wasn't angry about the decision, only concerned that the procedure would be carried out in a proper manner. And she did have thoughts about the hair.

"There is a *huge* difference between you choosing to do this and someone taking that choice away from you," Mom A said. "Now, I do think that a part of you might regret not keeping your hair when you're older. Your hair tells a story. To just throw it away would be like throwing away your past."

"But I don't like most of my past; I'd like to forget it happened."

"I understand where you're coming from, but you can never escape your past because it will always shape your future."

Kari tipped her head back on the loveseat and groaned. "I hate it when you make sense."

"I know," Mom A said with a chuckle. "And I also know that you understand what I'm saying."

"I do." Now she had to find someone she trusted enough to perform her epic haircut if and when the time came.

"Hey, since I have you on the phone and your Mom L left the room, can I run an idea by you that I had for our anniversary? I was thinking of—"

"Let me guess, you want to take her on a getaway?"

"How did you know?"

Her moms really were perfect for each other. "Lucky guess."

———

Kari prepared for a frigid morning ride on the tender to the mainland. She zipped her jacket to her chin and stuffed her hands in her pockets along with several dozen other people. As she overheard their conversations, she learned that there were a few running errands like her, nature photographers and marine scientists were meeting a different ship for a whale watching expedition, and WU students were awaiting different types of field trips. No one meandered over to her for small talk, which worked in their favor because, as the land drew closer, her stomach let her know it was not pleased about her fast for the blood draw.

St. John's was full of colorful, modest-sized homes dotting the hills along the water, while small and large fishing vessels, and impressive leisure boats, floated in the marina. As she took her gaze farther inland, the buildings became less residential and more commercial. Nothing towered like it did in New York, but the town had seen prosperity.

Most likely aided by Robert MacDonald.

The tender pulled up to the dock, and while she walked to her destination, she took in the quaint seaside town and noticed a few possible breakfast spots. Once she arrived at the clinic, she checked in and then sat in the corner while she watched the local forecast for the day. No one spoke to her. After a few minutes, the phlebotomist called her back, found her vein, and had her out in minutes. It was a total impersonal experience and she loved it.

Kari's stomach rumbled as she went to the nearest diner. She inhaled the delicious smells of coffee and greasy hash browns as she read the sign to seat herself. She headed to a large booth and, on the way, made eye contact with Finn. Despite her desire to spike her blood glucose in private, she waved at them. Not an excited wave, but one that could still be construed as an acknowledgement of one's existence. Finn waved back and, less than a second later, a red headed boy around four years old popped his head over the top of the booth.

"Who is that?" the boy yelled.

Finn smiled—not a smartass one, but an actual amused grin. "That's Kari. I know her from the ship."

"I'm Declan," he said with a broad, gappy smile. "I just ate *two* damper dogs with so much jam!"

"That's nice . . . I think." Kari had never heard of a damper dog and based on the name was a little afraid.

"You might have heard of a touton," Finn said. "Same thing."

Kari shook her head.

"It's fried bread."

"Oh!" Now she could get on board with the local breakfast lingo. "I'll consider checking the damper dogs out. Thanks." Kari started to walk to the far corner booth.

"Are you Peyton's friend?" Declan yelled.

Kari's brow rose at the name. She turned to see who she knew as Finn with their eyes closed, shaking their head. Declan, on the other hand, smiled wide enough for her to see more missing teeth. "Um, we work together."

A look of relief washed over their face. "That's right! And remember, I like the name Finn now."

The little boy nodded. "Do you dance, too?"

"Dance?" Kari asked with a chuckle, and then saw Finn's serious expression. She didn't need to read their mind to know that Finn needed her to keep up the ruse. "I don't dance, but I play guitar."

"Are you in the same boat show together?"

What the kid lacked in teeth he made up for in questions. "Yes, we are. But I'm really new and still learning the part I need to play. I'm sure Finn can tell you all about it."

"Yes, I can!" they said quickly. "And I have to get you to school by nine, so if I don't finish telling you about it here, I can still tell you there because I'll be there with you all morning to have fun."

Declan disappeared from view. Finn shot her a thankful look.

Kari took her seat, accepted a menu from the waitress, and eavesdropped on Finn's description of their current—and completely fictitious—show. According to Finn, the troupe performed twice a day, six days a week. The director was an absolute tyrant, but the choreographer was a genius. Kari had no idea what Finn's dancing background actually was, but the details integrated into the story were impressive enough for her to believe that they had taken dance classes. Finn was also a skilled storyteller. Kari particularly liked the anecdote of when they discovered that some cast members were allergic to spirit gum because the skin around their adhered elf ears broke into terrible rashes.

They almost had to cancel the Christmas show because of it!

The two red heads stopped by her booth before her breakfast of fish cakes with a damper dog arrived. She put down her phone where she had been investigating Iceland's clinical trial approval processes. It was her light breakfast reading.

"If you don't mind," Finn said, "Declan would like to ask you something before we leave."

"Sure." To Kari's shock, Declan climbed onto the narrow seat beside her, cupped her ear, and leaned in.

"Is Pey—Finn—a good dancer?"

The hope and innocence in his voice caused her to grin. Kari turned to him and whispered back, "The best on the ship." His gap-toothed smile while he shimmied back out of the seat was worth the lie. "See you at rehearsal, Finn."

"Bye, Kari, I'll see you soon," Finn said and then mouthed, *"Thank you"*.

———

Kari sat on a bench near the pick-up point with several bags at her feet and waited for the noon tender to come to shore. She had been able to get most of her items, but none of her bags had a shoe organizer. Maybe next time.

As the boat approached, several more people gathered in the area. She recognized a few. One man in a suit—who was much too close to her—was terrified about a job interview for a ship engineer position. Then, walking toward her was Finn with a tear in the knee of their dark skinny jeans.

"You have quite a few bags," they said. "Did you get everything you needed?"

"Mostly. But you just reminded me I should buy a sewing kit."

Finn looked down. "I was hoping it wasn't noticeable, but the fact that my skin is so pale I'm like a fluorescent light bulb probably doesn't help."

Kari smiled. "You're right. It doesn't help. Did you fall?"

"Yeah, I was playing with Declan at recess and tripped."

"How very undancer like of you."

"Yeah, about that . . ." They sat on the far end of the bench. *How do I explain to her?*

"Just so you know, we're close enough for me to do the thing with that skill that I have." With so many ears around, it was best to be vague.

Finn shrugged. "I got nothing to hide anymore, but it's Declan I'm worried about. It's him I have to lie to."

"Is Declan your little brother?"

"No. He's my son."

Kari liked to think that she had a poker face, but in this case she failed because she felt her skin stretch from her raised brow. How could she ask her next question delicately? "Okay, this is clearly none of my business, so feel free not to answer, but he doesn't know that, does he?"

Finn shook their head. "Due to my circumstances at the time and his age, my aunt thought it would be best if she told him I was a sibling. He lives with her now and she has legal custody."

A son who didn't know who his parent was. "I can't imagine how much that hurts you."

Finn sighed. "It does. But what was I going to do? All I know is that if I hadn't reached out to her, Declan would have been placed in foster care. At least this way, I know where he is. We can video chat and I can see him when my schedule allows it. When I'm done with my service to the

Hinewai, I'll ask for custody, and we'll attend a lot of therapy."

"Madeleine told me a little bit about your situation. How much time do you have left in your contract?"

"Around three years. By then I'll have money saved and I can show the courts I'm a proper adult and all that." Finn took a moment to study her. "You've got your own arrangement, right?"

"I do." The people gathered started to drift away from the bench and toward the boarding zone. "And I'm starting to think that's Henry and Madeleine's game. They find people with special skills, offer them what they want most, and hold a portion of their life hostage until their term is up."

Impressed. "It took me three months to figure that out. Can I ask what it is you want most?"

"Experimental brain surgery. Can I ask who Peyton is?"

More about who Peyton was. "The short answer is someone I'd like to move on from. The long answer is a conversation for another time."

"Fair." Kari pretended her combination of her paper and canvas shopping bags held her interest. "Then, can I ask what kind of dance you do?"

Finn snickered. "I would say contemporary but it's not formal. If a trained dancer watched me, they would probably laugh, but to Declan I'm the best dancer ever."

"Well, yeah, because I told him, and I'm a very trustworthy source." Given Mom L's ability of sensing her emotions from afar, Kari wondered if there was a history in Finn's family. "Do you know if Declan shares your gift?"

"The gift of amateur dance?"

Kari laughed, causing them to grin. "No, the other thing you have."

Finn buried their hands in their leather jacket pockets. "I

don't know, to be honest. I often think maybe my mom or dad did and that's why they left. Couldn't take it, you know? But they were gone before my ability developed and I could ask them."

"How old were you when they left?"

"Twelve. Aunt took me in too, but then . . . things got tough money wise and complicated because of identity struggles, relationships, and a baby."

Kari thought about reciprocating some of her story but thought better of it. The information could lead to Finn knowing about her family history. She didn't think she'd ever trust someone enough for that.

"Oh, my God!" a woman said, her eyes focused on her phone. She meandered closer to Kari. *They used a sleeps with the fishes joke about Robert MacDonald's death. That's so insensitive.*

Kari's heart jumped into her throat and the alarm on her face must have shown because Finn inched closer.

"What happened?" they asked.

"Let me confirm what I just heard." She typed in the businessman's name into her search engine with trembling fingers, and there on her rectangular screen was the face of the man who's mind she'd read for Madeleine and Henry. The headline read: Robert MacDonald, entrepreneur and businessman, found dead from a self-inflicted gunshot wound.

She scrolled below Robert's picture and read the preliminary details. One of his ships outside Norway was raided by maritime officials, where they found millions of dollars in drugs hidden inside of—what a surprise—ice core samples. "Oh, my Gods." She showed Finn as another tremor went through her. "I told Madeleine this information. Did I . . . kill him?"

"No, you didn't. Before he even stepped on the ship, they knew he was dirty. They just didn't know the details."

They used the information she gave Madeleine. If she hadn't done that, Robert would still be alive. He wouldn't have shot himself. The idea that she had somehow contributed to his death caused her breakfast of local delicacies to churn in her stomach and her breathing to increase. She leaned down so her head was between her knees and started her four-seven-eight breaths so she didn't hyperventilate.

Guilt. Finn placed a gentle hand on her shoulder. "This is not your fault."

Physical contact was so infrequent it reset her focus in an instant. Kari lifted her head to meet Finn's eyes. "I thought he'd just go to jail."

"And that still wouldn't be your fault. He did the crimes. The part that's weird to me is since when does a person that wealthy kill himself instead of getting a million-dollar legal team on it first? I can't imagine someone as rich and powerful as him would ever consider jail a real threat."

Kari's stomach settled at Finn's rhetorical question. That was an interesting point. Rich people always thought they could beat the system. "But then that means someone else killed him? They murdered him? Why?"

Powerful people have enemies. Finn shrugged. "He had something someone wanted, and this was the best way to get it? I don't know. He was into a lot of shady shit."

Still shocked, but not shaken anymore, Kari stood from the bench to join the rest of the crowd. "I thought he was just a sleezy rich guy at first, but he ended up being a lot more."

"No one on this ship is who they appear to be." *Including us.*

Chapter Fourteen

For the rest of the week, Kari focused on all things not related to her new involvement in the underworld: She made her new home more homey, she rewrote the portions of her proposal, and to add onto her busy week, she even hit the gym. She did everything possible to not obsess over her next assignment. If every person whose mind she read wound up dead—even if they were the scum of the earth—that would send her back to therapy.

Despite the distractions, soon it was time to don her business suit and go back to Madeleine's office. In case someone saw her enter the VIP access cabin, she concocted a tale that early in the ship's history an office was placed on that deck because there was water damage to a records room. That sounded believable enough.

"You're prompt," Madeleine said from the head of the conference table. "I like that."

Kari returned Neill's small wave. "Well, considering that assignments are money for the project, I didn't want any reason for a penalty."

"That's wise. Now, for why you're here. There's a press conference and you're going to act as one of those microphone people who circulate in the crowd."

This assignment was already hell. "Sounds reasonable." It was times like this Kari wished Madeleine didn't keep an intentional distance from her. She would love to know the nefarious machinations Madeleine had planned. "Why am I really going on shore?"

There was that wicked grin again. "There's a journalist, Adam Cho, who has developed an"—she paused to seemingly choose the precise word—"uncomfortable interest in the *Hinewai* and sends a colleague to all of Henry's press events. We want to know what's driving his curiosity."

Kari knew Adam Cho well. He was a celebrity journalist who aired investigative reports on ENN and wrote bestsellers. He sent Mom A a holiday card every year since she was part of the ENN family. "Okay, who's the colleague?"

"We don't know."

So not only did she have to siphon information from the target, but she also had to determine who the target was in a massive crowd. Although, unlike last time, this seemed lower risk. But the timing was odd. "Why is there a press conference here anyway?"

"Due to Robert MacDonald's untimely death, Henry's announcing he's bought the majority share as he feels it will help the stability of the company."

Her firestarter necklace practically bounced off her chest, her heart beat so hard. She received the request for this assignment before the news that Robert was dead. They knew. They planned his murder.

"Are you okay?" Madeleine asked. "You look . . . ill."

"I'm fine," Kari said and forced a smile. "It sounded like you were going to tell me more."

"Right. Well, Henry already flew over in his helicopter, since that makes a grander entrance." Madeleine picked up a lanyard with an identification badge off the table and handed it to Neill.

Neill walked the extra distance to her. *Good smile in the picture.* "Here you go." He handed it to Kari.

"Show that to the front desk and they'll tell you where to go," Madeleine said. "Neill will drive you there and then take both you and Finn back. They may be able to help ID the journalist, too."

Kari reviewed her ship identification and slipped the lanyard over her head. "Where's Finn now?"

"They left with Henry." Madeleine stood from the table, then left in the direction of her office.

Kari turned to Neill. Unlike the last time she saw him, the top button of his shirt was left undone. His lower neck was red between the ink of his tattoos like it had been rubbed. Was he strangled in a fight doing more of Henry's bidding? "Is that rope burn?"

I was hoping it wasn't noticeable. "I tried a new detergent that was on sale. It was advertised as gentle, but . . ." He shook his massive head. "I have very sensitive skin."

He had to be on the blackmail-employment deal. He was way too nice to work for them for no reason. "I hope it's not too itchy."

He shrugged. "I'll live. We should go now."

As much as Kari appreciated fresh air and nature in all its forms, she opted to ride to shore in the cabin of the VIP boat for warmth. Even if that meant she had to make small talk with the captain about her weekend plans.

"St. John's is small, but there's still some night life," the captain said and started to decelerate the boat. "You should go out."

"Not really my thing, but I played table tennis the other day and liked it."

The captain laughed.

"I like table tennis," Neill said. "You got a problem with table tennis?"

The captain shook his head with legit fear in his eyes, then turned to focus on maneuvering the boat to dock.

Kari gave Neill a nod of thanks, who responded with a grin. It was reassuring to have him in her corner, even if it was validation that the tabletop sport was a good time.

She followed Neill to the parking lot until they reached a black sedan. "I drive so I think it's fair that I choose the music, but if you hate it let me know."

Kari got in and, for the exception of listening to R&B classics, they drove to a hotel in silence. His thoughts were sparse, but when Neill did think about something it was only about the song or the driving. She was surprised to learn he focused on the lyrics and their meaning. He was deep in thought about his time in the South African National Defence Force during *Lean on Me* when he drove by a cluster of news vans parked at a hotel.

"Are all of Henry's press conferences this well attended?" she asked.

Neill pulled into one of the last open spots and cut the engine. "This is a smaller one. It's in a one-hundred-seater conference room."

Kari unbuckled her seat belt and moved to open the door, but Neill stayed where he was. "You're not coming in?"

"I've been told I draw too much negative attention, so I'll wait a bit and then come in the back way."

Yes, it was probably true, but he sounded so depressed when he said it. "I'm sorry, buddy." The 'buddy' escaped her lips before she could reel it back in.

"I appreciate that. See you soon."

Kari got out of the car and proceeded to the front desk, where she held up the *Hinewai* staff credential as a way of explaining why she was there.

"Second floor, ballroom three," the person behind the desk said. "The stairs will be quicker than the elevator."

Kari headed up the wide spiral staircase in the center of the lobby. Once at the top, she followed the brass signs for the ballroom, which happened to be accompanied by voices that gained volume with each step. She took a moment to prepare herself for an overcrowded room of journalists shouting questions, photographers snapping pictures, and people behind a camera waiting for a perfect close-up of Henry.

The room had an empty podium on a stage and four sections of twenty-five seats in front of it. Every seat was occupied. In the back, lined against the wall, were photographers and camera crews. In the far back corner, Finn waved her over with a portable microphone in their hand.

Kari walked up. "You missed a fun car ride listening to music with Neill."

"I'll have to hear those R&B classics on the return trip, then." *No targets standing out, sorry.* "This is for the questions." They held out the microphone for her to take.

Kari received the hand-off and looked over her shoulder at the crowd. One hundred minds she had to sift through. The payday after this better be huge. "I'll see you after."

Kari shuffled her way through the crowded room. The talking and thoughts of everyone approached intolerable levels. She hadn't been anywhere with this type of information density since the flight for her grandfather's funeral.

The press conference started five minutes later with Henry's announcement of the acquisition. He informed the crowd he had been able to convince a few minority shareholders to sell him their shares so he could hold the majority, and by doing so it would help protect the company image. People didn't associate Wibawa Enterprises with instability or failure.

What Kari found leagues more interesting were the thoughts as she roved the room. Most couldn't have cared less about the change of hands. They viewed it as one rich guy taking over for another. A few were optimistic the switch would bring better environmental policy.

He's human swine. Someday he'll get what's coming to him.

Kari stopped and backpedaled a step. To her left, in a seat near the aisle, was a man with laser focus on Henry and a jaw clenched. His laptop was open to his notes page, which was already filled with company names, ownership, and board members. The Wibawa name was all over it.

She took a closer look at the man. He looked like an English professor—complete with corduroy jacket and ponytail. His journalist badge said his name was Linus but he had no specific affiliation.

Kari took a place in the aisle behind him.

I wonder if anyone will notice that Robert died the same way as Sophia Beaulieu. I should ask. No, I shouldn't. If I ask then, I'll end up dead too. Shit.

Kari knew Beaulieu was wealthy, but that was it. She took out her phone and conducted a search. She read that Beaulieu was an heiress to one of Europe's largest fashion empires, but after a visit on the *Hinewai*, she died. The coroner's report labeled it a suicide via an overdose of pills, but there was no note left or history of depression. A week after her funeral, Henry took over the company with the majority share in the name of helping stability.

"At this time, I would love to take your questions," Henry said, with a photograph of him and the Canadian Prime

Minister posing with a halibut almost the same size as Neill behind him on the screen.

There were shouts and dozens of hands went up.

"Do you have plans to change how the business operates?" someone said into one of the room's other roving mics.

"Not immediately," Henry said, "however, overfishing is a problem and I would like to lead more as an example for the industry. Next question."

I need to ask something. This is bigger than me. People have to take notice of him and his ship.

Linus stood and gestured for Kari to hand over the microphone. Despite her vicarious nerves for him, she gave it to him. "Is it true that Robert MacDonald was a guest of the *Hinewai* right before his death?"

Henry folded his lips inward in a grimace. "Yes, it is true."

"Did you discuss business on the boat?"

Henry grinned. "I don't know how to *not* talk about business." Once a quiet murmur of laughter ceased, he continued. "We talked about our recent successes."

Be direct. Adam would want you to be direct. "Did you know about the drug smuggling in ice core samples?"

Henry stopped smiling. "Of course, not! And both the *Hinewai* and the company will cooperate with Interpol or whomever in any way we need to for that investigation. Now, if it's alright with you, I'd like to spend the remainder of the press conference addressing questions about the business. Or overfishing. Next question."

Same story as Beaulieu. Such lying scum. "Sorry, one more. One more!" Linus shouted into the mic.

Henry sighed. "Go ahead."

"Was Robert MacDonald's nose broken when he was on your ship?"

Kari tensed.

Henry braced each hand on the podium and leaned into the mic. The angry glint in his eyes was back as he stared Linus down. His deep inhale and exhale went through the foam of the mic and carried throughout the speakers in the room as an ominous, low muffle. "No."

The word carried like thunder through the room, but Linus didn't blink as he handed Kari the mic. *Such a liar. The original coroner's report timed it for on the ship.*

Her palm strike was in a coroner's report? Kari's chest tightened. But wait. Linus thought of the 'original' report. That meant there had been a revision. A revision that no doubt changed the cause of death from murder to suicide. How far had Henry and Madeleine gone to procure and protect Wibawa Enterprises? How far would they go?

The press conference lasted thirty more minutes. Questions were asked about the money invested, dedicated work groups, and even if there would be a mascot. Linus never asked another, but he took copious notes on his laptop. Kari watched him compose an email to Adam Cho, summarizing the press conference and including his thoughts on the matter.

"Thank you everyone for coming," Henry said, then exited the stage.

The room filled with sounds of people rustling and zippering their bags, folding and snapping their camera gear. Then, they started to leave in a slow stream.

Linus stood to leave and nearly walked right into her. His eyes went to her *Hinewai* badge. *Jesus Christ, they're everywhere.* His jaw clench returned, but then he looked at her face. *Just a kid.* "You should get out," he said.

Kari shifted from one foot to the other. "I'm just waiting for the AV person to come and collect this from me. Then, I can go."

"No, I mean you should get off that ship. They're dangerous people."

He couldn't be more on the nose, but instead she said, "I don't think so. They've been really good to me, and I have everything I could ever need there."

Young and dumb, and trusting of everyone. "In your spare time you should do some research about your boss. Know who you're getting in bed with—metaphorically speaking."

A sour taste made her mouth pucker as she watched Linus leave with a throng of others. He was right. She should have done more research about Henry. But she couldn't change the past and needed to focus on the present. She needed to ask Finn about Sophia Beaulieu's time on the *Hinewai* but do so in a way that didn't rouse suspicions. She had begun to like Finn, but trust was a ways off yet.

Standing right here. "Microphone, please," one of the hotel AV people said to her with their hand open.

She gave it to him and then looked at the podium. Everyone was gone. That was her cue to head back to the parking lot.

The lot had thinned by the time she had arrived. Once she was buckled in, Neill drove her and Finn back to the ship. Neill was preoccupied with *Sitting on the Dock of the Bay*. Finn replayed highlights of their time with Declan to distract from their building empath-induced headache. The crowd had varying emotions, apparently. Kari used her time to figure out how to best summarize the events to Madeleine without giving her information that would threaten Linus's life.

———

The elevator doors opened to an empty conference room. Madeleine walked out from her passage, sipping tea. "Well?"

Finn stepped forward. "The locals are worried about what

this might do to the economy. The out-of-town reporters are suspicious about his concern for overfishing and the hotel crew was agitated for the late notice. May I leave now?"

She nodded.

"Thank you, ma'am. Good luck," Finn said to Kari before they turned to leave.

"Now it's your turn," Madeleine said. "What little morsels of information were you able to pick up from this excursion?"

She needed to play it as normal as possible, which meant being an informative smart-ass. But she also had to dodge using Linus's name. "Well, other than the fact that Neill here also likes to play table tennis, I found Adam Cho's plant."

"Excellent! What did you learn?"

"He kept thinking about a similar suicide that had happened—Sofia Beaulieu—which allowed Henry to regain control of another company."

"Oh my God, are you serious?"

"I do like table tennis," Neill said.

"About the suicide!" Madeleine chided. "He kn—thinks we had something to do with that?"

"Yes." Kari left out the part where Linus emailed Adam Cho in real time all of his thoughts. "He asked about the broken nose in an 'original' coroner's report, but Henry said it wasn't broken on the ship."

"See, that's why we avoid the face." Madeleine tapped a manicured but unpolished nail against her tea cup. "Did you learn anything else? From other people even?"

"Like Finn said, the crowd thought the overfishing concerns weren't believable coming from him."

"I told Henry that! He saw a documentary and now he suddenly cares, so he just *had* to mention it. He'll probably want us to do an internet scour of all photos of him eating sushi."

Billionaires were the strangest people. "Is there anything else you need?"

"Indeed," Madeleine said. "What's this inquisitive reporter's name?"

Kari shrugged. "Sorry, I didn't catch it. He took off his press badge before I could get a look."

"You didn't get his name?" Madeleine yelled. Then, she closed her eyes and muttered to herself. When she focused those ice blue lasers at Kari, she took a step forward but still wasn't close enough to be in range. "In the future, when you gather intelligence . . . Always. Get. A. Name!"

Kari winced. "Does that mean I didn't earn all the money I could have?" Madeleine's mouth dropped open. "But, that's fair, from your perspective. I'll make sure I do that in the future."

"You better." Madeleine shook her head again. "We won't be needing you again until we arrive in Reykjavík. Now, go and think about what you've done, which is incur a $25,000 penalty for not getting a name." Madeleine made a shooing gesture.

Kari headed for the elevator and stepped inside. She may have earned less money, but she could sleep better knowing Linus wasn't in danger.

"Hey, Kari." Neill stopped right outside the elevator doors. *I hope this isn't weird.* "Do you want to play table tennis later? I can text you when I get off shift."

Sure, he most likely had killed people, but like everyone, Neill had layers. "Sounds fun."

Chapter Fifteen

Reykjavík, Iceland

Kari would soon understand how her brain was different.

After lying in bed and thinking about that for thirty minutes—officially making it a new day—Kari tossed the covers off and put on her running clothes. A quick 10k would exhaust her.

Except it didn't.

The only thing she got out of the run was more sweaty clothes and a craving for peanut lover's trail mix. But at least they were problems she had solutions to. After a quick rinse in the shower, she bundled in her sweatpants and hoodie and ate her post-midnight snack while she admired Reykjavík's late sunset from her balcony. Her belly was happy, but her brain was still agitated.

Kari calculated the time difference from Iceland to Oregon. It would be right around the end of the work day for both of her mothers, but when it came to weird, Mom A was the best mom to go to. Kari dug deep into her two sizes too large sweatpants' pocket and texted her.

Can't sleep. Nervous about the EEG.

After less than ten seconds, Mom A's response started.

Are you nervous about the test or the results?

That was an interesting question and the exact reason why she had chosen the right mom.

I guess the results.

I can understand that. Not only do you finally get to learn about this part of yourself but you also get to put what was once a theoretical experiment into practice. It's the ultimate test of your scientific mettle. I'd be nervous too.

How was it possible for someone to be that perceptive?

I didn't think of it like that. What if they don't find any activity?

Wouldn't that mean you're dead?

Kari chuckled.

Good point. But you know what I mean.

Then you still have data. You'll just have to spend your energies inventing a technique or machine that will test what you do have.

Like one of her professors had once said, the result you don't want is still a result.

I think I needed to hear that reminder. Thanks.

You're welcome. Do you need any other
assurances so you can sleep?

Kari yawned before she answered.

No, I'm good.

Okay. Love you, chickpea.

Love you too.

Kari stashed her phone back into her pocket and went back inside her cabin where the warmth of her bed beckoned. And extra comfort from home. She missed home.

She walked over to the small shelf near her TV and looked at the framed picture of her moms. Then, Kari reached between the frame and its stand to pick up the plastic bag that contained their special soaps. She closed her eyes, inhaled the mix of orange-ginger and evergreen, and imagined them both giving her a hug goodnight. She grinned despite the tightness in her throat. After a few moments of aromatherapy, she returned the soap and returned to bed. Physical exhaustion and mental relief washed over her for complete relaxation.

Then, she heard the *shh* of someone sliding something under the door.

Kari opened her eyes and saw the faint outline of an envelope. Was it better to stay in bed and let her mind wonder what was inside? Or was it worth it to get out of her comfy covers and learn the answer to her latest question?

With a groan, Kari tossed the covers off and went to the envelope. Madeleine's script was outside—no surprise there—and on the inside was the brief instruction:

Saturday 2:00 pm come to the conference room. Clothing doesn't matter. You'll receive a new wardrobe, hair, and makeup. You're going to a charity event in Stockholm with Henry. I'm actually jealous. Bring your passport, just in case.

Kari smirked and tossed the note on the kitchen counter. She'd let Madeleine's jealousy be the final push for sweet dreams.

———

Kari followed her colleagues to the railing of the tender. A stiff breeze, that carried faint sulfur fumes from the island's volcanoes, blew her ponytail around and made the hair on her forearms stand. She folded her arms across her chest. "It's cold out here."

Much colder over there. "I suggest you look slightly to the south for some perspective." Santos pointed to a volcanic rocky range that had a small amount of snow cover.

"I think I might check out some of the warmer features, thanks."

Yes! "You should check out the hot springs at some point while we're here," Mitchell said. "But get your Blue Spa tickets now. When I went to buy mine as part of the running club package, they were almost sold out."

Santos nodded. "The hot springs are one of the best experiences you'll get in Iceland. The hákarl, on the other hand, I didn't care for." *Neither did Charlotte.*

Kari had an adventurous palate, but fermented shark was something she was skeptical about. But she'd still try it. "I think I'll do both, if the opportunities arise."

"You're a brave young woman." Santos shook his head and moved his gaze back to the scenery before them.

The boat motored deeper into the harbor. The mountains in the distance were now blanketed with fog and could be viewed from every angle of the ship. The landscape was a mix of exposed rock and grass hills, but the city proper lay straight ahead with its mix of roads, multi-story modern buildings, and quaint shops.

"How far is our trip to the neuroimaging center?" Kari asked.

"Not far," Santos said. "We'll be there before you know it."

———

Mitchell clapped his hands together. "Are we ready?"

Kari leaned to the side, the tissue paper on the exam table she sat on crinkled, and she caught her reflection in the cabinet glass. Her scalp was covered with twenty electrodes. The wires were grouped in a bundle and fell over her shoulder like her usual ponytail. "I'm ready, but . . ." Kari hitched a thumb at the nurse who stood in the corner.

The technicians at the center had been asked to be present for technical support but not participate in the readings. They had also been told that Kari was a *Hinewai* VIP with her own medical team. Apparently, the memo hadn't circulated around to everyone.

"I usually stay when a woman is being examined," the nurse said.

"You don't have to stay," Kari said. Again, it was nice to see medical ethics at work.

The nurse's line-of-sight darted back and forth between Santos, Mitchell, and back to her again. "But . . . this is what is proper."

Kari nodded. The wires on her shoulder shifted and tugged at her scalp. "Normally, I'd agree with you, but I'd prefer if you left."

She took a few steps closer. *Underage bride and being held captive against her will.* "Are you sure?"

"I promise I'm safe. I know them very well and my parents know I'm here even though, according to US law, I'm legally an adult and I don't have to tell them anything."

That must have convinced her because the nurse backed away, but she still gave Santos and Mitchell a hairy eyeball. "I'll be down the hall if you need anything."

Once she was gone, Kari pushed off the exam table. To get as much distance between her and Mitchell as possible, she sat in a visitor chair against the wall. "Let's get this show on the road."

Mitchell sat on a rolling stool on the other side of the EEG cart, which had his laptop on top of the medical center's closed one, a port for the wires from the electrodes, and his laptop connected to that port. A penlight lay on the cart as well.

Santos stood in the far corner on the opposite side of the room. He took a laser measurer out of his pocket and aimed it until a red dot was centered on her sternum. "Can you hear either of our thoughts?"

"No. How far away are you?"

"Two point eight meters." He made a note in his tablet. "Okay, let's start."

"Close your eyes," Mitchell instructed, "and put the sleep mask on."

The first steps of her written protocol were the absence of as much stimulation as possible. No visuals. No sounds. No people within telepathy range. They would gradually introduce stimulation and she would perform tasks—math, reading, motor tests that looked like a sobriety check—and Mitchell would note it in the EEG software he'd downloaded to his laptop earlier in the week.

"I'm really excited to finally get to the good stuff," she said as her index finger touched her nose. And she stood on one leg.

"I think you'll find that even these mundane tests will have results that'll keep your interest, but, yes, let's get to the finale." Mitchell looked over to Santos. "You can start."

Santos took the laser measure, pointed at Kari once more, and began his approach and stopped. "Two point seven-five meters." When Mitchell gave him the go-ahead nod, he advanced again. "Two—"

"Whoa!" Mitchell said as he stared at the EEG read out.

"What?" Kari asked, alarmed. She wanted to get up and see the screen, but the bundle of electrodes tethered her in place. "Is everything okay?"

"Do you 'hear' Santos?" Mitchell asked.

"Not yet."

Mitchell pushed up his glasses while he continued to stare at the screen. "Fascinating. Well, tell me when you do. Santos, come in to two point five meters." Mitchell typed with rapid clicks to the keyboard.

"I don't know if this is pertinent information," Kari said, "but I also think it is cold in here."

Mitchell chuckled. "Santos, closer." He resumed the furious typing. "And closer."

She's right. It is really cold in here.

"I got him loud and clear," she said.

"Okay," Mitchell said. "Let me know if and when he becomes distorted."

Kari had never thought about her telepathy in that context before. "Can I answer that after he comes closer?"

Mitchell waved Santos in with his hand, then typed away once more.

"Clarity is the same," Kari said. "Can we do the imagery testing now?"

"Sure," Santos said.

They repeated the distance test and Santos imagined the items on the paper Mitchell handed him. Kari was pleased Mitchell kept the selection of mystical creatures, food, and items in a department store easy.

"Even though we haven't sat down and done the analysis of the data yet," Mitchell said, "your EEG activity does vary on his distance from you. I'd say we're done with our test."

"I'm going to try one more thing, off the record." Kari reached out with her mind to extend a warm greeting to those who may have the ability to hear her. A portion of her brain that was normally completely at rest jolted awake.

Mitchell squinted and leaned closer to the EEG screen. "Something is definitely happening. What are you doing?"

"Bah!" Santos jumped back and then pointed at the window.

An eagle with feathers of every shade of brown and cream, but with white tail feathers, perched outside the window. It opened its yellow beak, and a small, regurgitated fish fell out of its mouth.

"Interesting," Kari said. They never had said hi like that before.

———

"You have no idea how happy I am right now," Kari said to Mitchell and Santos as they stepped off the tender. "This is the true initiation of Project ORCA . . . It's the best day of my life!"

"You're just saying that because you got your shoe organizer too," Santos said as he crossed the gangplank.

"And it fits twelve pairs! But I think I'm going to modify the bottom with my new sewing kit for my boots. That'll be my activity after dinner since we aren't starting the analysis until tomorrow." She pouted with her lower lip extended for maximum dramatic effect.

Mitchell sighed. "I know you want to dive into the data as soon as possible, but I want to back this up first. Also, this was a long day and once we start with the data, I don't think we'll come out of the lab for a while. If I were you, I'd grab a lunch to-go tomorrow. See you then." Mitchell waved goodbye as he headed for the stairs.

"You're not following him?" Kari asked.

"I'm waiting for Charlotte so we can check out the hot springs together. I decided to get tickets when you went to the restroom to try and fix your hair." *Didn't work.* He checked his phone and then smiled. *Always running five minutes late.* "I don't know if this was the happiest day of my life, but it was certainly one of the most incredible. We really are going to change the field. Have a goodnight, Kari."

"You too. Enjoy those hot springs."

With her coworkers having gone their separate ways for the evening, Kari headed to her cabin to drop off her purchases, grab her dinnerware, and put on a baseball cap so those in the cafeteria didn't rubberneck when they saw her. The adhesive from the electrodes had given her a massive case of bed head. Brushing her hair made it worse.

Hat on, Kari took her tray, plate, and bowl with her as she left her cabin.

"Hey, stranger," Jade said as she came her way with her dinner. "I see you've learned from the master."

"My own dishes really has been a game changer. I can't thank you enough."

"I'm happy I was able to help." Jade maneuvered her tray, with the assistance of her thigh, so she could get her thumb on the scanner. *I need a third hand.* "The hat's a good look for you, by the way. Super cute."

"I'm just covering up the fact that my hair needs washed after I had a brain evaluation. You know, for my seizures." Jade opened the door and Kari saw a white envelope on the kitchen counter. The surprise on her face must have shown because Jade reacted by visibly scanning her cabin.

Is there a ghost? "Something wrong?"

Kari played disoriented. "Huh? Oh! Believe it or not, I just had an absence seizure. That's what they look like when I have them. My testing today must have stressed my brain more than I thought."

"I've been wanting to ask you more about that. I'm glad nothing extreme happens, but that's still worrisome."

"It is. That's why I'm doing tests." And now it was time to change the subject. "Hey, is that your mail laying over there? Do we even get mail here? I haven't received anything yet."

"It's not mail. That's a request that came in."

"Really?" Now they were getting somewhere. Did Jade have some kind of paranormal power Madeleine exploited? Could she cook with pyrokinesis? "Do you get requests . . . often?"

Does she know she sounds like a detective? "Yeah," Jade drawled. "It's a big ship, so it's always someone's birthday and people love their cake."

"Oh, it's requests for cake! That makes sense given you're a baker."

That test must have been a doozy. "Yeah, it does, and it's a nice side hustle for the students. People write down what kind they want and sketch the basic design. Then, I take it down to WU and help them make it." Jade cocked her head. "Are you sure you're okay? You look a little . . . off."

Dammit, she'd made it weird. "I just need some rest. You have a good night."

"Do the same, but knock if you need help or anything like that. I don't care if it's after eight o'clock."

The weirdness was gone and Jade cared about her enough to cut into her me-time. "I appreciate that. Goodnight."

Jade smiled and shut the door.

Everything was making her paranoid, including envelopes. She tucked—or sealed—those thoughts away and focused on her evening activities of eating her lamb stew and reading Adam Cho's bestseller, which she found in one of the ship's 'take a book, leave a book' bins. If she understood Cho, then maybe she could learn what he hoped to learn about Henry. Or what greater story he was on to.

———

Mitchell stood beside the large screen in their conference area. "These EEG readings are fascinating. All of the standard tests yielded normal readings in the four waveforms." He pointed to the diagram of her head where the electrodes had been placed on her scalp. "Your C3-P3 regions clearly show enhanced activity when you 'heard' Santos."

That meant the locations of the telepathy existed on the left side of her brain, starting at the rear of her frontal lobe and ending in the middle of her parietal lobe. It was a good thing she looked good in hats, because it would cover the area after they drilled into her skull.

"Can I see what that looked like on the EEG?" she asked.

"Sure." Mitchell advanced his slide to show twenty squiggly lines from the twenty electrodes.

Kari read down the side of the graph to the C3-P3 lines.

They looked like all the other lines. "Could you explain the 'enhanced' bit? Because I'm not seeing it."

"Just wait." Mitchell grinned and advanced the slide. One line showed a significant jump in activity. "Then, this happened." He clicked again and the line leapt into the adjacent line's space.

"Holy shit," Kari muttered. This was it. There on the screen before her was the evidence she had sought for so long. But what was so fascinating to her was the comparison of the three slides. The time points weren't visible on the screen shots Mitchell had prepared for them. "What happened in the testing between the slides?"

"The first was when you both started. This one"—Mitchell went to the slide with the minor spikes—"was when Santos approached you but you still couldn't 'hear' him."

"Wait." Kari shook her head. "That means my brain detects him even when I can't hear it."

Mitchell took a seat at the table and folded his hands. "You mentioned that when you first developed telepathy you had to try, but as you got older, all of a sudden, the waves came to you. I don't know how to tell you this but—"

"You think my telepathy could grow even stronger than it is now."

Yes. Mitchell nodded.

If that happened, even sitting across a room from someone or playing table tennis like a regular person was gone. Any prospect of healthy relationships was gone. "So, how long until we can do the fMRI and find out how deep this brain demon goes?"

"You have to wait over two months for the fMRI?" Mom A asked.

Kari brought the phone back to her ear, but then thought better of it and put it on speaker. It would be easier to sort her laundered clothes that way anyway. "Well, it's an estimate, but as we get closer, I'll have a better idea of the timing. As you know, weather is a major factor."

"How many stops are there between now and the imaging center in Madrid?"

"Four. Oslo, London, La Rochelle, and Lisbon. We'll take the train from Barcelona to get the scan."

After an uncomfortable period of silence, Mom A spoke again. "This is . . . This is really happening for you."

Kari couldn't see Mom A but could picture her smile. "I know, and it's amazing. The first time I saw the graph, I saw a tangible entity I could fight and not this invisible bully that's made my life impossible." Kari left out the part where if they didn't find a way to stop her ability now, they had reason to believe it could grow in power. "But enough about me, how are you and Mom L? I'm actually surprised she didn't join the call. She's usually yelled something in the background by now."

"Believe it or not, she's taking a nap."

Kari laughed. "Okay, that's even weirder than my brain stuff. What's going on with her?"

"She hasn't been sleeping well and I think it finally caught up to her."

Kari stopped pairing her socks. Was Mom L sensing her anxiety? "Is it me? While I think I've adjusted well, it's still stressful at times." Like when she was gathering blackmail for her billionaire overlord.

"Honestly, I think it's just menopause."

"That sounds really fun for you. I'm sorry I'm missing it."

Mom A chuckled. "Yeah, it's been a blast. I can't wait until we both have it at the same time. You'll certainly be glad you're halfway around the world."

"Agreed." Kari fished out a pair of black lacy panties that were not hers and tossed them to the side. Sharing laundry facilities did have some surprises. "I do miss you two. It's nice that I can be open and honest with Mitchell and Santos, and I'm friendly with my neighbor and a few others, but they don't get me like you two."

"And no one ever will, chickpea. But I'm excited to learn about these friendly 'others'. It's been awhile since you've had a social circle."

"Well, they're mostly peripheral to my translating side hustle, so I wouldn't get too excited about it. I've only had a few decent conversations or table tennis matches with them."

"It's still nice to hear that you're making friends. Are you doing anything with them this weekend?"

"Only in a work sense. All I know is I'm helping at a charity event in Stockholm."

"As in Sweden?"

"That'd be the one. What are you doing this weekend?"

"Adding a roof to extend over the chicken coop area since I'm paranoid about predators and packing for Michigan. We leave Monday afternoon after one of your Mom L's meetings."

An unexpected jab punched her in the gut. This was the first time she'd miss a trip to visit her Noko Ani and Ata Niq. "Please give them lots of hugs for me. Except Wade." They were roughly the same age, and he had been a cockwaffle since day one. On the other hand, her older cousin was amazing. "I miss everyone else but him."

Mom A laughed. "I know they miss you too. We'll get to see you around New Year's, right?"

"Yes. I'll go to the travel agent on the ship this week to make the arrangements."

Chapter Sixteen

Kari had assumed she would have her Stockholm makeover in the conference room, not in Henry's private jet, but to get to the jet meant they had to take his helicopter to Keflavik Airport. The land they flew over had a charming village where the residential areas were divided by brilliant green fields. It was a change from the charred rock she had seen earlier.

"Coming in for landing," the helicopter pilot said through the headsets.

"Excellent," Henry said from his seat closer to the front, then turned to her in the back row. "Was this your first time in a helicopter?"

It was strange reading his lips and hearing the slight delay through the headset. "Yes. Why do you ask?"

"I looked back once or twice and you had a gigantic smile each time. It was nice to see. We'll have to have more adventures so that becomes a regular occurrence."

He really was a perplexing man. Consumed by obtaining

more power and wealth, but also kind of sweet. In a way, he reminded her of Nana Sid.

They landed with a mild jostle and, once the pilot cut the engine, they headed to the tarmac. A woman in white pants, a burgundy polo, and white jacket jogged their way. "Your plane is undergoing the last of its take-off preparation checks in the FBO," she shouted over the airport noise. "Please follow me, Mr. Wibawa."

"Have the others arrived?" he asked.

"Yes, and per your instructions I told the stylist and your tailor they could set up in your study."

"Excellent. I love it when there's no waiting."

"Don't we have to go through security?" Kari asked. She picked up her pace so that she was within distance to hear his real answer. "I have a multi-tool in my pocket, and it has a knife."

I can do anything I want. Henry waved off the concern. "Your passport is all we will need to show Swedish customs and that's only if they ask. I'm hoping they got the message last time and will not." She followed his gaze down to her pocket. *I wonder how often she uses that.*

"I use it pretty frequently. I like knowing that I always have a tool with me to fix something."

"I love that sense of ingenuity!"

Kari didn't feel like tightening loose screws was ingenious, but it did raise a question that had been circling her mind for a while. "You don't keep your distance from me like Madeleine does, can I ask why?"

Interesting. "I didn't know that. But, I think it comes down to trust. I don't mind you knowing me now that you're in my inner circle. Plus, I am a big fan of your work."

She had made it to inner circle level? Wow. "Out of curiosity, is there anything I've done that you're not a fan of?"

Henry cocked his head. *Such a good question.* "Like Madeleine, I wish you would have learned that reporter's name back in Newfoundland. But mostly there are some things you do that I don't understand, like why you read books written by Adam Cho." *That was a good catch by Josef.*

"Good to know," she said, even though the knowledge that he knew she'd read Cho's book made her queasy. Were there cameras aimed at the book bin area? As soon as she thought it, she knew the answer was yes. It was a basic security measure. But still, Josef had seen the footage, noted her with the book, and reported it.

"Are you okay, Karishma? You're suddenly very quiet."

"Oh, just feeling a little topsy-turvy from the helicopter ride. I'll be fine." Kari continued to follow the crew member even though she knew where they were headed.

An impressively sized private plane with the Wibawa logo on the side was in front of them. A petite woman in the standard Wibawa uniform with shiny black hair pulled into the tightest bun Kari had seen stood at the bottom of the stairs leading up to the jet's hatch.

"Hello, Captain Ng," Henry said. "How is our flight looking?"

"We'll have some wind at our backs, so about a three-hour flight." After Henry went up the stairs, she made eye contact with Kari. *Doll he wants to dress up.* "Welcome aboard."

After Kari went up the stairs, she entered the plane and truly entered the world of the affluent. There were white leather chairs and a couch with the occasional multi-purpose table making up the layout. There were smaller screens mounted in front of each chair, but they paled in comparison to a larger screen that divided the main seating area from the bathroom, galley, and what she assumed was his study.

"Would you care for a glass of champagne, Mr. Wibawa?" asked one of the servers.

"Please." He took off his suit jacket. "And some chocolate-covered almonds before our main snack is served."

"Of course." The attendant looked at Kari. "And for you?"

Henry held up a hand. "She's eighteen, so no alcohol until we leave Icelandic air space. Sorry, Karishma."

"It's fine," she said, "and probably not a good idea to experiment with alcohol at altitude before a job anyway. I'll take some chocolate-covered almonds though."

Henry sat in one of the oversized leather chairs and pointed at the one across the aisle for her. Due to the spacious layout, he wouldn't be in range of her telepathy. "Once we take off and have a bite to eat, you will see my tailor, and then have your hair and makeup done. But don't worry, this is not a princess treatment. When they are finished with you, you will still look like you. You will just be a more elegant and powerful version of you."

It was so hard remembering he probably had sinister motives when he said words like that. "I like that idea."

"I didn't think you'd have any issues with my plan, but it's always nice to hear that people are on board. Then, I'll debrief you on the evening. Thank you," he said once the attendant placed a miniature bowl of chocolate-covered almonds and a flute of champagne on his side table.

The server placed the same sized bowl and an empty glass with a bottle of sparkling water on her table. He left before she could thank him. The plane, the service, the chair that paradoxically had lumbar support even though it resembled a marshmallow in several ways, were all next-level extravagant.

Henry chuckled. "You have a very clear-thinking face. Too bad I cannot read your thoughts."

"I'm just taking in my surroundings."

"You've been on airplanes before."

"Never a private one." She plucked an almond from the bowl and popped it in her mouth. Why she was expecting it to taste like every other chocolate-covered almond, she had no idea. It was perfect. "Can I ask you a question?"

"Absolutely. We have lots of time for conversation."

She had to determine a way to ask her question without being offensive. So, flattery first. "I've read your biography and understand how you built your amazing empire off the commercial real estate your father and mother built."

"Thank you for including my mother."

"Why wouldn't I? She had wonderful vision. Way ahead of her time."

He gave a small bow of recognition. "It's why I named the ship after her."

"Considering that, do you know how extravagant all of this is to someone like me? I grew up on a goat farm. Fancy dinner night was pizza in the outdoor oven that had the really good cheese."

"Ah." He crossed his legs and folded his hands on his lap, as if he were her grandfather about to launch into story time. "My family history is a complicated one at that. Yes, my family is wealthy and I inherited quite a bit of land and the seed company, but believe it or not, I do know what it is like to have a humble life.

"Like many rich boys, I was sent away to an exclusive boarding school in Victoria, Australia. Very proper, very strict. Naturally, I didn't care for it, nor did most of my classmates. One of their sources of fun was bullying me. I remember distinctly being told by this brat that if I ever retaliated, he would personally buy my entire family's business as a gift for his little sister."

"You're kidding?"

"I'm not. Most of them came from very old money. I was new money so my lack of social graces or knowledge of those families offended them. A good portion were also openly racist. Eventually, though, I did find a friend.

"On Saturdays, we had chaperoned bus trips into Melbourne, which was when I walked into a candy shop, *Coultier's Candies*, and met Madeleine. I was fourteen, obnoxious, and arrogant, and she wanted nothing to do with me. Naturally, I fell in love.

"Week after week I went back to get their homemade caramels to sneak a peek at her working in the back. After a year, she started as a cashier, where I guess I grew on her enough to talk to me. She lived above the shop, and that was when I truly learned how spoiled I was, even for new money. Her family had one full bathroom. She and a sister shared a bedroom. The home had only one television and they used their back balcony to air-dry laundry."

Kari said nothing even though he had basically described the moms' house as though they lived in poverty.

"My last year in boarding school, Madeleine told me her parents' plan for her was to take over the candy shop someday, but she confessed to me that wasn't what she wanted. She wanted to travel, maybe become a lawyer. I felt such empathy for her, so much so I asked my parents if I could go into my trust to help her financially with university. They agreed."

Kari absorbed all he had just told her. Was Madeleine working out a term of her own? Did she owe service to Henry?

"So, Madeleine went off to university and became even more brilliant. Created her own majors and changed her accent to the cultivated one you're familiar with now, but we lost touch since I had to go off to Oxford. Then, I became a father, got married, and"—he smiled a bit mischievously—"divorced. Once I established myself as more than just the offspring of wealthy people, I searched for Madeleine, found her, and asked if she wanted to work with me. Turns out, she did."

Maybe it wasn't a term of service after all. Maybe they genuinely liked each other? Kari had to ask the question on her mind even if it was none of her business. "Are you two . . . a couple?"

"No," he said with a laugh. "We are business partners only. The giant leaps my company has made in the last twenty years are largely because of her vision and imagination."

"And illegal talent scouting."

He shrugged. "You say potato, I say gets the job done."

And that, Kari thought, was the essence of Henry Wibawa. He was goal-oriented to a fault. He would find whatever people, methods, or tools necessary to see that it was done. And he did so while still thinking he was in some way in touch with the 'common people' because he had a crush as a teenager on a girl who worked in a candy store.

It was unsettling.

The attendant placed a tray of crackers with smoked salmon folded like roses and a small mound of caviar on the small dining table beside Henry. "Your snack, sir. Also, Captain Ng wants me to let you know we are preparing for departure."

"Thank you." Henry hitched a thumb over his shoulder. "Karishma, you're more than welcome to eat with me or do your own thing."

The same tray was placed beside her. "If it's alright with you, I think I'll watch a movie solo. We're going to be spending a lot of time together later."

"Very true. There might even be dancing," he said with his eyes sparking.

———

"Pardon the interruption," Captain Ng said over the plane's speaker, "but we are now at altitude, so feel free to move about and get ready for the party."

Kari popped another chocolate-covered almond in her mouth and unbuckled her seat belt. It was time to play billionaire quasi-date dress up.

"Excuse me, Kari."

Kari stood almost a head taller than the diminutive woman with poofy gray hair and a West African accent. "Yes."

"I'm Theresa, your tailor. Please follow me." She turned and headed toward the back of the plane. *Nathan'll need time to cover that forehead breakout.* "I don't think Nathan will need to do much to your hair. You have beautiful hair."

She wanted to undo her ponytail and hide behind her 'beautiful' hair. It was so dumb that she had superpowers but still got acne during her period. Whoever made that rule, she wanted a word with them. Or it.

Kari walked down the aisle, passed a full bathroom and then into an office with walnut shelves and an imposing desk with ivy carved into the legs. On the left, three extravagant dresses hung off a wardrobe rack. The first was a classic strapless silhouette of solid black, with an asymmetric cut chest and a slit that ran up to mid-thigh. The second was brilliant yellow, had a halter-style top and open back to go with a sheath bottom. The third was a ruched, mid-thigh, two-strap number made of red satin. They were all beautiful in their own ways, but for Kari there was a clear winner.

"Definitely the black one."

"A classic look," said a voice from behind. When Kari turned to see who it was, a thickset man with a full, blond quaff and thick glasses waved. "I'm Nathan, and I'm *dying* to work with those eyes of yours."

"Thank you," Kari said. "Maybe you can do something about my Quasimodo-like forehead too."

"Oh, that's nothing. The lighting is awful in the plane, except at my station."

Always about the lighting. "Please disrobe, except for your undies," Theresa said. "You'll want to put on a strapless bra."

"And I'll excuse myself while you do that." Nathan stood and dusted invisible lint from his thighs. "I'm going to see if there's anything in the galley to get rid of this lingering fish taste."

Kari wasn't as modest as he assumed. Granted, she didn't parade herself around naked, but at the same time, they were just boobs. And he had boobs, too. Where people got their ideas about body image and 'decency' she didn't know.

Standing in only her panties and an adhesive black bra, Kari gestured to her body. "Okay, what's step two?"

Theresa pointed to a pair of black, strappy stilettos, which could have been used as a tourniquet. Or for torture, actually. Kari didn't hate that theme. "You'll put those on to determine how much I need to hem your dress. Then, you'll be Nathan's project."

"Sounds like a plan."

"But first," Theresa lifted the cord of her necklace until the firestarter was in her hand, "this has to go." *I don't think it's even jewelry.*

"This might not look like much." Kari extended the cord of her necklace and lifted it over her head. "But it means a lot to me."

Theresa took the necklace from her. "It's usually the things that look the least impressive that are the most important."

The initial markings Theresa had to make for the dress took no time at all. After a few minutes, Kari was back in only her bra and underwear sitting in Nathan's styling chair. At first it was odd having someone do her hair and makeup while she sat in only her undergarments, but she got used to it. As a bonus, Nathan's thoughts were truthful and amusing—a little gossipy —but he wasn't a liar and held a good conversation with Theresa while she sewed away.

"Do you both work on the ship too?" Kari asked.

Nathan laughed, a fluffy blush brush in hand. "I hardly call what I do work. I track gauges in the engineering rooms." He put the brush away and picked up a small bottle of setting spray. "But due to the Wibawa Enterprises Promise, I get called to do makeup."

"Where did you learn how to do makeup?"

"Drag shows. In a younger life, I was one hell of a diva."

"And in my younger life," Theresa said, "I was a professor of anthropology at World University. When I retired, I became Henry's tailor."

"That sounds like an interesting transition."

She chuckled. "I loved traveling and didn't want to give it up, so I practically begged for ways to stay on the ship. Word got around." She cut the black thread with her sewing scissors and maneuvered the dress so its outside faced out again. "How much longer do you have, Nathan? The dress is done."

"Close your eyes," he directed Kari, then sprayed a light mist on her face. "I'm done! You are chef's kiss."

Kari studied her reflection in the mirror. She still looked like herself, but her skin glowed, her lips were the brightest red they had ever been, and the smoky cat eye solidified her international-telepath-of-mystery vibe. And no visible forehead breakout!

A click came from the plane's intercom. "We'll be starting our descent soon. Please wrap things up in the back and return to your seats."

"You heard the lady," Theresa said. "Out of the chair and into the dress."

The backs of her thighs stuck to the vinyl in the makeup chair and made a slight suction sound as she stood in her wicked heels. Kari resumed the chair pose once more so Theresa could fit the dress over her head and zip the back.

"Is there anything else?" Theresa asked Nathan.

"Oh!" he said and riffled through his suitcase. "I have a comb for her hair." He pulled out a velvet jewelry box, opened it, and pulled out a floral-patterned, diamond hair clip. "This is technically for weddings, but since we weren't sure which dress you'd pick, it seemed neutral enough. Back in the chair, please."

Kari marveled at her reflection in the dress. She resembled some sort of dark, powerful non-princess. More like the princess's best friend who received less attention but who was smarter and more attractive in a less commercial way. "I look . . . wow."

"And this will really seal the deal." He combed her hair again, gathered it along each side, and pinned it in place. He opened a drawer, pulled out a hand mirror, and held it so Kari could see the back.

The only time she had seen that many sparkles was a clear night's sky at her grandparents' house in the Upper Peninsula of Michigan. That led her to one conclusion. "Is this made of diamonds?"

Nathan stifled a laugh. "Do you really think Henry Wibawa would buy cubic zirconia?"

Kari gawked into the sparkly wonder that no doubt cost more than her salary for the year. And the year after that. "Can one of you take my picture?"

"Absolutely. You look stunning."

Theresa took her phone and snapped several different photos

showcasing every element. Once Kari hit send, she said her thank yous and returned to the main cabin area where Henry sat in a classic tuxedo. There were two flutes of champagne on his table.

He looked up at her in wonder. "Karishma, you are a vision."

"Thank you." She sat being mindful of her dress. "Too bad there's no place to carry my multi-tool in this. Then, I would feel complete."

"I will make a note of that for next time. You need all of your tools available to you to operate at peak performance." He handed her a flute of champagne. *Now, let's talk about our goal for the evening.*

Chapter Seventeen

Stockholm, Sweden

Henry sipped his champagne. "I've asked for us to sit at Gabriella Fermi's table. I believe she's involved with a specific circle I'd like a part in."

Kari had heard of the Italian heiress but didn't know any details about her life or fortune. "And you want me to get dirt on her?" she asked while she studied the bubbles in her drink.

"Believe it or not, no."

Kari looked away from her tiny bubbles and back to him.

"I've been told that Gabriella is bringing her son, Julius, who is an insufferable and terrible person."

"You really know how to make this evening sound exciting."

"I'm just trying to prepare you." Henry flicked the top of his champagne flute with his finger nail, causing it to ring. "You should try some of this. I can't guarantee the drinks at the museum will be of the highest quality, even if the per-plate charity donations are footing the bill."

"How much did you donate for our plates?"

"Half a million."

"Dollars?" Kari yelled in disbelief, then brought the flute to her lips without taking her eyes off Henry. The bubbles tickled her mouth and the slight sweetness and acidity brought her taste buds to life. And her eyes to open more widely. She took another sip. No wonder they served the beverage in such small glasses because this was delightful. "That's nice."

"It's a classic brut. I hoped you'd like it, and, I think, you'll like the bonus here as well."

Kari sat more at attention. "I'm all ears."

"If you can gather usable evidence against Julius, I'm prepared to give inCog that same amount as the plate donation for your experiment."

Kari nearly choked on her champagne. "Half a million dollars for ORCA?" That would be enough to cover the rest of the project. At least she thought it would be. They hadn't reached the bribing surgeons stage yet.

"Indeed." Henry picked up a tablet and walked across the aisle to hand it to her. *He is so vile.* "This is what he looks like."

Kari examined the picture of Julius riding a jet ski. He looked late thirties, early forties. Average build and muscle tone. Dark eyes, dark hair . . . everywhere. With his money, surely he could wax that monobrow or turn the shag carpeting on his chest into something more low pile. But the beard stubble was trimmed in a stylish manner. Two young ladies in bikinis clung to him. Kari hesitated to call them women because they looked younger than she was.

"What's he done?" she asked.

"There is no proof of anything, but there are all kinds of rumors." He gestured to the picture. "I'm assuming you can guess what one of those rumors is based on the picture."

"And I'm going to sit right next to him and get the evidence."

"Exactly right."

Julius was scum. But she had no issues with removing the world of scum. Kari's shoulders relaxed and she molded back into her seat as the plane continued its descent. "But how does pinning Julius to crimes help you with Gabriella? I would think that would antagonize her."

"In a typical family dynamic, you would be right, but the Fermi name has been synonymous with wealth and power for centuries, and Julius has tainted that. Furthermore, a substantial part of the fortune will go to him if she loses a legal fight regarding her recently deceased husband's will."

"But if it was her husband's money . . .?"

Henry shook his head. "The money is from Gabriella's side, which is why it is such a confusing, complicated mess. If I can get Julius out of the picture in some way, I believe she will do me this favor."

Okay, that made sense, but other questions still needed answered. "If she hates him that much, why would she come to this event with him?"

"Appearances. Despite the smiles, the wealthy often loathe each other. In this case, Gabriella and I may not be friends—she may even hate me, I don't know—but we can still help each other."

Sometimes it wasn't about the money. It was about favors. Politics. "There must be a lot of power in that circle you want to get into."

"Oh, indeed there is." A focused, dangerous glint passed over his brown eyes before he blinked it away. He picked up his flute but jerked in his seat as the landing gear touched down.

———

Of course, they were greeted at the airport with a limousine.

Of course, they walked onto a red carpet when they arrived at the museum.

Of course, their first view when they walked into the main gallery was an ice sculpture of the museum itself. The details included the line-up of limousines. It was a nice touch.

I guess ice is like glass. "The theme of the evening is Glass Houses and Stones," Henry said to her.

Kari kept her comments regarding the irony to herself. It was best she focused on not tripping or slipping in her heels, since the floor was a seamless, polished gray concrete. They strolled past the massive ice sculpture in the foyer and into the next room. Along the perimeter were black sculptures encased in glass and on brilliant white pedestals.

"Now we have reached the stones," Henry said.

They paused in front of the first piece, an obsidian jaguar. Kari read the plaque stating the Teotihuacan work was on loan from Mexico. "We're still in the glass, actually, just the volcanic kind."

"Well done, Henry!" a bass-level British voice said from behind. "You've brought a date who has both brains and beauty."

"Hello, Marcus!" Instead of shaking Marcus's hand, Henry hugged him, complete with slaps on the back. When they pulled away, Henry touched his gray goatee. *I look much younger than him.* "You're looking old, my friend."

"I would normally say the same, but you have the fountain of youth here on your arm." Marcus flashed a brilliant smile at her. "Introduce us."

"Of course! Marcus, this is Karishma. She's a scientist for one of my companies and a translator on the *Hinewai.* Karishma, this is Marcus, he's the curator here and an old friend of mine from Oxford."

Marcus extended his hand. *Scientist, interesting.* "It's very nice to meet you. What do you think about the exhibit?"

"I haven't really seen much of it yet, but I appreciate that this particular art is on loan and not simply stolen from its Indigenous peoples."

I knew changing the description would work! "Well, when you do have the chance to tour everything, I'll be interested to hear your opinion. For now"—he pointed to the wall with an inconspicuous door—"I need to check the kitchen to make sure we're on schedule. If the amuse-bouche is late, there will be hell to pay."

"I understand," Henry said. "We'll catch up later."

Marcus waved his goodbye and pushed his way into the next room. She'd write an email to the Teotihuacan Art Society when she arrived back in her cabin. "Was Marcus the one who assigned us to Gabriella's table?"

Indeed. Henry grinned. "It helps to stay in touch."

Kari veered off from Henry to observe the rest of the obsidian sculptures. A carved snowflake of snowflake obsidian. A brush and mirror, which reflected Kari's image in darkness. A massive carving of the Andes was the segue into the dining room.

She didn't know what the grand room was reserved for during typical operating hours—perhaps temporary walls were used to enclose different types of exhibits—but currently the room had twenty glass tables each with ten settings. The centerpieces of iridescent blown glass were modern art themselves. The various crystal glasses had diamond and wedge patterns leading to the stem while utensils of the finest silver that had been melted and molded so they each had unique patterns of flowers sat on the table. Off to the side of the room was a four-piece jazz band—all in tuxedos regardless of gender

—playing a soft tune. The person playing stand-up bass looked eerily familiar.

As she studied the performer, a clearer image formed of a past photograph. Instead of a tux, they had worn skin-tight, low red plaid pants with a mostly open white button-down shirt to reveal a toned torso and Adonis belt. Yes, the bassist was once featured on a poster in her childhood bedroom.

"Oh, my Gods!" Kari squeaked and tugged on Henry's jacket. "That's Bryce Reznik from The BroMancers." Even though Sweden had a tradition of generating pop music, it didn't cross her mind that an idol would be here.

Who is that? No matter. "Would you like me to get Marcus to introduce you later?"

Kari shook her head with such vigor she was surprised her extravagant hair comb didn't fly out. "I can't. I . . . I'm already freaking out."

Henry chuckled. *A crush.* "It's very endearing to see you star struck. I should have warned you about celebrity appearances on the plane."

Once Kari's adrenaline rush waned, her senses became more overwhelmed with the volume—internal and external—in the room. Fortunately, once they took their seats, the space between them was ample enough so she'd only be bombarded with maybe four thoughts at a time. But that still wasn't something she looked forward to.

You have got to be kidding me.

Kari followed Henry's line of sight to see Adam Cho looking dashing in a tuxedo. "What do you want to do?"

Running or avoiding him makes me look like a coward. Henry took a deep breath and exhaled through pursed lips. "Let's say hello. Tell him you read his book."

"Okay," Kari said, uncertain, as they walked over to the

famous reporter. "But don't tell him my last name. He might piece Mom A and me together from her work with ENN."

Interesting. We may be able to use that at some point.

Each step toward him filled her more and more with dread. She wanted to keep her moms away from Henry and Madeleine as much as possible, and now she had given Henry possible bait. But what else was she supposed to do? Not tell Henry, let him say her full name, see the recognition on Adam's face, and pretend everything was fine?

Nothing was fine!

Henry approached the journalist and held out his hand. *Be civil.* "So nice to see you here, Adam. I take it your book did even better than expected for you to have made the donation threshold."

Such an asshole and even brought a bimbo to the event. Adam smiled and shook Henry's hand. "What can I say? When half the world lives in poverty, they like to know how the other half lives. Especially that special percentage that earns more per minute than some do in a year. Would you care to share your secrets now in an impromptu interview?"

I hate him so much. "The secret is that I acknowledge my limitations and seek those talents elsewhere. For example, this is Karishma, a truly remarkable young woman."

Does a weak gag reflex count as talent? "And may I ask what those talents are?"

Disliking Adam was now something her and Henry had in common. Why did an attractive young woman automatically have to be associated with sexuality and a lack of practical or extraordinary skills? "I wouldn't call being a genius a talent, Mr. Cho, but Henry has brought me here this evening for trans-lation purposes."

"Very true," Henry said. "I only speak three, but Karishma speaks about a dozen."

"More than that. I've been working on becoming fluent in Swahili and Persian." Since Adam continued to look unimpressed and arrogant, she had one additional skill she wanted to showcase. "Of course, English is by far my strongest language, especially when it comes to rules of grammar. I would be happy to send you my notes regarding errors I found in your book. Although, I understand that, as a journalist, you were more focused on the content. I don't judge."

His smug face is so hilarious right now. "And what did you think of the content?" Henry asked with a straight face.

"I can't pretend to know how a lay book like that is supposed to read, since I'm primarily immersed in scholarly literature for my day job as a neuroscientist. So, I'll say it was interesting, but I would have appreciated more evidence and less speculation."

Dammit. Adam cleared his throat. "Please send my publisher those notes, but I promise my follow-up book is full of harder evidence," he said to Henry. *Where is Fiesler on that?* "Now, if you'll both excuse me, I should get to my table as the first course is arriving soon."

Henry's brow furrowed. *Second book?*

Kari didn't remember a Fiesler referenced in the first book. "Fiesler?" she quietly mused.

"Who is Fiesler?"

Shit. She said that out loud. "Um. He has someone named Fiesler working on it with him."

"I'm curious to learn more about that if the opportunity arises for you." He pointed ahead to a table farthest from the dance floor. "For now, let's go to our table. There's Gabriella Fermi."

The Italian billionaire was plainer than Kari had imagined. Modest makeup, simple curled dark brown hair, and a black dress with full sleeves that seemed more fitting for a funeral.

She sipped a glass of red wine and spoke to a couple with matching gray hair and a red-and-black theme to their dress and tux.

"Who is Gabriella talking to?" Kari asked.

"Angela Schultz, president of one of the largest banks in Europe, and some guy I don't know."

Kari cocked an eyebrow at him.

"What? I can only know so many people."

Once they approached the table, Kari saw a folded card with *Guest of Henry Wibawa* in a fine cursive at a place setting. Of course, she would be sandwiched between Henry and Julius. She started to pull out her chair, but Henry's light hand on her wrist stopped her.

"Allow me." *I need to show off my chivalry and etiquette.* Henry pulled the chair out for her. "Good evening, everyone."

"Henry!" A man off to the left came up and shook his hand. "I'm so glad to see you here. I was just thinking the other day that . . ."

The conversation behind her trailed off as Henry walked farther away, leaving Kari with Gabriella Fermi, Angela the banker, and what's-his-name. They all stared at her with the same inquisitive look. But didn't share the same thoughts.

Is she even old enough to drink?

Finally, someone new to talk to.

I hope Julius can behave himself.

The last came from Gabriella, and it set off the super creep alarm. "Hello. I'm Kari, also known as Guest of Henry Wibawa." She scooted in her chair and, almost like she had rung a bell, a server appeared.

"A drink, madam?"

She had seen the bottle on the flight over so she could appear somewhat knowledgeable. "Delamotte Brut."

The server grimaced. "My apologies, we only have Dom Pérignon this evening."

Kari had to act the part. "I suppose that's fine. Thank you." He left with a small bow and she returned her attention to the table who stared at her. "The service here is quite prompt."

"I thought the same thing." The man with no name smiled. "I'm Hans. Pleased to meet you."

"He's my companion for the evening," Angela said. "Are you Henry's . . . date?" *Please say no. I can't handle being pictured at another scandal.*

Kari chuckled and sipped the champagne that had just been placed in front of her. "No, I'm not a date. I work on the *Hinewai* and was asked to come in case there was a need for a translator given the diverse attendance of this event."

Gabriella grinned, her eyes bright and cheek muscles tight. "I didn't see that coming."

"Nor I," Angela said. The surprise on her face morphed into disgust. *I hoped he got hit by a train when he stepped out.*

Damage control before the night even gets started. "Julius!" Gabriella said. "You came back already."

He had cold eyes, a wide smile that showed the sharpness of his canine teeth, and a full dark beard and hair that spouted from the tops of his hands. He could have been morphing into a werewolf, but there wasn't a full moon. Before he said hello or asked any questions, he took a moment to picture her naked. His vision of her didn't include pubic hair and her breasts were a cup size smaller.

Yep. He was a pedophile.

"And who is this lovely sight, Mamma?" Julius asked.

"This is Kari. She'll be translating for Henry Wibawa this evening should the need arise." *I doubt that's true, but it's a good lie.*

Julius's eyebrows lifted. "It's a pleasure to meet you." *Look at her. Dressed as dessert.* He lifted Kari's hand from the table and kissed the back of it.

When Kari had seen the gesture in the movies, it seemed charming, possibly even romantic. In real life, she wanted to douse her hand with rubbing alcohol to disinfect her skin from his dehumanizing lip germs. She twisted her hand in his and gave him a firm handshake. "Hello."

Julius laughed. *Playing hard to get. Tiresome.* "So businesslike. Hopefully, you know how to unwind and have fun?"

"Karishma is a very focused and ambitious individual," Henry said and placed his hand on the top of her chair's back. "Aren't you?"

"That is a true statement," Kari said.

Henry joined them at the table. *Be believable and nice.* "How are you doing, Julius?"

Despise new money. "My newest thoroughbred won soundly a few weeks ago, so I've been busy doing interviews and gloating." Julius pulled out his seat beside Kari and sat. "Do you like horses, Karishma?" *All girls love horses.*

She smiled enough to appear polite. "Only Henry gets to call me Karishma; please, call me Kari. And I'm interested in the genealogy of horses. Was your victorious thoroughbred from a line of champions?"

She thinks she can tell me what to do. "Both of When in Rome's parents were competitive in their days on the track."

Horse names were so dumb. "All of that natural talent is truly amazing."

If only paying the jockeys to slow their horses was cheaper. "Yes, I'm excited to keep this lineage going."

"When's the next race?" Hans asked.

While Julius laid out the training and race schedule for the next few months, the others asked enough questions for her to gain more insight into his race fixing and blackmail of equine trainers, jockeys, and veterinarians. Meanwhile, their amuse-bouche arrived on a slab of slate: a poached prawn with micro-greens and citrus paired with a small pour of pinot grigio.

"Did you get what you expected?" Henry asked.

Kari understood he wasn't referring to the first course. "No surprises here." After she cut the crustacean with a knife and fork—she observed the etiquette of her tablemates—she savored the firm texture and bright flavor. "That's delicious."

Henry chuckled. "Pair it with the wine. It's sublime."

She did and a quiet moan escaped.

Oh, yes. Let's hear that again later.

Kari made a note to control her outward signs of enjoying what was bound to be a delicious meal and not to look down through the glass table because she was bound to see the bulge of Julius's erection at some point in the evening.

And it was going to be a long evening.

———

Kari refrained from indulging in every morsel of the subsequent four courses and sip of the accompanying wine pairing. If she stuffed herself to the gills, then she couldn't fully engage in the conversation at her table. The others at the table were pleasant and wanted to include her, but in doing so she couldn't focus on Julius. And he detested that Kari's attention was not on him.

His thoughts reflected his growing frustration.

Julius thought Angela was a whore who had emasculated Hans, he thought Henry had potential but was subservient to Madeleine, where it should have been the other way around, and he positively loathed the butch woman who played in the jazz band.

Julius wasn't only a misogynist, he *loathed* women.

Topics about civil contributions and issues about other recent charity events had led Kari to learning more about his crimes, like tax evasion and party drugs. But those and the horse racing corruption would only give him slaps on the wrist. That would inconvenience his team of lawyers, not him. Kari needed more and the only way she could get it was to isolate him and get closer.

And she knew Julius couldn't wait for that.

He touched her wrist. He bumped her leg under the table. He whispered in her ear to tell her that his personal chef made an even more wonderful sous vide duck. He whispered that she should finish her wine. He whispered that he needed to excuse himself for the restroom.

Thank the Gods. She hated his warm breath on her ear.

Kari needed to protect others from him. And to do that, she needed to use herself as bait, even if that did make the berries and créme anglaise in her stomach curdle. Kari scanned the room for her best option. She needed some level of privacy but at the same time didn't want to put herself in a risky situation. As confident as she was that she could handle herself, her grappling skills were rusty and her outfit wouldn't allow her to run or keep her balance easily. The rest of the art gallery was an option, but she had no idea what the lighting or security camera situation was. She spotted the parquet dance floor with a couple already engaged in a modified waltz. Dancing wasn't even a moderate skill of hers, but she was running out of time.

There she is. Need to keep her occupied a little longer. "Are you finished?" Julius stood over her and gestured to her empty dessert bowl.

"I have and it was delicious." She pointed to the dance floor. "Would you like to dance? But before you answer, you should know that I'm awful."

We could get her to pass for fifteen. "I'm an excellent teacher." Julius held out his hand.

The moment she put her hand in his, the fear in her heart rivaled that day on the farm when she was eleven. She recognized the sign she was about to hyperventilate when her heel struck the parquet floor. She had to calm herself and fast.

Her eyes went to the ceiling. Several security cameras pointed in multiple directions. Dozens of people had their phones out. Professional photographers were scattered throughout the room. Henry had a worried scowl but gave her a subtle nod. He understood and would be watchful. As long as she stayed in this room, she would be safe.

The pounding of her heart slowed as Julius turned back to her with a malevolent smile. Kari gave him her best demure grin.

What is the best way to start? "Alright, lesson one," Julius said over the upbeat number.

Every muscle in her eyes fought the urge to roll. He actually was intent on teaching her how to dance.

"Mind your posture, shoulders back and down, chest open." He waited until she complied. *Takes direction instantly. Good.* "Now . . ." He placed her left hand on his shoulder. "Keep your hand here, while I move mine to your waist." To his credit, he settled his hand at her waist and no lower, then he took her right hand into his. "Now, follow my lead."

"That's the part that's always confused me," she said. "How do I know where you're going? I'm not psychic."

"If you can feel my hips"—he pulled her in until they were pressed against each other—"you know where I'm going."

Luckily, the only hard part of him that grounded into her lower abdomen were the clasps of his suspenders. "I can see how that makes it easier." Kari peered over his arm and made eye contact with several women in the room. The frown lines in their faces were visible. Even the ones with recent Botox.

"You're doing well with your footwork." *Don't get greedy.* "You followed along with the conversations well at the table. Very inquisitive. Are you a college student?"

"No." It helped that Julius had arrived at the table when neither Henry nor herself noted her day job. "I thought I'd work and save money before I went to school again."

"And you're working on the *Hinewai*. Surely, that makes your parents nervous."

And it was time to lie some more. She had to be as vulnerable as possible for him to believe she was the easiest prey imaginable. "I wouldn't know. I haven't spoken to them in quite some time. I didn't really have a good upbringing, so I ran away when we lived in the Philippines."

Wonderful. "That's tragic! Do you have siblings?"

"No." While his face read concern, it was all an act, and an act she could match. "Please don't feel bad for me. I love seeing new places, and bouncing around the world as a military brat when I was young taught me all of those languages I know now. It's proven to be of great use on the *Hinewai.*"

"Do you speak Italian?"

"Yes."

"How am I supposed to believe that?" he asked with his brow raised.

Kari sighed. "Yes, I speak Italian. Do you get along well with your parents?" she asked in Italian.

"I was close to my father, but he recently passed. My mother . . ." *Fucking hate that harpy.* "We don't see eye to eye on many things." *Especially the changes I wrote in his will.*

"I'm sorry to hear about your father." Julius altered the will? That was definitely something worth passing onto Henry. "Do you mind if we continue in English? I'm a little drunk and it's a little difficult for me to dance and speak Italian at the same time."

"Fair enough, but I am impressed with your Italian." *Olivier will love her. No one will miss her. Henry isn't paying attention.*

She wore her faux-polite smile and continued to follow his lead even though Julius was actively planning on how he could traffic her. As much as she was revolted by him, she continued to play her part. She should win an Academy Award.

"Do you like dancing with me?" Julius asked.

"I do. Thank you for showing me some pointers."

He gave her a cocky grin and continued to lead. He actually was a good dancer and instructor, but she wasn't going to tell him that.

In any other situation she may have enjoyed herself, but she wanted the evening over and back into her regular clothes where a weird sticky bra wasn't pulling at her skin and her shoes weren't acting as vices. But the only way she'd get back into clothes and an environment where she felt like herself was to expedite getting information. Knowing who Olivier was wasn't enough. She had to offer Julius more and, for someone like him, the idea of a 'purity' in a young woman was like catnip.

"It feels a little strange dancing this close to you," she said.

Am I too close? "How so?"

"It's . . ." Kari whispered, "it's kind of sexy and I don't even know you."

He chuckled deep in his throat. "Well, a good dance is a lot like sex."

She bit her lower lip and then ducked her head in the hopes of appearing nervous. "I . . . um . . . wouldn't know."

Jackpot. "No need to feel embarrassed," Julius said. "Virtue among young women should be held in the highest regard."

It took every ounce of self-control she had not to push him away and launch into a rant about the hypocrisies in his patriarchal thinking. "I'm glad you think so because I get embarrassed sometimes by how much women talk about their lovers."

"That kind of woman is nothing but trash." The phone in his pocket buzzed. "Excuse me one moment, please. I'm expecting a stock tip from a friend." He took out his phone and read the text to himself. *Driver in the front of museum. Black luxury sedan, plate NLP 14E. Already paid half. Give her the candy, wait 15, and he'll take her to the airfield for Monte Carlo.* He tucked the phone away. "I'm terribly sorry about that." He pulled her even closer than she was before. This time she felt more than his suspender clips against her body. He lowered the hand that was on her waist to the top of her buttock. "I was thinking of getting some air soon."

Kari moved his hand back up to her waist. "There's lots of air in here. Very breathable."

Silly. "I'm talking about the fresh air outside. Smoking a cigar on a gorgeous evening with a beautiful young lady is one of my favorite things in life." His hand slid back down.

Thanks to the text, she had the information she needed. There was no need to keep up the charade any longer. Kari placed his hand back on her waist. Again. "There's a reason I moved your hand back up the first time. I don't want your hand there. We're not that friendly."

"But I'd like to be, and escaping the room is such a good way of getting to know each other. That's so hard to do when others are listening." He lifted his hand, but then she felt the slow drag of a single finger slide down her butt cheek.

Kari stopped the dance. "I said no. I'm going back to the table now, and if you touch my ass again, I'll put you down."

There's fight in her. Unexpected, exciting. "I think you're too nice for such a dramatic spectacle, Karishma." He drew out her name in her ear while his full hand returned to her cheek. And he squeezed.

Kari moved her hand from his shoulder to the hand groping her and tightened her grip above his wrist. In an instant, she twisted his arm so his ass-grabbing hand faced him, and she used her other hand to push his hairy knuckles toward him as hard as she could, forcing his hand at an unnatural ninety-degree angle.

The elegant room filled with his scream and the gasps of those around as he dropped to his knees. To the band's credit, they kept playing.

"I am nice," Kari said over his howls of pain and kept her grip. "I'm so nice that I could break your wrist right now, but I choose not to because I've already asserted my dominance over you." Kari released him with a throw that sent him on his back and clutching his wrist. "I told you not to touch my ass."

"Cunt!" Spittle flew from his mouth as he struggled to get to his knees and then feet. "I'm going to ruin you!"

"Yeah, we'll see who that happens to first," Kari said as she walked away with her back straight, shoulders back and down, and chest out until a fleet of people in security uniforms and Marcus rushed at him and her. Dammit. She held her hands out in front of her in a surrender-like posture. "I saw a text on his phone. There's a driver out front in a black car that was going to abduct me. Julius helped plan it."

Should have listened to my wife. "Check the front," Marcus said to the security guard in a suit. "Are you okay?" he asked her.

Kari watched as Julius refused to give up his phone from across the room and walked out. She was okay, but she knew there were others who were not. "I'm fine. I just want to go back to my seat."

The grin Bryce Resnik gave her and the different iterations

she heard of 'good for her' and 'he had that coming' helped her keep her confident strut even though she needed to clasp her hands in front of her to stop them from shaking. Every set of eyes at the table were on her. Henry was wide-eyed. Gabriella sipped her dessert wine like nothing had happened.

"Do you mind if I wait in the limo?" she asked Henry. "It'll be pretty awkward if he comes back to the table."

"He won't," Gabriella said and then a ghost of a smile formed across her lips. "And I insist that you stay."

———

On their way out of the event, Kari discretely did her 4-7-8 breathing in a quiet corner and watched Henry have a jovial conversation with Gabriella and shake a few hands. The gravity of the situation landed on her once Marcus came back to the table with a report of the driver out front. Due to the mild temperatures, the front windows had been down and, in plain view, was a dark bottle, cloth, pillow case, and zip ties.

She had been a hundred yards away from being drugged, kidnapped, and sold.

Every now and then between her cycled breaths, she'd catch a finger pointed in her direction followed by a whisper. Except for Adam Cho. He had stopped by to comment that she had left self-defense off her earlier list of talents.

What if this made the news?

"Do you mind if I make a call once we're on the plane?" she asked Henry as they walked out of the museum. "I'm worried my moms will hear about this before I have a chance to tell them that I'm okay."

Business first. "You can call after we speak to Madeleine."

"Do you understand I was almost sold into sex trafficking and I'm freaking out right now?"

Why suddenly dramatic? He cocked his head. "You seem so calm."

"Only because I have coping skills due to past trauma!" When his brow raised, she knew the volume wasn't appreciated. "I'm sorry for yelling." She went inside the limo where the driver held the door open for her.

Once Henry was seated across from her and the door shut, he pulled a glass bottle of water from the center console and poured two glass tumblers. "You may send them a text first, but a call will need to wait. Is that fair?"

She supposed that was the best she would get. Kari nodded.

Good. "I hope your tactic of getting him out there on the dance floor gave you the evidence I need."

"It did." She took a long drink of cool water that soothed her parched throat. "What did Gabriella say to you?"

"Ah! We had an excellent talk. We bonded over what it's like to be disappointed in our sons and she invited me to her private island in Malta when the *Hinewai* nears there."

Henry never discussed his son. She didn't recall reading about him in the news either. "At least your son's staying out of trouble."

"Only because real trouble requires ambition and Ray has none." *Ashamed he has my name.*

They continued their ride to the airport in relative silence. Henry even slept. She hoped sleep was in her future. Correction: sleep without nightmares.

"Welcome back," Captain Ng said when they arrived on the tarmac. Then she looked right at Kari. "Good for you." *Prick had it coming.*

Kari grimaced. "What do you know?"

Ng pointed to their driver. "The motor pool has smoke breaks with the wait staff."

At least she hadn't found out from the internet. Kari made

her way up the stairs to the inside of the plane, where her stylists watched a movie on the big TV and drank wine.

"Karishma, you may send your text now."

Not waiting another moment, she took off her torture shoes near her seat and then walked barefoot to the rear of the plane. The room that had been filled with makeup lights and sewing kits was now transformed back into a traditional office. She took a seat across from his desk and saw her clothes folded on an end table. Her multi-tool, necklace, and cell phone rested on top.

Gods, she wanted into those clothes.

Kari put her necklace back on, sat in the guest chair, and then texted.

> You might see something on the news about an altercation I was in with Julius Fermi. I'm okay. We can talk about it soon, promise.

Henry shut the office door behind him, opened a drawer from his gargantuan desk, and removed a small device. He plugged it into a laptop port.

"Please don't tell me that your method of super-secret communication is a regular encryption system?"

"I'll have you know my password is very long and has many special characters, too." After two dozen keystrokes and a few clicks of his mouse later, Kari heard a rhythmic chime.

"Hello, Henry," Madeleine said, "So, what did you learn? And it better be good since Kari is trending on my Feminists for World Change group."

Kari cringed. The moms were in that group and it was the afternoon their time. She flipped her phone over to glance at the screen. They had already texted back. She hadn't made out the words, but there were a lot of capital letters and exclamation points.

"I'm waiting," came Madeleine's annoyed voice.

Kari launched into every dirty detail she learned about Julius. Every misdemeanor. Every felony. Every person involved.

"Olivier!" Madeleine gasped. "You are very lucky that you didn't end up in that car."

Kari's brow rose. "You know him?"

"Yes. He has some extremely vicious rumors about him." After a few moments, she said, "I'm going to break our research team into shifts to work both angles of this."

"What do you mean by both angles?" Kari asked.

"The information that law enforcement can use immediately and the information about the will for Gabriella." After a pause Madeleine asked, "Were there any other notable people or thoughts?"

"We ran into Adam Cho," Henry said. "He thought about a Fiesler person when referencing a book he's writing, per Karishma."

"Doesn't ring a bell. I'll add Fiesler to my list of people to investigate. And Kari, that was a very nice wrist lock. You earned every dollar with this one."

Madeleine disconnected and Henry took the device out of his laptop. He walked over to a dragon bookend on the shelf and placed it inside its tooth-filled mouth. He pushed down on the tail until there was a crack and crunch from inside its bronze belly. "Such a fun toy." Henry turned back to her, pleased. "Please feel free to use my office to change and talk to your mothers. I'll tell Captain Ng to delay the take off for another fifteen minutes."

Kari waited until he was gone and the door was shut behind him to go to her clothes pile. A dress zipper was left for her so she didn't need Theresa's aid. Once she was back into her clothes, she took a moment to center herself once more. The call would test her emotions, too.

"Chickpea," Mom A said with a cracked voice, "are you okay?"

"Thank the Gods you're alright," Mom L said. "Where are you?"

"I'm safe and in Henry's plane."

"But are you alright?"

Kari inhaled a long breath. She would remember Julius Fermi's gruesome thoughts and her near abduction for the rest of her life. But she also knew that his reign of terror would come to an end. And she was the reason why. "I'll be okay."

Chapter Eighteen

Barcelona, Spain

Kari raised her eyes skyward as she gave praise to whomever or whatever could be listening that her thousand-point data analysis of a traumatic brain injury and depression study was over. "I never thought that would end."

"You were the one who insisted it was possible, so congratulations!" Santos gave her a fist pump in the air. "You can celebrate with . . . Tuesday is a table tennis night, right?"

Kari raised a brow. "Are you keeping tabs on me?"

"No, it's just nice to see that you allow yourself some fun. Between this and translating, you're busy all the time."

Each of the previous four stops in Europe had an assignment from Madeleine, but fortunately the only thing she had to do was clear plates at dinner. No drama involved. "You two have fun, too. I know Tuesday is a movie night for you and Charlotte, and when Mitchell and his running club do their 5k challenge on the treadmills."

"Just make sure you don't stay up too late," Mitchell added. "We have a big day tomorrow."

Kari nodded as she shut off her computer. After two months of waiting, tomorrow was her long-awaited fMRI in Madrid. "I promise no post-table tennis shenanigans. I'll be at the boat bright and early for our train ride."

They said a small chorus of goodbyes and she left the inCog office. Since she had started on the ship, she had settled on a Monday through Friday routine that suited her. It gave her variety, structure, and a chance for relaxation since her weekend assignments from Madeleine were the most anxiety-filled parts of the week, even though she only had simple tasks. Finn's theory was that ever since her viral take down of Julius Fermi, Henry and Madeleine didn't want her in the limelight.

Kari saw the logic in that.

Working with Finn had been pleasant even though they only spoke to each other in passing. But when they did, there was an ease to the conversation she appreciated. In addition, Finn was the only person who understood what it was like having a paranormal skill.

"I owe you for last week." Jade walked beside Kari as they took to the stairs. *I'm going to kick her teenage ass.*

"And what makes you think your luck will be any better than last week?"

"My hand isn't cramped from doing all of that intricate icing work for Henry's birthday cake."

This year, the baking masterpiece was a castle, complete with a working dark chocolate drawbridge, guards in the towers, and a circulating stream of white chocolate dyed navy blue that functioned as its moat. There was even a gluten-free, vegan tower.

"Even though you lost a few matches," Kari said, "there has to be some satisfaction over the compliments you received."

"I am quite pleased people noticed the engraving work on the draw bridge. But now Diana wants the same level of detail on her belated cake." Jade shook her head. "I hope I can pull that off in our rented house for the holidays."

"I'm sure she'll understand that it's an away game for you."

Can buy one if the kitchen sucks. Jade nudged her arm. "Hey, when's your birthday?"

"April. Why? Do you want to make my cake?"

She can't put that together? Jade put her arm around Kari. "I would. How about I make it as my present to you?"

"Deal!" Kari continued walking until they reached the club room. A familiar figure leaned casually outside of the door. "I was just thinking about you."

"Really?" Finn asked intrigued.

Jade looked between them with a tiny grin. *They're so cute!* "I'm going to give you both a minute to talk. I'll start my warm up."

"Oh!" Kari pointed to the room. "If no one is in there, change the music to that blues station we discovered last week."

Jade gave her a thumbs up and went inside.

Kari turned her attention back to Finn but kept her distance from them. "What's going on?"

"There's breaking news Madeleine wants you to hear."

"Why would she send you to tell me news?"

"I offered since I hadn't seen you in a while. Also, Declan says 'hello.'" Finn took a large step forward. *Thanks to you, Julius Fermi and two others were arrested on human trafficking charges fifteen minutes ago.*

"Seriously?" Kari yelled. Using herself as bait had been worth it. "That's amazing! That's . . ." Someone down the hall looked their way with an arched brow. "It's so nice that Declan remembers me!"

Finn smiled so that their crooked tooth stuck out. *I'll add that they rescued two dozen girls all under the age of fifteen from a hotel in Monte Carlo.* "I don't want to take away any more of your time with Jade, but we thought you'd like to know."

Her whole being froze. She hadn't imagined an outcome so soon. Or results so profound.

"Are you okay?" Finn asked. "You normally don't stay quiet this long."

Kari's eyes refocused on their face. Their beautiful and concerned face. Square jaw, full lips. "I'm a little shocked is all. Thank you for coming to tell me."

Finn stepped back and gave a small bow. "You're welcome, and I did want to tell you that Declan does say hi. He actually says it every time we talk."

Kari smiled. "Has he said anything else I should be aware of?"

"He saw the famous video of you and says I need to give you dance lessons." Finn laughed as they walked away.

In her eighteen years, nothing made Kari feel more accomplished than saving those girls. Yes, inCog earned ample funding for it. Although, she had to explain the large sum was because Henry was afraid she'd sue him for putting her in that dangerous situation. But she would have done it without the money. She knew there were more people out there who needed to be rescued and she didn't have to wait for Madeleine to put her in the situation where she could. Truth be told, she appreciated her telepathy when she could control it. She helped vulnerable people that way. If her remote system worked, it would change her life so she could change the world.

Kari went into the game room where Jade had found the blues station. The soulful guitar struck her ears, as did the sound of the ball bouncing off Jade's paddle as she hit it repeatedly in the air.

"How was your flirting with Finn?" Jade asked.

"I wasn't . . ." Kari sighed. "Finn was sent to give me some follow-up on an assignment I did a few months ago. That's all." Kari grabbed a paddle from the side of the room and took her place at the end of the table. "I'm set."

"But you were flirting." Jade served a lob to the back corner of the table. "Just to be clear. You did a hair flip."

"I did not." She returned the ball, but Jade let it pass. Her expression let her know not to argue the hair flip point. "Okay, I do enjoy Finn's company and may seek more of it in a friend capacity. But I have to focus on work right now. We have some really important stuff coming up at inCog."

———

After a train ride that primarily consisted of a brown landscape, Kari stood in front of a silver-gray medical center on the outskirts of downtown Madrid. Santos called his contact inside and quickly learned the plan had to change.

"My friend wasn't able to get rid of the MRI technician." Santos looked to Mitchell. "You'll have company in the booth. Are you okay with that?"

"I don't really have a choice," Mitchell said, "but I'll make it work the best I can."

Santos turned his attention to Kari. "I'll tell them I'm your father and you have claustrophobia, so I can justify needing to be in the room with you."

"Whatever you say, Dad." The motion of her mouth and the sound of her voice saying that word was unnatural.

They headed to the elevator bank where Santos pressed the button for the third floor. *Hope this doesn't raise questions.*

"Don't worry," Kari said. "You can always play the 'her symptoms are all over the place' card."

Mitchell raised a brow. "Because that's why we're disconnecting their computer system to use our own."

"Well . . ." Kari rested her hand on Santos's arm. "Dad here doesn't want to take any chances with delayed results."

Dad. That is weird to hear.

A woman with a plastic badge dangling off her waist squealed when she saw them approach. "Miguel!" she yelled and rushed over in her sensible black flats, her auburn hair bouncing along the way, to give him a hug. "It's been far, far too long."

"It's good to see you too, Amelia." Santos pulled back from the hug. "Let me introduce you to my inCog colleagues. Dr. Thomas Mitchell, our clinical specialist, and this is Karishma Okpik-Bakshi, our associate scientist and patient today."

"Pleasure." Mitchell shook her hand.

Then, so did Kari. "Thank you for helping us today."

What is wrong with her? "Absolutely," Amelia said. "I knew someday he would come back for a favor. Without his help, I don't think I would have ever finished medical school." She gave Santos a light slap on the arm. "Can you believe Alejandro will start college in the fall?"

"No!" Santos said in amazement. "Please tell him I said hi, and I still think of him when I see a bicycle kick."

"I will do that, but, for now, let's get you started."

They followed Amelia down the corridor with too bright fluorescent lights to a door marked *MRI Suite*. She pulled her badge and scanned the panel by the door. A green light blinked.

"Is there anyone else there aside from the technician?" Santos asked.

"No. I told them there was a sizable donation to our hospital in exchange for a speedy MRI with the highest discretion, so limited staff, but I still thought it best to take the back way in."

Kari continued to walk down the hall with industrial white

tiles and doors marked with signs of *Warning: High Voltage, Employees Only*, and *Supply Closet*. They took a turn and went through a double door where the floor transitioned into thin carpet.

Amelia stopped outside a changing room. "There is only a single room, so you two will need to take turns. I've already left two gowns out for you. When you finish changing, follow the signs for the *Procedure Room*." She turned to Mitchell. "Follow me to the *Equipment Room*."

After Amelia and Mitchell were a few steps away, Santos gestured to the changing room. "Ladies first."

———

Kari walked into the stark imaging room wearing only her cotton gown, underwear, and socks. She took slow and steady breaths to calm her nerves. Over her inhales and exhales, she could hear Mitchell and the technician speak about the procedure and the electrical hum of the MRI.

"Is Santos on his way?" Mitchell asked.

"Yes. Dad," Kari said without cringing, "will be here shortly."

"Good. Let's start with you laying on the table."

After she laid down on the padded table, they prepped her for the specialized reading. The brain coil, which was a plastic helmet of sorts, slid over her head. To aid in her immobilization, Mitchell tucked foam wedges between her head and the plastic frame. A mirror affixed to the top allowed Kari to see Santos enter the room. "Hi, Dad. Glad you could come."

"I wouldn't miss it."

The tech left Kari's view and reappeared with a beige device he placed in her hand. *Worst for claustrophobics.* "That has a call button in case you need us to stop for whatever reason."

"And I'll be talking to you the whole time through the intercom," Mitchell said. "Especially at those times I mentioned earlier."

Mitchell referred to the code they had developed. He would ask her to count backwards from twenty, and when she got to five, Kari would ask for Santos to come to her side. Then, she'd read Santos's mind.

Once Mitchell was in the control room, a click came over the intercom. "Give me a thumbs up if you can hear me." When she did, he continued. "Try to relax. Steady breaths until I ask you to hold it."

For the next several minutes her only activity was breathing and then holding her breath. Then came the functional part of the MRI. She recited words back to Mitchell. She worked on logic problems. Then, there was the cue to count backward.

"Dad?" she said once she got to five, but Santos didn't react. "Dad!"

"Oh!" He pushed himself off the wall and scrambled toward her. "Are you okay?" He took her hand and gave her a faux-comforting pat. "I'm right here." *Sorry, I was zoning out a bit over there. I was thinking about where I wanted to grab dinner. I'm thinking paella. There's only dozens upon dozens of spectacular places to choose from in Barcelona.*

To ensure they had enough time to collect the necessary data, she had to listen to Santos's detailed thoughts about each and every one of his favorite restaurants. He also mentally recited the lyrics to *Bohemian Rhapsody*. Part of Kari worried that during the test the magnetic force of the MRI could distort the telepathic waves, but she still heard him loud and clear. Now she laid in the noisy tube with her head frozen in place and wondered where telepathy fell on the electromagnetic spectrum. She guessed around radio waves.

The machine became quieter, and Mitchell's voice came over the intercom. "Good job, Kari. We have everything we need."

"Great," she said as she still lay immobile in her disposable cloth gown. "Can someone help me out of this thing?"

A short while later the tech came out and released her from her plastic and foam prison. Kari accepted Santos's helping hand to sit and then dangled her legs off the side. "So, paella for dinner?"

———

"To fMRIs," Kari said while she held up her glass of cava for a toast, "the gift I always wanted."

Santos clicked his glass of the same sparkling white wine while Mitchell toasted with his lemon water at their table overlooking the bay. Some patrons dined outside, but the breeze coming off the water made the December night too frigid for her liking. Kari gazed at the lights shimmering in the water, inhaled the delicious smells of the kitchen, and eagerly awaited the preliminary report Mitchell was about to provide.

"So," Mitchell removed his laptop from his bag, "I'm going to remind you both that this isn't the complete analysis. I'm only showing you the portions of the test that highlight the telepathy region in the before and after."

Santos shook his head. "I still can't believe you were able to do all of that in only a train ride."

"Well, it helped that I knew what region I should look at because of the EEG and the exact time you approached her. Not really finding a needle in a haystack." Mitchell opened his laptop, typed for a few seconds, and turned the screen to face them.

Kari leaned forward to see the different images of her brain on the screen. Four of them were black and white and only showed the outline of her skull, the many wiggly gyri, and the split of her hemispheres. Another two black and white images showed kidney-shaped white blobs in the same active spots her EEG showed. The final two images showed the kidney shapes, but this time the white area was replaced with brilliant red and surrounded by orange and then yellow.

Kari pointed sternly at the screen. "Found you, cockwaffle."

Cockwaffle, funny. "How deep is that in her brain?" Santos asked without taking his eyes off the screen.

"My estimate is four centimeters for the tissue sample."

Kari sat back and sipped her cava while she processed that information. To retrieve the cells for further testing, they would need to make a coin-sized hole in her skull, insert a computer-guided soft-tipped needle four centimeters into her brain, and remove a small amount of tissue.

"I'll reach out to the neurosurgery lead in Tel Aviv to let them know we'll have the measurements for the stereotactic programming soon," Santos said. "We'll see if they feel comfortable moving forward with the procedure."

Kari exhaled a long breath. "This is where it'll be tough to tell the moms."

Chapter Nineteen

Kari lounged with a blanket over her, sipped her chamomile, and admired the ultra-modern outline of the buildings against the night sky from her spot in the Barcelona harbor. The touch, taste, and sight soothed her while Mom L spoke in quick bursts. But mostly Mom L was thinking out loud about how she could get herself and Mom A to Israel.

She underestimated how much 'baby's first brain surgery' would impact the moms.

"Please don't fly halfway around the world for a little surgery," Kari pleaded.

"A little surgery! They're going to drill into your head and remove a portion of your brain!"

Kari didn't know what had happened; they were fine with the idea earlier. "Why are you freaking out all of a sudden? This procedure is actually very simple and the chance for complications is minor."

"I know my tune has changed a bit, but that's because it's no longer an 'if' question, it's a when question. And where and who questions. I want to make sure it's done in a good place with qualified people."

Kari laughed. "Considering we're using American health care as our benchmark, it's very good."

"I'm serious, chickpea. Who and where?"

Kari sighed. So much for adding some levity to the conversation. "It's the Tel Aviv Institute of Brain and Spinal Surgery. As for who, her name is Dr. Malka who is recently retired but still holds all the necessary certifications. Lately, she gets called in to consult on big-time things. Mostly tumor removals. From what I can tell she's basically like Nani Tanha. But, you know, ten years younger."

Mom L was silent except for the clicking of keys. "Okay, I just did a quick search and can verify that she's a real doctor."

"Sounds like a real thorough job, Mom L."

"Watch it! You might be in Spain now, but you'll be home soon where you can get a very powerful mom glare." After a beat, she asked in a much friendlier tone, "Has anything changed for your visit?"

Kari groaned. She didn't care what the travel advisor on the *Hinewai* said, but her new flight plan of Barcelona to London to New York to Portland was not quick and easy. "In a word, yes. I'll text you when we're about ready to take off from New York."

"New York? You have a layover in New York now?"

"Yeah." Kari turned her head at the *shh* of a white envelope sliding under her door. She groaned again. "Can you give Mom A the news for me? I have to go."

"Sure thing. I love you, chickpea, and see you soon!"

"I love you, too."

She picked up the envelope and, since she was alert this time, opened the door to see if the delivery person was still there. Long, wavy red hair fell over their shoulders.

"You usually come later at night," Kari said.

Finn stopped, turned, and walked toward her. "Or you stayed up. Had I known you were still awake I would have lingered to chat a bit. Why are you up past your bedtime?"

"I had to give my moms a call to talk about some stuff, so I aimed for their lunch break. But I only ended up getting one of them."

"You talk to them a lot, don't you?"

Kari shrugged. "How much is a lot?"

"The amount you do."

The cabin door beside Kari opened. Jade stared back at her with an expression that conveyed both annoyance and amusement. "Sorry, we were being loud."

"Flirt in your cabin," Jade demanded, then shut the door.

Finn smirked. "I don't mind relocating if you don't."

"Fine," Kari drawled and stepped to the side. "Although, I don't know why I'm doing this, because I am exhausted."

Does look tired. "I can only guess that it's because you like going to bed after some witty banter or"—they pointed to the envelope in her hand—"after questions have been answered."

She held it up. "You know what this is about?"

"This time I do, and we should probably sit down."

Kari pointed to the chairs by her dining table and desk combo, then went to her bed and crisscrossed her legs. Before she heard the explanation, she glanced at the time. It was already an hour past her usual bedtime. She knew she'd be hating life tomorrow, but knowing what was ahead would help her fall asleep faster. "Okay, lay it on me."

"Once we leave Naples, the two of us and Henry are making a quick stop at a tiny island near Malta."

"Oh, this is the Gabriella Fermi visit. Henry mentioned it in Stockholm." She thought their billionaire-we-hate-our-sons play date would have happened already. "What kind of meeting is it?"

"That, I actually don't know." Finn crossed their legs at the knee. "We're tagging along for the usual reasons, but also because Henry believes Gabriella is hiding something on the island of value, but he has no idea what. The only thing he knows is that it takes a lot of off-grid power."

"Sounds like typical Henry stuff. But why wait? Normally, he'd be on his plane by now."

"She's been busy with fixing her estate mess after Julius's legal troubles and also holiday plans. Gabriella spends December and most of January skiing, then she craves warm weather again."

"Sounds rich people reasonable enough."

Finn chuckled. "I saw you check the time. Do you have a date you need beauty rest for or something? Tomorrow's a weekend."

Were they fishing for romantic intel? Kari couldn't tell. "I happen to be leaving early tomorrow morning to go home to Oregon. So, I guess I do have a date."

"A date with your moms?" Finn grinned.

"Don't make it weird."

They held their hands up in surrender. "I apologize. I'm sure it'll be very wholesome. Maybe you'll have a mothers-daughter sleepover and do each other's hair or something."

She shook her head. "If any hair is getting 'done' it'll be me and my new buzz cut."

Finn laughed but then they stopped, uncrossed their legs, and leaned forward. "Are you serious?"

"I'm having a procedure in Tel Aviv when we dock there, which requires shaving a spot on my head. But, I figured I'd go for the whole thing."

Finn cocked his head and studied her.

"What are you staring at?"

"I'm trying to figure out what you'd look like with no hair, which is really difficult. But . . . I think your face could handle it."

"What does that mean?"

"It means that your features are strong enough to carry any haircut. Even with your hair gone, your eyes, your mouth shape, and your bone structure are more than enough to keep your appearance . . . satisfactory."

Kari laughed. "'Satisfactory' has to be the most flattering thing anyone has ever said to me about my physical appearance."

Finn smiled and leaned back in the chair. "While I've never shaved my head—"

"Thank the Gods. Your hair is very satisfactory."

"Touché. But what I was going to say is that while I've never shaved my head, I do have ample experience with my grooming kit."

"You have a kit? Not a razor or shaver? But an entire kit?"

"Well, different parts of my body require different tools and lotions because of different shapes, textures, and sensitivities."

"Can I ask you a personal question?"

"I don't see why not. You already know I'm an empath, did time in prison, and I have a son who thinks I'm his sibling. It doesn't get more personal than that."

"You have a point there." Kari uncrisscrossed her legs and sat on the edge of her bed. "All of that shaving sounds really time consuming. Why not laser everything?"

Finn laughed. And then they laughed harder. "That is not at all what I thought you'd ask me. But I like the ritual and it helps me feel more like me."

"I get that. I know society tells someone like me to shave, but even without that, I think I'd do it anyway. I just like the way it feels when I'm done. What did you think I was going to ask you?"

Finn pursed their lips. "I thought you were going to ask me about my gender identity."

"When it comes to that, I figured you'd tell me your story if and when you trusted me enough to know. I understand that's a heavy topic."

Finn nodded and then stood. "I appreciate your understanding, truly. But it is both a heavy and long conversation, and one that'll prevent you from getting more sleep. You have a big day of travel ahead, so I should head out."

"Yeah," she said, even though she was now contemplating skipping her breakfast time for extra sleep. She was also mulling over another thought. "This might sound really out there, but when the time comes, will you do it for me?"

Do it? They quirked a brow. "Sorry, I'm not the mind reader here, so you'll have to be more specific."

She could back out of her wild idea now but . . . it just made sense. "Would you give me my new haircut? Most people don't understand the significance hair can have to a person, but you do. You'll approach it with respect and not like it's a goofy prank or something."

Finn gave her a soft smile. "I'd be honored to. Just tell me when." They walked to the door and glanced over their shoulder, a few strands of wavy red hair obstructed Finn's face. "I'll see you when you get back. Safe travels." Finn left, closing the door behind them.

A warmth filled Kari's chest that she had only felt on a handful of occasions. It was a feeling of complete gratitude, and without having to have an awkward conversation about it, Kari knew she had a real friend in Finn.

Bonus points for having a friend who was easy on the eyes.

She looked down at the envelope in her hands—

Madeleine's cursive written on the outside—and opened it.
This time there were two cards.

Your services will be needed upon the return from your holiday. Please plan your brain surgery accordingly. Yes, I know about that.

Have a lovely time visiting your mothers. Your bonus will arrive when you're there.

Chapter Twenty

Oregon, United States

"Chickpea!"

Kari turned to the shout of her nickname at the airport arrival pick-up and saw Mom L outside a van. She alternated between waving her arms overhead and giving other drivers dirty looks for honking at her illegal park job. All of this while Mom A barreled toward her. Kari braced for impact. "Hi, Mom A. I missed you, too."

My baby. "I'm so glad to see you!" Mom A squeezed her, covered her with evergreen scent, and kissed her forehead and cheeks. "I missed you so much." She stood back and held Kari's hands. *She looks so much older.*

"I've only been gone six months."

"Is there any point in the next few minutes I can also hug our daughter?" Mom L asked. "I can only get away with parking this monstrosity here so long." A horn blared beside her to emphasize the point. "I know!" she yelled at the yellow taxi.

So impatient. "Come on." Mom A took her rolling suitcase for her. "Let's get you another hug."

Mom L's embrace was less crazed but just as loving. *Happy*

brain feels. "In case you couldn't tell, we missed you, and we can't wait to hear about all of your adventures, but first I have to get out of here before I get a ticket. Feel free to get all the way in the back."

Kari got into the van and climbed through the seats to reach the back row. "Why did you buy a gigantic car?"

"We didn't," Mom A said. "We're borrowing it from a courthouse friend for the journey home."

Mom L made brief eye contact with her via the rearview mirror as she pulled back out into traffic. "We figured you'd probably be approaching a migraine and or full rage-mode by now with the number of people who have surrounded you, so the least we could do was offer a reprieve from the voices for the next two hours."

"You are amazing people, really. Who's the courthouse friend?"

"You don't know him, but you'll meet him."

Kari caught the meaningful eye contact exchanged between her mothers. This is where reading their minds would have been helpful. "What's happening?"

"First let me say that I know we promised a quiet week centered around food and helping us find a dog to adopt," Mom L said, "but I have to do a work thing, and it would be really nice if you came. You might even have fun."

Mom A turned from her spot in the passenger seat. "She has to be at City Hall for the New Year's ball drop."

"That's so many people! Drunk people, at that."

"I got you your own room at the hotel across the street," Mom L said. "You can get some food at the party, say hi, and then disappear. It'll just be nice for people to see that you exist. You can brag."

"I can't talk about what I do! The NDAs I had to sign are like one of those phone books Ata Niq won't throw away."

"Fine. Don't brag. But most people when they're eighteen haven't left the country of their birth, let alone have visited the amount of places you've been to. You were docked off London for like a month in addition to all the other European stops. Pick some favorite moments to chat about."

Mom A turned back again with a frown. "I'm sorry you're missing Italy, by the way, but we promise this will be just as fun!"

———

All of her former comforts were at home. Her favorite blanket. Her favorite foods. Her brief hello and fly by with Brownie. But home was different now. It was smaller. The tiny house that she had once compared to winning the lottery was cramped. The goats smelled so much worse than she had remembered. And now there were chickens.

Loud chickens.

Kari sat in front of the fire and dug her hands deeper into her winter coat. She had already put another log on, so if she couldn't bear the cold after that, it was time to go inside. Inside to the cramped little box. She looked up to the millions of stars above, but even though she knew each star was over several thousand degrees, the idea of space chilled her.

"This will warm you up, too." Mom A held out a steaming mug. *A little apple cider.*

The heat of the ceramic unfroze her fingers. "With maple syrup?"

"Like there's any other acceptable way." Mom A took her seat from across the fire pit with her own mug. "You've been out here awhile. Usually, your threshold for staying outside was ten degrees ago, which is still more tolerant than your Mom L"

Kari grinned. "I'm getting lost in my thoughts."

"Would you rather I go in so you can be alone?"

Both moms always respected her need for space, which she knew was a trait not all parents gave their children. "When you moved out into your own place and then visited Ata Niq and Noko Ani for the first time, what did you think?"

Mom A blew out an audible breath. "Wow, that's going back a ways." She took a sip and then chuckled. "I remember being surprised how much Mom and Dad wanted to get me things. No longer were the days of, 'You know where it is. Get it yourself.' Let me guess, you're having similar feelings about that."

Kari nodded. "I don't think I've put away a dish, gotten my own food, or"—she held up her mug—"drink since I got here. But I'm struck by other things too."

"Like what?"

Kari grimaced, not sure how to articulate her feelings without upsetting her mother.

"Ah. Let me guess, it doesn't quite feel the same or as good. Like you know you're welcome, but you also feel like a guest because the home you've built for yourself is somewhere else."

"Yeah, I think that's part of it. Does that make you feel bad?"

"Bad isn't the word I'd choose. It makes me feel . . . a little sad. You've officially left the nest and the nest you've built for yourself is to your design with a few friends and a good job. That makes me happy for you, and on the scale of mom feelings, your happiness will always tip the scale."

"How are you two not freezing your asses off?" Mom L came out in a full winter parka, put another log on the fire, and took a seat beside Mom A. "I have a hot flash right now and even I can't take this. I can't believe I used to work outdoors year-round."

Mom A took her gloved hand and kissed it. "I was

wondering when you'd get jealous and join us. Also, if it's above freezing, it's not that cold."

While Mom A's focus went back to the fire, Kari shared a look with Mom L that suggested Mom A had the minority opinion on that one.

"Well, my back will seize if I get too cold," Mom L said, then bumped Mom A's shoulder. "Did you ask her yet?"

Kari sighed. "I already asked for the time off to do family summer vacation in Alaska."

"That's not what she wants to know," Mom A said. "Although it's good to have confirmation. I'll make Wade sleep on the couch since he hasn't done that yet."

"He could always sleep outside and guard us from grizzlies." Kari noted the disapproving cock of Mom A's head. "Okay, okay. I'll be nice. What do you want to ask me?"

"As silly as it sounds, we'd like to know more about your friends," Mom L said. "It's exciting for us."

"I told you. Neill is my table tennis buddy, Jade doubles as my neighbor and table tennis buddy, and I work with Finn and occasionally we have banter."

They stared at her. Mom A was the first to break eye contact and sipped her cider, but Mom L kept those big, questioning eyes on her. She didn't even blink. Kari knew precisely what they wanted to know.

"Fine. Neill is from South Africa who does a security detail and is progressing nicely in the finesse of his table tennis skills. He looks super tough but is actually very sweet. Jade is from Louisiana, divorced, has a daughter my age, and teaches baking at World University. Sometimes she'll bring me 'imperfect' bakes from the day. And . . . she's just really nice and looks out for me. I like that we can play or hang out and she respects my need for space. She teases me sometimes, too."

"She teases you?" Mom L asked with an arched brow.

"You know how friends barb each other in little ways. It's been awhile since someone who wasn't either of you felt comfortable enough around me to do that." Kari sipped her cider which had started to cool. "It's nice."

"Just as long as it's in good fun." Mom A took a long drink, the steam wafted ribbons around her face. "What does she barb you about?"

"Mostly Finn. She insists we're flirting and we're not."

"The plot thickens," Mom A said with a mischievous glint in her eye.

Mom L gave her a playful slap on the thigh. "Tell us about Finn."

"Well, first, I don't think we're flirting. I think that Jade wants to live vicariously through me because Finn is gorgeous. I won't deny that. They're—We haven't had a talk about gender identity yet, but Finn does prefer they-them pronouns. Anyway, Finn's from Newfoundland and a VIP assistant, which is how we met because that's where the need for translators usually comes in." That was all the moms were getting. She didn't think they would want her to discuss their empath skills or Declan.

Mom A gave her a slow nod as though she were digesting all the information. "How old's Finn?"

"Twenty-one."

"Long, wavy hair?" Mom L asked.

"Yeah," Kari drawled. "Why?"

"You have a definite type," Mom A responded. "How often do you work with Finn?"

"Not too often. Maybe once every other week." Kari thought about their pop-in visit just before she had left. "We had a good talk the last time we saw each other and, like Jade, they respect my space which is why I appreciate the friendship. At first, I thought Finn was annoying because of a little smirk they kept giving me. Like they knew something I didn't. I hated that."

"And that's definitely flirting," Mom A said.

Kari scrunched her nose. "You think?"

"Yes," both moms said in unison.

"Well, whatever it is, I just love the fact that I have Mitchell and Santos in my professional life who I can speak openly to and three people in my personal life where I can be almost a normal person. I'm practically an average citizen now."

"Right, because the average citizen acts as a translator for royalty, celebrities, and the richest people in the world. I still can't believe you do that as a side hustle." Mom L chuckled then reached for her lower back. "Okay, my body is telling me that I'm done with this outside nonsense. I'll see you inside, sweets." She kissed Mom A's forehead and then rounded the fire pit to Kari to kiss her forehead too. *Goodnight, chickpea. Dream of the puppy we saw.*

"Night, Mom L." She watched her go into the house and caught Mom A's devious grin. "What?"

"Let's expand on 'gorgeous.'"

———

Since she hadn't packed anything appropriate for the New Year's Eve party, she borrowed black tights from Mom L and a black skirt and bright blue sweater from Mom A. The snowflake beaded earrings her Noko Ani had made went perfect with the ensemble.

Better wake me up.

Kari got into the backseat of the family car and buckled herself in. "I can't believe you're drinking coffee."

Desperate. "How else am I supposed to stay alert past eight o'clock?" Mom L backed out of the gravel driveway and headed toward town. "I'm going to check us in first, so once you have your fill of a walking appetizer dinner, you can retire for the evening. Although, it would be nice if you stuck around for the ball drop."

"So I have to watch you two make out? No thanks."

I think your Mom L would love to know more about Finn's toned dancer legs. What do you think?

Kari understood the threat loud and clear. "I mean your love is beautiful. Everyone should see it."

"That's right it is." Mom L reached over the console for Mom A's hand. "Also, we'll save the making out for when the press isn't there."

Kari's brow scrunched. "Why would the press be there?"

"Because this is a small town and a big, bright ball being lowered on a pulley is news. You may have forgotten about that now that you're a world traveler."

In a way, Mom L was right. Not only was her childhood home small now, so was the town. The twenty-minute drive used to feel like forever, now it took no time at all since there were no boats to wait for or helicopter to airplane transfers.

She really did have a different life.

Mom L checked them in and they dropped their overnight bags off to their respective rooms before the trio headed across the street to the tavern for the local politics, hobnobbing festivities.

"Smells good, at least." Kari had already seen a few servers walk by with delicious-smelling finger foods. "Okay, I'm here. You kids have fun."

"We intend to." Mom L hooked her arm inside Mom A's and pointed a threatening finger at Kari. "Stay away from the bar."

She rolled her eyes. Now she had to visit the bar out of principle. But her first stop was to the bacon-wrapped scallops followed by the crab-stuffed mushrooms. In between bites, she made an effort to say hello or give a nod of acknowledgement to someone, even though they kept thinking about how much of a genius freak she was. Keeping her mouth full helped not speak with them. But party food was heavy on the sodium, leaving her parched.

"Champagne, please." She smiled broadly at the bartender.

Got to be kidding. The bartender shook his head. "I know who you are, Kari. How about a soda?"

"Fine," she said, annoyed. "I'll take a ginger ale, but can you do something fancy to it?"

Funny. He scooped ice into a large glass and sprayed the soda into it. Then, he tossed in a cherry with a plastic sword skewering it. *Oh, the thing.* "I also have something else for you." He ducked down, disappeared from behind the bar, and reemerged a second later with a white envelope in his hand. "This was dropped off for you."

She spun around in a panic looking for faces from the ship. "Who brought this?"

The bartender shrugged. "Sorry, I wasn't here. There was just a note when my shift started to make sure you got it at some point. You beat me to the punch."

Bar, really? "I thought I told you no bar . . . What's wrong?" Mom L's jovial voice turned to concern in an instant.

Kari played her shock at receiving the envelope off as annoyed. "I can't believe you gave the bartender a heads up about me."

"It's what I do." Mom L sipped her beer and lowered her gaze to the envelope. "What's that?"

"I don't know. I think I'll go up to the room and open it."

Not fair. "I didn't get a cherry and sword in my ginger ale," Mom A said, interrupting their awkward moment. "Oh no, what happened? You both have a face."

"Of course, we have faces!" Kari said.

Attitude! Mom L pointed a stern finger at Kari. "Don't use that tone with your mother."

Overreact much. "Relax, Leela. What happened, chickpea?"

"Nothing happened," Kari said. She had to diffuse this situation as soon as possible. She had no idea what was in that envelope. However, if Madeleine had been so bold as to deliver this in public, then the contents had to be innocuous. "This was dropped off for me. Here, I'll open it and read it so we can all move on with our lives." With an uneasy belly, Kari read the contents out loud. "We are delighted with your performance and have issued you a bonus for the year even though you have only been with us a short time. We hope you enjoy it as much as your fireside chat with your mothers. Happy New Year!" She had kept her voice even despite her heart dropping to the pit of her stomach. Madeleine had been watching her.

Wonderful. "That's so sweet," Mom A cooed and hugged her while Mom L shot her a skeptical eye. "You were already talking about quality time by the fire with us before you left."

"Why do you feel so anxious about it?" Mom L asked at the same time Mom A asked, "How did they know you were here to deliver the letter?"

"I . . . um." Quick lie. Quick lie. Quick lie. "You caught me," Kari said with a fake laugh. "I've been texting back-and-forth with Finn all week and told them about the party. They must have helped coordinate the surprise delivery for me."

I'm crushing too. Mom A put her hand over her heart.

"That makes sense," Mom L said. "The bonus is a nice surprise, too. Any idea how much?"

"No. I'll check that out on my banking app later. For now" —she had to get the topic of conversation back to the party—"I really want to check out those Philly steak egg rolls."

Kari left her moms, but instead of hitting the egg roll tray, she detoured to the restroom. She closed the stall door behind her and opened her banking app. A surprised "oh" escaped her lips and she leaned back on the door for balance.

There was nothing like starting the New Year $9,999 richer.

Chapter Twenty-One

Gabriella's Island, Malta

If possible, her travel back to the ship was even more complicated than her departure. She had just enough time to eat, shower, and power nap a headache away before her next assignment.

After leaving her cabin in bluish clothes—per Madeleine's request—and a wide-brim hat for the Mediterranean midday sun, Kari watched Jade come down the passageway. "Hi, stranger."

"Are you leaving again?" Jade asked, surprised. "I'm going to forget what you look like!"

"I promise we can hang out when I get back. We need to catch up about our holiday and I need to see the cake you made Diana."

Jade smiled in that way that made her nose scrunch. "The kitchen posed no problems. I nailed it! Oh, and I hear that club four got an air hockey table. We should think about mixing up where we go since the one in our spot is always hogged. Maybe we can go there before dinner today."

"I'd be willing to try. See ya!" Kari took the now familiar

route to the faux-office, stepped in the elevator, and ascended to the conference room.

"You're almost late," Madeleine said as she appeared to study her, "with your very large hat. Henry should be here in a moment, which gives us time to catch up." She leaned back at the end of the table and crossed her legs. "How was your trip home?"

"Nice. I don't know what was more of a surprise, getting a hand-delivered envelope, that you spied on me from a satellite, or that the editors of the local paper plastered my moms kissing on the front page with the caption, 'Our Mayor Loves the New Year.'"

"You also got a bonus."

"That *was* a nice surprise."

"We want you to know how much your obedience and discretion is appreciated, but also include a reminder that we know everything about you should you choose to abandon those tenets."

"Subtle."

Madeleine shrugged. "I do what I can."

The door beside the elevator opened and Henry walked in wearing a dark blue suit and a smile. "I love your hat, Karishma. Let's head down to meet Finn and get going."

"We're not going up?" Kari asked. "Like in the helicopter up?

"No. We're going down to the boat." Henry headed to the elevator and waved for Kari to follow. Once they were both inside, he leaned forward for the retina scan, and they started their descent to the bottom of the ship. "You're going on a new boat." *Very special. Should be a treat.*

"Now I'm curious about the boat and what we'll be doing on the island."

Making progress. "Nor I. It's important to play this by ear. I don't know what Gabriella will share and what we'll have to find out through other means."

"So, it's completely within the realm of possibility she'll be an open book."

"Yes, but I am doubtful. You'll need to be clever to get information." He stared at his custom leather Italian shoes and shook his head. *Hope this is the invitation.*

"The invitation to that special circle you wanted to be included in?"

Careful with thoughts. Henry waved her off and wasted no time stepping out of the elevator, increasing the distance between them.

"Whoa!" Kari followed and scanned an area of deck one she didn't know existed. Unlike the area where the marine science, VIP boat, and boarding for the tender were, this was its own separate room. With its own unique boat. It had to be the boat Gia had referenced back in New York. The craft rested on a trailer-like framing while dual motors the size of small cars took up the stern. There was a low-profile, covered cabin. Unlike most boats she had seen, the haul was painted a bluish-gray, the glass of the cabin was non-reflective, and all the unlit light bulbs were red. This boat was meant for speed and camouflage.

Yep, this was his getaway vehicle.

Kari sat on the blue pixel patterned seat across from Henry on the boat's perimeter and noticed their party was short a person. "I thought Finn would be here by now."

"Soon. They had a quick errand to run." Henry crossed his legs at the knee. "Between the two of you, I will have no doubt what Gabriella's intentions are." He pointed off to the side. "There's Finn and Josef now."

Both came in not in their standard black-on-black clothes, but in shades of blue. Not only was the boat camouflaged, so was everyone on board. Josef veered off to the side and hit a red button on the wall that rolled up like a garage door. Perhaps it was the sudden rush of sea air coming in, but Kari could have sworn Finn's hair blew back from their chiseled face as though they were in slow motion. Their lips formed that smirk, which she once hated but now found sexy.

Dammit, Mom A and her interrogation. Now she had a crush.

Josef took his place in the cabin behind the wheel while Finn sat away from both Henry and her. They were in a triangle at the bow.

"Did you have a nice visit back home, Kari?" Finn asked.

"I did. There was quality time with the moms and playing with dogs. Also, chickens." At their smile, she asked, "Did you have a good New Year?"

"We had quite the party on the ship!" Henry said. "I think they heard us all the way in Rome."

She couldn't have cared less about Henry's New Year. Like every day, she was sure it met his every whim. "How about you, Finn? Did you ring in the New Year with Declan?"

They shrugged. "Yes and no. We video chatted before midnight his time so he could go to bed at a reasonable hour. This was the first year he had questions about what the New Year meant. I did my best to explain Earth moving around the sun, but I think I confused him. And myself, actually."

Kari grinned as the platform they were on lowered with a mechanical groan. The rolling door of the ship opened wider, the sun blinding them in the process. Kari put on her sunglasses. The hat would have to wait or else it would fly off into the Mediterranean. With her hair up, at least she didn't have to worry about it knotting, but Finn would suffer. She dug into her pocket for an extra hair tie. "Here you go." Kari leaned across the space in the bow and handed it to them. "I know how easily hair knots."

Finn gave her nod of thanks and proceeded to place their hair in a high bun. "This will make my toque easier to pull on." Sure enough, they pulled a dark blue beanie out of their pocket.

Their red hair would have stuck out like a buoy.

The boat was now at a complete diagonal with the water like it was preparing for a nose dive. It lurched forward, then the water at the stern splashed. "Hold on," Josef said as the boat bobbed up and down. Those were the first words she had ever heard Josef say. She thought he was mute, but he sounded . . . maybe Czech? Once they cleared the *Hinewai*, he engaged the double motor.

Kari was pushed back into her seat and a wide smile covered her features as the wind whipped her ponytail around and sea spray from the Maltese water misted her sunglasses. It was nice to squeeze in some fun between billionaire brain picking and brain surgery. The volume from the motors made conversation difficult, but she had to ask one question. "Where's Neill?"

"For certain tasks," Henry shouted, "I prefer Josef."

She nodded, the message clear. Tasks which required clandestine approaches and as little speaking as possible were Josef's deal.

After a twenty-minute zigzag ride—far enough away where she knew they had disappeared from the *Hinewai*'s view and anyone who was trying to follow them—she could see the privately owned island's features as the boat bounced over the waves. The profile of the island consisted of layers of eroded honey-colored rock and a speckling of low shrubs marked the only vegetation. To take advantage of the consistent sea breezes and lack of shade, a cluster of wind turbines and a field of solar panels were on land. She'd bet money there was some sort of hydroelectric power set up near the shore.

Josef turned into a harbor surrounded by what looked like limestone cliffs, then pulled into a small marina with ten boat slips.

A young man with golden-brown everything—skin, hair, even shorts and polo of different yellows—stood with his hands clasped in front of him. Josef tossed him a rope the golden marina worker secured to the boat cleat with an intricate knot. Then, he did it again with a second rope. Josef opened the low door to the side of the boat.

Kari was struck by the perfection of the light aqua-colored water. She could see the sandy bottom below and tiny silver fish eating algae off the safety ropes that secured the dock.

"We're following you to Gabriella?" Henry asked the marina worker.

"Yes, Signore Wibawa," he said in an Italian accent.

Henry turned to Kari and approached. *Learn what he knows.* Once she gave him a nod of understanding, he continued the discussion. "I don't see the house. How far of a walk is this?"

"Not far. Just over the hill." *And under the hill.*

Behind her large sunglasses and hat, no one could see her brow raise to that thought. Of course, maybe that was how he thought of a basement. "How many floors is it?" Kari asked.

"Two. It is much, much smaller than her other homes." His steps increased so he was too far away for her to read.

Kari increased her pace on the worn white sand trail lined with solar lights. Finn walked beside him, so that element was covered. "Is there a basement?" she asked.

Henry quirked his brow.

Fed to the pigs if I talk. "I don't know."

Kari hated the next question she needed to ask, but since

she appeared like the spoiled assistant of a billionaire, she might as well act like it. "Are you not allowed in the house?" she asked in a laugh.

"No, I'm not."

"Really?" Kari couldn't contain her surprise and looked at Finn, who shrugged. Josef rolled his eyes. "Where are you allowed to go?"

"The grounds. I stay in the worker quarters."

"How many 'workers' on the island are there?"

He uttered an annoyed sigh. *So many questions.* "At this moment, only me since this isn't one of the larger gatherings."

"Like New Year's Eve parties?" Kari joked.

Fed to the pigs while I am still alive. Rather than answer, he walked faster.

Sensing that she had gotten all the information out of him she was going to get, Kari continued to walk until the ground underfoot transitioned to a sandy soil and they crested a hill. Then, she saw the cottage-style home. From the outside, it didn't appear to be extravagant. Solar panels and two skylights dominated its clay-tiled roof, whereas the exterior was a white-washed stucco. There were only two high, narrow windows on each floor. Possibly to allow heat to escape, but also maybe to make snooping more difficult.

Quaint. "I never thought she'd live in something so small," Finn whispered to her.

"And with hardly any windows," she whispered back, and in the process caught the slight citrus scent of bergamot in Finn's hair. Thank the Gods the toque was back in their pocket. That luscious hair needed to be seen.

Henry pursed his lips and placed his hands on his hips as he stood on the sandstone pavers outside the home. *There is more here.* "Is there farming on the island?"

"There are a few trees here and there, but only for private

use," the marina worker said. "Nothing for export." He gestured to the front door. "Go ahead and knock. I'll see you back at the boat."

When he went back up the hill, Kari searched for any signs there could be something under the home. She refused to believe that one of the wealthiest people in the world, who had enough solar, wind, and probably hydroelectric power to run a small city, had that infrastructure in place for a two-story house. Kari took off her sunglasses to see the landscape with unaltered colors and searched for anything out of place. She took in the texture and color of the soil, the small bushes and occasional lemon or olive tree, and the too perfect cluster of bushes with brilliant violet flowers.

Before Henry could lift the tacky mermaid door knocker, she tapped his shoulder. "I see something. A pipe sticking out of the ground—looks like a vent—at the top of the hill. There's a bunch of fake shrubs around it."

Henry turned and cocked his head. "How do you know they're fake?"

"Every flower is the same exact shape, height, and color."

"Why would there be a pipe?" Finn asked.

The small house, power requirements, non-exported food, and ground pipe led Kari to one conclusion. "Probably because there's an underground operation of sorts."

A dungeon! Finn's eyes widened. "Do you think there are people down there now?"

"I hope to Gods not!" Kari put her sunglasses back on. "Maybe this is left over from her son's trafficking day?"

Now, Finn's mouth dropped. *That's abhorrent!*

"But I'm sure Gabriella would have seen to their release if that were the case," Kari said in an attempt to assuage their fears. "Maybe Henry can find out?"

"Yes, let's do that." Henry lifted the tail of the mermaid knocker and struck the plate three times.

Kari listened for movement inside but didn't hear anything. Henry was about to lift the mermaid's tail again when the door opened. The last time Kari had seen Gabriella Fermi was in Stockholm where she wore evening attire. Now she wore white capris and a sky blue linen shirt with the sleeves rolled up.

"I made lemonade," Gabriella said and then went back into the house. "Please, come in."

There was no way Kari would drink that lemonade. While she liked Gabriella more than her son, she still didn't trust her.

"Josef." Henry directed a come here motion of his index finger and lowered his voice. "Stay outside and watch the perimeter."

Josef nodded.

Henry had the same thought about poisoned lemonade as they walked through the living room, which featured a cream couch and matching recliners, a few tables, and a TV on a hutch. DVDs—actual DVDs like at her grandparents' house— were lined up underneath it. The kitchen had a small island and basic appliances in white. The normalcy put Kari even more on alert.

Billionaires did not live like this.

"There is a powder room beside the pantry if you need to use the restroom." Gabriella went to the refrigerator, removed a pitcher of lemonade, and placed it on the counter.

Up until now, Kari had kept her distance from Gabriella, but now she inched closer as she opened the upper cabinet. "Do you need help?"

"No, thank you," Gabriella said with her head blocked by the cabinet. *Where are the tall glasses? That's right. Dishwasher.* She grabbed four wine glasses instead, took them to the kitchen island, and poured. "I don't like ice. Hurts my teeth and dilutes the flavor of my lemons." *Henry brought an assistant and his translator? I clearly speak English. Might as well use them.* She handed Kari two glasses and gave Finn the other two. "Take those to the patio. Let's enjoy the sun, Henry." Gabriella opened the sliding glass door and walked through.

Kari hung back while Henry walked ahead. "What vibe are you getting?" she asked Finn.

Whole thing is weird. "She's apprehensive for sure. Does that track with what she's thinking?"

"I suppose, considering she's mostly concerned with beverage service and why we're here."

She and Finn walked out into a picturesque but simple courtyard. Potted plants with herbs grew, as did tomatoes and cucumbers. The four walls surrounding them alternated between the white stucco and large windows that included the second floor. The courtyard was vaguely reminiscent of the best feature of the biomedical building in Boston.

She still couldn't believe they turned her down!

Kari and Finn joined Gabriella and Henry at a dining table for ten. She took her seat across from Henry and catty-corner from Gabriella and Finn. She could hear Gabriella—and her notes about making bruschetta later—but not Henry.

Gabriella observed Kari. She rested her arm on the table and rested her chin in her hand. *Looks like such a regular girl now.* "Do you regret doing what you did to my son?"

"I told him not to touch me in multiple different ways and he didn't listen. So, no, I don't regret protecting myself."

That's good. Gabriella nodded. "A young woman needs conviction and to look out for herself. But, I am curious why you're here, since Henry clearly doesn't need a translator or my son restrained today."

Before she could answer for herself, Henry spoke. "I asked both Karishma and Finn to come with me today, because I was not sure of the nature of the visit. They both assist me in various capacities. Karishma, in addition to being excellent with languages, is a keen observer of the world and a scientist."

Gabriella pointed to Finn. "And the red head?"

"Finn is a master of understanding what people want. They can also test the lemonade, so I can make sure you aren't trying to poison me."

"Henry," Finn said, clearly hurt.

Gabriella laughed. She picked up her lemonade and traded it with Henry's. "Here. Now, please relax. If I wanted you dead, you all would be already." She sipped from her new glass. "Even with your muscle walking around the house."

The rich lady had a point. Kari sipped her lemonade and her taste buds sang. "Is there ginger in this?"

Gabriella gave her an enthusiastic nod. "I add some root for a few hours, and then take it out so it doesn't overpower the flavor. I also think my Sicilian lemons are far superior to what you are probably used to. Now . . ." She turned her attention to Henry once more. "While I understand that you didn't know the nature of this visit, I must insist that they both leave. What I want to discuss with you is for your ears only."

Both Kari and Finn looked at each other and then to Henry for direction.

"Go ahead inside," he said to them as if they were children and the adults had to do the 'grown-up' talking.

Finn led the way back into the cottage, drink in hand, and closed the sliding door behind them. "I can't help but think that Henry views me as expendable now."

"Because he's willing to sacrifice you to poisoned lemonade to save his own ass?"

"That'd be the reason." Finn went to a recliner, kicked the foot rest up, and assumed the optimal relaxed position. "So, what movie should we watch?"

"Do you really want to watch a movie?"

"What else can we do? Snoop around and find this underground whatever that Gabriella no doubt has massive security on and will know the second we attempt to go inside?"

"You make a good point." Rather than head to the collection of DVDs, she went to the matching recliner across from Finn but kept the footrest down. She placed her hat on the end table beside her. "Before we jump to the movie, I have a work-type question."

"I'll answer only if you answer one of my own."

"Fine." She trusted Finn now, which was something she couldn't say back when they were in St. John's. "Were you on VIP duty when Sofia Beaulieu visited?"

Finn sat up from the fully reclined position but kept their feet up. "Yes, actually. Why?"

"What was her demeanor like?"

"I mean . . . She was pretty snobby, even by VIP standards, and wasn't in the least bit nervous or intimidated by Henry. To be honest, I was shocked when I learned she committed suicide. I felt terribly for Ahmed, another VIP assistant, since he found the body."

Kari leaned forward and rested her elbows on her knees. "Interesting."

"Why is that interesting?"

"In the past three years, Henry has become the majority shareholder in four companies that all net over $400 million in worth, individually. All four of those companies had key people die in suspicious ways: two suicides, one helicopter crash, and one venomous snake bite."

"Who got bit by a snake?"

"Hanjun Liu was done in by a black mamba in Mozambique. That's how Henry got into textiles."

Finn squirmed. "It's a stretch to say that he had something

to do with all of that. Henry only wants more diversity in his investments. That's what he's always saying, at least."

Kari shook her head, but not because she didn't believe in investment diversity. Her gut told her that he was behind the deaths and the guy walking in circles outside probably pulled the metaphorical triggers. "I have a weird feeling it's all related to something bigger and I'll leave it at that. Now, what's your question for me?"

"You didn't like me when you first met me, did you?"

The question caught her off-guard and she laughed so loudly she was surprised nobody—including Josef—rushed in. "Please don't take this personally, but up until a few months ago I really didn't like anyone who wasn't one of my mothers. Also, there was that surprise morning visit, which I know wasn't your fault, but you had this smug smile that rubbed me the wrong way from the get-go."

"I wasn't smug! I was surprised you answered the door wearing only a towel! Who does that?"

"I do when I notice I'm in the middle of the ocean and I'm not supposed to be!" As she said it, she felt the pull across her cheeks from her smile. "If I had a redo, would I do it the same way? No."

"Well, that's a shame. Good thing I've etched it into my memory." Finn winked.

The smiling continued, but this time she added a non-threatening finger wag. "You better watch it."

"Or you'll do what?"

"I don't know yet, but it may involve poisoned lemonade."

Finn laughed, which brought out the chuckles inside her as well. But the good times came to an immediate halt when the sliding door opened again. Gabriella appeared as calm and collected as before, while Henry had a grin like the cat who ate the canary. Or the billionaire who now owned the Canary Islands.

He extended a hand to Gabriella. "I'll get in contact with you as soon as I have secured the asset. Finn, Karishma, time to go."

Finn said a quick goodbye and followed Henry. Kari started to leave as well, but doubled-back to pick up her hat on the end table.

Gabriella rushed to her and placed a hand on her shoulder. *I need to tell her.* "Be careful with Madeleine, but be even more careful with Henry."

The information didn't come as a surprise, but Gabriella acting as the messenger did. "What did he say to you?"

Method of asset collection for In Virtute. "I know he wants power and he intends on doing anything to get it. Including using you." She eyed Kari up and down. *A smart girl, but just a girl.* "Although, I still don't know how."

"Why are you telling me this?"

Guilt. "Because my late husband and son took advantage of many young women—and girls—the least I can do is try to start to make amends. I'm starting by looking out for you."

Chapter Twenty-Two

Tripoli, Libya

After the visit with Gabriella, Kari hadn't heard a peep from Madeleine or Henry. That was for the best. The more time she had to think about it, the more unsettled Gabriella's words made her. How were they going to use her? They could already put her anywhere in the world, with any person, and learn their innermost thoughts. What more did they want? And what was this 'asset' Henry needed to secure for In Virtute? What was In Virtute?

"Have you heard anything?" Kari asked Finn as she fired the air hockey puck at them like a bullet.

They returned the disc by banking it off the side. "Nothing about our visit with Gabriella. Although, I did learn one of Adam Cho's contacts is in Brisbane. Took a while for Madeleine to track, because he recently changed his name."

She went for a more direct line to the goal slot. "Who?"

Finn had no choice but to try a quick deflection, which caused the puck to bounce between the sides several times. "I want to say . . . Fiester."

"Fiesler?"

"Yes!" Finn said with a bright grin. "That's the one! How'd you know?"

"Something Cho thought back in Stockholm." Finn struck and slid the puck back-and-forth several more times before she asked, "Do you know any super-wealthy, powerful people with highly questionable moral fiber we'll be visiting soon?"

"Only at least one in every stop we make."

Kari laughed and in doing so let down her guard enough for Finn's puck to slide past her defenses. "Dammit!"

"Yes!" Finn's hands went in the air in triumph.

"I thought you two would go on forever," Neill said from his spot on the sideline. "I'm tagging in."

"Thank God." Finn pulled at the front of their button-down several times in an attempt to cool themselves off. "She's ruthless."

"Don't pretend you don't like it." She didn't care if that was considered flirting.

"Oh, I do. See you soon, Kari. Good luck, Neill."

"Bye!" She waved with the bright red slide pusher in her hand. Then, she squared her shoulders to face Neill in his off-duty jeans and T-shirt. One of these days she was going to have to ask him about the assortment of tattoos that covered his neck and forearms. "You ready?"

"I am, but can I make a request?"

"Sure."

"I don't want to talk about work stuff. All of that really gets me down."

The many layers of Neill continued to develop. "Okay. What do you want to talk about while we play?"

"I like art. Can we talk about that?"

Perfect timing! "Absolutely. What's your favorite tattoo?"

Chapter Twenty-Three

Tel Aviv, Israel

Kari heard the quick knock on her cabin door and glanced at the time on her phone: 8:05pm. She paused her movie, tossed the remote on the loveseat, and answered it. "You're late."

Finn stood with a bag slung over their shoulder. "Sorry, I was talking to Declan and . . . it was a little tough to say goodbye this time around."

It was hard to be annoyed when that was the reason. "Is everything okay?" Kari stepped aside to let them in.

"He's afraid to go to soccer practice, but loves soccer. I was able to pull it out of him that there's a kid picking on him for being smaller and having red hair." *Calls him a leprechaun.* "Really got to me."

"As someone who was once called bug-eyed, I can sympathize."

Don't we all. Finn patted the bag. "Where do you want to do this?"

"I thought outside on the balcony might be nice. Easier cleanup too." Kari didn't move from her spot in the entryway. If she started walking then her hair would be gone for good. "Sorry, I think I'm a little nervous."

I get it. A smile crossed their lips. "Maybe call your moms for extra encouragement?"

She mulled his suggestion over but she knew where her mothers stood. Both of them supported her decision and they respected that it was *her* decision. "I'm good, but maybe you can do a before and after picture for them."

"I think they'd like that."

Kari handed Finn her phone and posed for a quick picture. And then another. And then another where Finn snuck into the picture too. Once on the balcony, she tied her hair back in a ponytail with a series of three ties while she looked at the red-and-white-striped carousel roof on shore. She couldn't quite make out the people walking around the port market at dusk, but she knew they were there.

"What's the ponytail for?" Finn asked.

"I want to keep the hair you cut bundled for safe keeping. I thought I might pick up an ornate wooden box and store it there."

Makes sense. "Are you ready?"

Kari gripped the bottom of her chair and braced herself for the most dramatic physical transformation of her life. "Ready." There was a slight pull on her ponytail, then the sound of the metal scissor blades sliding together. Her head felt lighter, and a detached ponytail dangled in front of her eyes. She took it in her hands and marveled at the bundled strands. "This is so weird. I feel like I'm holding an arm or something."

Understandable. Finn snickered. "It was a big part of your life for a long time. Part of your identity, even. I get it."

Their clear understanding of the situation meant that she had without a doubt chosen the right person to do this job.

"Okay, for the next part—the clippers bit—can you distract me?"

Distract her?

"Just talk to me to take my mind off what's happening."

"Gotcha. Well, I've got some news for you about Gabriella's property." Finn started the electric clippers and a low buzz drowned out the sound from a random boat horn. "She has a bunker down there."

"That makes rich people sense." She fought the instinct to wince when she felt the shaver make the first pass against her scalp.

"Right? And apparently, Henry earned a private tour of it while we were in Tripoli. There are supplies to last five years. I was eavesdropping between him and Josef, so I may have missed some of the details."

Kari didn't understand people. "If the world is so dangerous that you need to go into hiding or humanity's on the brink of extinction, why would you want to survive that? If people find you, they will eat you."

That's dark. "I'd like to think I wouldn't eat anyone."

A clump of hair fell onto her chest. It was unnerving; even more so than cannibalism. "You say you wouldn't eat someone now, but you're not starving."

"True." Finn made another pass with the shaver. "I wonder which part is the most delicious."

Kari's shoulders bounced with laughter. "I can't believe we're talking about this."

"You told me to distract you! And I think I'm doing a very good job, thank you very much."

"You are and . . ." She might as well answer the question to keep the surreal conversation going and ignore the sensation that one side of her head was cooler than the other. "I don't know if it's the most delicious, but I'm going for the glutes."

The clippers were lifted from her scalp, presumably so Finn could howl with laughter. "The confidence with which you said that is alarming."

"Well, it just makes sense given the mass, and I understand there are a lot of jokes within that area, but I'm choosing not to engage in them."

"As long as you acknowledge the jokes." Finn moved the clippers over areas they had already passed. Her haircut must have reached the missed patches stage. "Aside from your willingness to eat someone, do you think you could live in a bunker?"

"No way with this telepathy thing. It's bad enough now, let alone being trapped in an underground box with who knows how many people." After a moment to reflect on the end of the world, she did reach a conclusion. "I bet I could make it better though."

Huh? "What's that?"

"Society 2.0."

"Out of curiosity, why don't you think you can do that now?"

That was a magnificent question. Why didn't she think she could do that? She had accomplished everything she had ever set her mind to. "I guess because there's other things I want to do first and if I'm going to save society, I should like more of it."

Doesn't make sense. "I'm society. You like me."

Kari grinned. "Give it time."

Finn turned off the clippers and then stood in front of her from the far side of the balcony with pursed lips and a cocked head. "Alright, I'd say we're done."

"It worries me that you intentionally stepped that far away. How do I look? And be honest, because I'll find out eventually anyway."

"You look . . ." Finn gave her a soft smile, "like how you

were meant to. No more hiding." Finn handed Kari her phone. *You are stunning.* "See for yourself."

Kari opened the camera and gawked at her new self. Her eyes were still bold, but her jawline was stronger. Her ears didn't stand out as far as she'd feared. Her neck was long. She had only one conclusion. "I look hot!"

Finn laughed. "You do look . . . very nice."

"Nice? I am so much better than nice. I look amazing!" Kari continued to marvel at her image on the phone and angled herself to view every bit of her new do. "I don't think I have any weird skull bumps or crevices either."

"You don't. And I would tell you."

Kari proceeded to take several pictures, each with a different angle and expression. She chose four and sent them to the moms. When she gave her attention back to Finn, they shook their head, amused. "Sorry, I got carried away."

"Something like this doesn't happen very often, it's okay to be excited." Finn gestured to the balcony with the clippers. "Do you need any help sweeping up? Or anything else?"

She glanced down at the patchy, dark brown carpet of her own hair. "No, I can do it." Kari grabbed her detached ponytail and headed inside with Finn trailing. "So, now that you've gotten this out of the way, do you have any actual fun plans for the evening?"

Finn closed the sliding door behind them and turned to her. *Why would she say it that way?* Their red brow lifted. *Ah.* "You know you're not a chore, right?"

"I mean . . . I kind of am. You did something you didn't have to do to help me."

"Right, but that's what friends do, and that's what we are."

The sentimental tone gave her a slight lump in the back of her throat. She turned her sudden nerves into a confident grin.

"That's right, we are. So, as your friend, do you have fun evening plans?"

"Nah. I'm doing the usual gig with one of the VIPs. A pretty important one, too."

"I wonder why Henry or Madeleine didn't ask me to come?"

"As narcissistic as they both are, they know tomorrow is a big day for you. Also, I think your next assignment is in India, which you'll learn about soon enough." Finn unzipped the grooming kit and pulled out a white envelope. "Maybe right now."

Kari snatched it out of their hand. "You're sneaky."

I am. Finn saw themself to the door. "Good luck tomorrow, and good night."

"It's really the doctor who needs the good luck, but I'll pass it on."

Once Finn left, Kari leaned her back against the door and tapped the white envelope in her palm. She should have known the pleasant evening of buzz cut would have had some sort of twist. With a shake of her shaven head, she tossed the envelope on her kitchen counter and went under her kitchen sink for the handheld broom and sweep pan. Before she could make it to the balcony, her phone rang. She threw her head back and groaned at the caller. However, being the good daughter she was, she answered. "Hi."

"I didn't want to put doubt in your mind," Mom L said, "but you really pulled it off."

"That's her way of saying you look fantastic," Mom A said. "How does it feel?"

"I had no idea how heavy my hair was."

Mom L snickered. "I bet. Is your head cold? Back in the day when I tried a stylish haircut, I remember the wind was the first thing that surprised me."

Kari started sweeping her hair. "It is weird that there's a breeze off the water and my hair isn't moving with it."

"Did you keep it?" Mom A asked.

"I did," Kari answered with a yawn. "Sorry. I've been working more this week to make up for time I'll miss during my recovery."

"We should let you get to bed," Mom L said. "But promise that you'll let us know you're okay after the surgery."

"I'll be groggy, but I'll have Mitchell text you."

"Thank you. We love you, chickpea."

"We love you so, so much!" Mom A added for emphasis.

"I love you too." Kari ended the call and tucked her phone in her pocket.

After she swept her hair clippings, there was only one thing left to do before bed. It had become part of her ritual to stare at her name written in script before sliding her finger under the crease and opening the envelope.

Good luck tomorrow. Your next assignment is dress-up in Mumbai. Stay tuned.

Kari tossed the note on the counter and headed to the bathroom for a change to her nighttime routine: a shower with antiseptic soap. Afterward, she wiped the condensation off the steamed mirror and was transfixed by her new appearance. Yet she'd have another change soon.

An incision in her scalp and holes in her skull.

———

Kari tossed and turned during the night. The combination of getting used to her pillowcase touching her scalp and worst-case scenarios kept popping into her mind. Just when she was about to drift off something like, 'What if the anesthesia wears off?' or 'What if they biopsy too much or in the wrong place?' would pop into her thoughts. She could end up still a telepath and lose the ability to read or play the guitar or speak.

The alarm sounded while she was awake.

After a morning shower with antiseptic soap, Kari headed to the tender's waiting area with her orange-flavored sports drink breakfast. There were a few double takes as she passed people on the stairs, but no one said a word. There were a couple thoughts that she embodied a punk persona, though. "I didn't think you'd both be here," she said.

Mitchell and Santos turned from overlooking the railing to her in unison. Santos's brow went to his hairline, Mitchell nodded.

"I like it," Mitchell said. "I bet it feels strange."

"It does." Her gaze went to Santos, whose surprise still hadn't left his face. "I didn't think you were coming with us, it being Charlotte's birthday and all."

The statement seemed to shake Santos from his stupor. "I still wanted to wish you luck. Today is going to be incredible. Mitchell has promised to give me updates."

"If you could add my moms to that list, I'd appreciate it." Kari glanced over to where the crew started the gangplank preparations. "We should get going. See you soon, Santos. I hope."

"Yes, you will! Take care of her, Mitchell." With that he turned and walked away.

Kari scanned her thumb and took a seat near the bow.

Mitchell sat in the same row but gave her plenty of space; he looked at his watch. "Our car is already at the dock, so we're ahead of schedule."

Kari took a deep breath and released it. "Good."

"Kari," Mitchell said and waited until she looked at him, "if I had any concern that this would put you in danger or wouldn't work, Santos and I would never have arranged this."

She wasn't sure if it was the words or the confidence he projected, but it helped. "Thank you."

He gave a single nod and turned to face forward with his hands folded in his lap.

The other passengers spread themselves out, leaving them to their row in peace. As they made their way to shore, they watched the sun rise over Tel Aviv in comfortable silence. Like all the major cities Kari had visited, the early morning dock bustled with activity. Workers unloaded cargo from ships, shops on and near the water prepared to open for the day, and traffic started to build.

According to their driver's thoughts, traffic was light.

Twenty minutes later, they pulled up in front of an intimidating, glass-walled building but with simple landscape to add some green. The building's lobby smelled like the antiseptic soap she had used to bathe.

"Neurosurgical reception is on the fifth floor," Michell said as they walked toward the elevators. "I'll stay with you the whole time. Including when you're wheeled into ICU afterward."

"Is it normal for a 'personal physician' to do that?"

"I mean, not much of this is normal, but I think them knowing that I'm your primary care neurologist makes them more comfortable." Mitchell pressed the button for the fifth floor.

"Good." The elevator doors opened and Kari stepped inside. "We should all be comfortable."

———

What was that noise? It wasn't her alarm. Sound wave by sound wave, the noise formed words. A woman spoke but it wasn't either mom. Whoever it was, they needed to leave. She hadn't invited them into her tiny house! Wait. She didn't live there anymore. She hadn't invited them into her cabin.

They were intruders!

"G-ou!" Kari yelled.

Why couldn't she talk? The intruders must have placed tiny weights inside her tongue and lips because she couldn't move her mouth. She struggled to open her eyes to see who they were, but they had placed the weights in her eyelids too. And arms. And legs. What had they done to her?

There were too many problems to solve at once. She focused all of her energy into opening her eyes to the brightness of . . . not her cabin. A woman with a salt-and-pepper bob—not one of the moms—spoke to Mitchell. Who was that lady?

Now that her eyes were open, her next goal was to work out the mouth problem. Kari stretched in a yawn-like motion and moved her lower jaw side-to-side. Then she forced her tongue to the roof of her mouth and in a circle. Success!

Now, she was ready to kick some ass.

"Get out!" She tried to point to illustrate her demand, but instead of a rigid, strong gesture, her arm flopped only a few inches off the bed.

"Kari," a voice said in a non-threatening tone, "this is Dr. Mitchell. You had surgery and you're in the recovery room. Dr. Malka is with me."

Surgery. Malka. Oh, that's right. She was in a hospital. "You saw my brain?"

The corners of Malka's lips turned upward. "I did."

"That's pretty jazzed. I'm real excited to learn why I hear people's thoughts."

"Um . . . ah . . ." Mitchell stammered. "What Kari means by

that is she worries excessively over what people think of her. She and her therapist have been working on that."

"I see." Malka approached her bedside. *Sad to see young women fixated on what others think.* "The nursing staff will monitor you and can get you anything you might need. I'm sure Dr. Mitchell will be keeping a close eye as well. I'll be back in the morning where we can hopefully talk about your discharge."

Malka left the room—which seemed to spin—to leave Kari and Mitchell alone. Kari closed her eyes.

"It might be another hour or two until the general anesthesia wears off. Do you want some water?"

"Not right now." There was something she wanted to ask but she couldn't remember what it was. She thought about her time before the surgery. Her arrival at the hospital, her review with the doctor about the procedure and what to expect after, and her talk with Mitchell. "Oh. Can you let my moms know that I'm okay?"

"I texted them when you came out of surgery, but I'll do it again to let them know you're awake. Mostly." After a pause he added, "I have another text, too. From Santos."

"What did he say?"

"Now the real science of Project ORCA begins."

Chapter Twenty-Four

The Red Sea

After the required overnight stay in the hospital and six days of bed rest in her cabin—with daily check-ins courtesy of Mitchell—Kari was ready for her follow-up telehealth appointment with Dr. Malka.

"Is Dr. Mitchell there?" Malka asked.

He leaned to the side so he was on the screen. "Present."

"How are her vitals?"

"All normal," Mitchell said. "Well, Kari's brand of normal." *Still can't believe how low her resting heart rate is.*

"Right," Dr. Malka drawled. "Can you lean your head forward so I can view the incision? It would help if Dr. Mitchell shined a light on it."

Kari leaned forward and heard the click of his pen light, then saw the extra brightness in her periphery. Over their conversation of stitching and cleaning, she would rotate her head as instructed. Her view of the keyboard reminded her that it needed to be cleaned, too. Her J key was borderline tan. So gross. "Can I lift my head now?"

"Yes, you may," Malka said. "No headaches or sensory

issues? Itching around the areas where the stereotactic frame was placed?"

"No. The incision itself is a little itchy but I was told to expect that."

"Alright then. You're progressing nicely, but I do want to do this again the same time next week so I can give Mitchell the go-ahead to remove your stitches."

"Sounds like a plan." Now was the time to ask the million-dollar question that would satisfy her other itch. "Do I have your permission to return to work?"

"As long as it's desk work, that's fine. You should still refrain from any vigorous activity that might disturb the area. No exercise."

Well, that ruled out table tennis and air hockey. "Okay, I can handle that. I'll see you next week." Kari closed their tele-health session and turned to Mitchell. "Can I analyze my brain now?"

Excited. "Santos has everything set up."

———

"While we know these cells are unique," Santos said, "I'm hoping that they will be similar enough to other neurons—my guess is a variation on a Purkinje cell—to use that method of cell culture to artificially grow more of your cells."

Kari nodded. Then, her eyes drifted over to the computer monitor set up near the microscope without its dust cover on. "You looked at them already, didn't you?"

Sorry. "I did," Santos said. "I know you wanted to be first, but we were concerned about the viability of your cells if we froze and then thawed them. On the upside, you'll be glad we upgraded to a three-photon."

Rather than a traditional light microscope or electron

microscope, a three-photon microscope allowed them to view her cells alive with extreme detail. They could interact with each other and fluorescently labeled targets would make specific areas glow. It was fascinating, as well as pretty.

"Did you find something?" Kari asked with a grimace. "I hope."

Santos grinned. "View the control cells first. It's a recording of Purkinje cells from another neuroscience lab. I have it cued for you."

Kari rubbed her hands together then took her seat in front of the monitor. She saw the complex, branched network of dendrites that made up the neurons and the different green and red fluorescent tags outline the cells in a field of blackness. It resembled a willow tree with Christmas tree lights on it. "What proteins did they label here?"

"Calcium pump and cytoskeleton."

After she had their basic patterns memorized, she looked up at Santos, who was texting Charlotte. At least that was what Kari guessed based on the list of movies he was thinking of. "Can I see my sample now?"

"You got it." Santos put his phone away and took control of the mouse and keyboard until her sample was brought up on the screen.

"Oooh," was the best way to describe her thoughts regarding what her telepathy cells looked like.

"I'm interested to hear what you think about this," Mitchell said.

What Kari saw before her was a slow, pulsating, solid green and red blob. That had to be a mistake. "To confirm, you used the same process as the control cells?"

"Yes. And I've adjusted the contrast to try to make more sense of it but I've had no luck."

Kari pursed her lips. The first and most obvious reason

would be that her cells had quadruple the number of proteins as the controls. But Kari had her doubts. It seemed too easy for that to be the reason. She stared at the nearly stationary image on the screen. That also didn't make sense. The control cells moved as they interacted. There was no way her cells were stagnant; her brain was the opposite of lazy.

"Can you slow the recording?" Kari asked. "I think the changes are so rapid, it appears like a solid image."

Huh? Santos's eyebrows arched high on his forehead.

"Let's break it down into frames," Mitchell said. *Interesting idea.*

"Worth a shot." Rather than pressing play, Santos clicked each millisecond forward.

Kari's eyes honed in on one branch of the psychedelic tree. "Next frame." The branches didn't sway. They connected.

"The hell . . ." Santos went to the next frame, where the same thing happened. "They are moving together."

More than that. "Working together," Mitchell said. "And doing so instantly. Something is either in or on those cells directing that line of communication. Like in an orchestra."

Kari leaned back in her chair as frame upon frame of her cells jumped in some sort of choreographed dance. "And the next step is identifying the conductor."

———

For days Kari couldn't tear herself away from the images. She now had evidence to substantiate her hypothesis and, because of that, there was no stopping her. Except for meals. It was aggravating that Santos would force her to leave the lab so she could eat.

"There you are!" Jade bellowed from the other end of the passageway.

Kari stood outside of her cabin door with her rice and lentil bowl. As soon as she saw Jade's annoyed face, she knew why. "I'm sorry I didn't come to the club room. I got caught up at work."

I was worried sick. "You couldn't have let me know? I haven't talked to you since your seizure surgery thing—which I still don't understand—and thought something bad happened when you were under the knife."

"It was more drill than knife."

Jade placed her hands on her hips. *Oh, she did not take that tone.*

"You're right," Kari quickly said. "I'm sorry. I'm not used to having friends and letting them know about things like that." Kari unlocked her door and gestured to the inside of her cabin with a tilt of her head. "Do you want to come inside and I can update you?"

Jade's angry posture relaxed. "Yes. Let me get my tea first."

Kari left the door unlatched and took a seat at her table. Jade came in a few moments later, hot tea in hand, and made herself at home on the loveseat.

"I take it since you're not still in the hospital or have your head wrapped in gauze, everything went to plan?"

"That is correct."

"And you're not going to have seizures anymore?"

"Not quite." Kari dipped her spoon into her dinner. "I require a follow-up procedure. We still need to identify the specific molecules in my brain tissue that cause . . . the seizures. Once we find that, then they'll go back into my brain to insert a genetically-modified—"

"Please tell me you're done after that."

"Yes and no," Kari said with her mouth full. "I have to wait several weeks for the molecule they put in to take effect before we try turning on the light of the fiber-optic cable."

Jade blew out a long breath and shook her head. "That's a hell of a lot more complicated than most surgeries I know." Jade's eyes peered over her mug as she sipped her tea. "When does the next surgery happen?"

"I'm hoping we'll have everything ready by the time we reach Australia. That's not much time, but I'm going to work my ass off to get it done. Santos, too. He's really excited about the project."

Jade waited a beat then gave a short laugh. "How can you speak about it so calmly? I'd be a nervous wreck."

Kari shrugged as she dipped her spoon down for more. She really shouldn't have skipped lunch. "I think it helps that I understand the process, but it beats the alternative."

"Yeah, but you speak about it like you're getting a mole biopsied. This is your brain! I'd be freaking out if I needed brain surgery. Twice!"

"I think if you had to live my life, my choices would seem less alarming." The lentils really were amazing. Too bad she couldn't go back for more.

"That's a fair point. How easy was it to shave your head?"

"Emotionally or in practice?"

"Both."

"I was nervous, but again, it needed done so I didn't really have an option. Doing it was easy because I didn't wield the clippers," Kari said with a flourish of her spoon.

Jade's brow scrunched. "Who did?" When Kari remained silent, a burst of laughter erupted from her. "I guess I don't have to keep my eyes peeled for potential dates when you have Finn on the line. No! Scratch that. I settled too young and look what happened. A young woman should play the field. See who else is out there, like maybe there's a tall, square-jawed blonde at WU who I saw in the office this week checking out the sapphic club flyer. You're cool with that, right? You're an everysexual?"

"Okay. One, it's pansexual. Two, I don't need to or want to date right now, even if flirting is fun. I'm perfectly content with two jobs, traveling the world, and having friends. I'm not used to having friends and I need to learn how to be a good friend before I date. Three, I think it's weird and a major conflict that you'd set me up with one of your students."

"I see your point, but just so you know, Belle isn't one of my students. According to WU's policy the only problem would be if I dated her, which I have no interest in doing."

"Glad to hear you're not compromising your teaching ethics." Kari was about to load her spoon once more when there was a knock at her cabin door. Aside from Jade, there was only one person who would do that. Kari pushed herself away from the table. "You can't laugh."

"Why?" Jade smirked. "Are you expecting a certain red head?"

Kari grumbled and went to the door. Before she opened it, she wiped the corners of her mouth with thumb and forefinger and pulled down her bunched shirt.

"You look fabulous," Jade said with a snicker.

"Shut up." Kari opened the door, but Finn was not on the other side of it. "Mitchell?"

Urgent. "We have to talk," he said in a grave tone. "Right now."

Jade got up from the loveseat. "I should probably go, then. Don't be a stranger, Kari."

Once Jade was back into her apartment, Mitchell still lingered in the hall despite Kari's gesture for him to come into her cabin.

This is bad.

"What's wrong?" Kari asked as Mitchell wrung his hands in the passageway.

Not here.

"Okay. I'll follow you." Despite her long legs, she struggled to keep up with Mitchell as they left her cabin. He hadn't said a word and they weren't heading in the direction of the lab. "Where are we going?"

He closed the distance between them. *A place that isn't bugged. Like our lab is.*

About a dozen different questions rushed to Kari at the same time, but she kept them to herself until they were at the railing on deck ten with a fuzzy view of the moon behind a cloud.

I found a bug in an outlet.

Kari took a breath. This wasn't the end of the world. They hadn't discussed anything in the lab that Henry and Madeleine didn't already know, but Mitchell and Santos didn't know that. She couldn't tell Mitchell the details, but for his safety he couldn't investigate this any further. "Does Santos know?"

No. I came to you first since it's you I'm worried about. Aside from us, only the highest level of security on the ship know our code and, because of our conversations, they know you're a telepath! He paled as though he was going to lose his lentils over the rail. "They'll strip my medical license. Santos will probably be evicted and be fired from inCog. God, what have we done?"

Kari placed a gentle hand on his forearm. Maybe she had powers of healing intention she hadn't discovered yet? "First, please calm down. I promise you won't lose your license and Santos won't lose inCog."

Mitchell scoffed and walked out of range. "Because you can hack into their auditory systems and memory? I don't think so."

Okay, no powers of healing intention. She had to come

clean or Mitchell's frantic state would be how everyone on the ship learned. "Okay, so I'm going to tell you something, but you *can't* tell Santos and you *have* to remain calm. Okay?"

With his hands on his hips, he closed his eyes and gave a nod.

Kari supposed that was good enough since there was no way he could guess where this was headed. "Henry and Madeleine already know I'm a telepath."

"What? How?"

Kari had to give him credit for not screaming those two complex but short questions. "I can't give you the details, because that would put you at risk, so let's just say that they know and are using it to their advantage."

"Their advantage?" Mitchell cocked his head and folded his arms. He stood perplexed for several moments. Then, he gasped. "They're using you to get information from people. To spy on them!"

"Stop yelling," she said through gritted teeth. "There are non-hidden surveillance cameras all over the decks. Just come closer."

His jaw dropped. *She didn't deny it.* "Why would you agree to do that? It's not because of the surgery, is it?"

"No—although, that is a perk. Let's just say that, hypothetically speaking, the people they would want me to extract information from would be very flawed people. They'd be cheaters and traffickers and spousal abusers, and I would get to do something about it. I could see that there were less victims in this world."

This isn't hypothetical at all. He inhaled a sharp breath. *That's why she was with Julius Fermi.* "This is why the lab has been getting so much money for the project."

Kari gave him an almost imperceptible nod.

This is insane. Mitchell rubbed the stubble on his face and leaned back against the rail. But walked to her again. "I'm intentionally getting closer." *If they're using your telepathy, then why would they finance our research? We're partially removing your ability.*

"It goes back to the four years of service in my contract."

He stood with his hands on his hips and looked at her. *How could she be so stupid?*

"I'm not stupid and I didn't seek this out! I'm making the best of a situation I had no control over."

No control? She's so delusional. Mitchell paced along the rail and then in a circle, all while never making eye contact with her. He eventually walked back to her, leaned his forearms against the railing, and looked out to the sea. *How do you know they won't stab you in the back? Or inCog?*

"I know that as long as I play by their rules, we're all safe."

I hope you're right. Mitchell walked away and into the belly of the ship.

Chapter Twenty-Five

Mumbai, India

Kari stared at herself in the full-length mirror on Madeleine's bathroom door. The spike-heeled boots were shiny, white, and reached her knee. The pink and yellow paisley dress fell just under her butt cheeks and the material missing to the scoop-neck must have gone to the sleeves since her wrists looked like they had their own skirt. She slid open the closet door. "I feel like jail bait from the 1960s."

"I can't help how you feel," Madeleine replied from her secret office. "And given that you'll be nineteen *very* soon, you've passed the age of consent almost everywhere in the world, so no baiting here. How's the wig feel?"

The black hairy mass still lay on the sink's countertop like a passed-out terrier. "I didn't put it on yet."

"Well, get to it! You and Henry have to leave for the party in ten minutes."

Kari still had difficulty coming to terms with the fact that she had to go to a 1960s themed costume party for a famous Bollywood—and a little Pollywood—producer's sixtieth birthday. She pulled the cap on and then tugged and moved the wig into position. Kari had to admit she looked as though she had stepped into another era.

Telepath and quasi-time traveler, at your service.

Kari took the comb that had been laid out and gave herself a perfect part down the center. The wig had bangs, which made the styling even weirder. She leaned forward on the counter and brought her face closer to the mirror. So many parts of her life had changed, but at least this still felt like dress up.

She entered Madeleine's office at the same moment Henry did from the conference room side. He wore a loose suit, circular-framed glasses, and a messy white wig.

"I'm Andy Warhol! Are you ready, Karishma?"

"If by ready you mean, 'learn Pawar's dirty secrets,' then yes, I am ready."

———

Like the New Year's party back in Oregon, Kari spent the first half of the party in a quiet, dark corner observing the crowd. Unlike New Year's back in Oregon, this corner was in a swanky, skyrise penthouse. She watched the debauchery of the rich and famous unfold before her eyes while she sipped sparkling water from a short, glass tumbler. She added her own ice and a slice of lemon to make it resemble a cocktail. There was less pressure to drink from the others that way and thus was more difficult to slip her something.

Which could happen anywhere, but with visible drugs around, the odds seemed higher.

Sobriety allowed her to take in the scene more. And there was a lot to see. Beside the copious drugs and alcohol, there were fit, attractive, and sometimes naked people walking about.

She imagined somewhere in the penthouse there was an orgy. There had to be.

Once she spotted Syed Pawar in his orange and gold kurti with his coiffed black hair and trim beard, she kept a careful eye. He spent an unusual amount of time with a specific waiter who circulated champagne. Kari learned the server's name was Aarav and he was delighted she spoke Marathi. Via his thoughts she learned he believed she was sexy even with her clothes on, and when he wasn't working parties he helped with inventory on an opium operation in Kashmir that Pawar ran. Aarav feared Pawar who would beat, if not straight-out murder, anyone who messed with his opium poppies or final products.

She didn't feel terrible about giving Henry the scoop on him later. Pawar was a cinema king by day and a drug lord by night. And during the day, too.

The opium took up a lot of his time.

Kari excused herself from Aarav's company and found an area on the terrace to tell Henry the details she learned about the illegal drug trade. That was when he referred to Pawar as "the asset" and could soon appease Gabriella. With his blessing, she left. No part of her wanted to party, and every part of her wanted to take the wig off and sleep in the limo. Since Neill was the driver, she could let her guard down.

Thank the Gods it wasn't Josef and his psychopath vibes.

She knew Neill was worried about her, but he had good reason to. She had been pulling fourteen-hour days in the lab performing detailed lab work so they could beat the clock and have everything done before Australia. She was stressed and exhausted, but inCog saw the finish line up ahead.

———

"Good morning!" Santos said with zeal.

Kari glanced over to the molecular portion of the lab. She could see his hands donned in blue gloves inside the laminar flow hood. On the stainless-steel surface were a variety of different solutions and small plastic tubes. "Hi," was the only word she had the energy to say.

"Did you have a good day off?"

She shrugged. "Eh."

His pleasant demeanor morphed into one of neutrality. "Well, I appreciate you coming in—especially on a Sunday morning—but I have good reason, and I'm sure you'll be just as excited." He took his hands out from the hood and tossed his gloves into the biohazard trash. "We found the protein."

Kari never knew sleep deprivation could disappear in an instant, but now she did. "When?"

"I came in yesterday to tend to the cells, do the mass spectrophotometry analysis, etcetera. I finished pretty late, so I sat down with the results this morning, and that's when I found it. Why don't you get logged in and we'll pull everything up on the conference TV."

"Absolutely!" Kari headed to her computer and saw Mitchell. "Have you seen the data?"

Her conversations with Mitchell since the discovery of the lab's bug were limited to only work. Every so often he would look at her and shake his head. His disapproval grated on her nerves more than she would have thought, but she reminded herself that he didn't understand the complete situation, so she let him be judgmental and angry. It was another side of Mitchell.

Maybe it was this side that caused his wife to cheat on him.

"Santos was waiting for both of us to get here." Mitchell waited for her to boot up her computer before he said, "You look exhausted. Did you have to *translate* yesterday?"

To Santos and those listening via the bug, the question was

innocuous, but the edge in his voice was clear. "I did need to speak some Marathi last night, but now I'd like to put that to the side and get to work."

On the large TV was a graph of several black vertical lines. "This is the analysis of the proteins in the control neuron sample. Everything is standard. No surprises." He clicked the remote, and the graph overlapped with a new one that had green vertical lines instead. "Almost identical to your tissue sample, except for one." He used the red laser pointer and circled the single green spike. "Meet—what I believe is—the conductor of the telepathy orchestra."

"Have you verified this?" Mitchell asked.

"I ran the sample three times. Every time with the same result."

Kari approached the screen. It was all she could do not to reach out and touch the thin green line. "When can we isolate it?"

"We can start immediately. The sooner we do that, the faster we can create the vector."

"What can I do while you two are in the lab doing that?" Mitchell asked.

"Call your contact in Melbourne and try to get a surgical suite," Santos said. "Also, you can order the remote and wireless transponder we found earlier. It's time."

———

Kari's cabin door practically jumped off the hinges from whoever pounded on it. All she knew was it wasn't Finn. That wasn't their style. She put down her rehydrated spaghetti—she missed dinner service, again—and answered.

Don't scare her. "I need help!" Jade yelled in her face and ran back toward her cabin.

Kari followed without question. When she entered Jade's cabin she froze in the doorway from what she saw before her.

"Surprise!" Jade and Finn yelled, while Neill blew into a party favor that made a honk noise. A Happy Birthday banner that had seen better days hung over a colorful but understated cake. The dominant white frosting was smooth on the top and ridged along the sides. The decoration and birthday message were a lush green with lavender and daffodil flowers that reminded her of a springtime field. There were presents on either side of it.

Kari cried on the spot. She hadn't had a birthday with more than one true friend ever. "I'm sorry," she wiped away her tears, "I'm just really happy. No one's ever . . ." Kari didn't think it was possible, but she cried harder. The combination of stress and the thoughtful gesture broke her.

"Oh, come here." *Hope she'd like it, but this degree surprises me.* Jade gave her a hug while also closing the cabin door behind her.

"Thank you so much. All of you." Kari pulled herself together and took the tissue Finn offered.

Snot bubble. "Happy birthday, Kari," Finn said. "Unfortunately, Neill and I can't stay long, so . . ."

"Open our presents now!" Neill bounced at the knees. "Mine is the one wrapped in aluminum foil because that's all I had in my cabin."

Kari discretely dabbed at the mucus trickling from her nose and giggled. Actually giggled and went to the shiny and shallow rectangular box. She tucked the tissue in her pocket. Even though Finn and Neill were in a rush, she savored peeling away the aluminum layer and lifting the cardboard lid. Inside, the rubber of a table tennis paddle's surface had been removed and in its place was a painted scene of her and Neill playing. "Wow. This is . . . Did you do this?"

Neill gave her a shy smile. "You know I appreciate art; I just didn't tell you I liked painting, too. I thought that'd ruin the surprise. Flip it over."

On the other side, the rubber was also removed and he'd burned into the wood, *Happy 19th birthday, Kari. From, Neill.*

"I was able to borrow one of the tools from engineering to write it myself."

"That makes me love it even more. Thank you." Kari looked to Finn, who gave her a sweet smile. "I guess yours is next." She picked up the gift bag with balloon print and read the tag. Five names had been crossed out, including Finn's, before her name was written. "I guess I should keep this for the next birthday."

"Correct," Finn said. "I hope I didn't overstep and that you like it."

Kari grinned and dug through the pastel tissue paper to pull out a wooden box that had the tree of life burned into the top. Curious, she opened it up to find that its black velvet-lined inside was empty.

Confused. "It's for your ponytail," Finn said. "I didn't know if you found a place for it yet. If you already did, maybe you could use this for tea or something."

The tears came again. She had to focus on getting simple, intelligible words out. "I didn't get anything for my hair yet. Just stuffed it in a big envelope."

"Finn made the design too," Neill said. "We learned how to do it together."

Her smile grew at the imagery of the two of them learning how to do arts and crafts together. Since they were both standing side-by-side, she placed her arms around both of them at once.

She's so tiny.

You're very, very welcome. Please blow your nose again.

"I love both of my presents." She released them from the hug, blew her nose with a new tissue, and saw Jade, who waggled her eyebrows and had a flashlight in her hand. "What's that for?"

"We can't do candles for your cake because of the fire regulations, so we're going to sing and you can blow out the flashlight." Jade approached the cake and turned on the flashlight so the beam hit the ceiling. "Ha . . ." she started until Neill and Finn picked up the cue and started singing *Happy Birthday*.

Her cheeks hurt from smiling during the out-of-tune number. When they reached the conclusion of the song, she made her wish and then blew across the flashlight, which Jade turned off with a *whoosh* noise. Kari couldn't wait to dive into her third gift, the two-tiered baked masterpiece. It didn't matter what the flavor profile was. She knew it would be delicious, but it was a shame they'd have to ruin the artistry.

"Can I get a picture of everything and everyone before Finn and Neill have to leave?"

"Absolutely. This is your day." Jade took out her phone. "Let's do a group photo; I'll set a timer." Jade directed them into perfect positioning and, after a five second countdown, the flash went off. She went to her phone and studied the picture. *My boobs look good. Neill's a stud.* "I'll send this to you. I'm sure your moms will like it."

"Thank you so much. I can't really put into words how I feel right now, but I'm twitchy in a good way."

I'll never top this. Jade cackled. "We're glad you liked it. I'm just sorry I had to scare the hell out of you to get your ass over here." Jade turned her attention to Finn and Neill. "Cake to go?"

Kif! "That'd be wonderful," Neill said, not wasting any time. *So kind.*

Jade cut four generous pieces, placed two into to-go

containers and two slices on plates. She stacked the to-gos and handed them off. Neill and Finn gave their thanks and headed Kari's way toward the door.

"It was great to finally talk to you, Jade," Neill said and paused in front of Kari. "Happy birthday."

He headed out and Finn was next in the leave line. *Good to see her happy.* "I'm glad you like the box." Then, Finn hugged her. "Happy birthday."

She held on long enough so the bergamot scent of Finn's hair products enveloped her. "Thank you. I'll see you soon."

Finn gave a quiet nod and left. Kari shut the door and then leaned against it. "Holy shit, Jade."

"Surprised you, huh?" Jade chuckled and put a plate on the dining table. "Eat your cake."

Kari wasn't going to fight that request. "I think 'surprised' is putting it mildly."

"I hope you don't mind that I didn't invite Mitchell and Santos." Jade took her cake to her recliner. "But I thought six people in here might be a little much for everyone, let alone you."

"I appreciate that." Kari took her first bite and an explosion of coconut, lime, and mint hit her taste buds. "This is the best cake ever. Thank you."

"Oh, I should have offered you a drink."

Kari shook that idea off. "I want the flavor to linger."

Jade laughed and then sighed. "Can we have some serious talk now?"

"Is this about Finn?"

"No." She pointed her fork in Kari's direction. "You look awful."

"I haven't really been sleeping well or . . . at all. I'm a bit obsessed with the project at work."

"Sounds like you're letting it consume you. You're nineteen

years old now and have bags under your eyes so deep they're like shelves. I could store my spices there."

"Maybe I have been burning the candle at both ends." Time pressure with ground-breaking work in the lab. Assignments from Madeleine. Trying to learn Henry's ultimate goal and what kind of dirt Cho had on him. It was a heavy burden.

"I know you're not over there thinking about how I mastered the texture of that cake." Jade kicked back in her recliner. "What's on your mind?"

Kari scraped icing off the plate. "I think I'm a lot like my grandparents—my Mom L's parents, not the other ones. They were obsessed with work too, basically neglected Mom L when she was growing up in the process. I don't want to do that. I don't want to forget about my family or friends."

"So don't."

"I think that's easier said than done. This project is everything to me."

"You do realize you just contradicted yourself, right?"

"How?"

Jade sent her that universal look for, 'Are you kidding me?'

Kari sighed. "Look, I would appreciate it if you just told me. I'm not a mind reader."

Jade pointed her fork at her again. "First, you can have an attitude sometimes." At Kari's offended scoff, she added, "Yes, you can. Secondly, you can only have a single top priority at a time in life. That's what makes it a priority! It's up to you whether you want that to be your relationships or your work. It can't be both.

"When you're young, it's easy to let your passion consume you because you have other people in your life reaching out. Me pounding on your door. Your moms texting you. That goes away, eventually. Faster if you don't reciprocate."

Kari thought about Jade's comment—and criticism—while

she tapped her icing-smeared fork on the plate. Mom A had sent her a picture of the chickens with their new dog, a one-year-old shepherd-Pyrenees mix named Sage, but she never replied. "I haven't been the best at responding to the moms lately."

"Then I suggest you do that when you're finished with your cake. Have you talked to them yet today? I'm sure they want to talk to their birthday girl."

"Not yet. Time zone issues."

"Make that and sleep your next two agenda items. At the mention of sleep, I swear your eyelids drooped. Plus, you devoured that slice like a starved animal."

Kari looked down at her almost empty plate. If she was in her cabin, she would have licked the crumbs and icing smears clean. She stood with the plate in hand. "Thank you very much for everything, and I'm sorry I gave you an attitude."

"Well, admitting you did it is the first step toward prevention. And I hope you don't mind me sounding like a third mom." Jade pushed in the recliner and walked toward her. *God, she does remind me of Diana sometimes.* She took the plate from Kari and put it in the sink. "Let me get this cake in a box for you."

"I get the whole cake?" Kari asked in happy surprise.

"You do. but I'm sure Mitchell and Santos wouldn't mind a piece or two." Once Jade had the cake in a white bakery box, she handed it over. *How does she look more tired?* "You get a good night's rest, birthday girl."

Once Kari was back in her cabin, she picked up the phone. It was morning back home, so they would be awake. She dialed Mom L's number first but it went to voicemail. Then, she tried Mom A's which ended with the same result.

"Hi, moms. Sorry I've been out of communication lately. I've been busy in the lab—I know that's no excuse for not texting you back—but I wanted to let you know I'm okay. Actually, I'm more than okay, I just had a surprise party thrown for me. But I do need to get some sleep, per Jade's orders. I'll call back later. Love you both. Oh, and the farm animal family is very cute."

Before bed, she reheated and finished her spaghetti dinner and, because she could, had another small piece of cake. She could go to bed happy and full on the first day of her nineteenth year.

Chapter Twenty-Six

Melbourne, Australia

Piece together the telepathy protein encoded with the light-sensitive opsin and promoter. Check.

Insert all of that business into the vector. Check.

Measure the fiber-optic cable so it was long enough to reach the telepathy region. Check.

Ensure the remote makes the light turn on and off with the click of a button . . .

Kari released a long exhale, pointed the thumb-sized remote at the coin-sized receiver resting on the stainless-steel surface inside the sterile hood, and pressed the single on/off button. A small blue light turned on at the end cable. "Check!" Kari turned the light off, scrambled back to the computer, and made the notes in her lab journal. "Okay, all aspects have been triple checked by Santos and me."

"I'll be honest," Mitchell said with one of Kari's fMRI images in front of him, "I started to get nervous about the time-line when we ran out of buffer solution in Jakarta."

"And weren't able to pick up the cable in Singapore," Santos added. Fortunately, a small tech company in Perth had what they'd needed and were able to build the remote system to their specifications. Now, they were two days away from the last procedure.

She scratched her scalp and was reminded that she needed to head straight to Finn's cabin after work for another haircut. It had been months since the last one in Tel Aviv. Her hair had reached the point where it was more soft than stubbly.

Santos spun away from his computer monitor. "If you're done with that, it sounds like you're both ready for the day's inCog work. Mitchell, I still need the PET scan analysis of that prison study. Kari, you have that traumatic brain injury-deafness data."

"Another one?"

Santos nodded. "This one comes from the same group as the last one, just a different research angle. This one has chin-chillas."

Analyzing the data would make the remaining hours of her day go faster until it was time to see Finn.

———

"Are you cold?" Finn asked before setting the hair clippers to her scalp. "I can get you a sweater if you'd like."

Kari resisted the urge to take the offer, even though she was chilled on Finn's balcony. The people doing cannonballs off the massive yacht in the near distance must have been freezing. "I'm fine. This won't take long."

If you say so. Finn started the clippers. "Did you hear the news about Syed Pawar?"

"Let me guess," Kari said over the buzzing, "he was found dead by an apparent suicide and now Henry owns the largest movie studio in India."

So close. They glided the clipper against her scalp. "Pawar was murdered by some drug cartel—as were other members of his entourage—and now Henry owns the studio."

Kari performed the financial math. "Between Beaulieu, MacDonald, and Pawar he's gained over one billion dollars in assets in just over a year."

He's ambitious. Finn moved the clippers behind her ears. "I wonder what or who is next? Or when he'll have enough?"

"I don't think he'll ever be done." Kari let the silence hang as they both had the shared thought that Henry had more money than he knew what to do with yet he still sought more. More money. More power. More influence. But more power and influence to do what, specifically? Just be in Gabriella's club of the über-powerful? What did she call it? In Virtute? "What do you think Pawar got Henry?"

"A spot in Gabriella's bunker for the end of the world, maybe? I'd think you'd know since you've spent time with him."

"Ever since we visited Gabriella in Malta, he's kept an intentional distance from me. Even in Mumbai. But I kind of doubt she and Henry are sharing types. Maybe he was getting tips to build his own? A super bunker is on-brand for someone like Henry."

It really is. "Wonder where'd he put it?"

Bunker talk dominated the topic of conversation while Finn finished. The possible locations. The size. Who would be invited to stay. If it would have a bowling alley or pool.

Look at the goose bumps. "I should have insisted you wear one of my sweaters," Finn said. "You're freezing."

Kari folded her arms to aid her warmth. "I am sorry I declined your chivalry. Can you make it up to me by opening the door? It's *so* heavy."

Finn snickered. "I can handle that. But if I'm going to be

doing that and giving you haircuts, then I think I should ask for something in return."

"Like what?"

Here it goes. "I don't want to wait until the end of the world where we might be in separate bunkers to go on a date with you. What do you think?"

Kari's back straightened, her eyes widened, and her pulse quickened. They said the 'd' word. "Like a date-date where there's obvious flirting and possible kissing?"

So nervous. "Yes, that kind of date," Finn said with a grin. "But, I know you have more important and . . . stressful things in your near future. You should focus on that. I don't need an ans—"

"Yes! I say yes to date-date. Can we plan something after I've healed a bit?"

"Of course." Finn slid open the sliding door. "After you."

Kari stepped into the warmth of their cabin. She had only taken a cursory look when she came in before, but now she focused on the details. Declan's picture was centered on an end table in the living room, the refrigerator, and a nightstand. Finn's comforter was white with a massive black prop-up pillow. The kitchen, living, and mini-dining table/desk setup was the same in her cabin, but the table was pushed into the farthest most corner to allow more space in the middle. Did they dance here?

"It feels weird that I haven't been here before," Kari said.

Hardly anyone has. "That's my fault. I tend not to invite people, but you're always welcome."

Kari smiled and continued to the main door. "Thanks again for the haircut."

"I'm glad I could help." *Really, I am.*

She put her hand on the door knob to leave, but then stopped and turned to face them. After the time they had spent together and their future date somewhere on the calendar, she couldn't leave with a comment about gratitude for shaving her head. "I want you to know that . . ."

Finn didn't interrupt as she trailed off. *It's alright. Take your time.*

She gathered her thoughts and feelings and inhaled a steady breath. "On the off chance this surgery changes my personality, leaves me incapable of communication, or kills me, I want you to know that I appreciate you for more than just haircuts. You're a good friend and you make me feel like a normal person."

Her emotions are all over the place. "Kari, I have no doubt your surgery will go to plan and, I mean this in the best way possible, but you will never be normal. Telepathy or not, you're an extraordinary person."

Kari's insides buzzed and her skin grew even warmer. Without thinking, she leaned forward and pressed her lips to Finn's.

Unexpected. Don't get carried away. Finn didn't seek to deepen it, only to reciprocate what Kari was willing to give.

The contact lingered a few seconds more before she pulled away, embarrassed by her boldness. "Okay, bye." She opened the door and headed down the passageway. "I'll see you after my surgery!"

———

On her dining table, Kari had her laptop and ten envelopes laid out, each with the recipient's name in the center using her best handwriting. Kari had spent the evening drafting personalized letters to her loved ones and friends in the event something tragic happened. She was confident, but the surgery risks were higher due to the secrecy. If something went wrong Mitchell would step in the best he could, but that was it. They couldn't call for help. And there would be no record of the event.

This was a ghost surgery.

Before any major procedure like this, it was appropriate to set time aside to talk to those who meant the most. Kari opened her laptop and clicked the link to videoconference with her moms.

"Hi, chickpea," they said in unison. They were both smiling but Kari could see the crumpled tissue in her Mom L's hand. Sage's face was at the bottom of the screen, panting as his hello.

"I would have thought Mom A would be the one crying."

"Before we logged on," Mom L said, "I looked at the first family picture and the tear monster got me."

Kari knew the exact picture she was talking about. It was a hinged frame with two pictures, the first was of the moms on the day she was conceived and the second was a sonogram of her. Back on the screen, Mom A unraveled her braid and Mom L pulled at the tissue in her hand. Sage was trying to eat it. She needed to reassure them and maybe in the process, she could reassure herself. "Everything will be fine, I promise."

"We would feel so much better if you told us who was assisting Mitchell."

The less the moms knew the better. And the fact that the surgery was being led by someone who lost their medical license over substance abuse issues during a procedure was not something they needed to know. "It's Regina Specht."

Mom L narrowed her eyes, and then Kari heard the typing. Hopefully, the first thing that popped up in her internet search wasn't her obituary. Picking the name of a neurosurgeon who recently died seemed to make the most sense.

"Oh," Mom A said pleasantly, "she's very qualified."

"See," Kari said. "Everything will be fine. I will be fine."

Kari's eyes drifted to where she had written her letters. If she believed the procedure would be a success—and she did—then there couldn't be an insurance policy. It didn't make sense to have one when all it did was place unreasonable doubt in her mind.

Fortunately, she had written on paper that would biodegrade in a week.

"Can you give me a minute?" Kari asked. "I have to tend to something real quick."

Before either mom could respond, she turned off her camera and grabbed her letters. She went to the kitchen, put them inside a paper bag, crumpled it for the sake of aerodynamics, and then went to her balcony. There were worse crimes than the one she was about to commit. She threw the brown bag in an arch that landed in the Australian waters below and then went back to her computer. "Alright, now how's Sage adjusting to his new home?"

Kari listened to the moms go on and on about the hilarity and fluffiness for what seemed to be an hour, but it was worth every minute and reminded her once again how much she loved dogs.

———

"There's the woman of the hour!" Santos said from his seat on the tender. "I thought maybe you were getting cold feet."

"How do you feel?" Mitchell asked. The materials necessary for her surgery were in a red cooler by his feet. There was no biohazard sticker since that would draw attention.

Kari pulled the knit hat down over her ears. She had a cold head, not cold feet. "All things considered, pretty good. Let's just enjoy the ride in, shall we?"

Melbourne's atmosphere was leagues more bustling and

populated than she had anticipated. Logically, she knew the city was five million people strong—much larger than Los Angeles, even—but navigating the traffic and taking in the skyscrapers made her realize she had underestimated the city. But for all the activity, the air and land were clean. Kari had a good feeling about this city.

"Hello," Kari said to the neurosurgery receptionist and adjusted her bag. "I'm checking in. The name's Meg River." She hoped her Uncle River in Michigan had a shiver or sixth sense that she was thinking about him on the other side of the world.

The receptionist nodded. "You're scheduled for . . . a deep brain stimulation procedure? Is that correct?"

That wasn't the truth, but it was the correct lie. "Yes, that's right. My personal physician is here too, that may not be in the notes." Kari knew that was in the notes because she had written them when she had hacked into their computer system.

"Yes, the notes are here. Says that Dr. Mitchell is assisting Dr. Specht, who is a visiting surgeon." The receptionist raised a brow while she typed away. "Okay, I have you checked in. You and your"—she looked past Kari to Mitchell and Santos—"surgical team can wait here. A nurse will show you to your room shortly."

Kari went to the waiting area and tossed her bag under a seat positioned away from the dozen or so people there. One elderly man was in a wheelchair. A small child with a seizure helmet dangled his feet off the chair and pointed at pictures in his book so his mother and father could see. Nearest to Kari was a middle-aged woman with a floral-print scarf wrapped around her head who stared out the window.

Is she shaking? "Don't be nervous," Mitchell said. "I know that won't help, but I have to say it."

Kari gave him a soft smile. While writing Mitchell's letter, she had come to the conclusion that he had reacted the way he did about Henry and Madeleine's scheme because he was trying to protect her. "Yeah, I know. You're just looking after me."

She gets it. He nodded. "That's exactly right."

There were so many emotions coursing through her: happiness, anxiety, excitement. "I'll be right back. Nervous bladder."

After she took care of that business and washed her hands, she caught her reflection in the mirror above the sink. Stress had a way of speeding the aging clock on someone, especially around the eyes. She could have been Mom L's identical twin. Kari took off her knit cap to regain a better sense of her identity and brought her focus to the initial incision area, above and a little behind her ear. It was wild to think in less than twelve hours they'd open up that part of her again. This was what she was willing to do for a 'normal' life when, according to Finn, she was anything but.

When she left the restroom, Mitchell, Santos, and a third man were speaking to one another.

"There she is," Mitchell said and waved her over. "This is Steve, your nurse for tonight and tomorrow. Dr. Specht hand-picked him for your operation."

Code: Steve had questionable ethics.

"Should I follow you to my room?" Kari asked as Santos handed her the overnight bag.

"Yeah," he said in a broad Australian accent. *This better be worth the money.* Steve had quick steps down the hall. Clearly, he didn't want to be here any longer than he had to or be seen by more people than necessary. He turned to Mitchell and Santos but continued his pace. "You two are going to the room where Specht will meet the rest of the surgical team."

Kari's ears perked. "I'd like to go to the pre-surgical meeting, if I could."

"You can't. That would draw extra attention and, from what I understand, that is something we wish to avoid." Steve stopped outside a door labeled *Conference Room D*. A *Closed for Renovations* sign was on the door. "This is stop number one."

Mitchell turned to her. "We'll fill you in later."

"Make sure they know what they're doing," Kari said.

Mitchell laughed. "I promise. You should try and relax as much as possible."

Kari said her goodbyes and followed Steve down the hall and up two stairwells, all of which reeked of antiseptic spray. They stopped at the seventh floor and passed a dozen patient rooms before stopping at the last door in the hall.

Welcome to purgatory. "No one will be coming down here," Steve said.

"What about whoever is in these last few rooms?"

Vegetables. "This is the section for patients who are unresponsive and family members won't remove life support. I think the last visitor I saw down here was a month ago. Nurses on rotation will leave you alone, but I'd still be quiet if I were you. No loud shows or music; avoid flushing the toilet. That sort of thing."

She'd spend her night surrounded by forgotten people who were barely alive. It was official: This was the most depressing place she had ever been. The ventilation system above Kari kicked on and blew a wave of Arctic air at her. "I'll hang out quietly until the morning."

"Good. I'll tell the team which room you're in." Steve turned to walk away but stopped. "Oh, and don't eat anything after six pm. Not that they bring food down here anyway."

Once he was gone, Kari took in her accommodations. Her room was dominated by large machines, a bed not much better than a gurney, and no TV, but at least she had a private bathroom, which was good because she had the urge to pee again. Due to the rules of her stay, she'd abide by the 'if its yellow, let it mellow' rule.

She watched a movie with closed captioning on her laptop to pass the time. She was midway through the horror-comedy when there was a knock. Out of instinct, she almost said "yeah," but stopped herself. If it wasn't someone she knew on the other side of the door, her story was that she was an American tourist who had lost her credentials and needed a place to stay.

The door opened a crack. "It's us," Santos said. "Are you decent?"

Kari rolled her eyes. "The orgy just ended, but I'm clothed again." They remained in the hall. "Yes, you can come in. Although, I don't have much in the way of seating to offer you." She pointed to the single chair in the corner once she saw Santos peek his head into the room.

"We won't stay long," Santos said and held a white paper bag out to her. "Steve told us you wouldn't have any meal service, so we picked up something for you."

"Thank you." She took the bag and opened it up. An apple and chips rested on top of the wrapped sandwich. "How's tomorrow? Any changes to the plans?"

"None," Mitchell said. "What 'Specht' may lack in ethics she makes up for in preparedness. She walked everyone through their role—not that there are many of us. We were even able to cut the number down by one; Santos will act as an assistant of sorts."

Kari cocked a brow. "You've assisted in surgery before."

"I wouldn't really call a 'look out' assisting surgery."

———

If the goal wasn't to attract attention, then they shouldn't have put her in a wheelchair that rattled at every turn and bump on the way to the surgical suite.

Maintenance needs to tighten the screws on this. Kari didn't say she agreed with Steve since she kind of hated him, but she did. "Here we are," Steve said as the elevator doors opened.

The surgical floor was several degrees colder than her room and the thin hospital gown and compression surgical stockings she wore did little to ward off the chill. The colorless walls, sleek glass, and stainless steel made the environment feel even cooler.

"Good morning," Mitchell said through his surgical mask. "How are you feeling?"

"Right now, I'm freezing, but I'm ready."

That wasn't a line. Kari's nerves were steady, her bladder wasn't hyperactive, and she woke up to a reassuring text from her mothers. *A hilarious thing happened to Sage. We'll give you details and a picture later. We love you, chickpea.* They were calm or at least playing it like she wasn't going to die. That helped.

"If it's alright with everyone, I'd like to get started," said a petite woman in an accent that sounded like Josef's. That had to be the woman who stole Specht's identity. Her hair and fair-skinned, freckled face were obscured behind the teal surgical cap, goggles, and mask. Faux-Specht focused her gaze on Steve. "You may go now."

Once he left, Kari followed Specht's directions for how to position herself. Kari reclined on the gurney so that her upper body was angled forty-five degrees. To her surprise, the set up was more comfortable than the bed she had tried to sleep in. As she pulled her gown down more over her thighs, a new character came over. Whereas Specht had fair skin and hair, this person had shades of mahogany.

I don't care if this takes care of the down payment, I have to hear consent. "Is it alright with you if I administer the sedative to you now?" His cadence and accent sounded exactly like Nana Sid.

"More than alright." Kari moved her hand on top of the bed rail so he had access to the vein in the back of her hand. She felt the pinch and watched as the needle disappeared into her skin to set up the IV. This time the anesthesia was meant to knock her out only for the initial portion of the surgery.

"Now," Mitchell said, "what I'd like you to do is count backward from hundred."

"Can't I do something more original, like recite pi?"

"If that's what you want, go ahead."

"Three point one four—"

———

Muddled sounds came through a fog and to her ears.

"Hi there, Kari, it's Dr. Mitchell. You're doing great."

"What . . ." She opened her eyes to see several people dressed head-to-toe in scrubs. "Oh, I know where I am. Is my head in the cage yet?"

Hope it doesn't scar. "It is," Mitchell said. "In fact, we're about ready to unscrew the plate. You'll probably feel some vibration traveling down through your jaw. That's normal."

"Thanks all for operating on my brain." The whirring of the screwdriver started and sure enough the vibration traveled down her bone. She snickered. "That kind of tickles." Then she heard the light clang of metal on metal.

"The plate is off," Specht said. *Distract her.* "I'd like you to tell me about your favorite childhood memory."

"That would be when I was five and got my dog. I love dogs so much. It's nice my moms just got one." Kari continued to describe Sage to anyone who bothered to listen. "And I have no doubt he will protect those chickens."

"Very good. We are in proper position." *I wonder what this will actually do.* "Injecting in three . . . two . . . one . . . now."

"I miss having a dog," Kari said. "I said hi to a white-bellied sea eagle in Perth, but it's not the same."

Duh. "I'm sorry to hear that," Mitchell said in a calm, collected voice "We have one more step, so we're going to increase your sedative drip again. You're going to feel a little vibration now. This time she's screwing the new plate in with the transponder."

"That's jazzed. Can I still talk about dogs?"

"Sure," Mitchell said. "Name all the breeds of dogs alphabetically."

Kari only reached basset hound.

———

Kari opened her eyes. She was no longer in the surgical suite, rather in her hospital room. Mitchell sat in the corner, phone in his hand. She opened her mouth to speak but had the worst cotton mouth of her life. "Hey," she forced out of her throat.

He put his phone down and approached the bed. "You're awake!"

"Am I not supposed to be?" She mumbled and tried to reach her bedside drink.

"Don't move too much." He got the drink and placed a straw in front of her mouth. *Easy does it.*

She sipped from the bendy straw. "How did it go?"

Santos got queasy. "Surgery went great. Your scalp is probably still numb from the local."

With caution, she took her hand and moved it toward her head.

"Don't touch it! I'll show you the picture I took earlier." He grabbed his phone off a thin white box from the window ledge and turned his phone around so she could see the picture of her scalp from the operating room. *Don't want infection.*

The round, black transponder was raised a few millimeters above the marked and brown iodine-stained skin of her scalp. There were marks on her forehead above the outer corner of her eyebrows from the stereotactic frame's titanium pin sites. "That's so wild. Did you let my moms know I'm okay?"

"I did. But if you give me a moment, I can let them know you're awake. Do you want me to send them the picture?"

"Picture, no. Update, yes." The picture would freak Mom A out for life. She'd call them once the drugs were out of her system. "What's that white box on the ledge?"

"Steve brought it up an hour ago." He walked the box over to her. "There's a card that goes with it."

When she read the name of the store on the box, *Coultier Candies,* Kari didn't need to read the card to know who they were from. "Yeah, I bet she does want me to get well soon."

Chapter Twenty-Seven

Coral Sea

A week had passed since the surgery. Every hour of every day she had thought about whether or not the procedure worked but they had to wait. Not only did she need to heal, but the injection needed time to settle in with the specific cells. And like the first surgery, she was confined to her cabin to rest and limit her exposure to pathogens.

"Looks good," Mitchell said as he hovered above her while she sat at her dining table. He turned off his pen light with a click. *How does she heal so fast?*

"Does that mean I'm cleared to wash my own hair and leave my cabin?" She missed the outside world. She missed table tennis and air hockey with Jade and Neill. Joking in the lab with Santos. Possibly flirting with Finn. Okay, definitely flirting with Finn.

"As long as you use the baby shampoo I left and are very gentle, you should be fine." Mitchell walked around and took a seat in the dining chair across from her. "And yes to getting out of your cabin. You can return to light activity, like coming back to work or playing guitar."

"Until when?"

Probably a month. "I want to monitor your healing progress and conduct basic neurological tests to make sure you're not experiencing side effects. Infection isn't the only thing we need to be concerned with. We did something never done before to the human brain. Let's be cautious."

"But . . ." How could she ask without sounding rude? "But we can do that in the lab, right? You don't have to come here anymore."

Space invader. He grinned. "Am I cramping your style?"

"It's less about style and more about my living space feeling like a hospital. You have a very clinical demeanor, which I appreciate and it gives me fond memories of my Nana Sid and Nani Tanha, but I'd like to keep my cabin more fun and carefree."

"I can live with that." Mitchell stood to leave. "So, what are your plans now that you're free?"

Kari smiled. "I have some ideas."

———

Since it wasn't quite dinnertime, she sent a text, walked up to deck ten, and bought a Jamaican blue mountain coffee. She claimed a lounge chair overlooking the sea while the breeze tickled her scalp. It felt like ages since she and Mitchell sat here, talked over coffee, and admired the view of New York City. Now, she was on the other side of the world on their way to Papua New Guinea, where they would spend a month for the ship's annual maintenance. A whole month in one place.

She hadn't done that since London.

"Well, well, well," Finn said from behind her. "Look who's out again in the world."

They arrived faster than she had thought. She looked over

her shoulder to see Finn's wicked smirk. Why was it that depending on the relationship you had with a person, it changed the meaning of their expressions? "Thank you for the get well texts and funny animal videos," she said, "but Madeleine sent a chocolate sampler. Just saying."

"I'm always being outdone." Finn shook their head and tsked. "Regardless, it's very nice to see you out and about. You can only get so much from texts and pictures, even if I did enjoy the banter and brainstorming date ideas."

"About that, remember that I'm still only cleared for light activity, which includes, but is not limited to: sitting on my ass in various places, consuming calories, and talking."

"I think we can make that work." They sat in the lounge chair on the opposite side of the round table between them and reached for her free hand. *Nice way to spend a few minutes.*

Kari smiled behind her mug. "Where are you off to?"

"Helipad. And before you ask, all I know is that the VIP is the richest person in Darwin, and they're mad the ship didn't dock there."

Madeleine was sure to start putting her to work now that she could work at inCog again. "I'll probably be called for the next VIP."

"Are you up for it? That may not be a 'light activity.'"

"Depends. If it's clearing dishes, I can do that. If it's ballroom dancing turned into self-defense, probably not."

Finn puffed out their chest. "I'll protect you," they said in a dramatic, low voice.

Kari laughed. "Just because I had a little brain surgery doesn't mean I'm a damsel in distress."

Hardly. "You at five percent are more formidable than one hundred percent of most people." *And I do mean that.* "So," Finn drawled, "before I leave, I had another idea about our date. We dock at Henry's private island Saturday and the beach is right there. I can bring lunch. Sound good?"

The date was actually happening. "I'd love that."

"Great! I'll see you Saturday, eleven o'clock your cabin."

"Yes—oh! Can we meet at the tender? It's only because Jade might come out and make it awkward."

I can also see that happening. In response, Finn held her gaze and kissed the back of her hand. "Eleven at the tender on Saturday, then. See you soon."

Even after they left, Kari relished in what was probably the sexiest thing that had ever happened to her. Way sexier than when Julius Fermi kissed her hand. She thought about Finn's kiss as she finished her coffee, headed back to her room, and ran into Jade.

"Hey!" Jade said with a smile. "I appreciate that note you left on my door indicating that you weren't dead and were healing in your cabin staying away from germs. Good job!"

Kari grinned bashfully. She could be taught! "Thanks."

"So, how are you feeling after the surgery?"

"I'm so great! Do you want to get dinner later? If you say yes, I can also tell you about my upcoming beach date with Finn."

Jade gasped. *Finally! Neill owes me twenty.* "I would love that. I have all kinds of unsolicited advice to give you."

Chapter Twenty-Eight

Henry's Island, Papua New Guinea

Kari stood in front of her full-length mirror and gave herself a once-over. The bikini wouldn't 'wow' Finn since they had already seen her in it during the infamous hot tub assignment, but at the same time the swim wear was comfortable and matched her floppy beach hat. She pulled on a pair of fashionably distressed denim shorts and a tank top to complete her beach look. That was date preparation in record time.

Not having hair to style really helped.

Kari grabbed two towels and left her cabin. She wasn't even halfway down the passageway when she heard the squeak of Jade's door open. Kari turned to see Jade with a grin. "You need to oil your hinges."

"And you need to remember what I told you," Jade said in a serious tone. "Beach makeouts sound fun in theory, but the sand goes in all the crannies and gets uncomfortable fast. On the flip side, pay attention to whether or not Finn applies lotion under your bikini strap. You don't want to get burned just because they might be bashful."

"That second part is a good point." Kari walked away then hollered, "I'll see you later."

"I want a full report!"

Kari waved in response and made her way to the tender. The vessel had a new element: armed guards. "What's with extra security?" she asked the queue monitor while she scanned herself to board.

Pirates spotted. "Just a precautionary measure. We ask that you stay on the beach or the island's amenities at all times."

"Will security be on the beach?"

Less kidnapping. "Yes."

Kari sucked in her lower lip and released it with a pop. "Okay, then. No adventuring for this lady beyond the beach."

"I'm going to agree with you, even though I do like to live a bit on the wild side."

Kari turned and was face-to-face with Finn, who dressed in a white sarong tied at the side, a loose cornflower blue v-neck, and a cloth bag slung over their shoulder. Their muscular and hairless leg escaped from the sarong's slit. They ran a hand through their red hair and brought most of it forward to fall over their shoulder. The copper tones in their oversized sunglasses matched well.

Is she staring at my leg? "You look very nice."

Kari's eyes quickly looked away from the definition in their quadriceps to Finn's eyes behind the tinted lenses. "Compared to you, I feel underdressed. And then I'll feel really underdressed once I take off my clothes."

They lowered their sunglasses and grinned. *Care to rephrase?*

"Oh! I meant because of my bikini. That kind of underdressed. This isn't a naked date. I'm still not permitted to have vigorous activity."

Vigorous? Wow.

"Oh, Gods." Why was she still talking? "Anyway . . ." Kari ducked her head.

Oh, she's embarrassed now.

She hated confirmation that she had made a fool of herself and even more so that she then acted coy about it. "Do you want to grab a seat beside the serene, crystal blue water and the guy with the machine gun?"

"Sounds perfect." Finn followed until they reached their seats. They were ignored by the security guard clad in full tactical gear and an earpiece. *Guy is armed to the teeth. Has to be boiling in that outfit.* "Thank you for remembering the towels."

"It's the least I could do since you brought lunch." Kari studied the guard's vest. Was that a grenade? "Was the security like this last year when you came to PNG?"

"I didn't go last time." *Oh no. She's stressed.* "Is this too uncomfortable for you?"

Terrifying was more like it, but what were their other options? Stay on the boat where they would definitely be spied on. "I'm good. What did you bring?"

Finn opened the bag to reveal two silicon cups and different insulated bags. "A little charcuterie, wine, and water."

This was like a real, adult date. They were about to head off to a secluded beach with food and wine, but with no chaperones or curfews or even roommates. Armed guards, yes, but they wouldn't break up a makeout party. Was making out vigorous activity? Shit. Okay, she could figure this out. Her maximum heart rate was 140 beats per minute due to her abnormally low resting heart rate. Now, 80% of that was—

Now she's anxious. Also, tension? "Is the picnic idea alright?" Finn asked. "Your"—they waved a hand over Kari— "emotions are changing. Fast."

"I love the picnic idea. I just got a sudden case of the first date nerves, that's all."

"You're sure?"

"Yeah." Kari decided to come clean because it was better than lying or hurting their feelings. "You're only the second person I've ever gone on a date with and that first date was over two years ago, so I'm not real experienced." She smiled, but it was more of a grimace. "And now I'm making it weird."

"No, you're not." Finn placed a hand on Kari's knee. *Oh, probably too much.* They lifted their hand. "Let's focus on having a good time."

Kari exhaled and nodded. "Good. That's good. Also, knee touches are fine."

Even though they were surrounded by armed guards, the fifteen-minute ride to the beach—complete with reciprocated hand-on-knee action—relaxed her. Finn noted the peak of an inactive volcano on the other side of the bay. A pod of dolphins that raced beside the boat caused any remaining tension in her shoulders to melt away. There was beauty everywhere Kari looked, including the lush green of the island's palm trees as they grew closer.

They pulled up to the pier and the boat hands tied them off while the security guards stayed vigilant.

Kari turned to Finn. "I'm going to let you take the lead since you have a more solid plan than I do." She followed Finn as they disembarked and walked to a worn, sandy path. There was a sign with arrows pointing in the direction of the snorkeling shop and the beach. Kari had expected Henry's private island to be more isolated, but considering they were a short boat ride away from cities, like Kimbe, it made sense that there was a stable, local economy based on Henry's activities. Especially when the *Hinewai* was docked.

Finn took the turn for the beach. Both of their steps

crunched on the combination of sand and pebbles as they headed in the direction of the gray sand, no doubt influenced by the nearby volcano. Once they stopped, Kari handed a towel to Finn, who laid theirs down in a palm tree's sliver of shade. She put hers down beside them, allowing a narrow strip of sand to come between them.

Finn sat with their legs crisscrossed and took the different items out of the bag, one by one. "I'm sorry to say that the ship store did not have any sparkling wine or champagne." Finn pulled a bottle of white wine out of one of the insulator bags. "I hope pinot grigio is okay."

"I'm sure it's fine."

Finn searched in the side pocket. *Where is it? Dammit.* "You wouldn't by any chance have that multi-tool with you, would you?"

"You know I do."

My hero.

Kari pulled the tool out of her pocket and flipped open the corkscrew. She used the end to cut the foil, then uncorked it, and handed the bottle back. "So, when did you start thinking about asking me out?"

Getting right to the good stuff. Finn chuckled and poured the wine. "Once I was pretty sure you didn't hate me anymore . . . I would say it was when you asked me to cut your hair. Then, I knew I had won your trust, but wasn't sure if you were attracted to me. I had to work up the courage to find out."

Kari cocked her head. "You couldn't see that I was attracted to you with the emotion reading you can do?"

Finn shook their head. "That only works in . . . arousal situations." *Hope not too much.* Finn handed Kari a glass.

Yeah, she wasn't going there. "So, what are we cheersing to?" Kari asked.

"How about to friends in unlikely places?"

"I like that. Cheers." Their silicon cups touched without a sound.

Kari sipped the light-bodied and tart wine. It'd be more delicious and fun with bubbles, but it was the thought that counted. "That's good."

It was the only one they had. "When we were in France, Henry made me take a sip of some sort of wine that is considered to be one of the top ten in the world." Finn puckered their mouth. "But it tasted like pure vinegar."

"I think there's a code somewhere that once you're rich, you have to like expensive things just because they're expensive."

"I work around a lot of wealthy people and I'm going to have to agree with you. Money doesn't buy taste or class."

"I'll cheers to that, too. Does Declan know about all of the lavish lifestyle items you see?"

"He knows there are wealthy people who visit the ship, but he thinks I'm isolated from it. That I live in traditional cruise ship quarters, share a room with another dancer in our show. For his own good, I'll keep that lie going."

"How about the other secret?"

Finn sighed. *That's tougher.* "I know I'll have to tell him I'm his parent someday, but I have no idea when. Probably when our therapist recommends it. I'd like to do family counseling with him once I'm released from my contract with the ship."

"That sounds wise."

She let the comfortable silence hang until Finn spoke again. *I should bring up the elephant in the room now.* "Thank you for never pushing the Peyton thing."

Gods, it had been months since she heard little Declan call the person she knew as Finn that name. "You're welcome. I figured you would tell me if and when you were ready to and you trusted me knowing that. Just like if you ever wanted to elaborate on your identity."

Not many understand. Finn nodded. "I feel like Peyton was my old life where I was forced to live as a teenage boy, and got me in trouble. When I started on the ship, Madeleine told me this was my new life, so I asked if I could have a new name to go with it. In that regard, she gave me a wonderful gift."

Kari thought about the arrangement for her surgery. For Madeleine, it was less about giving a gift and more about securing the long-term investment of her worker bees.

"Redefining myself non-binary was really freeing. I simply don't conform to the gender practices or roles I don't feel comfortable with, like having a hairy chest, and accept the ones I do feel comfortable with. I can be my own person and I finally feel comfortable being in my own skin."

Kari grinned. "I think that's great. Thank you for telling me."

"You're welcome, and thank you for never pushing." Finn released a small chuckle. "I was worried how Declan would react, but he understands more than most adults."

Children did have a flexibility with their thinking that many adults lacked. "Do you have an idea of where you and Declan will live?"

Good question. Finn cocked their head. "I don't know, actually. I hate the winter in Newfoundland, so I'm not against moving. Maybe I'll rent an RV and travel around with him until we find a place we'd both like to settle." Finn had a unique smile reserved for when they spoke about Declan; it was pure warmth and caring. But then a sadness crossed their features. *Miss him every day.*

"Have you ever thought of wearing something that reminds you of him?" Kari lifted the firestarter out from under her tank top. "My moms gave this to me before I left. It's simple, but when I miss them I can feel this against me and . . . it helps."

Incredibly sweet. "That's a good idea. Maybe we could

make bracelets together during some kind of arts and crafts activity."

"I think Declan would really like that."

Finn finished their wine and reached for the bag. "Would you like a snack?"

"I would but we have to get into the water before we eat. There's a rule."

"For swimming laps maybe." When she responded with a frown, Finn sighed. "Fine, but only a quick dip because I haven't put my sunscreen on yet."

"Deal, let's go." Kari hadn't grown up near the ocean, so any time the opportunity arose she couldn't wait to dive in. The ocean was powerful, and the more you fought it, the more it pummeled you. She respected that.

Before she took off her own clothes, Kari watched as Finn stripped off their shirt revealing more lean muscles in their chest and abdomen. Then, she mirrored Finn's actions and tossed her tank top to her towel. It was tempting to close their distance to learn what they thought, but she hesitated. It wasn't because of what they might think of her body—she knew she looked good—but knowing precisely why would arouse her.

And that was something she knew she couldn't hide from them.

Kari stood with her shorts pooled at her feet. The titillating eye she received in return told her she had all of their attention. "No dunking." She flicked her shorts at them with a kick and jogged to the clear water—surely that was light activity—until her awkward steps splashed in the warm sea. She turned once she was waist-deep to see that Finn had shed their sarong and entered the water like they were a graceful merperson. "How do you do that?"

"Do what?" Finn dipped their head underwater and reemerged with perfect, dark red ringlets.

"That. All of your movement is so lithe regardless of where you are."

Finn shrugged, causing water from their hair to drip down over their chest and shoulders. "I think it's because I'm a magical creature."

"I'm serious. What's your secret?"

"I don't fight. I always go with the flow, which may make me appear smooth but it certainly has its disadvantages. You, on the other hand, have fight, but I don't necessarily mean that in a violent way. Unlike Josef."

Yes! Office gossip! "What's the deal with him?"

"Other than he's walking aggression and Henry's pet." Finn shook their head. "I have no idea, which is weird in and of itself."

Kari waved her hands back and forth in the water to keep her balance. "What do you mean by that?"

"I mean . . . I'm not even sure Madeleine knows everything about him. When she and Josef are in the same room together, I sense a lot of confusion with her. Like she doesn't know what to make of him. No one else brings that out in her."

So Madeleine wasn't an omniscient being on the *Hinewai*. Fascinating.

"You also emit something no one else does." Finn stepped toward her with their eyes unfocused and their hand hovered inches off her heart. *Never seen anything like it.*

Kari gulped. Was there an energy that emerged when you were a magical birth? Possibly a demigod? "What do you sense?"

"I can literally see the power covering you. It's a purple-silver shimmer all around you." *It's beautiful.* Finn's eyes focused on her once again. "You're beautiful."

Rather than swoon into the water, she met them halfway for a kiss. Warm, soft welcoming lips touched hers and were joined by the slightest caress of her jaw and cheek. The waves lapped against them as they kissed more deeply in the shallows. Kari rested her hand on Finn's waist partially for balance and partially because they were picturing her touching them there.

This is amazing.

"Uh-huh," was the most she could articulate before she leaned in again.

TAT-TAT-TAT-TAT! A sudden burst of machine gun fire from the beach stopped her from parting her lips and, instead, dropped into the water until only her mouth hovered above the salt water.

Another round pierced the air, causing both her and Finn to turn to the beach. She expected to see the armed escorts engaged in a firefight with pirates, not to see a single guard waving at them with the gun at their side.

"You have to come in!" the man in tactical gear yelled. "There's an emergency!"

———

After dressing on the shore, taking the VIP boat back to the *Hinewai*, and cursing the entire time, Kari and Finn went to the secret conference room. Henry was at one head of the table. Madeleine was at the other. Josef stood near Henry, Neill was by the wall screen.

"I'm sorry we interrupted your date," Henry said. "Gabriella, myself, and others have a situation that needs to be tended to."

"Because of this," Madeleine said and pointed to Finn, "you need to go to Palermo with Josef and Henry. Now."

"Like now-now?" Finn asked.

"I didn't stutter," Madeleine said.

"You'll need to pack," Henry added. "I recommend for a

week and we need to leave in thirty minutes. I'll meet you on the helipad."

What will I be doing in Palermo for a week? "Yes, sir. May I ask what I'll be doing there?"

Henry grinned. "What you do best. Now, go dry, change, and pack." Henry headed toward the exit to the open deck. Josef followed close behind.

Finn turned to Kari. *Stupid.* "So much for a romantic end to our date."

"Not your fault. Don't get poisoned by lemonade." She gave Finn a brief goodbye kiss—after all, it was the end of their date—and watched them leave until the elevator doors closed. Kari turned to face Madeleine. "What's the emergency that machine gun fire needed to be used to break up my date?"

"Let's just say that Henry's offered to handle a situation discretely as a favor to his new billionaire best friend, Gabriella."

If Kari didn't know better, she'd say Madeleine was jealous. "Well, can I leave then?"

Madeleine shook her head. "Related to all of that, you have to go to Brisbane—"

"We were just in Australia!"

"Like I was saying," Madeleine said with a sharp tone, "you're going to go to Mr. Fiesler's office. Hopefully, you won't have to break in."

"You said I wouldn't have to commit crimes!"

"Don't. Get. Caught," Madeleine said as if it were the simplest answer in the world.

"But . . . you said—"

"It's not like I'm asking you to kill someone. Besides, he may leave his office door unlocked, then you're having a moral quandary over nothing." While Kari remained speechless over the sudden turn of the terms and conditions of her unwritten contract with Madeleine, she added, "I don't know what you're looking for once you're there, but an analyst is working on something to help you. Once that gadget is done and tested, you'll leave via more traditional transport. So, it'll be a bit slower and you'll need to go through airport security."

Kari did the travel math in her head, then her brow rose. "Will I miss work?"

"This is your work. Your most important work."

"No," Kari said with a laugh. "This is your and Henry's most important work that I happen to do part-time. I work full-time for inCog."

Madeleine's eyebrows raised. "That's certainly an interesting perspective, but I'm sure you'll make it back before Monday morning. Stay close to your cabin. I'll send directions your way via Neill."

Chapter Twenty-Nine

Madeleine sat at the head of the conference table for the early afternoon debriefing. She really did go to every length imaginable to make sure Kari couldn't read her mind. "You took the instruction of 'dress like a college student' seriously."

Kari's outfit of jeans, red T-shirt, and a baseball hat was one of the most comfortable ensembles she had been in for an assignment. Her backpack really added to her character. "Well, Neill was very serious when he said it. Of course, that was after he told me that he couldn't come with me due to pirate watch. Maybe the tone trickled over."

"Pirates are nothing to scoff at. Now, have a seat so we can get to business. You have gifts."

Kari sat at the other head of the table where there was an eyeglass case and small fabric pouch. She opened the larger case and took out the square-framed eyeglasses.

"You'll need to add those glasses to your look. They will record everything you see in Fiesler's office. There's an audio and live video feed with a sensor on the inside of the nose bridge which turns it on and off when you wear them. Do you know how to pick a lock?"

Thanks to being grounded once when she hacked into the parental controls for the TV and having an assortment of paper clips and bobby pins, she did. "Yes, I can." Kari took a wild guess what was in gift number two. She unsnapped the pouch and inside were several hooks and picks. There was also some cash.

"Excellent. Now, lockpicks aren't illegal, but, if airport security starts asking questions, just leave it behind. I'm confident we'll still learn plenty even without whatever is in the drawers. For the higher tech issue, while Fiesler takes his laptop home with him, we have it on good authority that his password to the cloud is written on a sticky note underneath a coaster."

"You're kidding."

"I know! It's like he's begging for someone to come and rummage through his things. And that someone is you. Questions?"

"A few. How am I getting there? How much time do I have?"

"You'll take the tender to the dock, a cab to the Port Moresby airport where you'll pay in cash, then fly commercial to Brisbane. You'll have a car waiting for you there. All other instructions of where at the university and timeline will be provided by the driver. Any other questions before you go?"

Kari had several, but there was only one Madeleine had any control over. "Do I have to fly commercial?"

"Look who's become bougie," Madeleine said with a laugh. "Your seat is first class if it helps. I emailed you your tickets, you're already checked in. Your return ticket is a red-eye, so your work at inCog—which is so *very* important to you—won't be disrupted."

———

Madeleine set up expedited security, so her bag wasn't an issue; first class had leg room, and the business and honeymoon travelers wanted nothing to do with her. For traveling commercial, it was the best option, but there was still a concern. Six weeks was the recommended minimum time for post-brain surgery air travel. But she was a fast healer and tried to put those worries to the side. Instead of thinking about the air pressure changes in the cavities around her brain, she reviewed different lockpick videos on her laptop.

Then, she researched her target.

Matthew Vale was an award-winning investigative journalist of combat zones, but he retired from that line of work due to threats. He changed his name to Fiesler when the threats continued and was subsequently offered a teaching position. A deeper dive into him via the website Grade My Professor found a mix of comments regarding his dramatic teaching style, overpowering cologne, and his contempt for anyone who strayed from cis-heteronormativity. One anonymous student went so far as to say he had made a formal complaint to his advisor regarding a slur he used in class, but it fell on deaf ears.

Okay, now she could hate him.

Once her flight landed, locating her driver proved to be more of an adventure than she would have liked. Kari scoured the arrival area for someone with a sign but saw no one. She was about to go back inside the airport when she felt a tap on her shoulder. She turned and was face-to-face with a young woman who could have easily been mistaken as her sister.

"Are you Kari?" she asked in a British accent.

"Only if you're my driver."

About time! "Brilliant! Please follow me." She led her to the most average gray sedan in existence and opened the back for her. "I'm sorry it took me awhile to spot you, I was looking for someone with longer hair. The picture they gave me must be old."

"Not a problem. I was looking for someone holding a sign."

"I was told not to do anything to draw attention." She punched in the address for the university. The estimated time of arrival was fifteen minutes. "Once we get there, I'll drive around just a little more so we are more on the desired timeline."

Kari nodded and took in the interior of the car. It wasn't messy, nor pristine. She picked up a receipt off the floor hoping to learn more about her driver. Based on the time stamp, someone made a stop at the gas station before coming. A someone who paid cash. So much for clues. "I didn't catch your name."

Supposed to give her a fake one? Hannah so common it doesn't matter. "Hannah."

No one who was contacted via car service would have any problems providing their name. "May I ask what company you work for?"

Auntie Amara a company? I supposed the whole Gupta, Inc is. "I'm an independent contractor. Now, if you don't mind, I need to focus on driving. Getting out of airports is tricky business."

That was fine with Kari. What raised questions was who Amara Gupta was. The last name was so common it didn't strike her in any way, but she did have a hunch. Kari took out her phone and performed a quick search. Amara Gupta's head-shot—complete with perfect bob haircut—popped on her screen within a second.

After Amara's father's death two years ago, she became the head of the family empire that had grown exponentially due to investments in technology and communications. She was past the level of Pawar, MacDonald, and the others. Amara had to be working with Henry. And, most likely, Gabriella.

Hannah drove around a few of the tree-lined campus streets, and Kari took the glasses out of her bag and put them on. They slid down her nose, and while the lenses weren't prescription, the slight difference in light refraction would be enough to give her a headache later.

Hannah parked in front of what was most likely the target building. "Room 226. Stand outside here when you're done. I'll arrive around 8:10pm to create the illusion you called for the same car."

"Works for me. I'll see you then."

Kari headed inside the journalism building. For the exception of a few lingering students in the lobby with their laptops open, the building was vacant. An advantage of the time of day or semester break, she supposed. Kari made a note of all exits, elevators, and stairs if she needed to make a hasty exit later. There was a person waiting at the elevator, so she took the stairs up to the second floor and with each step the glasses slid down her nose. She pushed the glasses back up the bridge of her nose once she was at the top.

From what she could tell, the hall was only for professor offices. All the doors were shut and the lights were off behind them, including Fiesler's. Before she tested the door, she took a breath and reminded herself of what she had found on the internet regarding his hatred for people like her moms, Finn, and herself. She put her hand on the doorknob; it turned.

Excellent. No breaking and entering charges today.

When she pushed the door open, a wave of musk struck her nostrils. The comment about his cologne had been correct. Her eyes would adjust to the darkness, but Kari was cognizant that everything she looked at and said was recorded, so she went to the blinds and opened them a fraction so the light from the street illuminated the space. Kari lingered her gaze on every object, file, or stack of papers in the office of clichéd academic chaos.

She began the detailed search by lifting the cork coaster by his keyboard. Not only was there a sticky note with his cloud password, but the note had his passwords to *everything*. Madeleine could get into his cloud storage and could check his banking or subscriptions. She could even change his gym membership if she wanted to. Kari returned the coaster to its appropriate location.

Next were the drawers, but before she started picking locks, she pulled the handle. It opened easily. Hidden away in the unlocked drawer were composition books with black-and-white-marbled covers filed in a row like folders. She took the first one closest to her. The cover was labeled with the current year and the inside was filled with ideas about lectures, news events, and story ideas. The pages were written in a neat script with black ink to the margins.

She put the first notebook away and grabbed the second. Then the third. Halfway through the stack, the edges of the paper began to yellow. His notes went back twenty years. But shoved in the back was a new journal with crisp, white pages.

It might as well have had a red, blinking light and alarm.

Kari opened the journal and began to leaf through the pages. Underneath Adam Cho's name was a list of phone numbers, no names, and a schedule of conversations. There had been one the previous day with the summary:

Wibawa acquisitions have reached financial threshold

A threshold? That was why he went on a rampage scooping up business. Henry had been trying to reach a value of worth. Kari was stuck on the why when she turned the page. Listed on the page were the world's most powerful and wealthy individuals, listed by region:

Europe – Gabriella Fermi
Africa – Jasi Monye
Western Asia – Botan Ito
Southeast Asia – Amara Gupta
North America – Jack Weatherby
South America – Ricardo Rojas

Henry was not on the list, but he was on the next page. Everything he owned was listed, which took multiple pages. Homes, cars, boats, companies—including inCog—were all in categorized and numbered order. The last was Pawar's studio. Beneath that and circled was:

New region? Australia and South Pacific member-Henry Wibawa

Kari stopped for her own pondering. This had to be the organization Henry wanted included in and what Gabriella thought of as *In Virtute*. More importantly, Fiesler was on to them for Cho's book. Gabriella and Amara must have found out and Henry offered to help squash the evidence since he was now a part of it in some way.

She flipped through blank pages for more information until she reached a folded paper tucked inside. She spread the paper out to see that it was a sketch of a building. No, it was a blueprint. The light pencil made it impossible to read, so she took it near the window until she could make out the design and read the numbers, but the blueprint was rudimentary at best. The most she could tell was that the building didn't have windows but did have a massive, arched entrance. For the structure's interior, there appeared to be an open, circular room, surrounded by several columns. There were no dimensions except *20m* written at the top of the column. Talk about high ceilings.

Was this a temple? Or a meeting room? And where could it be without drawing attention?

The questions swirled around her mind until she heard a whistle down the hall. Aside from possibly getting caught, Mom A said to never whistle at night as it brought bad luck. This was definitely an unlucky situation.

Kari rushed to put the notebook away without making a sound and returned the blinds to their original position. Depending on how close the stranger was, she had to make this bad situation look like an even worse situation. She made the decision for a grand exit. Kari unzipped the fly on her jeans, spread the fabric so her hot pink underwear really popped, and left the office with a flirty and whispered, "Bye, Matty," and silently closed the door. She saw the person in her near periphery and deliberately turned toward them. "Oh!" She exaggerated a startled jump. "You scared me."

The stranger who had bags under their eyes and was still in the office wing had to either be a professor or a graduate student. "What are you doing here at this hour?"

Kari shrugged. "Special office hours. Needed help with . . . headlines."

He looked her up and down and paused when they reached her pants. *Rumor is true!* "I hope you got the help you needed." He walked away with an impressive speed but with no whistle.

Her time in the building wasn't quite up, but now that she had been spotted leaving, she had to commit to a departure.

The AV elements were still engaged, so she said her apology out loud. "I hope you got what you need."

"Bravo, Kari." Madeleine gave her a light applause from her office. "The situation has now disappeared into the ether since the evidence in the cloud has vanished. Your acting was quite impressive, too."

"Thanks," she said with a yawn. Her red-eye had been full of turbulence and a toddler who had their own first-class seat. "Did you know who my driver was going to be?"

Madeleine inhaled deeply through her nostrils. "I did not."

Interesting. She had been left in the dark again. "Do you know about that list, then? Or what that blueprint is all about?"

Madeleine sucked in her upper lip and released it with a pop. "Those, my dear, are mysteries to us both. You're dismissed."

Chapter Thirty

Philippine Sea

A new, massive inCog project with a tight deadline had turned Kari's forty-hour week into sixty. It was exhausting, tedious, and the team missed a fire drill on the ship because of it. Her social life was nonexistent. Socializing with Jade consisted of playing note tag on each others' doors. She missed Jade's laugh and energy. She missed and worried about Finn. She had sent several unreturned texts since they had left for Palermo *weeks* ago.

But she had seen Henry and Josef.

Henry thanked her for the work in Brisbane, but when she asked about Finn, the most she got was, 'They're safe.' To her surprise, Cho and Fiesler were also safe. Kari had checked the news daily to ensure they both were still alive. Although, Fiesler was suspended for inappropriate behavior pending an investigation for inappropriate content in the university's cloud storage.

An additional form of stress took the form of the small, black remote that dangled from a lanyard on Mitchell's wall at inCog. Sometimes he would bump it when repositioning his monitor, causing it to swing like a pendulum. Each back-and-forth was almost a taunt as if it said, "Press the button. Press the button," to learn if the final surgery had worked.

It was too much.

"Is there any chance I can take a mental health day?" Kari asked Santos. "I feel like I'm going to crack, and if that happens then nothing will ever get done."

"No problem." Santos rubbed his eyes as if feeling the same strain she did. "We've all put in crazy hours this week, and I'll be leaving early anyway since I have a meeting with the management office."

Kari saved her work and closed her windows. "Why do you have to go to the management office?"

"Probably to get yelled at for skipping the fire drill."

"Maybe they'll buy that we don't hear the alarm down here," Mitchell said.

"By all means," Santos said, "you can come with me and tell them that obvious lie."

"Nah," Mitchell said. "I'll let you handle that. I'm going to stay down here until I get through my current stack of CTE brain slices."

Kari didn't bother participating in any witty banter as she left. The most she had the energy for was a weak wave good-bye. She needed to get in her cabin and out of her head as soon as possible. Since they were in the middle of the ocean, she couldn't use a point on land as a focal point for meditation. But a faux candlelight meditation app on her TV would suffice. If she did that followed by a cat nap, she'd still wake to the same problems but with a clearer mind to solve them.

———

Kari woke to a drool-covered pillow and banging on her door. "I'm coming," she said as she dragged her bare feet. The banging persisted. "It better be you, Jade, with a cake for me!" She opened the door. "Hey, Neill. What's wro—"

"You need to come with me, now." He didn't wait for her to respond before he started down the passageway.

Kari closed the door behind her and ran without her shoes on to catch up. "What's happening?"

"Finn is back and there is major change happening, but we can't talk about it here." Once they were in the VIP office, but before they entered the bathroom elevator, Neill tapped her shoulder. *Nod if you understand.*

"Wh—" His meaty hand covered her mouth. His eyes focused on her with such intensity he might has well have been trying to see through her.

The words, tone, and actions gave her a chill. She nodded.

"Up we go, then," he said with a more relaxed tone. *I'm not supposed to know this but some kind of deal just happened between Henry and Gabriella, because of it they're setting up a place for Finn in Palermo. They're also planning something with you but I don't know what.*

She observed Neill's posture in the elevator. His shoulders were high, arms were crossed, jaw twitched, and skin flushed. Kari had never seen him this angry before and wanted to ask a dozen follow-up questions—the biggest being what they wanted to do with her—but she knew she had to keep her mouth shut.

The elevator doors opened and she saw Finn in the otherwise empty conference room. "What's g—"

Finn's lips silenced her in what was leagues beyond a hello kiss. This was hello, goodbye, and I missed you so much rolled into one. *Want to linger.* "We don't have much time before I leave again."

"Where did you go the first time?" Kari asked breathlessly and wondered how she could grow so hot, so fast. Also, apparently one's toes could curl when they were kissed. "I tried to reach you."

"They took my phone, so I couldn't take pictures or record anything." *Listen. You have to be careful. These people don't know what you can do, but they know how much you mean to Henry. He wouldn't give you up.*

"That makes no sense."

It does if you view us as pawns and not people. Don't let down your guard. Something behind her must have caught Finn's attention because the thoughts stopped and the kisses started again. *Please be careful.*

What in the world was happening? Kari's sleepy brain was too overwhelmed to make sense of it all.

"I would say get a room," Madeleine said as she entered from her office, "but that's more complicated now that Finn no longer resides on this ship and guests aren't allowed."

"What?" Kari yelled, which caused Neill's hand to go to her back. No doubt it was his reminder to her to stay calm. She turned to Finn. "You're leaving for good?"

Don't want to. "Yes. Apparently, I work for Gabriella Fermi now."

"Technically, you're subcontracted, so think of it like a transfer between offices." Madeleine sat at the conference table. "I know you two have become close, but I'm sure you'll see each other every once in a while. Gabriella and Henry are best pals now and will be working together more often moving forward."

Now she understood the gravity of the situation. Kari turned to Finn. "When do you have to leave?"

"Now," Finn said and directed a contemptuous stare at

Madeleine. "In fact, the only reason I was invited back was so I could get my things."

"Which you've now done," Madeleine said, "so up to the helipad you go."

I hate every molecule of her. "Walk me up?" Finn asked.

"Not so fast," Madeleine said. "Kari needs to stay, but I promise I'll send her up before you leave."

Every. Single. Molecule. Finn took Kari's hand and gave it a comforting squeeze before they left the room.

"Now, on to you," Madeleine said to Kari. "You were asked to come because Finn's absence creates a gap in our VIP services, so you'll be replacing them."

That didn't make sense. She couldn't have two full-time jobs. The contract Madeleine wrote forbade it. "I can't do that. I work for inCog full-time."

"Your contract stipulates that during your off hours from inCog you work for us to fulfill your Wibawa Enterprises Promise. Therefore, if there is no inCog, you don't have any conflict."

What happened to inCog?

Kari had the same question as Neill and was glad he had placed a light hand on her shoulder because she may have fallen over from shock. "What do you mean no inCog? I was there a few hours ago!"

Madeleine's lips formed a diabolical grin. "inCog—or rather—Santos, ignored an emergency drill and that's grounds for termination. And Henry, who owns the company, is using this opportunity not to seek new management and is closing the business. And since neither Mitchell nor Santos have other employment on the ship, they are also being evicted effective immediately."

This is unreal.

"inCog is gone?" Kari asked, even though she knew the answer was yes.

"Indeed, it is."

Her job was gone. Santos and Mitchell were unemployed and homeless. They hadn't even concluded if the ORCA procedure had worked. Just like the first time when she was in the conference room, she swallowed the bile that climbed up her esophagus.

"I would recommend saying your goodbyes to Finn as they will be leaving soon via helicopter," Madeleine said. "For the other two, you have a bit more time since the VIP boat is going through its checks and fueling."

"Wait! Stop!" There were too many changes too fast. "What about the lab?"

Madeleine shrugged. "Henry owns the lab and"—her eyes flashed a look that was nothing but malicious—"everything in it."

Kak.

Kari's frantic heart froze. That could only mean one thing: Madeleine or Henry had the remote. They had the control to her telepathy.

I got you, Kari. Steady breaths. Neill put his arms around her, and it was then she realized she had started to hyperventilate.

"Neill," Madeleine said, "perhaps you should carry her to the helipad for her goodbyes to Finn. Her legs are unsteady."

"She's strong," he said. *You can do this, Kari.*

The patronizing tone in Madeleine's voice juxtaposed with Neill's support replaced her fear and shock with determination. "I can walk," she said in the fiercest voice she could muster. She walked on shaky legs to the helipad. The pilot was already in the cockpit, but rotors hadn't started yet. The other seats, except the seat behind the pilot, had suitcases and boxes. When she reached Finn, they stretched for her hand.

I just found out about inCog. No idea they would do this to you. They wrapped her in a tight hug and there was the bergamot. "I know you're angry, but please don't challenge this."

Kari shook her head against their chest. "This is surreal," she said in a soft voice. "You're gone, inCog is gone, my remote . . . I don't even know where to start to process this."

"If it helps, I think we'll be able to talk and my time with Gabriella hasn't been awful, so you don't need to worry about me." *Sorry.* Finn kissed her temple. "But I think it would be best given the distance and uncertainties if you live your life, and I'll do the same." *Such a jerk.*

Finn's abrupt departure was the cut and there was the salt to go into the wound.

Logically, she understood, but understanding the situation didn't take the sting away. "I get it. Goodbye, then."

Finn's fingers grazed her cheekbone with a feather touch. *Goodbye.* They took brisk steps up the metal stairs leading up to the helipad and didn't look back once they got in the passenger seat of the helicopter. Soon, the blades whirled overhead, causing her polo shirt to whip around her body. The helicopter hovered and flew west.

Got to hurt. Neill's heavy footsteps came beside her. "I can't say anything to make this better, but I'm here for you."

Kari appreciated the sentiment but couldn't give voice to it.

"We should head down to deck one so you can catch Mitchell and Santos before they leave," he said in a gentle tone. *Can't believe this.*

Kari followed him to the elevator and descended to deck one while anger, disgust, disappointment, and fear consumed her. And Neill.

"Kari!" Santos ran to her and put his arms around her as

soon as she entered the VIP passenger area. *Must hate me even more than Charlotte.* "I'm so, so sorry. I never meant for any of this."

"It's not your fault." Kari caught movement and her eyes grew wide when she saw that Mitchell had a new look: a blossoming black eye, broken glasses, and a split lip. "Oh my Gods, what happened?"

"I tried to stop him," Mitchell said, while he rested his hand on his ribcage. "I'm sorry, but Josef took the remote." *Know rib is fractured.*

All she could do was give him the gentlest hug since he was in so much pain. "No, I'm sorry. You were right! I should have listened to you about them. I'm sorry." Her voice cracked as tears started to form. She really was losing them.

Mitchell cradled her head like she was his own child. "I don't want you to think or worry about that. You're a brilliant young woman, okay? And even though they're kicking us out, I want you to keep in touch. You have our personal numbers."

"I will." Kari wiped away her tears with her fingers. "I promise. Where do you think you'll go?"

"Charlotte wants me to go back to the US, but where . . . I don't know." Santos pointed to the VIP boat. "The captain says she's taking us to Lanyu, which is an island off Taiwan. So, I figured Mitchell and I have plenty of time to brainstorm places on the ride there."

Kari craned her neck to see the boat and captain. She had never seen that boat captain before.

"We're fueled and ready," the captain said. "Your belongings were loaded as well."

"How did they have time for that?" Kari asked.

"Apparently," Mitchell said, "they worked as a team and started when we were at work."

"Gentleman," the captain said as a warning. "Let's go."

"What a cockwaffle," Kari muttered, causing them both to softly chuckle and give her one more goodbye hug. But the comforting cocoon was gone too soon. She watched them board and wave to her even as the boat became a speck in the distance.

They were gone. And inCog was gone.

"It's always tough to say goodbye," Madeleine said from behind. "I understand you'll need some time to process all of this. As a gesture of good faith, you don't have to start your new, full-time role as VIP assistant until after the weekend."

Kari turned from the water and marched toward her until Neill stepped in front to block her. "This is such bull shit!"

Calm down, Kari. Don't make this worse.

Madeleine reacted as though she had been scolded by a small child. A hint of surprise, anger, and amusement. "I think you're forgetting that while our operation is unorthodox, you have been well paid and have made the world better by ridding it of scum. But, let's not forget the biggest gift, an experimental surgery completely paid for so you could have your dream realized. You need to remember the positives that come with working for us."

"Positives!" Kari screamed. "You just stripped three people I care about from my life so you can use me as a puppet."

Kari, stop it. Now.

"That's just business, Kari," Madeleine said. "Now, I recommend you reign in your anger or there will be consequences."

"She means it," Neill said. "Let's just go." *Jade and I can help you through this.*

Kari wasn't going to let it go. She wasn't letting any of this go. She had never been consumed with so much rage in her life. Her entire being shook and angry tears fell down her cheeks. "Fuck you and Henry. That's how I feel about your 'business.'"

Madeleine closed her eyes, took a breath, and reopened them. "I don't think you mean that."

"Yes, I fucking do! Even you don't even know what his business is anymore. He's keeping you in the dark and you've been replaced by Gabriella. You're jealous! It's as simple as that. And you're doing all of this just to prove you have some power left!"

Oh, no. Reel it back. "I'm sure she didn't mean that," Neill pleaded.

"I think she did." Madeleine's posture shifted and she walked to the side of the room. "Josef, hand me your radio."

Josef stepped out from the shadows and Madeleine took the radio he offered. Kari saw the cuts on his knuckles from where he had beaten Mitchell.

"You think that I'm nothing," Madeleine said. "That I'm worthless to Henry. That I'm all talk. Well, I can assure you that I am needed more than you will ever know to keep the mission of this ship in line, and the success of that mission requires both obedience and discretion. You failed both!"

"No, I didn't!"

Madeleine shook her head. "You knew the journalist's name in Newfoundland, Linus, and didn't tell us. We spotted it on camera after the fact. I advocated that we reprimand you, but Henry insisted we let it slide and create a contingency for the next time you went solo. Why do you think when you were sent alone into Brisbane we gave you a recording device?"

Kari's eyes widened.

"And," Madeleine continued, "you told Mitchell about our arrangement when he discovered the bug in inCog."

"I never—"

"Oh, please. A child could have read through that one-sided dialogue. But once again, Henry insisted you still provided value without causing headaches and we could 'take care' of the problem later, which is what you're about to see."

"What do you mean? I just saw it! They're gone! Problem solved."

So naïve.

Madeleine shook her head and dialed to a channel on the radio. "I was going to ask Josef to do this later, but you're a person who appreciates evidence. And you're a person who needs to witness the consequences in order to fully grasp what I mean by *complete* obedience and discretion." She pressed the talk button. "I need more ice."

There was a crackle of static. "Understood," the captain of the VIP boat said.

The eye contact Madeleine held caused Kari to freeze. Whether it was terror or shock, she didn't know, but they stared each other down for what was the most intense pause of Kari's life. "What does ice—"

There were two faint pops in the distance. Then, a third.

"What was that?" Kari asked, panicked.

Oh, no. Neill turned to look in the direction of the VIP boat.

Madeleine handed Josef the radio. "If you use that big brain of yours, I think you can figure out exactly what that was."

Kari pieced together the circumstances and the sounds. Mitchell knew too much. Santos knew too much. They were loose ends that needed to be tied via execution. "You bitch!" She lunged at Madeleine, but Neill's arms around her stopped her progress and lifted her from the ground.

This is awful, but please calm down. They are capable of more.

"Josef," Madeleine commanded while she locked eyes with Kari, "I think enough time has passed. Finish the job."

He walked away, pulled a cell phone out of his pocket, and dialed. A *boom* pierced the air with deafening force. Neill's grip loosened on Kari, allowing her to run to the side of the deck and look into the distance where a black cloud rose into the blue sky. She watched in horror as another explosion erupted.

"No!" Kari wailed as she fell to her knees. There was a chance they could have survived a gunshot, but now there was no hope. Santos and Mitchell were both dead. "No," she screamed over and over, each time becoming less and less coherent through her sobs.

"Actions. Have. Consequences," Madeleine said. "And it's time you learned that attitudes also have consequences."

"Did you have to do that?" Neill asked through Kari's bawling.

"Oh, Neill. You, out of all the people on this ship, should understand the chain of command. Or, rather, what happens when you break it."

I do.

Still on her knees, Kari lifted her head to try to make eye contact with Madeleine. Cold, icy blue eyes locked on hers. Neill positioned himself between the two, arms spread like he was a referee in a ring.

"Do you understand the full scope now?" Madeleine asked Kari.

For the love of God, just nod and stop antagonizing her.

Kari nodded.

"Good," Madeleine said. "Because I can promise you that cars explode just as easily. All that fuel and wiring makes them very dangerous. Tell me, do you know anyone who likes to drive around Oregon or is planning to rent a car in Alaska?"

Gods, not her moms. "Please, no." Kari pulled herself up using the railing and hesitated to face the monster who would murder—had murdered—the people most important to her if she didn't comply. But Kari did face her.

Madeleine grinned. Then pulled the remote out of her pants' pocket, pressed the button, and approached Kari. Each click of her heel against the deck's cement floor added to the soundtrack of her living nightmare. Once Madeleine was close enough for Kari to smell the Earl Gray and lemon on her breath, she asked, "Didn't you catch my thought just now?"

"No," Kari meekly said. ORCA worked and she couldn't celebrate it. Instead, she wanted to vomit off the side of the ship.

"Congratulations! Your brilliant science worked. How about now?" Madeleine pressed the button again. *Never forget. You may have powers, but we are in control. Always.* Madeleine pressed the button and pocketed the remote once more. "Did you catch that?"

"Yes," Kari whispered.

"Yes, what?"

Kari knew what Madeleine wanted to hear, as she had heard Finn say it time and time again. "Yes . . . ma'am."

"Then, we have an understanding." Madeleine walked away, the click of her heels resonating in the space. Josef followed. "See that she gets to her cabin, Neill."

Kari stayed on the deck and sobbed into Neill's chest as she watched the burning wreckage without his comforting thoughts in her head or voice in her ears. He stroked her back until utter exhaustion took over and she had no more tears.

Chapter Thirty-One

Anchorage, Alaska, United States

"Both Watanabe brothers are interested in joining Henry's deep-sea mining venture; however, they're worried their board won't go for it because it conflicts with environmental policies their company prides itself on."

"That's interesting," Madeleine said from behind her desk in the secret office. A matte black box with a small, square glass panel on the top was the only item on the desk. Or *in* the desk, really. The box and desk were glued and screwed together from every angle. "Although, now that I think about it, they were asking a lot of ecosystem questions. Anything else?"

Kari took her eyes off the black box. "They think our scotch selection sucks."

"Preaching to the choir, there," Madeleine muttered and placed her thumb on the box's glass panel. After a quiet but audible click, the top opened and Madeleine took out the remote. She pointed it at Kari and clicked before returning the device to its home. "You're dismissed. Oh, when you come back from your vacation, there will be another VIP assistant of sorts. An intern, Belle, from WU's hospitality program."

"Thank you for the notice, ma'am." Kari's feet stayed planted. For full dismissal, she waited until Madeleine headed to her proper office on the ship, waited for the all-clear sign, and went in so she could exit through the cubicles that made up the ship's main management office.

"All clear," Madeleine's voice carried through the bathroom closet.

Kari went through the bathroom passageway that connected the offices. It still pissed her off that the first thing she saw when she entered Madeleine's traditional office was a picture of her and her family standing in front of that stupid candy shop. There was also a new pillow on the other guest chair that said, *Thankful Grateful Blessed.*

She was such a phony bitch.

Kari said nothing as she left her office telepathy-free and entered the main administration center that was full of conversation. The air smelled like a mixture of old coffee, burned popcorn, and some kind of air purifying spray that was probably supposed to cover up the popcorn but failed.

"Hi, Kari."

She turned to the middle-aged man with a constant state of blush and short, chestnut hair. "Hey, what's going on?"

He came closer and dropped his voice. "It's a little embarrassing, to be honest. My fingers hurt like hell after I've only practiced one song. Is there anything I can do?"

She winced at her new guitar student. "Not really. The only thing I can suggest is more pain early to create your calluses faster. Practice after your shower while your fingers are soft."

"That'll hurt more!"

"It will, but only for a short time, buddy. Keep practicing while I'm gone, but stay away from those cheat chords." She gave him a slight smile before she walked away.

That was her first smile in several weeks.

Over a month had passed since the traumatic events in the Philippine Sea. Kari still mourned Santos, Mitchell, and inCog, but the primal devastation of daily crying jags was gone thanks to the help she had received from friends and family.

Her moms were available any time she needed to talk, day or night. Text or video. Her special soap was now almost fragrance free she had to open the bag so much.

Jade advocated for counseling early because of the nature of their deaths. For a corrupt enterprise, she had good healthcare and started telehealth therapy again. This was nothing like when she went to therapy as a kid. For one, this was her choice as an adult. And two, the only time she had telepathy was when Madeleine wanted her to.

Of everyone, Neill had helped the most. He knew the darkness her real job caused her to see and hear and suggested that to offset that she should try volunteer work to do some good. So, she put her name in the music club room to offer guitar lessons and a few other places where she might be of service. To her surprise, she didn't hate teaching or helping people problem solve.

"Kari."

She stopped and turned at the exit doors to a petite young woman with a round face and hijab. "Marhaban, Fatima." In exchange for tutoring Fatima in biology, she was teaching Kari how to speak Arabic.

"Your pronunciation is getting better. Would you mind sending me that animation link of the metabolic pathways again. I accidentally deleted it."

"I'll make sure I do that before I leave for shore."

"Thank you, and have a nice vacation with your family."

"Will do. And keep up the studying for that nursing exam!"

Fatima smiled. "Only if you stop asking me how to say insults and swear words."

From the office, Kari made her way to the café. An expensive coffee was a good way to mark the beginning of vacation. While she waited for her beans to grind, she pulled out her phone to return Finn's text. Earlier in the day they had sent her a picture of their new suite in Palermo. To say that it was lavish was an understatement.

Is your dance space between the four-poster bed and complete seating arrangement?

Finn had also helped in the aftermath, but there was nothing romantic about their relationship. Just a few texts here and there to remind her that they were thinking about her had helped. As did the knowledge that Gabriella had no plans to put Finn in risky situations. At least, Finn hadn't disclosed it to Kari. The only coded message she had ever received was that Gabriella didn't know how Finn was so perceptive of her and others' moods but was impressed by it. That was how Finn earned a bonus week to go back to Newfoundland.

Declan was ecstatic.

Once Kari's coffee was in hand, she continued her journey down to her cabin. Since she had been packing bit by bit over the past two days, the only thing left to do was change out of her black-on-black VIP uniform and into clothes that were truer to summertime Alaska. She had pulled on a light hooded sweatshirt over her tank top when there was a knock at the door. Kari opened it without seeing who was on the other side. She knew who it was. "I still have five minutes."

"I know," Jade said matter-of-fact with an empty canvas bag slung over her arm. "What can I say? I'm excited to meet the moms."

In Kari's one year at sea, she had seen dozens of different views as the *Hinewai* or its other boats approached land. There were dormant and smoldering volcanoes, skyscrapers that lit the night sky, couples who got engaged at sunset, and the scene before her now, her mothers holding a massive poster board that read *Chickpea!*

"Gods, this is embarrassing."

Jade nudged her shoulder. "But look at how cute they are."

"Yeah, they're super precious. Come on." Kari rolled her suitcase behind her as the two made their way down to the welcoming committee. As she approached, she saw an almost imperceptible frown on Mom L and she knew why: She couldn't sense her emotions. Kari had discovered she could no longer communicate with eagles when the device was activated, but she wasn't sure if it had also cut off the link to her mother. Apparently it had.

"Hi, Moms!" Kari abandoned her bag and hugged them both as a single unit. Then, the required kisses on her cheeks landed and the touching of her hair.

"It's so bouncy," Mom A said with a large smile. "I can't even see your little brain knobber."

"Bounciness and—I will not call it a 'brain knobber'—aside, I'd like you to meet Jade. Jade, these are the moms."

"It's so great to meet you." Jade shook both of their hands. "You're practically celebrities Kari talks about you so much."

"Likewise," Mom L said. "I hear you're quite the formidable table tennis opponent."

"And baker," Mom A added. "I'm still in awe over chickpea's birthday cake."

"It was absolutely my pleasure. Now, before I run off to the farmers' market, I have to tell you what a wonderful daughter you've raised. I know how challenging that can be, so good job to you both."

Mom A *aww*'d. Mom L smiled and scrunched her shoulders like a little kid.

"Kari," Jade said. "I'll see you in a week. Don't miss the ship."

"Bye!" Kari called after her and turned her attention back to the moms. "That's Jade. Sorry you can't meet Neill, but maybe when I leave."

"That'd be nice, but speaking of leaving." Mom L hitched a thumb to the direction of the parking lot. "Our meter time is almost out. We may have gotten here earlier than we had to."

They walked across the parking lot to a lone SUV in the back row. "It's so great to meet one of your friends." Mom A gave her a caring smile, but the glint in her eyes was suspicious.

"You know it's times like this, reading your mind would be helpful."

Mom A gave her a rueful smile. "I had been wondering if staying on the ship was the best thing for you after everything that had happened, but you look and sound really good. Are you happy?"

That was the million-dollar question. "I'm getting there. My friends help. My therapist helps. And I think teaching and learning from others has helped, too. As it turns out, I don't hate as many people as I thought. Just the cockwaffles."

Mom L laughed and she unlocked the car. "I hear that, and I guess I'm going to have to get used to not feeling how annoyed you are. I appreciate the warning you gave me about that, by the way."

Kari put her suitcase in the back and then sat in the back-seat. "I know it's going to be weird for both of us not to have that special connection, but I have to say it's amazing not having to hear your thought process of what the best way to get to the cabin is or if we should stop for food."

Mom L turned and gave her the kind of pat on the knee that only parents can give. "Then, it's worth it so you can be happy."

"And speaking of food," Mom A said, "I ran into a mutual acquaintance of ours at the ENN dinner in San Francisco last week: Adam Cho."

"Really?" Kari said, clearly surprised. "I don't really think of him as an acquaintance, but it was neat meeting him in Stockholm. I'm shocked he remembered me."

"Oh," Mom L said, "you made quite the impression even without the wrist lock, didn't she?"

"She sure did." Mom A turned to face her in the backseat. "He was very impressed by how well-spoken you were and how you advocated for yourself. He hopes to see you again sometime."

"Ah . . . That would be nice, I guess." But Henry and Madeleine would absolutely despise that. She chuckled at the thought of her being buddy-buddy with Adam Cho. But then her mild laughter ceased.

This was exactly what she needed to do.

"What's so funny, chickpea?" Mom L asked. Kari could see her large brown eyes focused on her in the rearview mirror.

"Oh . . . just something else that happened in Stockholm." Kari smiled pleasantly. "But enough about that, what kind of family activities did you plan? Bonus points if there is something with dog sledding."

As Mom L drove and Mom A explained the light agenda, Kari looked out to the coastline and dense forest of the Alaskan wilderness to plot her next moves. She'd have a wonderful vacation with her family, return to the *Hinewai* to perform her duties on the ship to the best of her ability, and contact Adam

Cho. Kari had no doubt he would help her with her next project.

To destroy Henry Wibawa and Madeleine Coultier.

353

Kari's story continues in . . .
Project Duplicity
The Kari Chronicles Book 2

Acknowledgments

My wife: The past two years writing this book have been WILD! You've done small things to support me (like buying me a map that covered the cork board you also bought me and then I stuck notes to the adjacent wall and not the cork board), to big things like giving me the time in my schedule to really try to "make it" as a creative. Since the publication of *Heroes*, not only have you supported the Kari series but you also encouraged me to pursue narration, which includes the famous(?) go-ahead to turn a space in our house into a recording studio. If any spouse or partner needs an example of how to be there for their special person, they just have to look to you to as a role model. I love you so much! Lastly, the use of "tawny" was done for you. I can't wait for you to read *Project ORCA* and hear what you think!

My Mom: You're coming in a close number two in terms of my support team. No matter what, you are a great remedy for when my self-esteem is low, especially in terms of my stories. I don't know many people whose parent's pre-order ten paperbacks so they can give them away to their friends. You're such a special woman and the absolutely best mother! I love you!

To little man: I won't lie, you mostly laid in your little doggie bed and looked at me while I typed or clicked away (even now). But you're always a source of love and smiles, which is what I need when the days of my imposter syndrome are especially high. I love you!

My best friend, Carl Nummyhands: You put the wheels in motion for me to interview Adam, which I don't know how I'll repay you for, but I'll try by bringing cookies in addition to giving Kari a love of cargo pants. While I did feel that choice of pant aligned with Kari's character, I thought of you every time I wrote about them. You are a true fashion icon. I can picture you wearing those pants now (possibly wearing your dinosaur hoodie) while you write the card about your thoughts on the book. Love you, friend!

Jen: This is probably sound silly, but the excitement you radiated when I described this novel to you on January 1, 2022 during out walk on the canal gave me an extra boost of encouragement that my idea of nefarious folks on a modified-cruise ship wasn't terrible. Writing is a pretty scary process, especially when one starts to change lanes, but you helped me feel more comfortable with that decision.

Adam: Thank you. Thank you. Thank you for the post-holiday Zoom you had with me to discuss optogenetics and how I wanted to use it in this novel. Unfortunately, I had to edit quite a bit of science out to make the story more lay friendly, but I hope what is there is still enough to maintain accuracy. You know, maintain the "accuracy" of what a telepath would do to regulate her ability.

Las Vegas: When the research cruise trip was unexpectedly canceled in September 2023, you provided just as much creative fodder in terms of extravagance and future sub-plots for the Kari series. You're tacky, but fun.

Vicki Holt: As a reader of the *Dreams* trilogy and a sci-fi writer, I can't thank you enough for beta reading this draft. Even though I want Kari to have her own adventure now, it is important to me to have series continuity while shifting genres. I sincerely appreciate the notes you gave me.

Ricky: As a scientist familiar with the *Dreams* trilogy, thank you for beta reading this draft. Even though I want Kari to have her own adventure now, it is important to me to have series continuity while shifting genres. Much like what I wrote from Adam, I needed to cut down a lot of science content to make it more lay-friendly.

Salt and Sage/Lune: Honestly, without you I don't know where I'd go. You consistently make my stories cleaner and more engaging with the suggestions that you make. While I've killed plenty of darlings because of you, I've learned so much about the story creation process. I hope the final product of Project ORCA makes you proud and you enjoy it...mostly because you have three more to read in the series 😊

Nan Campbell: Thank you for swooping in and giving my draft a final look before it went into line edits. (You know there's still too much science when both two people are calling it out) Your observation about the structure of the thoughts Kari "hears" really resonated with me and I hope the changes I made reflect that. Also, you get another kudos for telling me that "tender" was the word I needed.

The waiting room of the Honda dealership: Whoever was there that day, thank you for making sure I was okay as I cried writing the Kari surprise birthday party scene. That was good customer service. Although, your vending machine prices are too high.

Eanna Webb: I always enjoy working with you. And, once again, I must apologize for not having mastered basic rules of grammar (I have to remember FANBOYS). It's slow process, but I am learning! I also really appreciate the time you spent working on the blurb with me. We made a banger of a blurb!

Janice: I appreciate the extra eyes and questions when it comes to the final stretch of the editing process. Just when you think you have everything wrapped in a nice little bow you find the of-off and sparkles-sparkling. Thank you so much.

May Dawney: Thank you for working with me as we brought Kari to life on the cover. I know I asked for a few unexpected things, but you always deliver on producing an amazing cover. This cover better become a finalist in this year's awards (you know which one I'm talking about)! I can't wait to work on the next three books with you.

Readers of the *Dreams* trilogy: It means the world to me that you liked Aurora and Leela's story enough to give Kari's journey a try. I hope you enjoyed the little Easter eggs I sprinkled throughout and find their life trajectory to be as interesting and authentic as I do.

New Readers: Of all the new books and authors out there, I appreciate that you gave this story and me a try. While I want to keep my prior audience happy and turning the pages, you are who I need to grow my audience and be successful enough to sustain this profession I've chosen.

The Lesfic Sprinters: While I don't really do writing sprints anymore, the daily check-ins with you have kept me motivated and productive for around seven years. Someday I'll meet all of you in person.

Golden Crown Literary Society: Okay, so I haven't won any awards or been nominated (yet), but I appreciate the platform you've given me over the last few years to share my work and what skills/knowledge I do have.

Sapphic Lit Pop-Up Bookstore/Sapphic Literary Collective: You're part of the best company that includes my wife, mother, and best friend. Each one of us understands the challenges that writing and publication poses, and that brings a specialized type of support. You have all have been my purple-shirted rocks! I'm so happy that I can call you (and your partners) my friends.

About the Author

Serena J. Bishop is an accidental author. After writing technical, science-based pieces, in 2015 she decided to start turning her daydreams into stories. She writes witty, sapphic character-driven novels in the speculative fiction, thriller, and sapphic romance genres.

When Serena's not writing, narrating, or working at some job that probably falls within the realm of biology, she enjoys being a nerd, time with friends and family, and drinking coffee. Black, no sugar. Deck time or dock time with her wife is another favorite.

Serena lives in Maryland, USA with her magnificent wife and precious Chihuahua. She's also a member of the Sapphic Literary Collective, LLC. You can follow her by signing up for her newsletter at www.serenajbishop.com or following her on Facebook, Instagram, Threads, and maybe other ones (so many socials come and go) @serenajbishop.

Also by Serena J. Bishop

Dreams: Book 1 of the Dreams trilogy

The mind has a heart of its own.

Aurora's life is perfectly mundane. She has a job she hates, an ex that ran her out of her hometown, and the highlight of her week is Monday breakfast with her best friend. That changes when Aurora starts dreaming of a woman. A woman who Aurora falls head over heels for. She knows the romance that develops between them isn't real, but the dreams make life so much better that she hurries to bed every night...until she discovers that her dream woman isn't imaginary. Her name is Leela and she is in a coma.

Aurora must risk everything—her job, apartment, friends, and her sanity—to save Leela, a woman she's only ever met in her mind. But in order to help, Aurora must convince Leela's neurologist and parents that she and Leela have a bond that transcends the physical plane.

Can Aurora fight through a progressively nightmarish landscape to wake Leela? And if Leela wakes, will she recognize

Aurora as the one who saved her? As the one Leela said she loved? Their dream-relationship might not be real, but if there is any possibility of making her dreams come true, Aurora has to try.